Dedicated to my biggest fans:

June Sevier Riley

Perry Riley

Deborah Davis

Richard Espy

In Loving Memory of Christine Alexander

PART 1

INTERLUDE
JUNE 1972

Four days before her sixth birthday, Glory Hallelujah Bishop knew a whole lot of things. As a matter of fact, she knew more things than anybody else in her kindergarten class. She knew all her letters, and she knew C-A-T didn't say "cuh-at"—it said "cat," like a real cat that said "meow." And S-T-O-P didn't say "stop sign" or "red light" or "stop it" or "freeze"—it was plain old "stop" and meant *stop* just like the word said. And Glory knew not just school things—she knew important things, too, like how to spell and write her whole name and her mama's name and her daddy's name and her address and her phone number and her mama's phone number at work and the license number on her daddy's truck and the phone number on the door on her daddy's truck.

But that day, the most important thing Glory knew was that weddings were dumb and wedding ladies were crybabies and wedding boys were dumb and flower girls were the biggest, meanest dummies in the world. They were so mean and dumb in their big, dumb, fluffy dresses with their dumb ribbons, throwing their dumb flowers—and they were all doing it wrong anyway—that God was going to get them and make them ugly one day because it was a sin to act pretty in church.

Glory stood on the balcony, looking down on the empty church sanctuary where that day's wedding had taken place. The only kids allowed down there were wedding kids, so Glory and the

2

other children had watched from the balcony. Everybody said it was happy, but almost all the ladies had been crying. Glory hoped there wouldn't be another wedding the next day. It seemed like lately, every time they came to church, there was a wedding. There'd been two the day before, and her mother hand sung in the choir and cleaned up both times, and today after church there was another one, and her mother was *still* in there, talking and cleaning up.

"Hey. Whatcha doin'?"

Glory sighed. "Nothin'." She glanced out of the corner of her eye but didn't look directly at the boy on his hands and knees beside her. Josiah Jackson wasn't one of the wedding kids because he was a *bad boy*. He always had to sit out in the hall because he acted up in Sunday school, and his mom or dad always had to come and get him out of the nursery during church service. Sometimes, they even had to take him into the bathroom to *straighten him out*. When he stood up beside Glory, close enough that their shoulders touched, she moved over a step.

"How come you wasn't a flower girl?"

"I don't wanna be a flower girl." Glory wouldn't say out loud that they were mean dummies because she didn't want God to get her and make her ugly for saying mean things in church.

"Flower girls are stupid anyway. Trina is the stupidest."

Glory's eyes went wide, and she gaped at the very bad boy standing beside her. "You can't say *stupid* in church!" Glory whispered as loudly as she could. "God is gonna get you for saying that!"

"Well, you just said it!" Josiah didn't whisper at all. "Is God gonna get you?"

Glory turned away from the bad boy and took a giant step to the side. Of course, Josiah followed, so she took another step and another. After many more steps, they'd moved almost halfway around the balcony that encircled the sanctuary, and their battle of wills had turned to giggles. The game paused when a teenage couple walked into the sanctuary, looking around. Glory and Josiah watched the pair hugging and kissing. Well, at least, Josiah watched. Glory covered her eyes when the kissing started.

"It's okay. You can look now," Josiah whispered.

Glory peeked through her fingers. The teenagers were still kissing. She covered her eyes again and heard a thump as Josiah fell over, laughing. She peeked again to see the teenagers looking and pointing in their direction. The teenagers laughed and waved as they walked out, the girl with her arm around the boy and the boy with his hand on the girl's bottom. The girl tried to push the boy's hand away, and he whacked her. The girl just laughed. Glory decided teenagers were dumb too.

"Hey, c'mon!" Josiah said suddenly. "I wanna show you a trick!"

Glory watched the bad boy *running* down the spiral staircase.

"It's not bad—I promise! Hurry up!"

She followed him but didn't run. Even though she wanted to see the trick, following Josiah had gotten other kids in trouble, and watching him do a trick in church was probably a bad idea. At the bottom of the stairs, Josiah gave her a handful of flowers that had been left lying around from the wedding.

"Wait right here," he said. "I'll tell you when."

Glory watched him running again to the front of the sanctuary and shook her head. No matter what the trick was, she was not going to run in church.

"Okay, you can come here now!" Josiah called. "Bring the flowers too!"

Glory looked around and then walked to meet Josiah. She wondered if she looked like the flower girls walking up the aisle, even though her dress was yellow and she didn't have ribbons and she wasn't acting pretty.

At the front, Josiah bounced on his toes, grinning. "Okay. Do you like ice cream?"

Glory scrunched her eyebrows and looked at him. She wasn't going to be tricked into saying a bad word in church, so she just nodded.

"I promise it's not a bad trick." Josiah laughed. "You hafta talk. Do you like ice cream?"

Glory sighed, shifting her weight from one foot to the other. "Yes."

"No, you don't." Josiah said

"Huh? Yes, I do."

"Nope. You dooon't," Josiah sang.

"I do!" Glory said again as loudly as she dared.

Josiah broke into a wider grin. "I do too. Okay. Here's the good part. Close your eyes."

Glory folded her arms and stared at him.

"C'mon. It's not gonna be bad. I promise." He smiled at her again. "Trust me."

Glory took a deep breath and closed her eyes. She felt Josiah's hands on her shoulders, and then it was over so fast she wasn't sure what had happened. Her eyes flew open, and her hand went to her mouth. She stared at the grinning boy in front of her. "Josiah, you just kissed me?"

"Yup!" He smiled like he'd just done the best trick ever. "Now we're married."

Glory gasped. "No, we're not!"

"Uh-huh." Josiah laughed. "This is our wedding. We said I do, and you let me kiss you. That means we're married!"

Glory looked at the flowers in her hand and dropped them like they burned. "You tricked me! You take it back right now!"

"Nope, Mrs. Glory." Josiah picked up the flowers. "It's too late. You're married to me now." He offered her the flowers again, still smiling like he'd won.

"No! I'm not married to you, Josiah!" Glory pushed him down, and she didn't care if it was mean. She didn't even care if God was going to get her for it. There was no way she was going to be married to a bad boy like Josiah. When he didn't stop laughing and kept calling her *Mrs. Glory*, she hit him in the head with the flowers, and when he kept laughing, she bent down and hit him in the arm with her fist, and when he still wouldn't stop laughing, she sat on him and kept hitting him. Josiah shielded his face with his arms, and Glory hit him everywhere she could, demanding that he take back their marriage until she felt herself being pulled off a laughing Josiah by the teenage boy they'd seen earlier.

"How y'all gon' be fighting in church?" The teenager held Glory up by her wrists so her toes were barely touching the floor.

Josiah sat on the floor, leaning back on his elbows, smiling up at her. "Sometimes married people fight." He shrugged.

"We are not married, Josiah!" Glory didn't care about being quiet in church anymore.

"We just got married today." Josiah stood up and dusted himself off. "Now she mad."

"Married, huh?" The teenager laughed. "I don't know, li'l man. This one might be too much for you."

Glory was so angry she had to fight back tears. Struggling against the smirking teenager holding her wrist, she kicked at Josiah. "Let me go, you mean dummy!" She pinched the teenager, and he grabbed both of her wrists in one hand.

Josiah was starting to look not so happy.

"Li'l man, if you wanna be married to this woman, you gon' need to control her, or you might get hurt."

Glory kicked the teenager as hard as she could.

"Okay, let her go now," Josiah said. "We'll stop fighting, right, Glory?"

"I'm not married to you! Leave me—"

The hard smack on her bottom stunned her but not as much as the roar that came out of Josiah as he rammed his head into the teenager's belly, sending everybody tumbling to the floor.

"Don't you ever hit my wife!" Josiah kicked and pummeled the overwhelmed teenager while Glory scrambled to her feet. "Glory, run!"

Glory took off running and didn't stop until she reached the back of the sanctuary. She turned to see the teenager on his knees, laughing, and Josiah using karate moves just like the robots on TV. "God is gonna get you for tricking me, Josiah!" she yelled as she climbed the stairs to go find her mother.

AT HOME, SEATED AT the kitchen table, Glory watched her mother spoon and stir the brown chocolate powder into a tall glass of milk. After church, after the walk home, after changing clothes and eating dinner, mother and daughter had sat down to enjoy a dessert of flower-shaped butter cookies and, for Glory, a glass of chocolate milk. Her mother, Mary, had a cup of coffee and a cigarette. Glory dipped a cookie into her milk and counted to one—any longer, and the cookie would fall apart and sink, leaving muck at the bottom of her glass. Her mother sipped her coffee and took long, slow puffs on her cigarette.

"That was sho' a nice wedding today, wasn't it?" Mary said, blowing smoke into the air. "Jamette was so lovely. They gon' have a blessed life." She sipped her coffee.

"Mama, what happens when you get married?" Glory asked. "I mean after the wedding part. What do you do next?"

Mary coughed and put down her coffee cup. A puff of smoke blew out of her nose. "Well, baby, after the wedding..." She sipped her coffee again. "They start married life. They live together and have a family."

"So they hafta live together to be married?" *Aha... I can't be married to Josiah because we don't live together.*

"Well... sometimes married people don't live together. Like, your daddy mostly lives in his truck, but we're certainly married. His job makes him be gone a lot. And Jamette's new husband is going away to the army, so they're not gon' live together. She's gon' stay with her mama, but they still married."

Glory's heart sank. She dipped another cookie and forgot to count, realizing too late that she had only half a cookie in her hand. "What do you hafta do when you're married?"

Mary sighed a little and took a deep drag on her cigarette. "Well, baby, Bible says husband take care of the wife, love her, give her what she need, protect her, teach her, make her godly. Wife obey the husband, do whatever he say, don't shame him, take care of the home, take care of the babies."

Glory thought about Josiah, and her heart sank even further. He had tried to take care of her. He'd fought the teenager to protect her. "Oh." Glory picked up another cookie. "How do you stop being married?"

"Bible say what God has joined together, nobody can take it apart. Once you married, you married."

"But I don't wanna be married!" Glory blurted. "And today, Josiah—"

"What?" Mary sat up straight in the chair, her eyes wide. "What you say?"

"I said I don't wanna be married," Glory whispered.

"Don't you ever let me hear you say no mess like that!" Mary snapped.

"But—"

Mary stood up from the table and grabbed the extension cord hanging by the back door. "You hear me?"

"Yes, ma'am!" Glory cried, pulling her knees up to her chest, making herself as small as the kitchen chair would allow.

"I'm raisin' you to be a good, godly woman, and tha's what you gon' be, understand?"

"Yes, ma'am!"

Mary shook the extension cord in Glory's face. "You 'a be a good wife and a good mother and obey yo' husband. You understand me? Answer me!"

"Yes, ma'am." Glory trembled, tears streaming down her face, not daring to look away from her mother.

"Ain't gon' have you runnin' around like yo' Aunt Ruth, all them demons up in her, tryin' to be a man. I'a give you back to God first! You be a good wife just like God made you, understand me?"

"Yes, ma'am," Glory sobbed.

Mary dropped the cord on the table. "Good. Now, finish yo' milk." She sat down and lit another cigarette.

Glory wiped her tears, drank her milk, and suddenly understood why wedding ladies were crybabies.

CHAPTER 1
February 1984

Just breathing in the crisp night air made Glory feel free. The February wind was cold, but the sky was clear, and she could see the stars. Even though her whole body ached and burned, and she was covered with cuts and welts from her mother's extension cord, on this bitter-cold Valentine's eve, Glory slowly made her way up Seventy-Fifth Street.

She had always loved Seventy-Fifth Street in the South Shore neighborhood, with its bright lights and beautiful—and not-so-beautiful—people. In warmer weather, it would be alive nearly all night with traffic and music and pulsing neon beer signs in the tavern windows. Seventy-Fifth Street was where she'd dreamed of living one day. A cute little third floor apartment... just she and JT, looking down on the streetlights or up at the stars. They would have been Mr. and Mrs. Jackson, living happily ever after.

Glory had taken maybe thirty steps when she realized she was getting near the gangway—*that* gangway. She slowed her pace. The opening between her building and the next looked like a black cave... a black hole... a black doorway to her nightmares. Getting closer to the gangway, Glory moved to the curb. That night was her first time out alone since Malcolm had rescued her from a rapist in that gangway—since the twenty-seven-year-old minister had become her gallant protector.

After nine o'clock on a Monday night, Seventy-Fifth Street looked like a ghost town. Most of the shops were closed and dark, their metal gates locked tight. The tax office was still open, its fluorescent light casting a greenish glow on the sidewalk. Up the street, a local tavern spilled music and smoke every time the door opened, and a few men stood huddled in the cold outside the corner store—Glory's destination, the only open business in the area with a pay phone.

Glory stepped from the curb into the dirty-snow-covered street. The dark gangway loomed in her peripheral vision as she gave it wide berth, barely shielding her face in time to keep from being sprayed with slush by a speeding car. As she lowered her hands, she felt her four gold bracelets slide down her wrists. They had been a gift from her fiancé, Malcolm, this past Christmas. She'd been thrilled and flattered when he'd locked the engraved bracelets onto her wrists: *I am my beloved's, and his desire is toward me.* The jingle of the bracelets was a constant reminder of Malcolm's love and protection.

Each step she took, she prayed the cuts and welts wouldn't start bleeding again. Fighting against the biting winds of the frigid February night, with her bracelets jingling softly, Glory tried to pick up her pace, but the moist bandages on her legs rubbed against her long skirt and loosened. Her head ached from that fall against the metal bed frame, and the gauze covering the gash was barely enough to staunch the blood flow. The purging shouldn't have been a surprise. She must have been possessed by demons to say the things she'd said to her mother. *Did demons of doubt make me question God's will?*

"What if God sent somebody else for me?"

Did demons of disrespect loosen my tongue and cause me to speak against Malcolm?

"Mama, he's too old for me! I'm only seventeen! I don't wanna marry him!"

Did demons of worldliness make me forget my place, make me ungrateful, make me argue?

"Why can't I be normal? I hate this!"

Pulling her collar tighter, Glory walked the two blocks up Seventy-Fifth Street to the store with the pay phone. She had no idea who she'd call. She wished she could call her friends Tressa and Christy, but having no phone at home, she hadn't bothered to learn their numbers. She could call the salon, but her boss and best friend, Herschel, was not likely to be there on a Monday night, and what would she tell him? He'd want her to go to the hospital, but that was out of the question. *And what would I tell a doctor?* They might lock her up if she said she was injured in a demon purge.

Glory shivered. The small movement sent lightning bolts through her aching head and caused her undershirt to rub against the open wounds on her back that she hadn't been able to reach. That old extension cord, cracked and jagged in places, had scraped across her skin, raising welts and opening cuts, digging into the flesh on her left side, arm, and leg and on her back. Her mother wielded the weapon, shouting prayers to bind Glory's demons, and Glory sobbed and screamed for Jesus and begged for mercy. And when she could scream and cry no more, when she had no energy left to fight, when the pain was so much that she could no longer feel it, Glory drifted off to sleep while her mother pressed a pillow over her face to see if God would take her this time.

Glory looked up at the stars and whispered a prayer for strength. Each step felt heavier than the last. *What if I call Malcolm? I could convince him not to take me to a hospital, couldn't I?* Maybe she could hide her wounds, just tell him she had a bad headache. *But then what?*

She glanced at her watch. He'd likely be getting ready to preach the night ministry service at the South Gardens Mission and wouldn't be able to get to her immediately. Inside the store, she picked up the phone to dial Malcolm's pager and paused. Malcolm might ask why, and she would either have to tell him the truth about her behavior and risk *his* anger or allow her demons of lies to deceive him.

Glory hung up the phone, her bracelets jingling, reminding her that she was Malcolm's beloved and that he'd do anything for her. But after her outburst, she wasn't sure she even deserved Malcolm's love and protection. She left the store, turned up her collar again, and headed back home.

The Jezebel spirit is gone. God sent Malcolm to save me, and demons of lust and dishonor, lies and deceit made me shame him, but the demons are gone now. I'm a good girl, a godly woman. The demons are all gone.

PULLED FROM SLEEP BY the distant buzzing of her old electric alarm clock, Glory awoke, shivering. In the predawn quiet, she could hear the hissing of the old radiator, so she knew the heat was on, but with her goose bumps and chattering teeth, she felt like a window was open. As she sat up in her small bed, her whole body hurt, and a headache still thundered and burned in her skull. When she stood, the room swayed. She sat back down, feeling the cracking and splitting of crusted-over welts and cuts. The wounds she'd been able to reach—some warm, wet, and oozing—hurt at the slightest touch. Standing again, she steadied herself against her dresser, then the doorframe, and then the wall, lurching painfully down the hall to the bathroom. With trembling hands, Glory splashed her face and used a warm washcloth to carefully clean the dried blood from the matted spot at the front of her hair where she'd hit her head. She applied ointment and fresh bandages to the open welts and bleeding cuts she could reach and took three aspirin tablets.

"You should hurry. Malcolm be here soon, baby. How you feel this mornin'?"

Glory jumped at the sound of her mother's voice outside the bathroom door. Mary wasn't usually up this early. Glory wrapped herself in a towel to cover her blood-encrusted nightshirt.

"I'm still tired, Mama," she said, answering as best she could. Her throat burned, and the grating sound of her own voice hurt her head. Moving carefully to keep her balance, she opened the bathroom door to face her mother. "I just have a headache." She carefully met her mother's gaze because demons couldn't look a godly woman in the eye.

"I'm not surprised, baby." Mary shook her head. "Been so much devilment buildin' up in you. I was scared." She wiped a tear. "I was scared God was gon' hafta take you."

Glory wanted to reach out to hug her mother, to assure her the demons were all gone, but any extra movement made her head spin.

"I got rid of all that evil stuff in yo' bag—that picture of you like the whore of Babylon and that letter with you shamin' Malcolm."

The blush rising in her face made Glory's head throb. *How could I have been so careless?* She had almost forgotten about the cute artist she'd met on the train last Christmas. At least, she'd forgotten about him until she received a copy of drawings he'd done of her as a sexy supervillain. He even wanted Glory to be his girlfriend, and she'd written a letter saying yes. She shouldn't have left the incriminating letter and drawing in her bookbag.

"I burnt it all," Mary said. "Threw away all that mess in yo' purse too—them pills and stuff. Malcolm's gon' be yo' husband. You don't need none of that."

Yes, Malcolm will be my husband and savior.

Glory gripped the doorframe. She would have to dress carefully and bundle up tightly, but there was no way she'd hide her red eyes or her scratchy voice from Malcolm. She tried not to flinch when her mother reached out and touched her face.

"You kinda warm this mornin'. Demons all gone, baby?"

"Yes, Mama. Demons all gone."

Back in her bedroom, Glory dressed slowly. She easily pulled on her right stocking leg, but she had to stretch the nylon fabric and gently ease her foot and leg into the left stocking. She always wore pantyhose a couple of shades darker than her light-brown skin, the better to hide the scars on her legs. With her dark-brown hair tied back into a ponytail and a headband holding taped gauze in place, Glory pulled her undershirt over her head, wishing it were looser on her slender frame. The thin cotton fabric snagged and stung as it slid down her welted back. She slipped on a wool skirt and gray blouse and sweater, one of her many church-girl uniforms—shapeless, drab, and ugly.

Glory opened her ballerina jewelry box to retrieve the pair of gold earrings that matched her bracelets. The box with white flowers and a blond ballerina had been a gift from her father when she was six. It held a few harmless trinkets she'd collected over the years: a crackerjack pinball machine, the paper tabs off of her good-citizenship ribbons—her mother had cut up the actual ribbons so Glory wouldn't become prideful—the pearl earrings JT had given her for Christmas when she was seven, and the neon-orange Barbie shoe JT gave her when they'd gotten engaged last spring... after he'd made love to her, before he'd left for the navy and completely disappeared from her life.

Looking in the tiny mirror, Glory decided that when Malcolm arrived, she'd blame her bloodshot eyes on her headache. Their normal morning routine was pickup at five forty-five, and they'd get to the Red Apple restaurant in the Englewood neighborhood by six thirty, but Glory absolutely did not feel up to a huge restaurant breakfast, let alone school. When she heard the doorbell buzz, she made her way to the living room closet to get her coat and book-bag.

"MALCOLM?" GLORY HAD waited until she'd stepped out in-to the dimly lit hallway and heard her mother lock the door behind her before trying to speak.

At the bottom of the short, narrow staircase, Malcolm paused, holding the door open for her. He hadn't heard her. She closed her eyes and slowly descended the three steps to the foyer. The cool-er air briefly lifted the fog, but Glory knew there was no way she'd make it through school. She needed quiet and rest.

"You're movin' kinda slow. Are you okay?" Malcolm asked, lay-ing a hand on her shoulder.

"I have a really bad headache, and I think I have a fever. I don't feel up to school today."

Malcolm laughed a little, opening the heavy glass front door and filling the foyer with freezing February air. "Well, my first Valentine's Day present to you will be a day out of school. We'll go to the mission, and you can rest there. I'll take care of you till you feel better."

Glory steeled herself against Malcolm's guiding hand on her in-jured arm as she walked to the car. She concentrated on breathing and walking. Even though the brown vintage Cadillac rode smoothly, Glory felt every bump on the worn Chicago streets, and she was more than grateful when they arrived at the mission and Malcolm guided her to his office.

"Glory, you're burning up, and you're bleeding!"

Glory's hand went to the cut in her scalp. The bandage and headband must have come off with her hat. "It's just a small cut. I fell and hit my head last night—"

"No, sit down. Don't move."

Glory sat in the chair beside Malcolm's desk while he grabbed a handful of tissues. "Woman, why didn't you say anything?" he snapped. "You might need a stitch or something—"

"Please, Malcolm," Glory begged. "No hospitals, okay? It's small. I probably just bothered it taking off my hat. Please?"

Malcolm pressed the tissues to Glory's head and looked down into her eyes. "Hold this in place. Lemme find somebody to look at it."

Minutes later, Glory sat still while a young lady named Brittany reassured Malcolm that the cut was indeed manageable. The bubbly nursing student used tiny scissors to discreetly trim the hair in the area and bandaged the cut. While Glory rested on the couch, Brittany pulled Malcolm into the hall, saying she needed to talk to him about searching the women's clothing pantry for suitable headbands.

GLORY TRIED TO STAY awake, and when Malcolm returned, she watched him with sleepy eyes. He looked exhausted or upset—she couldn't tell which. Sitting at his desk, he bowed his head then looked up and wiped his eyes. "Glory, how did you bump your head?"

"I fell."

"How did you fall?"

"I tripped."

Malcolm sighed and wiped his face again, his light-brown eyes staring through her from under thick lashes. Glory and Malcolm had dated for two months before she decided he was nice to look at. He was tall and lithe like a runner, and Glory had once laughed at him and called him "just plain brown," but his complexion and hair color changed with the seasons. He went from warm tan with dark auburn hair in the summer to pale brown with dark-brown hair in the winter.

"Glory, Britt says you winced when she touched your left arm, and there's blood stains on the back of your top. She sent you another shirt to put on." Malcolm walked around his desk and knelt in front of her. "Tell me what happened."

"Malcolm, I can't. It's too embarrassing."

He reached out, stroked her cheek, and pushed her hair back behind her ear. "You're gonna be my wife. You don't get to be embarrassed with me."

Glory closed her eyes. "The devil got in me, and I got a whoopin.'"

Malcolm's hand left her face. "What?"

"Malcolm, I'm sorry. Sometimes I'm just so bad—"

"No. Stop. What do you mean a whoopin'? Like a little kid? With a belt?"

"Well, kinda. Not a belt. But I was really bad and—"

"Woman, no! You're bleeding." Malcolm stood up and held out a hand. "Stand up, and take off your top. Let me take a look."

The day before, she might have argued, but her demons were all gone now—there was no rebellion left in her. Glory moved slowly to take his hand and stand. With embarrassment and a modesty she had no reason to feel, she turned her back to him, unbuttoned her sweater, shook it from her right arm, then carefully peeled it from her left, hearing Malcolm's sharp intake of breath when her sweater was all the way off. She did the same with her blouse and stood still while Malcolm used scissors to cut away her thin cotton undershirt, which had become stuck to the oozing wounds on her back.

Glory waited, arms crossed in front of her, shivering, her bare back exposed to Malcolm's view, knowing he could see evidence of her demons from times before she could remember. For what seemed like an eternity, she heard nothing, only the ticking of the wall clock and the hum of the fluorescent lights. Then suddenly, the opening and thunderous slamming of the office door made her jump. Malcolm had left without a word. She wrapped herself in her bloodstained blouse and sweater and lay back down on the couch. The Jezebel she'd been the previous day had made so many plans for Valentine's Day. At barely seven o'clock in the morning, she cried softly and prayed that Malcolm still found her worthy.

GLORY OPENED HER EYES as Malcolm placed a tray on the coffee table in front of her. "I know you're having a rough morning, but you hafta eat, and it's still Valentine's Day." He held out his hand, helping her to sit up. Glory couldn't stop herself from smiling at the breakfast tray: heart-shaped French toast, bacon, and a parfait cup of fruit. A thin vase of red-and-white carnations sat next to a small box of chocolates.

"Thank you." She smiled up at him.

"Happy Valentine's Day, Glorious."

Glory heard warmth in his voice but saw none of it in his smile or his eyes. She pulled her blouse and sweater tighter around herself, lowered her eyes back to her breakfast, and tried to sit up straighter. She would be so good. She would even drink the coffee.

"Here, wrap up in this."

Glory turned slightly, letting the sweater and blouse fall from her shoulders. Malcolm wrapped a clean sheet and blanket around her, gently lifting her hair off her neck and laying it over her shoulders. "Now, eat. Somebody will be here to fix you up real soon."

"Okay. Thanks. Malcolm?"

"Yeah, Glory?"

"I'm sorry for making you mad. I shouldn'ta been so ba—"

"No!" Malcolm snapped. "You don't—"

Glory flinched.

Malcolm covered his face with his hands and took a deep breath. "I'm sorry. Eat your breakfast. Take a nap. I gotta make some phone calls. I'll be back as soon as I can."

Before she could say anything else, Malcolm left the office.

"HEY, GLORY, COME ON, time to wake up."

Glory moaned a little as a soft hand stroked her cheek and tucked her hair back behind her ear. She opened her eyes to look into Malcolm's. His anger of earlier seemed to be gone.

"Hi, Malcolm." She smiled a little, the pain in her head down to a dull ache. "I really need some water."

"Okay," he said. "I'll be right back—"

"And while you're at it," a voice behind Malcolm interrupted, "bring me two pans of hot water, hot as you can get, halfway full, and a pitcher of cold water, and a few clean towels, coupla face towels, and some bath towels."

Glory closed her eyes and tried to wish away the intimidating woman with the heavy voice and deep Southern drawl.

"And after you bring me those things, go to Bonwit's up on Michigan. Get there before noon. At customer service, ask for Jewel. Tell her your mama has an order waiting. She thought it best to get little Glory something decent to wear and not impose on the donations here."

Glory opened her eyes. Her wish hadn't worked. The Porters' tall, snobby housekeeper was still there.

Malcolm brushed back Glory's hair again, and she could see the silent apology in his eyes. "Mrs. Beyers is gonna take good care of you, okay? I'm gonna go get that stuff. You do what she tells you, okay?" He kissed her forehead.

"Okay, Malcolm." Glory sighed. With every muscle in her body aching, she sat up by herself but avoided stretching.

Glory waited quietly until Malcolm returned, pushing a cart of items. He looked more anxious than she'd ever seen him as Mrs. Beyers, the woman who'd helped raise him, placed a reassuring hand on his shoulder and ushered him from the office then returned to Glory's side. Glory couldn't decide whether the imposing woman was friend or enemy. She waited for instructions while Mrs. Beyers sorted through a large plaid tote bag.

"Well, dear heart," Mrs. Beyers said finally, "Malcolm says you've got some scratches that need attendin'. Stand up. Let me take a look."

Glory stood and slowly lowered the sheet and blanket from her back and shoulders.

"Oh, my lawd, sweet Jesus. That crazy..." Mrs. Beyers whispered then cleared her throat. "Okay. Let's get you outta the skirt and stockings too. I'll have you fixed up in no time, bless yo' heart."

Glory pulled the covers back up over her shoulders and finished undressing. Angry tears burned behind her eyes and nose. Malcolm's righteous fury was one thing, but this uppity woman's judgment was something else. Glory lay still on her side, facing the back of the couch, while Mrs. Beyers used the hot water mixed with peroxide to clean her wounds.

Where the blood had dried, the housekeeper left the warm cloth in place to soften the hardened areas. She used tweezers dipped in alcohol to pick out flecks of lint and long threads trapped deep in crusted welts. She let some bleed again. "To get the poison out," she said.

Glory alternately held her breath and bit down on the edge of the blanket as Mrs. Beyers applied salves—some burning and some cooling—and taped tight bandages to her wounds. The older woman's soft humming, sighs, and *tsks* of pity were often punctuated by outright curses of disgust.

"Child, I just cannot hold my peace any longer." Mrs. Beyers wrung out a towel in a tub of water. "What could you possibly be doing to get beat like a slave?"

"What do you mean?" Glory asked. *Beat like a slave.*

"Girl, don't play dumb. It's unbecoming." Mrs. Beyers dabbed at a long welt. "You know what I mean. No child deserves this. You have scars that go back years. That crazy woman needs to be locked up."

"You don't know me or my mother," Glory answered, fighting back demons of disrespect.

"You're right, I don't. But I do know what crazy looks like—"

"My mother is a strong, godly woman," Glory said quietly. "You don't know what she's been through, and you don't know what kinda demons I have that she—"

"Oh. Somebody beat the devil outta her, so she beating the devil outta you? Well, I do hope you'll leave disciplining your children up to somebody else. I don't believe the Porters will stand for you beating the devil out of their grandchildren. I mean, really, do you honestly believe you deserve this? Did you kill somebody? It's okay, no need to answer, bless yo' little heart."

"HEY." MALCOLM QUIETLY pushed the office door open, carrying four large white-and-purple-flowered shopping bags. Glory lay wrapped in the blanket and sheet, still facing the back of the couch, praying for sleep while Mrs. Beyers sat at Malcolm's desk, reading the newspaper. Glory rolled over and sat up, her headache nearly gone. Mrs. Beyers stood to gather her belongings.

"Mrs. Beyers, before you go..." Malcolm held up the bags. "Mother sent a lot of stuff. Can you help Glory get dressed, make sure she—"

"Malcolm," Mrs. Beyers said, cutting him off, "I'm sure little Glory can dress herself, but of course, I'll stay a bit and help. Why don't you go find us some lunch? There's an awful good smell coming from out there."

"Yes, ma'am. I think it's lasagna." Malcolm looked at Glory. "I'll be right back. You look a lot better."

Glory stared at the closing door. *Who was that? That wasn't even Church Malcolm. Unsure, nervous, soft... Little-Boy Malcolm? Malcolm who takes orders? Malcolm who doesn't run everything? Malcolm who calls this bossy old woman for help?*

"C'mon', dear heart, let's see what your future mother-in-law sent. I'm sure it's beautiful. She has excellent taste. Oh, of course, Valentine's Day. Such pretty buttons." Mrs. Beyers held up a black cardigan with red heart-shaped buttons. "It goes over this dress. Look how shiny the belt is."

As Mrs. Beyers unpacked the bags, knots grew in Glory's stomach. These clothes were wrong. Wearing worldly things with red decorations—flashy, gaudy—was inviting prideful vanity.

"Of course, she sent something lavender and pink." Mrs. Beyers held up a fluffy sweater. "That's her sorority colors. I'm sure that's what she *wants* you to wear, but we'll go with the dark colors for now. I patched you up real good, but let's not take any chances."

Glory chose the black outfit and dressed herself while Mrs. Beyers repacked the bags. Her muscles still hurt, and she could still feel the stinging of the welts, but standing in Malcolm's office, bandaged, comforted, loved, and protected, Glory felt blessed.

"Mrs. Beyers?" Glory said.

"Yes, dear heart?"

"Thank you." Glory kept her head down. "I really don't deserve—"

Mrs. Beyers reached out and lifted Glory's chin. "Chin up, dear heart."

Glory met her eyes.

"That's a good girl. *Nobody* deserves what you got. I know that's not what you was gon' say." She adjusted Glory's collar and smoothed her hair. "It's right that you speak up for your mama. But the God in the Bible, that I'm sure you've read, never *beat* the devil outta anybody. The missus says you're real smart. You think about that."

After lunch, Glory settled back onto the couch, listening to ice pelt the window, while Malcolm helped Mrs. Beyers pack up to leave.

"Your mama will have everything ready by tonight. She's actually very excited." Mrs. Beyers patted Malcolm's shoulder as she gathered her things. "I'll just take these extra clothes with me. Help me get this stuff to the car, Malcolm."

"Yes, ma'am, right behind you." Malcolm loaded the shopping bags onto the rolling cart.

Mrs. Beyers turned and nodded to Glory. "See you soon, dear heart."

Malcolm followed Mrs. Beyers out of the office. When she was finally alone, Glory marveled again at how differently Malcolm behaved in the company of Mrs. Beyers, his play mother. There was no sign of the street thug he used to be before the accident and deliverance that changed his life—no sign of the troubled young man who nearly took his own life. He wasn't the leader of anything. He was just a well-mannered young minister. Looking down at the bracelets, Glory felt a wave of gratitude. Malcolm loved her and was intent on making her part of his family, and even if he wrapped her

in gold chains, Glory knew Malcolm would eventually be her freedom.

Chapter 2

As much as she wanted to stay awake, Glory found herself dozing on the ride home, and when the car stopped in front of her building, she kept her eyes closed, wishing the day didn't have to end. Thanks to the pain medicine Malcolm had given her, Glory had slept much of the day, with Malcolm and occasionally Tutu—the wizened old man with the magical Caribbean voice from the reception desk—checking on her. Despite the morning's drama, Valentine's Day had turned out pretty nice. She hadn't been able to cook dinner at the parsonage like they'd planned, but the candlelit tray of baked chicken and dressing they shared in Malcolm's office was pretty good, and they had fun playing a question card game. Glory was both amused and relieved to learn that Malcolm's middle name was as bad as hers.

"Malcolm, I think I left my backpack in your office." Glory started to stretch, but the tug of the bandages made her change her mind. "How 'bout we go back and get it? It's still early. Maybe stop at White Castle's, get milkshakes. They're open all night, right?"

"Don't worry about your backpack. You're not going to school tomorrow, anyway. You're hurt. Mrs. Beyers is gonna take care of you."

"Malcolm, I'm fine. I'll probably be a little sore—"

"Glory. It's not up for discussion."

Glory opened her eyes and looked over at Malcolm. His eyes held none of the warmth and light of earlier.

"Glory, you have scars all over, don't you?" he said.

Glory didn't answer.

"Mrs. Beyers said they're old. She's been beating you... bloody... for years."

"It's not like that. You didn't understand—"

Malcolm slammed his fist against the steering wheel. "Then make me understand!"

"Sometimes I do bad things," she tried to explain. "Sometimes I let worldly things rule me and invite demons in. She tries to protect me... get the demons out. Like when I fell asleep in the car with JT—"

Malcolm pressed his head against the steering wheel. "For falling asleep..."

"Or when I was greedy and didn't come straight home, and that monster—"

"No!" He pounded the steering wheel again. "No! No! No!"

"Malcolm, she suffered a lot from lettin' demons in her. She's trying to get 'em outta me!" Glory hid her face in her hands. When she said her mother's reasons out loud, they sounded ridiculous. Telling them to Malcolm was a horrible betrayal and made her mother seem psychotic. "Please, Malcolm. Try to understand. She's just trying to protect me."

Malcolm reached out and lowered her hands from her face. He pushed her hair back and wiped the tear from her cheek then opened the driver's-side door. "Fasten your coat. Time to go in."

"Wait, what are you gonna do?" Glory asked, taking Malcolm's hand as he helped her from the car. She still ached, and the bitter nighttime chill didn't help.

Holding on to Malcolm, she moved slowly, feeling the pull of the bandages with every step. She didn't look up at him. From the tension in his arm, she could tell his face would be that mask of darkness that scared her.

"Malcolm, please. Don't do anything. Everything's okay. Really." Glory begged. Inside, she prayed. There could be no good outcome from this.

At the door to the apartment, Malcolm placed his hand over Glory's before she could insert her key into the lock. "Look at me, Glory." He reached out and gently lifted her chin. "You know I love you, right?"

Glory nodded.

"I need you to answer me out loud, okay? You know I love you, right?"

"Yes, Malcolm. I know you love me." She tried to keep the fear out of her voice, but looking into his eyes, she saw only cold darkness that terrified her.

"Here's what's about to happen. We're gonna go inside. You're gonna go to your room and pack up what's important to you. You're gonna say goodbye to your mother, and you're moving to my mother's. Do you understand?"

"Malcolm, no!"

"No, what? You don't understand?" he asked quietly.

"I can't just move in—"

"You'll be safe there."

"I'm not gonna just leave my mother—"

"Glory, it's safer for *everybody* with you living with my mother."

"Malcolm, please don't make me..." Glory couldn't even get the words out, hearing herself begging Malcolm not to free her from the life she was growing to hate, not to save her again, not to take her to a place full of books and light—not to answer her prayers because she had to honor her mother.

"Woman, understand. I will come after anybody who hurts you. You are my lady, and I love you, and it's my *job* to protect you. No matter where you are, even in your mother's house, I will always fight for you."

Glory stared up at the same Malcolm who'd defended her from her mother's attack in the hospital after he'd nearly killed the rapist. "But, Malcolm, she's been this way my whole life. I know how I'm supposed to act. I just got caught up in the world. Please!" Glory wrapped her arms around him. "I'll behave. She won't do it again. I'm almost eighteen, and then I can move out—"

Glory's protest was cut short by the sound of the apartment door opening.

"Y'all know it's not right to stand out in the hall like that. Give people cause to gossip." Mary stepped back and held the door for Malcolm and Glory to enter then closed it behind them. "Good evening, Malcolm."

"Evening, Mother Bishop." Malcolm moved to stand in the middle of the living room.

Glory stared at him. *Please, Malcolm, no.*

"How was school, baby?" Mary asked, going to the kitchen and turning off the kettle.

"She didn't go to school today, Mother Bishop," Malcolm answered before Glory could speak. He spoke in the same coldly pleasant voice he'd used in the store with Mr. Harris. "I kept her with me. She wasn't feeling well."

"Ain't you sweet, Malcolm!" Mary beamed. "Taking care of her like that! Baby, you okay?"

"I had a headache this morning and a fever." Glory placed herself in front of Malcolm. Not caring how inappropriate it appeared, she wrapped her arms around his waist and laid her head against his chest. "Please, Malcolm," she whispered. "See, it's okay now."

"Well, you didn't say you felt bad last night, but I guess you did tell me you had a headache this morning." Mary poured the boiling water, sending the scent of sage wafting through the apartment. "I hope she didn't give you no trouble, Malcolm. She can be devilish sometimes."

Glory squeezed with all her might and tried to resist as Malcolm pulled her arms from around him and gently pushed her away. "No, Mother Bishop." He laughed. "Glory is not devilish. Now, Glory, go do what I said for you to do. It's getting late."

Glory didn't move. She stood between Malcolm and the kitchen door—between Malcolm's cold, cruel smile and her mother. "Malcolm!" Glory wailed. "Please!"

"Glory Hallelujah Bishop!" Mary snapped, stepping into the living room. "This man spent all day taking care of you, and you gon' disobey? Go do whatever it is he told you."

"Mama, he's making me—"

"I thought we got all that out last night." Mary turned to Malcolm. "Sometimes she get demons in her, and I hafta get 'em out."

"Ha!" Malcolm's mirthless laugh was like a gunshot. "You cast out demons by the prince of demons."

Glory moved again to stand between Malcolm and her mother—between freedom and the mother who, the previous night, had tried to give her back to God. "Mama," Glory cried into her mother's confused face. "He's making me move out of here."

"Move out?" Mary looked confused. "Y'all ran off and got married?"

"Mama, no. We didn't get married. He's making me move to his mother's. He's mad because of... the... the... demons..."

Mary moved around her daughter. "Malcolm, you don't hafta worry about that. I'll just work a little harder to get the demons outta her. I'll set her right before y'all get married—"

Malcolm advanced on Mary, knocked the steaming cup from her hand, and backed her into the wall. "Woman, you are possessed by Satan, and by the prince of demons, you cast out the demons!"

"Malcolm, no!" Glory screamed.

"Your daughter is still bleeding from what you did! She has permanent scars from what you did for years and years! Jesus on the cross had less stripes than you gave to your own child!" Malcolm's gloved fist hit the wall.

Glory forced her way between them, straining against Malcolm, moving him back a step, feeling her bandages pulling on her skin. "Malcolm, please don't do this! I'll come with you tonight. Right now. Please, Malcolm!"

"I know my child, and she got demons all up in her!" Mary shot back. "She got rebellion and deceit in her! She was born in sin, and I work and pray every day to keep demons outta her! I call on Jesus—"

"No! Jesus cast out the legion by his *words*!"

Glory pulled Malcolm's arm, and he moved back another step. "Please, Malcolm. Come help me pack," she begged, pulling him harder, feeling loosened bandages moving under her clothes. "C'mon, Malcolm. Please!" She reached up and turned his face to look at her, praying her tears would move him. "Please, Malcolm? I'm coming with you."

"As my anger and wrath have been poured out on those who have harmed her, so will my wrath be poured out on you. You will be a curse and an object of horror, a curse and an object of reproach. She will never see this place again!"

Glory pulled him after her down the hall to her room. Into her old gray suitcase, she tossed her tattered apple-printed blanket and the rug woven of neckties that her grandmother had made. From her closet, she gathered the clothes she'd picked out for Christmas, ignoring the dowdy, ill-fitting things her mother had chosen. Finally, at her small chest of drawers, she grabbed a few unmentionables, her savings sock, and her ballerina jewelry box.

Glory stood looking around the small room with the faded striped wallpaper and pale-green curtains and felt like her heart was breaking. She shouldn't be leaving like this, in tears, with Malcolm threatening her mother. She looked up at him. He stared at the bloodstained linens on her small bed—gray-washed sheets smeared with dark brown. He wiped a tear then picked up Glory's suitcase and left the room.

Back in the living room, Mary leaned against the kitchen door fame, puffing a rolled-up brown-paper cigarette with a shaking hand. "I know y'all engaged." Mary took a short drag. "But you cain't just come in here and snatch a child without askin'. Not even you, Malcolm Porter."

"Child welfare does it all the time when they see bloody sheets, bleeding welts, and years and year of scars. You should be locked up with nothing *but* demons!" He snatched open the apartment door and stepped out into the hallway.

"I love you, Mama." Glory hugged her mother until she felt Mary's arms around her. "I'm sure it's only for a few days," she whispered. "I'll be back when he calms down."

"Malcolm!" Mary called out. "Mark my words. I know my child. She needs purging. She wants to be worldly. Devil get at her real easy. You takin' her over to your mother's with all that fancy stuff, gon' turn her head if you don't watch out. Demons of lies and rebellion, Jezebel spirit—"

Glory heard the suitcase drop and swift, heavy footfalls over the threshold. She threw herself at Malcolm before he could reach her mother.

"If you again lay a hand on her, you will remember the struggle and never do it again!" His voice was an icy snarl promising the wrath of God.

Glory pressed all her weight against Malcolm, the bandages under her clothes ripping from her skin, the medical tape roughly, agonizingly, scraping against her cuts and welts.

"Malcolm, God, please, let's go! Mama, just stop! I promise I'll be good!" Glory pushed against Malcolm until he backed up into the hall and grabbed her suitcase.

"I will bring you to a horrible end, and you will be no more. You will be sought, but you will never again be found!" Malcolm's biblical threats hung in the air as he backed toward the stairs.

Glory stared into her mother's impassive face. Mary took a deep drag on her rolled cigarette, nodded once, and closed the apartment door. Glory didn't move until after she heard all three locks click into place.

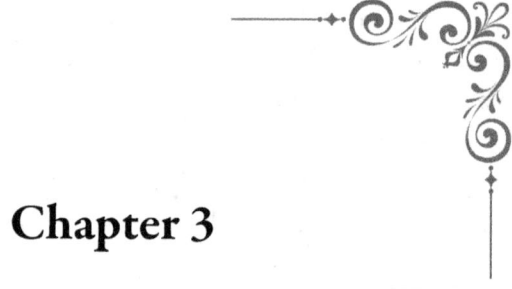

Chapter 3

In the dark room, Glory sat up in the center of the bed. To her right, a thin sliver of white daylight forced its way in at the top of the curtains. To her left, a soft blue light crept in under the bedroom door from the marble-tiled hallway. Far in front of her, she saw a faint glow from the night light in the bathroom. The clock on the bedside table flipped to 8:00 a.m., and the fancy old-fashioned telephone rang. After three rings, she wondered if she should answer it.

She finally lifted the heavy receiver on the eighth ring. "Hello?"

"Hi, Glory," Malcolm said in a cheerful voice. "It's okay to answer. It's your phone."

"Oh. I didn't know. I wasn't sure." Glory couldn't help smiling a little. She hadn't lived with a phone since she was nine years old.

"How are you this morning?"

"I'm okay." Glory wasn't exactly lying. Physically, she did feel mostly okay. She was stiff and sore and covered in painful bruises. She knew the pain would go away, but she couldn't think about the night before without crying, so she pushed those thoughts away.

"I'll be by to see you around lunchtime. I've got a lot to do this morning. Mother and Mrs. Beyers are gonna look after you."

"So, what do I do today? This is two days outta school—"

"Well, you heard Mrs. Beyers last night. She said for you to sit still and don't move. You're gonna spend today relaxing and healing—"

"Malcolm, I'm not sick, and I hafta go to work tonight. I could just take a note and sit outta gym—"

"Glory." Malcolm sighed. "You had a bleeding head wound and... and... you're covered with open cuts. If you wind up in the hospital with some kinda infection, how are you gonna explain your scars?"

"I don't know," Glory answered, feeling stupid. "It's just that..."

"Listen. It's not up for discussion. You're gonna sit there today. I know how much you wanna get at that library. We'll see what Mrs. Beyers says about you going to school and work tomorrow."

"Malcolm, what about my mother? I can't just—"

"The Lord has taken away your punishment." Malcolm's voice went cold. "He has turned back your enemy. The Lord is with you—never again will you fear any harm."

"Malcolm, stop it!" Glory moaned. "My mother is not my enemy. She does what she thinks is right—"

"She could have killed you, so she's *my* enemy."

"That's not true." Glory pushed away the memories of the pillows, the times God didn't want her back. Her mother loved her. Period.

"But you're safe now," Malcolm continued. "So *she's* safe."

A soft knock caught Glory's attention. "Malcolm, somebody's knocking."

"It's probably Mrs. Beyers. I'll see you later. I love you."

"I love you, too, Malcolm. Bye." Glory hung up the phone. "Come in!"

The door opened, and the petite silhouette of Mrs. Porter stood framed in the doorway. "Good morning, sunshine." Her voice reminded Glory of the slightly mischievous Southern belles in old movies. "I knew you were up because I tried to call, and the line was busy. My goodness, why are you sitting here in the dark?"

Mrs. Porter glided to the window and threw open the curtains, flooding the room with light, nearly blinding Glory.

"It's a lovely morning, Glory! Ha ha... morning glory! Since you're to be confined for a while, I'll breakfast with you in here. I'm sure you don't mind, right, Precious?" She looked over her shoulder at Glory.

Glory nodded, watching Mrs. Porter flit around, opening curtains, fluffing pillows, and lighting the gas fireplace. With her long brown hair held back from her face by a pink headband, Anita Porter reminded Glory of a lady on the soap operas. Her pink-and-purple robe trailed behind her just like someone on TV. She even had on matching high-heeled slippers with feathers on top.

"So you up and at 'em, and attend to your personals. Mrs. Beyers left you a fresh nightie, and your dressing gown is hangin' on the bedpost. How do you like your eggs?"

"Malcolm orders 'em scrambled hard," Glory answered.

"And when you cook eggs for yourself, how do you cook them, Precious?"

"I cook them kinda soft."

"Well, soft scrambled eggs it is, then." Mrs. Porter headed for the door. "Coffee or tea?"

"Malcolm always gets me coffee," Glory answered, immediately regretting it.

Mrs. Porter stopped at the door, turned, and looked over her glasses. "Glory, Malcolm is my son, and I know perfectly well what he likes. When I ask what you want, I do not expect to hear what Malcolm wants. Understand, Precious?"

"Yes, ma'am," Glory said. "I like tea... with lemon."

"Very good. Now, wasn't that easy?"

"Yes, Mrs. Porter. Thank you."

"You're welcome, Precious. Now, get freshened up. Mrs. Beyers will be in with breakfast presently. And, Glory, I'm only Mrs. Porter at church. Here, call me Miss Anita, okay?"

"Yes, ma'am... Miss Anita." Glory smiled at the butterfly lady flitting from the room.

When the door closed, Glory got out of bed and took a good look around the room she had been too upset and sleepy to look at the night before. Pale-yellow walls. Bright-yellow drapes over white sheers dotted with tiny white, yellow, and green flowers. Two yellow-flowered armchairs and a matching footstool were grouped with a coffee table and floor lamps near the fireplace, her grandmother's rug lay in front of the coffee table, and her apple blanket was draped over a chair. She almost squealed with delight at the television and stereo against the wall between the windows. On the opposite side of the room, a dresser stood topped by a fern, a bouquet of flowers, and a few knickknacks.

In the deep closet to right of the fireplace, Glory found all her clothes and the new outfits Anita had sent to Malcolm's office the day before. Behind the door to the left of the fireplace was the biggest bathroom Glory had ever seen. *Oh my God, the bathroom has two rooms!* The first part was pale yellow and had two sinks, a stack of fluffy towels, a mirror covering the whole wall, a vanity table with a lighted mirror and a thick, padded white bench, and a tall, narrow chest of drawers full of her unmentionables. In the second part of the bathroom, Glory found the toilet and a deep clawfoot tub.

Glory freshened up and changed into the nightie and dressing gown. *Oh my God, this is so silky!* Standing in the center of the bedroom, she wanted to throw her arms out and twirl in the patch of sunlight that fell on the thick butter-yellow carpet, but her arms and legs still ached, and Mrs. Beyers would probably fuss about her pulling the bandages again.

There was a sharp knock, then the door opened before Glory could respond, and Mrs. Beyers entered, pushing a cart, followed by a fussy Anita. "At least wait for her to answer! What if she wasn't dressed?" Anita said.

"She's got nothing I haven't seen," Mrs. Beyers said. "And if she's still abed, she's in worse shape than I thought."

Glory waited for the bickering women to notice her while Mrs. Beyers wheeled the cart toward the fireplace. "See, I knew she'd be up." The housekeeper began setting out breakfast on the coffee table in front of the armchairs. "Probably starving. That bit I gave her last night knocked her right out, and she didn't eat a thing."

Anita floated forward and took Glory's hands. "Don't you look simply breathtaking this morning. So much better than last night. I hope you like the ensemble I picked out for you. It so complements your beautiful complexion."

Glory felt a blush rising and tried to hide her face, only then noticing that her attire was a soft-pastel version of the ensemble Anita wore.

"Oh, no!" Anita reached out and lifted Glory's chin. "If you plan to be a Porter woman, you will hold your head up and accept a compliment. If you must blush, you may dip your head slightly and fan your bosom, but we do not hide our faces. Understand, Precious?"

Glory smiled a little. "Yes, ma'am."

"The proper response is, 'Why, thank you, Miss Anita. I love it. You have such wonderful taste.' Now you try."

Glory took a deep breath and giggled. "Why, thank you, Miss Anita—"

"Fan your bosom, sweetie, fan your bosom. That's a good girl."

Glory tried to fan her bosom, but a fit of giggles overwhelmed her, bringing tears to her eyes.

"Miss Anita, please stop!" Mrs. Beyers chided. "Let this girl have breakfast."

"Okay, enough bosom fanning for now." Anita laughed, taking Glory's hand and leading her to the armchair with her apple blanket. "I know it doesn't seem like it, but I can get a bit silly, and I've always wanted a daughter." She spread the blanket across Glory's lap. "So you'll forgive me if I overstep, won't you, Precious?"

Mrs. Beyers placed a platter of catfish, grits, eggs, and toast in Glory's lap. "Yes, Miss Anita. I'll forgive you," Glory said. She couldn't stop smiling even as she said grace and dug into her breakfast, surprised at how hungry she was.

"Good, good." Anita took her seat in the other armchair. "So, tell me the truth, Precious. Are you and my son having relations?" Anita accepted a plate from Mrs. Beyers. "This looks simply wonderful. Gimme a dash of hot sauce before you go, please."

Glory quickly chewed the mouthful and silenced the cough that threatened to choke her.

"Here ya go." Mrs. Beyers passed the hot sauce to Anita while lightly patting Glory on the back. "I'll leave you two to chat and be back in a bit. Miss Anita, don't let her do any stretching. I'm hoping to keep the scarring down if she keeps still enough. I'll check the bandages in a while. The worst of them are on her back and arm, so she needs to favor her left side."

"Yes, Mrs. Beyers, I understand. I'll be gentle with her." Anita giggled as the housekeeper left the room and then dug into her breakfast. "So, Glory. Are y'all doin' the do?"

"No, ma'am," Glory took a deep breath. "We're waiting for marriage."

"Mm-hmm." Anita nodded. "I admit I am surprised, but I honestly think I believe you. I mean, really, Malcolm is a grown man with a history, and you *are* a beautiful young girl. You wouldn't be the first to give in to him."

Glory fidgeted while she tried to summon courage she didn't feel. She and Malcolm had barely talked about sex, and Glory was in no way comfortable discussing it with his mother. "Miss Anita, we really haven't. Malcolm loves me, and he wants to wait till I'm older."

"Ah. Older is different than married, isn't it? And you say *he* wants to wait, hmmm?"

They ate in silence for a moment, Glory enjoying the best breakfast she'd ever had, in a sunlit room straight out of a magazine, with the lady who acted like a movie star.

Anita stood and removed Glory's empty plate and handed her a teacup. "Careful, Precious. It's hot."

"Thank you." Glory accepted the cup and saucer.

"Well, pardon my forwardness," Anita said, "but I had to ask. There's so much to plan, and it won't do to have you in the family way, ruinin' all the fun, now, will it?" Anita poured her own tea and returned to her chair. "It's too late for the debutante season, so your parties will be solely in your honor. You'll share the spotlight only with your attendants."

"Parties? I don't know—"

"Nonsense, Precious! Every girl deserves parties to mark becoming a young woman. I know you have your little prom thing at school, and there's the church cotillion, but there's a whole world outside of church and school, and you need to meet the right people. Don't look so scared," Anita continued. "We'll host a few small brunches to introduce you to my sorority and other clubs—they'll help you get into the right college. Maybe a few luncheons with businesswomen and at least two dinner parties before the grand bow for your eighteenth birthday. Then we'll go to my hometown for a few parties and a grand soiree for you there."

"But, Miss Anita—"

"If you're gonna be a Porter woman, you *are* gonna be properly introduced."

"But I don't have party clothes or anything—"

"Sweetie, you are moving into a position of power and privilege. There are people you hafta meet. With me as your sponsor, you will have everything you need."

"But, Miss Anita, it's not right for me to—"

"Look a gift horse in the mouth? Deprive an old woman of the pleasure of grooming a beautiful young lady into adulthood? Be ungrateful to your soon-to-be mother-in-law?"

Glory blinked twice and lowered the hot cup to her lap. She didn't know what to make of this fancy lady who only weeks before had called her a "dumb mama-fearing little girl who can't say her own name and hasn't read *The Cat in the Hat*." Herschel had said that fateful luncheon was Anita's attempt to humiliate Glory and get her out of Malcolm's life, but here she was, planning to turn Glory into a debutante.

Anita chattered on. "We have a lot of shopping to do. I promise not to treat you like a Barbie doll, but I do plan to touch up your wardrobe. When Mrs. Beyers unpacked your suitcase, we noticed you didn't bring any brassieres. What size should I have her pick up while she's out today?"

"Um, I'm not sure." Glory hid her face in her teacup, praying the scalding liquid didn't burn her.

"Don't tell me you're one of those bra burners?"

"No, ma'am. I just wear undershirts and tank tops."

"I don't understand." Anita blinked. "How do you take gym? What about running?"

Glory felt herself blushing, this time with genuine embarrassment. "I have one I keep in my gym locker." Glory couldn't bring herself to explain that Herschel had taken her shopping for a bra when school started because her mother thought such things made her chest attract attention. "Otherwise, I don't really need one." Glory concentrated on her tea and didn't look up again until she felt sure Miss Anita was no longer staring at her.

"Well... we'll go to Mary Del, near Evergreen Plaza. We'll get you properly measured, and you'll see what the right foundation can do. I mean really, your mama should've taken care of that. How does she expect you to attract anything, all sagging and drooping?" Anita sipped her tea then laughed. "Oh, wait. You did manage to catch my son, didn't you?"

Anita leaned back in her chair, and Glory did the same, enjoying the warmth of the fireplace. Listening to Anita's talk of parties and shopping and travel, Glory found herself forgetting that all this was temporary. But then, catching a glimpse of the dresser mirror and seeing her satin-draped self reflected in this beautiful room full of light, she was surprised at how she seemed to fit right into this gilded world. She fought down a twinge of guilt. Maybe the demons weren't gone after all.

"YOU KNOW YOU BELONG here, don't you?"

"Huh?" Glory looked up from her lunch of Harold's chicken wings, french fries with mild sauce, and spicy green beans. Mrs. Beyers had thrown in the beans, declaring the "ridiculous thimbleful" of coleslaw the "most inadequate" vegetable serving she had ever seen.

Malcolm reached out with his napkin and dabbed a bit of sauce from Glory's cheek. "I shoulda moved you in here a long time ago."

"It's awesome, but do you really think I belong here in this fancy place?" Glory waved her napkin around the sunny music room—conservatory, it was called—with its grand piano, soft, flowing fabrics, and fluffy furniture. It was her third favorite room in the giant apartment, after the library and her bedroom.

"Yeah, you do." Malcolm sipped his drink. "You're just not used to it yet."

"Malcolm, how long am I gonna be here? Your mother is making all these plans—"

"Glory, this is your home now. You're not going back to your mother's. Ever. I'm not having you where... where... let's just drop it, okay?"

Glory looked at Malcolm and tried a different approach. "I saw your old room. I love the colors. Aren't you gonna miss it?"

Malcolm smiled. "'I go to prepare a place for you,'" he quoted, laughing a little. "Actually, I'm kinda looking forward to living at the parsonage. I'm getting new furniture, painting. I'll let you see it one day but not anytime soon.'"

"Why not soon? How bad can it be?"

"Um... yeah. Turns out somebody saw us leaving at Christmas."

Glory gasped.

"Nobody knows it was you, but I've got a bad reputation now. Dad got pretty mad. I kinda had to make a deal with the devil to get the parsonage." He took a swallow of ginger ale from a glass. Anita didn't allow drinking from bottles or cans in her house.

"Elder Porter is not the devil," Glory scolded. "That's a terrible thing to say about your daddy!"

Malcolm laughed. "I'm not talking about my dad. You have *met* Mother, haven't you?" he said. Glory's eyes went wide, and Malcolm laughed again. "Don't worry. It's nothing, really. I hafta spend more time at the 'real' church, and *you* can never be seen going up to the apartments there. Dad was annoyed when he thought I was bringing women in. He doesn't really even know about you and me."

"What? I'm staying in his house, and he doesn't know about us?"

Malcolm reached across the table and took Glory's hand. "Woman, Elder Riley Porter would hit the ceiling if he knew we were engaged. He knows I care about you, but he knows you're in high school, and he won't tolerate a scandal in his church. Mother told him you were having trouble at home and needed a place to stay. She wanted to offer one of the guest rooms, but he thought it would be bad to have a foxy young girl around, tempting me... even temporarily."

Glory rolled her eyes at Malcolm's wink.

"Then she reminded Dad how much he needed me at the church," Malcolm continued, "and Dad just up and decided it was time for me to move out—insisted on it, even. I thought everything was cool till Mother suggested I 'earn my keep' at the parsonage by taking over Friday-night Bible study. It's okay, though."

Glory stared at the smug look on Malcolm's face. "You and Miss Anita tricked the pastor?" She imagined Elder Porter sitting in his study, carefully considering the issue, while his wife and son stood there like snakes. Suddenly, Glory knew she didn't belong in this place at all.

"Woman, no." Malcolm squeezed her hand. "And honestly, she tricked me too. She hates that I go to the mission so much, so she took my Friday nights. And my dad has only one concern: what's best for the church. When it comes to anything else, he listens to Mother."

Glory wrung her hands in her lap. "So your dad really wouldn't be okay with this, would he?"

"Glory, he is fine with it. He's actually gonna talk to your mother, but he knows Mother won't let you go back. Like I said, he won't tolerate any kind of scandal in his church. No bad publicity whatsoever. If you go back home, and something happens to you, Mother knows I'll cause a whole lotta bad publicity."

Glory stood up and walked around the room. She didn't like when Malcolm talked tough like that. She knew he was joking, mostly, but still... "Hey, Mrs. Beyers said I could go to school tomorrow. What am I gonna do for a note?"

"Already got one from the nurse at the mission." Malcolm stood up from the table. "I put it in your backpack."

"Oh, yeah, Miss Anita wants me to have breakfast with her every day. I tried to tell her we like going out early, but she insists."

"Don't worry. I'll talk to her." Malcolm pulled Glory into a hug. "She'll come around."

"Um, Malcolm... you have *met* your mother, right?"

"YOU HAVE NO IDEA HOW to break up with somebody, do you, Glory-Glory?" Herschel asked as he closed the gate on the front of the salon the next night. At ten o'clock, the party inside was still going strong, but Herschel was slipping out to drive Glory home to the Porters. "Back in my day, you broke up with somebody, you were done with 'em. I guess it's the new math or something. You take something away, and you end up with more."

Getting into the car, Glory laughed. "Herschel, stop!"

"Or, maybe *I* been doin' it wrong. First time you plan to break up with him, you get an engagement ring. This time, you get a penthouse. I guess I been breakin' up with the wrong people. Break up with 'im again—get us some lottery numbers!"

Glory and Herschel laughed loud and long while she directed him to the Porters' building. He stopped the car, and Herschel held Glory's hand as she reached for the door handle.

"Glory, listen. Serious for a second," he said.

Glory looked at her friend and was surprised to see hurt in his eyes.

"Darling, you know I love you like my own. I'm worried about you. *This* is not right. If you needed something, you coulda came to me."

Glory felt herself tearing up. "I don't need anything. I had a fight with my mother, and Malcolm found out, and things just blew up. I'm going home soon... when things calm down."

Herschel squeezed Glory's hand. "Listen, darling. Next time, you call me. I've got that whole building. There's always some riffraff I can kick out. You can have your own cute little apartment. You don't need to keep getting sucked into owing Malcolm. You hear me?"

"Yes, Herschel, I will."

"Promise?"

"Yes, I promise," she said. But as much as she loved Herschel, if there *was* a next time, Glory knew she would not betray her mother again.

Glory was surprised when her key opened the lock. Granted, Mrs. Beyers had made her practice it several times the previous day, and Malcolm had made her try it again that morning before leaving for school, but Glory hadn't been sure, yet, whether the whole fancy world of the Porter household wasn't just a dream.

When the lock clicked and she pushed open the door, Elder Porter greeted her with a hearty "Hello, young lady!"

Glory exhaled, smiled, and locked the door behind her. After dropping her backpack in her room, Glory headed for the library. She walked on tiptoe to avoid slipping on the marble floors in her stocking feet. The wall sconces, only lit in the evening, gave the halls a golden glow.

The library was dark when she opened the door, and Glory realized she had no idea where the lights were, but her attention was drawn to the tall windows. In the darkened room, the nearly full moon cast just enough light to make the space look magical. Glory stood at a window, staring, until she heard somebody behind her clear his throat before turning on the light.

"Tried not to scare you," a young man said. "I'm Dexter."

"Hello." Glory turned toward the voice and found herself facing a young man wearing khaki pants and a light-blue polo shirt. "Nice to meet you." She moved away from the window and headed for the door. "Good night."

"Um, okay?" Dexter waved a little. "See ya."

Glory wasn't scared, but being alone with a stranger just didn't seem proper. She'd made it almost to the door before Anita waltzed in.

"Good evening, Precious. I see you met my nephew Dexter. Isn't he dreamy?"

"Hi, Miss Anita," Glory answered. "Actually, he just introduced himself, and I was just leaving."

"Nonsense! Let me properly introduce you." Before Glory could escape, Anita grabbed her hand and led her over to the light panel, where Dexter appeared to take great pains to keep a straight face. "Glory, this is my nephew Dexter St. Jacques. He's a sophomore at Northern Illinois University in DeKalb."

Glory smiled a little and nodded.

"Dexter," Anita continued, "this is Miss Glory Bishop, the young lady I told you about. Isn't she simply glorious?"

Dexter smiled and offered his hand. "It's nice to meet you, Miss Glory. My aunt told me a lot about you." His Southern accent wasn't thick like Miss Anita's. It almost sounded like he was trying to hide it. His slightly crooked smile showed a chipped front tooth.

"It's nice to meet you too." Glory shook his hand. It felt as soft as Malcolm's.

"Glory," Anita said. "Dexter's feelin' a little homesick, so he's gonna spend some weekends with us. He'll be right down the hall from you, in Malcolm's old room. Won't that be fun?"

"Uh... sure," Glory said. *No, I don't belong here at all.*

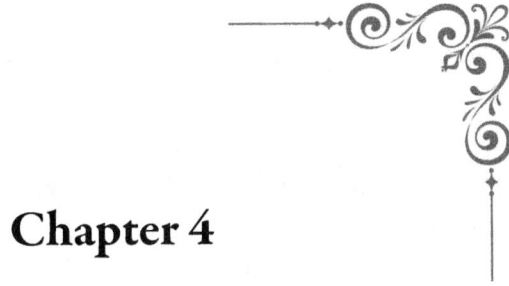

Chapter 4

Five days after moving into the Porter household, Glory didn't recognize the person in the mirror—the girl with hair twisted high on the sides and held in place with gold pins like a crown, some left flowing loosely in the back to her shoulders. The winter-white velour dress that barely touched her fell softly straight down from padded shoulders and then flared just at her hips. The cowl neckline plunged low in front, but the gathered fabric revealed nothing. The trim on the cuffs matched the trim on her gloves. She looked tall and elegant and, for the first time in her life, felt beautiful. But she also felt sinful pride and vanity trying to sneak into her heart, so walking into Lake Shore Christian Fellowship Church with Mother Porter that chilly Sunday morning, she prayed for strength to fight those demons.

Her arrival at church had been surprisingly normal. A few people remarked on her hair and dress, but otherwise, nobody treated her any differently. Kind of like her first Sunday at church after her night with JT or after getting her ears pierced or after getting engaged, her life had changed dramatically, and she felt so new and different. She was *glorious,* secretly living in a palace, quietly being a princess... and nobody seemed to notice the change in her beyond the obvious hair and wardrobe. Everybody just said hi and kept moving.

As the time for morning worship neared, Glory paced the balcony near Malcolm's office, peering again and again over the balcony railing, looking for her mother. Mary's choir wouldn't be singing that morning, so she would be seated as usual in the seventh or eighth row on the far right. Glory wasn't even sure her mother would be in church. She had no phone, so Glory couldn't call her, and Malcolm had forbidden her to visit. As quickly as she'd come to enjoy life with the Porters, Glory still missed her mother.

She almost squealed when she saw Mary walking toward her seat. With the eagerness of a little girl, Glory grabbed her purse and Bible, pushed her way through the gathering crowd, and took the seat beside her mother. "Hi, Mama," Glory whispered.

"Shush! What's wrong with you, girl?" Mary whispered back. "You know you ain't supposed to be talking in church."

Glory hung her head and pressed her lips together. She felt her mother reach over and hold her hand as service started.

AFTER SERVICE, THE church social hall—the Robinson Room, they called it—buzzed as always with the week's gossip. Glory overheard snippets of conversation about Malcolm's new apartment and his Bible study on Friday, with Cheryl and a few other women planning to attend every week. Glory felt more than a little annoyed. She wanted to flash her ring at them, show that Malcolm wanted no part of them. *Greedy old heffas.*

The room had emptied of all but Glory and the few diehard church families who refused to leave between services when she heard a small flurry of activity as Elder Porter and Mary Bishop arrived for coffee and cake. Whatever their talk had been, it was obviously good—her mother was smiling and laughing.

"Hi, Mama," Glory said, restraining herself from hugging her mother even though there weren't many people around.

"Hey, baby!" Mary looked her daughter up and down. "You look so different. Almost didn't recognize you. I see Anita's hand in that outfit—yes, I do."

Glory felt a hand on her shoulder. "Don't be modest, Mary," Anita gushed. "Your lovely daughter is the spitting image of you. Simply glorious, isn't she?"

Glory lowered her head to avoid watching her mother struggle with the compliment.

"Yes, Anita, and thank you," Mary said finally. "That's a very nice dress. Baby..." She turned to Glory. "Pastor says you're real quiet—spend all your time reading. You're not being rude, are you? You're helping out, right?"

"Why, of course she is, Mary," Anita said before Glory could answer. "She's helping by being her delightful self and concentrating on getting a proper education—"

"Anita," Elder Porter said, "I haven't had a cup of coffee yet."

Anita looked up at her husband.

"I'd really like one and a piece of pound cake if you can find one," Elder Porter said.

"Of course, dear." Anita spoke in a happy voice that scared Glory a little. "I'll get that for you." She squeezed Glory's shoulder before walking slowly away.

"You'll have to pardon Mrs. Porter," the pastor apologized. "Sometimes she gets carried away. I'll leave you ladies to your talk."

As the pastor left them, Glory gave in to her impulse and embraced her mother. She didn't cry, and she didn't want to go home—she just wanted to hug her. She held on until Mary pulled back.

"No need to carry on like this." Mary adjusted her hat. "Now, fix your dress." She reached out and smoothed Glory's collar. "You behave yourself at the Porters', right?"

"Yes, ma'am."

"And you being a good girl? Y'all ain't disrespecting—"

"Maaa! Nooo!" Glory giggled. "Malcolm doesn't even live there anymore."

"Well, good." Mary flicked a speck from the front of Glory's dress. "You better not be, 'cause I didn't send you over there to be bad... let them demons of lust get at you... have yo' Jezebel spirit—"

"Hello, Mother Bishop."

Glory looked to her right. Malcolm stood beside her, his hands behind his back, a church smile plastered on his face.

"Well, hello, Malcolm." Mary smiled. "Good to see you today. I was just telling Glory how I expect her to be while she's visiting. No messin' around." She shook her finger at Glory.

Malcolm didn't seem amused. "Glory never misbehaves, Mother Bishop."

As if on cue, Anita appeared on Glory's left side with a gentleman in tow. "Good to see everybody's still here. Elder does so love his coffee and pound cake." She slipped her arm through Glory's. "Mary, Deacon Strahan is gonna take you home. Don't want you out walking in this cold weather. Malcolm, can you go check if the van is back and get the good deacon the keys?"

"Yes, Mother." Malcolm turned to leave.

"Wait," Mary began. "That's kind of you to offer—"

"Nonsense!" Anita interrupted. "Elder insisted that since your talk lasted so long, you get a nice, comfortable ride home. Run along now, gentlemen. Mary, you must join us for lunch one Saturday. I'm having some sorority sisters over to meet our Glory... after she's fully recovered from her injuries, of course. They'll help her get admitted to some of the best schools in the country. Won't that be fun?"

"Anita, you know I don't want nothing to do with that mess," Mary scolded. "All I want you to do is see that she stays a good, godly young woman. She don't need none of your highfalutin worldliness. Don't be trying to change her into no younger version of you. That's not 'our' Glory. That child is *my* Glory, and she'll be back home with me soon enough." Mary reached out and pulled Glory into a tight hug. "I'll see you soon, baby, okay? You keep being good, hear me?"

"Yes, ma'am," Glory said, hugging her mother back.

"Anita." Mary nodded at the first lady.

"Mary." Anita nodded at Glory's mother.

GLORY STOOD STILL WHILE Anita bundled her tightly in her red wool scarf. "We can't have you tiring yourself out, Precious, and Malcolm is much too busy to look after you. Mrs. Beyers is outside, waiting to take you home to rest. We'll be there in a few hours, right after second service, okay?"

"Yes, ma'am," Glory wasn't tired, and she was barely sore anymore, but Anita insisted she go home, almost like she was getting rid of her.

"And, Glory, I know we won't be home before Dexter has to head back to school. You'll be a dear and give him a great big good-bye hug for me, won't you, Precious? Real tight, now. Make sure he knows he's always welcome to visit anytime."

"Yes, Miss Anita." Glory tightened her scarf and headed out to the housekeeper's waiting car.

INTERLUDE
JULY 1972

On the morning of her sixth birthday, it was all Glory could do not to jump out of bed and run screaming from her room—but she was in her panties and undershirt, and married ladies didn't run around like that. The smell of her daddy's cigar and his deep rumbly voice singing "Open Our Eyes" made her so happy she thought she would burst. As fast as she could, she dug a blue dress out of her bottom drawer and wrestled it on then carefully smoothed the pleats all the way around. She tugged at her pony-tails, checked to make sure her baby hadn't been kicked on the floor again—and then she ran screaming from the room.

"Daaaddy!" She barreled down the hall and jumped into the open arms of the singing giant standing in the living room.

"Heh, heh, heh!" the big man laughed, scooping her up and swinging her around. "Been singing that song for an hour. What took you so long?"

Glory wrapped her arms around her daddy's neck and squeezed with all her might. His fluffy gray hair smelled of green shampoo and a little bit like the inside of his truck, and his fuzzy cheeks smelled like cigars and coffee. Glory wasn't sure if it was okay for married ladies to hug their daddies, but she sure hoped so. He squeezed her back but not too tightly, and they danced around the living room until he finished singing their song.

"SO, MY GLORIOUS IS a big girl now, huh?" Paul Bishop III set a plate on the table in front of Glory. "This might not be enough food for you, sittin' there all grown up."

"Daddy, I'm only six!" Glory laughed. "I'm not that big. I'm just a *little* bigger—that's all." She hunched her shoulders as her daddy rubbed her head and sat down at the end of the table with his own plate of grits, eggs, bacon, and toast.

"So I got the whole day planned." Her daddy dug into his meal. "First, we goin' to the show, then maybe we go grab us a hotdog in the park, and then we go to Sears and get you some new big-girl clothes. Maybe grab some lemon ice and hot peanuts before we leave." He shoveled food into his mouth as he spoke. "Sound good, birthday girl?"

Glory pushed the food around on her plate. "Is Mama going?"

"Nope. She at work. Couldn't even stick around for breakfast." He picked up the newspaper. "It's just me and you today."

Glory sighed. "Well, we hafta ask Miss Joyce to watch the baby. I don't wanna carry her around all day, and I think you can't leave babies in the car."

"Okay, I guess, but why can't we leave your doll at home? I'm sure she'll be all right here."

"Daddy, a good wife takes care of babies. Maybe we should just stay here."

Her daddy lowered the newspaper and looked over his glasses. "Glorious, what are you talking about?"

Glory put down her fork. "Daddy, I got married, and now I just hafta watch the baby and do what Josiah says—"

"Wait a minute. Slow down, baby—"

"Yeah." Glory sighed, pushed her plate away, and rested her chin on her hands. "Josiah tricked me and made me marry him, but I beat him up, and he still wouldn't take it back, and a teenager was holding my arm and whacked me, and Josiah beat him up, so he's kinda a good husband except for the tricking part, but God is gonna get him for it, so I'm just the wife now." Glory shrugged and looked at her daddy. "I just get tired of taking the baby everywhere."

Her daddy sat with both hands covering his mouth and nose, his eyes squeezed tight. After a minute, he blew out a long breath. "I see. And what does Mama say about this?"

Glory sighed again. "I tried to tell her I didn't wanna be married, and she said demons made Aunt Ruthie a man, and if God makes you married, you just stuck." She looked at her daddy. His face was in his hands again, and his shoulders were shaking. His eyes even had tears in the corners. "I'm sorry, Daddy. I didn't mean to get married, but Josiah tricked me, and he wouldn't take it back." She had seen some men cry at weddings, but seeing her daddy with tears made her feel bad inside, like one of those crybaby wedding ladies. "Please, Daddy, don't cry. I'm really, really sorry! Please?"

The big man wiped his face, turned in his chair, and patted his knee. "C'mere, Glorious." He dabbed his eyes with a paper towel and cleared his throat.

Glory scrambled down from the chair and rushed to her daddy. "I'm sorry. I promise I won't get married anymore."

Her daddy lifted her onto his knee. When he hugged her to him, she looked up into his face. His mouth was serious, but his eyes were smiling.

"Daddy, you're not really sad, are you?" Glory accused.

"Now, listen, baby," her daddy said, his rumbly voice very serious but his eyes still crinkled. "I know you're a big girl, what with turning six and all, and yo' mama is right about one thing, bless her heart—when you married, you stuck. But you ain't married."

"But, Daddy, I said, 'I do,' and Josiah kissed me—"

"Oh, he did? He kissed you?"

"Yeah!"

"Is that a fact?"

"Yeah!"

"Well, Imma hafta talk to Josiah, but that don't mean you married."

"But he took care of me when he beat up the teenager for whacking me on the bottom. He said, 'Don't hit my wife!' and then boom!" Glory punched the air. "Knocked him right down!"

"I see," her daddy said. "Sounds like my kinda fella, but you still ain't married."

"But we said 'I do,' and I walked down the aisle with flowers and everything—"

"Mm-hmm. And this boy tricked you into all that, huh?"

"Yeah! Josiah is really, really bad and tricky."

"Well." Her daddy laughed, squeezing his daughter close. "He might be bad and tricky, but he ain't too smart, 'cause he forgot the two most important things."

"What?" Glory giggled as fingers poked at her ribs.

"I bet he don't have a job, does he?"

"No, Daddy! He's a little kid like me." Glory curled into a ball to keep from laughing.

"Well, then, that settles it. You ain't married 'cause he don't have a job, and he didn't ask me if he could marry you. Cain't nobody marry my Glorious unless I say so, understand?"

"Yes!" Glory screamed with laughter as her daddy's giant fingers won.

"So we going out and having a happy birthday and leaving the doll here 'cause *my* Glorious don't hafta listen to no husbands or look after no babies! Understand?"

"Yes!" Glory screamed sliding from her daddy's lap to the floor, her sides aching from the tickles and laughing and hiccoughs.

"Good," her daddy said. "Now that we got that straightened out, you go get washed up, and bring me somethin' to fix your hair, then let's get this birthday started!"

Glory squealed again and skipped from the kitchen, with her daddy's laughter echoing behind her.

GLORY BALLED UP THE pink dress and pushed it way back under her bed. She had really liked the dress with yellow flowers and the back out, but it had made her daddy cry, and now he was yelling at Mama.

"Ain't no damn devil in her! That baby is only six! She cain't do nothin' bad enough for you to beat her like that!"

"Paul, you don't be here all the time!" Mary pleaded. "She sneaky. Only the devil can make a child so young be sneaky like that. I do what I hafta do to protect her from—"

"Woman, I love you, and I'll never do you wrong," her daddy shouted. "But if you ever mark my child again, I'll whoop you like a man. Ya hear me? I'll whoop you like a man!"

Glory heard the front door slam and listened to see if she could hear anything else. She opened her bedroom door and tiptoed a few steps down the hall and paused. *Is tiptoeing being sneaky?* Glory continued down the hall, letting her bare feet slap loudly against the shiny wooden floor. She found her mother in the kitchen, lighting a cigarette. Mary's hand was shaking, and her eyes were red from crying.

Glory hugged her mother around her waist. "I won't be sneaky no more. And I won't let no more devils get in me either." She snuggled into her mother.

"I pray that God protects you from all harm." Mary squeezed Glory tightly. "And keeps you free from demons. In Jesus's name, a-man."

"A-man, Mama," Glory said.

Chapter 5

Glory loved almost everything about her life at the Porters'. It wasn't just the clothes and the books. It was the sunshine and light in every room. It was the fresh air and music in the apartment every day. And mostly, it was the freedom to be like other people. The day she came home from school and found a stack of new record albums and the artwork in her room replaced with posters of Michael Jackson and Prince, Glory actually cried.

Every time Elder Porter found her in the library, he'd challenge her to discuss whatever book she happened to be reading, and if she was looking at a map, he quizzed her on ancient geography. She tried to be a proper guest and help with chores, but she stopped when Mrs. Beyers yelled at her. Glory successfully negotiated a compromise in which she mostly did her own laundry and cleaned her own room but left the linens and vacuuming to Mrs. Beyers.

Glory slowly made friends with Cousin Dexter, although Anita insisted, "Y'all are *not* cousins, Precious." On his weekend visits, he seemed to study a lot, smile a little, and devour anything that Mrs. Beyers cooked.

With Malcolm's church duties keeping him busy all weekend, Dexter often served as Glory's driver to work on Saturdays, and sometimes, if they were both hungry late at night, he'd make a run to White Castle or Italian Fiesta, and they'd watch music videos in the library until they fell asleep. Sometimes, she thought about James, the boy she'd met on the train last Christmas, and laughed at herself. In one day, she'd gone from pretending to be engaged to Malcolm to being James's girlfriend—a boy she hardly knew—to truly being engaged to Malcolm. Other times, she thought about JT and the life she'd almost had, the baby she'd desperately wanted, and the streetlights and stars that she hadn't counted in so long. She still remembered how he felt and how he made her feel... so many dreams.

But mostly, even though she saw him almost every day, Glory was starting to miss Malcolm. They didn't get to have long mornings together anymore, and Anita had taken over Glory's college search, so their only real time together was limited to car rides to and from school. Even Mondays at the mission, he was working, and since she was now recognized as Malcolm's lady, she was pretty busy too. When he dropped her off every day, his hugs were long and lingering, and his goodbye kisses were short and hungry. Sometimes he raged at the eleven o'clock phone curfew on school nights. Malcolm had brought her into his beautiful world, and he was slowly being pushed out of it.

Under Anita's guidance, Glory's college options had widened. She now heard from schools as far away as California. She learned not to mention those schools to Malcolm after his reaction to a trip she and Anita took to the University of Wisconsin in Madison. She'd listened to him go from interested to angry, and then he forbade her to consider any more out-of-state schools. Looking back on it, Glory realized she probably shouldn't have dared him to tell that to his mother.

"So you're telling me that our precious Glory, *your* precious Glory, doesn't deserve the best education?" Anita had looked over her teacup at Malcolm, standing across the breakfast table from her. Even at six o'clock in the morning, Anita sat at the head of the breakfast table like a queen.

"No, Mother," Malcolm said. "You know that's not what I'm saying—"

"Please sit down, son. Have some breakfast. There's no need to pace like that. It's impolite."

Malcolm sighed and took a seat opposite his mother. Glory tried to catch his eye and signal that this wasn't a good conversation to continue—it was a case of an immovable object faced with an irresistible force. She saw Mrs. Beyers watching with an amused smile.

"Mother, you know Chicago has some of the best colleges in the world—"

"Then you mean to say this bright young lady doesn't get a choice in what opportunities to pursue? I see." Anita sipped her tea.

Glory looked away while Mrs. Beyers set their breakfast plates on the table.

"Why are you doing this, Mother?" Malcolm leaned back in his chair and folded his arms. "I thought you liked having her here."

"I do, son. You know that." Anita paused and recovered coolly. "But she should have every opportunity to pursue whatever she wants. You remember... like the unlimited educational opportunities you had."

"So, then, you'll explain to Dad why I'll be leaving Chicago to follow her to Wisconsin or California or wherever she chooses to go to school?" Malcolm's smirk was triumphant.

"Malcolm, for God's sake, let the girl grow up! You've got years before the wedding. I don't see why she shouldn't be out experiencing the world. Just because you didn't take the chance doesn't mean she shouldn't."

Malcolm winked at Glory and quickly finished his breakfast then got up and kissed his mother's cheek. "I love you, Mother.

This was fun." He nodded at Glory. "See you downstairs. We'll grab coffee on the way."

Glory watched Malcolm leave and then turned to see a proud smile on Anita's face.

"You hafta give 'em small victories sometimes," Anita said. "Remember that, Precious. Anyway, we're flying to Ann Arbor, Michigan, next Saturday so you can check out the University of Michigan. I'm still waiting to hear back from Spelman and Jackson State."

"But, Miss Anita, Malcolm said—"

"Precious, this is *your* life."

"But... I wouldn't have this life it wasn't for Malcolm," Glory said. Those were the words that her mother had drilled into her head and her heart, and sitting in this beautiful place, Glory knew them to be true. "It's not right for me to be ungrateful and rebellious."

"Wanting things for yourself is not ungrateful, Precious. In fact, important men, like my son is gonna be, need rebellious women at their side. He's gon' make some stupid decisions, and you'll need to rebel to protect him. This is lesson one."

"But... I don't know—"

"Don't worry, Precious," Miss Anita said. "I can handle my son. Grab your things and run along, now." She sipped her tea. "If he wanted you to stay docile, he brought you to the wrong place." She winked at Glory. "I'm from the South. Where do you think rebels come from?"

Chapter 6
SPRING 1984

Glory hated these brunches. "Networking," Anita called it—meeting the right people, knowing who could do what for her and prepare her to take her rightful place in society. She loved everything else about life with the Porters, but she absolutely hated dressing up every other Saturday morning and memorizing the names of Miss Anita's friends. She hated smiling bashfully when Miss Anita described her as a "girl Friday to a salon owner whose products are distributed in the most exclusive North Side boutiques." She hated these uppity people who talked about golf and fancy stuff and laughed at their own jokes—and their kids, snobby girls who were small versions of their mothers and snooty boys who were just like every boy in the world except they wore their sweaters tied around their necks.

The guests that day were Mrs. Gentry and her twin sons, Eric and Marc. Glory tried to listen politely and nod appropriately to the conversation. Anita grilled the boys on their hobbies and future plans, and Glory fielded questions from their mother about her own goals. After what felt like hours, Glory restrained a sigh as she was asked to entertain the boys in the library while the adults finished talking.

This was the worst part. As soon as the library door closed, the perfect angels were gone. The kids tried to smoke or asked for liquor. The boys always assumed she was fast because "all rich church girls are horny." Anita was always "simply mortified" when Glory told her, yet every other week, Glory walked another teenage nightmare into the library.

That morning, she kept the heavy double doors open, and to her surprise, the boys seemed genuinely interested in the Porters' book collection. She stayed back and pointed out her favorite sections while they wandered the room. When Eric—or maybe it was Marc—asked if they were too loud, Glory assured them the noise was fine and that it was okay to have the door open. She'd already fallen for that trick once.

"Hey, Glory, can you settle something for us?"

Glory looked up from the book she was reading. The twins stood in the corner near the map table, talking rapidly and loudly. Eric, in a green polo shirt, had his arms folded. Marc, in a red shirt, had his hands in his pockets. Eric motioned for her to come over.

Glory joined them at the map table. "What's up?"

"Well," Eric said, "My idiot brother thinks the Silk Road went through Prussia—"

"Call me an idiot again!" Marc pushed his brother, prompting Glory to step between them.

"You're actually going to fight about this?" Glory rolled her eyes. *Nerd boys fighting over geography.*

"All I'm saying," Marc said, "is that the Silk Road traveled through what eventually became Prussia—"

"No way! It never went through Europe—" Eric cut in.

"Um, guys," Glory interrupted, "you have the Silk Road map right here in front of you." She sighed. These boys weren't nerds—they were just stupid. "Europeans might've come down from Prussia, but the road barely went into Europe—"

"That's what I was saying," Eric said. "But this moron—"

"But this map is only showing major roads." Marc pointed at the spaces on the maps just outside the roads. "These parts had small roads and trails too. Who knows how long and hard people traveled to get to the main Silk Road?"

"Man, you're crazy," Eric said. "You see how wild this road looks? There's a front way and a back way. People pounded it hard and deep from both sides."

Glory looked at the two boys acting like they were staring intently at the map. *Are they really doing this?* She had to admit it was original. She turned to go back to her book, but Eric blocked her path, not pretending to be polite anymore.

"Excuse me." Glory tried to move around him. "I need to go."

"They came in and out, back and front, fast and slow," Eric continued. "That road was probably a whole lotta fun."

They had her effectively cornered, but Glory realized she wasn't scared, just annoyed. She'd faced real monsters, and all these stupid little boys could do was talk dirty. If they touched her, she'd scream. If they denied it, Anita would believe her, and Malcolm would kill them.

"What is it with you people?" Glory shook her head. "Don't you have a girlfriend or something? Oh, wait. You probably don't."

"Ha!" laughed Marc. "That's harsh!"

"You shut up too!" Glory snapped and then shoved Eric as hard as she could and stomped past him. She was almost out the door when she found her way blocked once again by the two smiling boys.

"Please, guys." Glory sighed. "I really don't feel like screaming. You'll deny it, I'll cry, maybe tear my dress and blame it on you, lotta commotion. I might even faint. Do you really wanna go through that?"

Eric grabbed Glory's hand, not letting her pull away. "I can't tell if you're playing hard to get or if you're really just no fun."

"She's not playing at all. She's really no fun." Dexter's voice came from the open doorway.

Glory snatched her hand back and smiled as Dexter stepped between the boys and stood next to her.

"Hi, I'm Dexter." He offered his hand. Neither boy shook it. Dexter shrugged. "I'm a lotta fun, but you shouldn't touch her. See these bracelets?" Dexter held up one of Glory's hands. "She's spoken for. Her owner already killed somebody for touching her without asking. Y'all should keep your hands off."

"Are you her owner?" Eric asked.

Dexter looked at him and shook his head then turned to Marc. "You must be the smart one. Y'all get back out there with your mama before you get in real trouble."

Marc tapped his brother's shoulder, and they left the library, but not before Eric made a slurping sound at Glory.

"I have an owner, Dexter?" Glory growled at the young man who'd just rescued her from a situation that she'd had well under control. "That's the best you could come up with?"

"What?" Dexter asked. "I don't get a thank-you?"

Glory made a fist and punched him in the stomach as hard as she could then went to her room to listen to Prince.

"GLORY, PRECIOUS!"

Glory looked up and removed her headphones as Anita entered her room. "Yes, ma'am?" She knew Anita couldn't hear the music on the tape player, but still, Glory blushed.

"Dexter told me about those awful boys today. I'm sorry."

"It's okay. I handled it."

"Nonsense! You've already been through enough, and to have such lowlifes in your own home—"

"Well, did Dexter tell you what *he* said?"

Anita sighed. "Yes, he did. I told him you shoulda punched him twice. Owner, indeed!" She punched her palm with her delicate little fist. "Well, anyway, Precious, get dressed 'cause Dexter's taking you to the movies to make it up to you. My treat."

"But, Miss Anita," Glory protested, "I'm not sure—"

"Nonsense! You've been cooped up here for much too long. Malcolm is too busy to entertain you properly, and obviously, the people I know leave a lot to be desired. You're a young girl who needs to get out and have fun. There's more to life than school, church, and work, Precious. You wanna have some good times to remember when you get to be my age, don't you?"

"But, Miss Anita—"

"Hurry, hurry, Precious!" Anita headed for the door. "Your cab'll be here in ten minutes."

Glory stood staring at the closed door and then took a deep breath. Normal girls dropped everything and went to the movies. She could do this. She had just enough time to call the mission and leave a message for Malcolm that she wouldn't be home when he called.

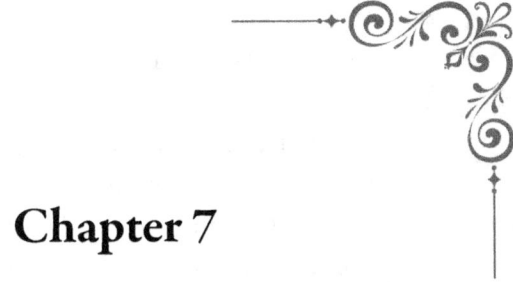

Chapter 7

After the incident with the twins, Dexter stayed around for all of Anita's get-togethers, sparing Glory the trouble of being alone with *those* people. And as the April party season started, and Glory was taken to make the rounds, Anita always called Dexter to come and escort Glory home early in the evening, insisting they take their time and have fun along the way.

Sometimes, Dexter just dropped Glory at home and headed off. Other times, they hung out together and watched cartoons or played board games. One unseasonably warm night, after somebody's sweet-sixteen party at the South Shore Country Club, Glory found herself moving to the beat of African drums at the Sixty-third Street beach, feeling the music so deep she wanted to shout, and after two or three wine coolers, she realized Dexter was really cute... and she knew it was definitely time to go home.

Glory could never understand why Malcolm had chosen the street life over the fancy life his mother wanted for him. The rough, hard world of the mission was so far from the safe, shiny one he'd grown up in. Glory had to wonder if there really had been a demon in Malcolm when he was young—something that had made him choose to go looking for evil.

***

"SHHH! NOT SO LOUD," Dexter whispered. "Why are you so giggly tonight?"

"I don't know." Glory tried to muffle another laugh. "Maybe because you're so goofy." Glory stood in the Porters' foyer, untangling her red silk scarf and shawl, while Dexter hung up his jacket. "I'm still mad at you about that 'owner' thing."

"C'mon, that was almost a month ago. You should really learn to forgive and let things go." He tweaked her nose.

Glory slapped Dexter's hand. "This was the third party I've had to sit through, and still, all of those snobby boys—"

"Are too dumb and afraid to come near you. And the girls are jealous because the boys stand around drooling over you, and you don't even put out."

"Dexter, did you really hafta grow up doing this kinda stuff? Meeting the right people and all this... mess?"

"Back home, it was worse." Dexter hung up Glory's scarf and shawl. "I was in two clubs. In the spring, I had to go to at least two parties every Friday and Saturday night. Boys just wanted to get some, but the girls were hunting for rings, especially in high school. A boy would flash his fancy car or something, and a girl would try to whip it on you—"

"Dexter!"

"It's true. And Auntie missed Malcolm's turn 'cause he got sick. Now she gets to relive her own debutante days through you, but everybody's scared to touch you."

"You know, tonight, somebody actually tried to tell me these"—she held up the bracelets—"are illegal in America. I should punch you again!"

"Well, do it quietly. You don't wanna wake everybody," Dexter said. "You hungry?"

"Oh my God! You're a bottomless pit, aren't you? C'mon." Glory grabbed his hand and pulled him toward the kitchen. "I'll find you something." Even though she wanted to be annoyed, Glory really was grateful to have Cousin Dexter around. "So, what would you like?" she whispered, pulling Dexter into the dimly lit kitchen. It was well after midnight, and everybody else in the Porter household was asleep.

"Not really hungry anymore." Dexter loosened his fingers from Glory's.

"Huh? You just said—"

Dexter nodded toward the kitchen table as Malcolm rose from a seat in the corner.

"Malcolm!" Glory dropped Dexter's hand and ran to her fiancé. "You're supposed to be on the night ministry." She looked up at him. "Is everything okay?"

"Everything's fine." Malcolm didn't look at her. "What's up, li'l cousin?" He nodded to Dexter.

"Hey, Mal." Dexter shoved his hands in his pockets. "Uh, good night."

"Yeah." Malcolm wrapped his arms around Glory, pulling her close, still not looking at her.

"Good night, Glory," Dexter said, leaving the kitchen.

"Night, Dex," Glory said.

"Good night!" Malcolm said, watching Dexter leave the room.

Glory pulled back from Malcolm and looked up at him. "Malcolm, what's wrong?"

"Where've you been?" he asked.

"At a party with your mother. She called Dex to come and get me."

Malcolm bowed his head, taking a deep breath. He pressed his forehead to hers, his voice lowered to a whisper. Glory felt his fingers grip her arms. "Woman, Mother has been home for hours. Where have you been?"

"Malcolm, please." Glory winced. He hadn't touched her like that in a long time, not since before Christmas. "When Dex picked me up, Miss Anita said to take our time, so we went to a movie. Please, if I knew you were coming, I would've been here."

"I'm sittin' here worrying, and you out in the streets—"

"Malcolm, I was with your cousin!" Glory snapped, pulling away from him.

"Don't you walk away from me!"

"Then stop hurting me, and stop being so silly!" Glory heard her own defiant tone and felt the wind of Malcolm's motion as the words left her mouth.

She didn't flinch or even blink. It didn't really hurt that much. He'd hit her a lot harder before... before he'd promised never to hit her again. Malcolm stepped back and looked at his hand and then reached out to touch the spot where he'd just hit her. She just looked at him.

He pulled her into his arms. "Oh God, I'm sorry!" Malcolm buried his face in her hair. "I'm not mad at you. I'm just upset. I was worried—"

"I know." *Have I been in this place so long I've forgotten* this *Malcolm?*

He held her tighter, shaking. "We haven't had any real time together in so long. I miss you so much... I'm leaving tomorrow. I blew off work tonight, and when you weren't here—"

"I know," Glory said. "I miss you too." *Has this place made me forget how to hold my tongue and not provoke him?*

"And then I saw you and him—"

"I'm sorry," Glory said honestly. Dexter had been right. She did belong to somebody. She was Malcolm's *beloved*, and she shouldn't have been holding Dexter's hand.

Malcolm choked back a sob. "I swear, I'll never raise a hand to you again."

"I know." Glory accepted his apology and his kiss. And she knew he meant it this time. Again.

EVEN COLD, HAROLD'S chicken wings were great. Seated across the kitchen table from Malcolm, Glory hoped they'd always make up this way. "You look tired," she said.

"And you look fine as wine." Malcolm reached across the table and took her hand. "I keep forgetting to tell you, every time I see you, it's like you're turning into this goddess—"

"Malcolm, stop." Glory blushed, pulling her hand back.

"No, really. It's like you're blossoming here. You're more glorious than I thought possible."

"Please, stop now."

"Okay. But yeah, you fine... good enough to eat." He kissed his fingers.

"Malcolm! One more word, and I'm going to bed!"

"Okay." Malcolm said. "You know, I didn't think I'd miss living here. But it's really quiet at the church. Lonely."

"Well, you could hang out here more." Glory laughed.

Malcolm sipped his pop and twirled the cracked ice in his glass. "No time. Dad's got me doing a lot more work at the church now. I only get to the mission to preach on Mondays and Thursdays and on Friday overnights. And after I graduate next month, they'll want me at the church full-time."

"Isn't that why you're going to Bible college—to be a real minister at a real church?"

"Wow." Malcolm shook his head. "I keep forgetting how young you are."

"Oh. Well—"

"No, don't get mad. It's just that you don't know... I don't minister to people in that church. I preach, but I don't help nobody. Any real good I do, I do on the street. I haven't changed a single life in that church—"

"You changed mine," Glory said.

Malcolm sighed. "You know what I mean. That's a place full of people who already know the Lord and expect to be entertained. On the street, I work with people in need. I make a difference. I can't get my dad to see that. For him, that pulpit is all that matters, and me gettin' up there is his dream."

"You hate it that much?" Glory asked. She'd always thought of Malcolm as a real minister at church and the mission as only a hobby. *What if he actually leaves the real church?* "You wouldn't leave Lake Shore, would you?"

"Nah, I'm not leaving. And I don't hate it." Malcolm leaned back in his chair and stretched. "If I get stuck in a pulpit, I'm just gonna change things, shake things up, step outside of all the high life... get down and dirty, like Jesus did."

"But, Malcolm, you can't just change people's church—"

"You just let me worry about runnin' churches, okay, woman?" He reached out and touched her cheek. "All I need you to do is be my *helpmeet*."

Glory yawned. "I can't believe I'm not gonna see you for my entire spring break. Do you really hafta go on this mission trip?" She got up to clear their plates from the table.

Malcolm came up behind Glory and wrapped his arms around her. "I tried to get out of it. Dad *wants* me to go, but Mother, she's *making* me. I mean, I get it—she wants me to keep an eye on Dad. He's too old for this stuff. And it's a good cause, but a mission trip to Haiti when we could do a mission trip right here in Chicago?" He hugged Glory tighter, kissing the top of her head. "Anyway," Malcolm continued, "it's only a week. You know Mother is gonna keep you busy, planning your parties and all that stuff. We'll talk every day, and you'll be so busy you won't even notice."

"Malcolm, when you were my age, did you hafta do this 'social calendar' stuff?"

"I told you I did." He laughed a little. "Until I got to be unmanageable, and nobody wanted me near their kids."

"Yeah, I guess."

"I was a bad influence. The girls wanted... a taste, and the boys wished they were as bad as me. Mother was always apologizing."

"I still can't believe you actually messed with those girls."

"I was a stupid teenager. I was wild, and I'm not proud of it. I still apologize to them when I see 'em. At least, all the ones I remember."

"Wow, stupid teenager, huh?" Glory pouted. "Um, I'm a teenager, too, you know."

"But you're not wild or stupid." He turned her to face him. "Now, kiss me good night, and get to bed. It's way past your bedtime, woman."

Glory let him guide her to her room, and then, outside her bedroom door, they kissed until he pulled away. Inside her room, she leaned against the door and listened to Malcolm walk down the hall. Her protector. Her savior. The man who loved her and had changed her life. She looked around the bright-yellow room then walked across the deep, soft carpet and leaned against the fine wood dresser and examined her face in the fancy gilded mirror that she would never have had were it not for Malcolm. There was no mark where he'd hit her, only a little redness. Malcolm loved her and had given her this wonderful life. All she had to do was respect him and love him back. Climbing into bed just as the sun came up, Glory prayed for the strength to stay godly and the wisdom to remember to hold her tongue.

MALCOLM HAD BEEN ABSOLUTELY right. Planning began the following day, moments after she'd watched the men of the church board the bus to O'Hare Airport, when Anita rushed Glory home to pack a bag, and then they hurried to Midway Airport to board a plane to Atlanta that very afternoon.

"We're having dinner with Kelly Anne Thornton, my sorority sister, at Spelman College." Anita accepted a tall drink from the stewardess. "I've told her all about you. You need to just be yourself, and don't mention you plan to marry my son anytime soon."

Glory stirred her hot tea and tried not to fidget in the itchy lavender suit. "What if she asks?"

"She won't. She'll ask about your future plans but not about marriage. Nobody expects a girl your age to ruin her life by getting married so young. You just talk about your educational goals, liberal arts degree, seeing the world, maybe missionary work overseas—things like that."

"But—"

"Spelman is one of the finest institutions in the country. This is a wonderful opportunity for you." Anita sipped her drink.

"But Malcolm won't let me go away for college." Glory knew she sounded pouty. "You know how he is."

"And how's he gonna stop you? Sweetie, I know you love him, and he is my son, but he's only a man, and if he's trying to hold you back—"

"But if it wasn't for him, I wouldn't be going to any college at all." Glory slumped in her seat, no longer caring that she didn't look elegant.

Anita lightly tapped Glory's hand, and she straightened up. "The object, Precious, is to get enough scholarship offers that you don't owe anybody anything and can go wherever you want with or without Malcolm. Understand? Now, grab your notebook. Let's go over our itinerary. We've got dinner tonight, and then you have a fitting at Harlica's in the morning. They're the best, you know—booked sometimes years in advance—but they're good friends, and I called them the day you moved in. We'll concentrate on dresses for the church cotillion and prom next month and maybe look at a few things for your eighteenth-birthday parties."

"Yes, ma'am." Glory sighed, settling back into her seat.

THE FOLLOWING MORNING, as Glory stood on the pedestal in the boutique for the third straight hour, she prayed that she wasn't committing blasphemy by silently calling on Jesus to purge the demons of dressmakers and high heels. She'd given up arguing about the party dresses and had resorted to praying for a natural disaster to get her out of the cotillion and prom. The cotillion would be bad enough—all the girls in their white gowns, trying to act like young women. But prom would be worse. Glory had never dreamed she would go, but Anita had not only insisted—she'd arranged professional makeup and photographers and had even considered hiring a date.

Looking at herself in the mirror, Glory admitted she liked the designs Harlie, Erica, and Anita had picked. The young designers hadn't hidden their dismay that everything had to cover her arms and work with Glory's jewelry that couldn't be removed, but they rose to the challenge, choosing Roman and Egyptian styles that made Glory feel like a queen. But still, since Malcolm couldn't escort her to the church cotillion and was too old for the prom, too, one of the boys from church might have to take her, so Glory would just rather not go.

During their time in Atlanta, Glory and Anita had a poolside lunch with Ariana Seaton, a retired navy officer. Though she wanted to ask questions about navy life, it was all Glory could do not to stare at the six-foot-tall woman who reminded her of an earthbound goddess—if she believed in such things. They then went on to meet with Mrs. Janie Hilton and her son Norman at Howard University in Washington, DC. The school was awesome, and visiting the capital was beyond Glory's wildest dreams. *And Miss Anita acts like it's nothing!* While the women talked, Glory enjoyed campus and city tours with Norman and added Howard University to her list of places to go if she ever broke up with Malcolm.

On the flight home, as Glory settled into her first-class seat, sipped a cup of tea, and watched the lights of Chicago approach, she knew her head had been turned in the worldly way that her mother had so warned against... and she wondered again why Malcolm had turned away from this life.

INTERLUDE
MAY 1976

The feeling was just wrong. A strange pressure in her stomach and chest. It didn't really hurt. There was no actual pain, just an ache. At the end of the math lesson, Glory asked Mrs. Stockman if she could go to the bathroom. Of course, the teacher asked her why, and all of the fourth graders waited with bated breath for Glory to say number one or number two.

"I think I'm gonna throw up," Glory said. "I feel sick."

"For goodness' sake, don't do it here. Go to the bathroom!"

Glory picked up the large wooden hall pass with Room 155 painted on it and left the classroom. In the bathroom, she splashed her face with water just like the ladies on TV did. She stood bending over a toilet until her knees ached, but she didn't throw up. When Mrs. Stockman came looking for her, she couldn't explain what was taking so long. All she knew was that she felt so bad she wanted to cry. She spent the rest of the morning sitting at her desk with her head down.

At noon, Glory joined the throng of children who walked home for lunch. Her babysitter, Miss Joyce, would have a buttery grilled cheese sandwich and a glass of milk waiting for her with fruit and a piece of candy.

Glory pushed open the heavy wood and glass door and slipped into the foyer before the ancient door could smash her fingers again. Then she reached up to ring Miss Joyce's bell. She wasn't tall enough to listen at the talking hole above the bell, so she pressed the button three short and one long time and waited until Miss Joyce buzzed her in.

Once she was seated at the gold-flecked table in the sunny kitchen, Glory ignored the afternoon cartoons and nibbled at a corner of her sandwich.

"Girl, why you not eatin'?" Miss Joyce asked when she came into the kitchen to light her cigarette on the stove. "You sick?"

"I don't know—" Glory's answer was cut off by a cough, then she burst into tears. "I just feel really bad!" she sobbed.

"Aw, baby, sometimes we just feel bad." Miss Joyce pulled Glory from her chair pressed the nine-year-old's head to her belly. "Sounds to me like you growin' up a little early. Yo' mama told you about sanitary napkins yet?"

"No," Glory cried. "What's that?"

"Well, I'll let her tell you about it. Got pains in your belly or back?"

"No, why?"

"It ain't my place to say, but crying for no reason is a sure sign of growing pains. How 'bout you stay here this afternoon? You like that?"

"Yeah." Glory sniffed and wiped her tears on her sleeve. "Can I lay on the couch?"

"Of course, baby."

Glory followed Miss Joyce into the living room and lay down on the plastic-covered couch with her head on a cigarette-scented pillow. She quietly cried herself to sleep to the sounds of *All My Children* and Miss Joyce's cussing at the characters.

WHEN GLORY WOKE, IT was nearly six o'clock, and the sun was starting to set. She hugged her babysitter and then walked down two flights to the Bishops' first-floor apartment. The metal gate with the huge padlock was open. Glory knocked on the door and waited. She counted all the way to fifty before knocking again. When she turned the doorknob and pushed, the door creaked open.

"Mama?" Glory called out into the dim stillness.

The drapes were drawn, and the TV was off. Glory looked around the living room. The giant family Bible lay on the coffee table. Next to it stood a tall glass candle with Jesus on it, his face glowing from the flame flickering in the glass. Her daddy always said the candle was a lie because Jesus wasn't white, so Mama usually kept it in the china cabinet. That day was the first time it had been lit.

Glory found her mother in the kitchen at her usual seat near the back door. Mary Bishop sat smoking what looked like a brown cigarette, but it smelled like burnt paper. Beside her was a plate piled high with broken cigarettes. The other smell Glory noticed was like beer and the brown liquor that her mama sometimes drank when she thought Glory was asleep.

Mary silently smoked the paper cigarette.

"Mama?" Glory said again. She looked at her mother's red, puffy eyes and the tracks that looked like scratches in her makeup. "What's wrong?"

"Yo' daddy's dead." Mary took another drag on the piece of brown paper.

"No, he's not," Glory assured her. "He's coming home today. He's just a little late, that's all."

Mary's hand reached out and slapped Glory hard enough to knock her to the floor. "Don't call me a liar. Bible say honor yo' mama. Ya hear me?" Mary spoke just above a whisper.

"Yes, ma'am," Glory whimpered. She tasted blood where she'd bitten her tongue.

Can it be true? Her mother would only hit her over her daddy's dead body. The ache she'd felt earlier welled up again and pushed out of Glory's throat as a retch, emptying her stomach of what little she'd eaten.

THERE HADN'T BEEN A funeral. Her mother had said he was donated to science. They had a special church service where people stood up and said nice things about him and told stories. Glory saw some people crying, especially Uncle Bobby and Aunt Martha, but mostly, people sat there just like regular church. People kept giving her hugs and patting her head. Somebody gave her a teddy bear wearing a T-shirt with *Paul* on it. Glory didn't know what that was supposed to do.

She didn't cry. *It's church, that's all. Just plain ol' church.* She held the piece of paper that had her daddy's picture and his life story on it. It said he drove trucks for thirty years and that Mama was the love of his life.

"Hey, Glory."

Glory looked around, expecting an annoying boy to be there... and of course, he was. She knew Josiah Jackson had liked her when they were little, but now he was just a regular boy, telling toilet jokes and making armpit farts.

"What?" Glory didn't feel like hearing a stupid joke.

Josiah held out a fluffy white flower. "Here. I'm sorry you're sad. Do you miss your dad?"

"Yeah. I wish I coulda saw him at least." Glory accepted the flower and took a deep breath. She was not about to cry in the crowded church social hall, especially in front of Josiah.

"Your dad was a giant, but he wasn't scary. Remember when he shook my hand? I tried to squeeze his hand real hard. He said I had a good handshake." Josiah's voice trailed off. "I'm sorry. My dad said I should talk to you about happy stuff."

Glory held her head back and tried to control her tears. She felt them fall out of the corners of her eyes and creep down to her ears. *Tears in my ears.* The little rhyme made her smile a bit, and Josiah smiled too.

"My mother said everybody is going to your house after church," Josiah said. "It's just gonna be a bunch of grown-ups talking all day. I'm bringing my G.I. Joe."

"Okay. I gotta go." Glory walked as fast as she could to the ladies' room. Once there, she pressed the teddy bear over her mouth and sobbed.

IN THE PACKED APARTMENT, even with two fans blowing, the air was hot and muggy. At one point, Glory counted fifty-two people. And the food... so much food. It seemed like everybody brought something—fried chicken and chicken and dressing, macaroni and cheese, a roast, and potatoes. There was a Crock-Pot with gumbo and rice and so much other food and dessert that Glory couldn't count it all. Somebody went to the store for paper plates and ice and came back with what he said was her daddy's favorite liquor. Glory was disappointed that Josiah hadn't actually come, but Trina was there with her grandparents. Glory wouldn't say Trina was her friend, and she hated sharing her Barbies with her because Trina kept calling them sexy.

After everybody ate, the prayers started. It seemed like everybody had a prayer for Paul and his family. Lots of "God's will" and "heavenly throne" and "blessed are they who mourn." Some people left after a couple of prayers, while others sat down and pulled out Bibles. By the time it got dark, people had eaten twice and started the second round of prayers. Glory slipped, unnoticed, out of the crowded apartment and into the hot spring night.

Sitting on the steps next to the front door, Glory bounced a tiny red ball and picked up imaginary jacks. *Why are so many people praying, and what are they praying for?* They couldn't make her daddy come back, and she already had peace, and she knew that even from heaven, her daddy was still with her. *So why all the prayers? Do I hafta ask God for the same thing over and over?*

Glory stared down at a dandelion pushing its way up between the broken slabs of the sidewalk. When a pair of red high-heeled shoes came into her field of vision, Glory's eyes followed long legs up to a tight red dress and then the made-up face of their other upstairs neighbor, Miss Aletha.

"What you doin' out here this late?" the older woman asked. Aletha took a seat on the step above where Glory sat and pulled a bottle from a brown paper bag that she'd set between her knees. "Damn, it's hot out here." She opened the green wide-mouth bottle with a pop and took a long swallow. "Mmm, that's good." She wiped the beer foam from her top lip. "So, yo' mama know you out here at nine o'clock?"

"I don't know. Maybe." Glory looked up at the green bottle sweating in the heat and glistening and sparkling under the streetlights. She could smell that it was a grownup drink, but it still looked cold and delicious.

"Yo' daddy know you out like this?"

"Yeah." Glory knew her daddy was in heaven, watching her, so it wasn't a lie. "But he died." Saying that out loud on this hot and lonely night made Glory's heart hurt.

"Aw, that's too bad." Aletha took another loud swallow. "Little girls need daddies. When he die?"

"Monday." Blinking back tears, Glory tried to be as strong as her mother. Mary Bishop hadn't cried once that whole week. She said the Lord gave her strength.

"Oh, just a few days ago. What happened?"

"He had an accident with his truck."

"Aww, I'm sorry. That's real sad." Aletha raised her bottle and drained most of the contents. "Here, hold this." She handed Glory the bottle. "I left a swallow for you. It won't hurt you. We gon' drink a toast to yo' daddy." She pulled another bottle from the bag and opened it. "Yo' daddy like beer?"

"Yeah."

"Good man." Aletha poured a little beer on the sidewalk. "Here's to the brothers who ain't here. What's his name, yo' daddy?"

"Paul."

Aletha raised her bottle. "Raise it up, now. Here's to Paul, who's watching over his little girl just like he was here." She touched her bottle to the one Glory held with a clink then took a long swallow. "Ah... that's good. Go on, drink up. That's how you do a toast."

Glory put the bottle to her lips, and the wide mouth nearly covered her nose. She turned up the bottle and let a few drops slide into her mouth. *Yuck.* It was both bitter and sweet at the same time, and it smelled kind of like old dishwater. But it was a little cold, and that felt kind of good. She turned up the bottle again and swallowed the last bit. *Yup. It is definitely gross. It must be something only grown-ups can like.*

The door behind them opened, and Glory jumped up from her seat on the steps. The glass bottle in her lap went crashing to the sidewalk. Luckily, most of the pieces landed close to the building, so Glory didn't think she'd get into trouble. Aletha remained in her seat. She didn't even move over a little so the people could walk past. The man said "Excuse me" loudly, and the woman just clucked her teeth and mumbled something about "hose."

Glory moved to sit down again, but the door opened, and a crowd of people came out. Again, Aletha kept her seat, but she did move over slightly. Glory guessed the praying was over because the crowd was church members leaving her apartment, with her mother standing in the building foyer, giving hugs and receiving blessings from all the departing guests.

As the last of the guests left, Glory caught her mother's eye. "Child, what are you doing out here?" Mary snapped. She glared at Aletha and pulled Glory to her side. "I thought you was in bed. Get your tail in this house!"

"Good night, baby," Aletha said to Glory.

Glory tried to say good night to Miss Aletha, but her mother snatched her arm and pulled her into the foyer.

"Good night, Mary!" Aletha called, laughing into her beer.

Back inside their apartment, cigarette smoke still hung in the air, but everything else had been cleaned up. She watched her mother blow out the flame in the Jesus candle and stare at the swirling smoke. Glory thought her mother was finally gonna cry, but Mary Bishop cleared her throat and straightened her back. "Girl, don't you let me catch you with that filthy hussy ever again, hear me?"

"Yes, ma'am." Glory sighed.

"Why you sighin'? God don't like no rebellious attitudes! Now, come on—gimme a good night kiss, and get to bed."

Glory followed her mother into the kitchen, where Mary bent down, and Glory kissed her mother's cheek.

"Jesus!" Mary screamed. "You been drinkin' beer?"

"No!" Glory lied. It had been a long time since she'd heard her mother call on Jesus like that.

Glory felt her mother's grip on her shoulder, fingernails pressing into her flesh. "And you got the demons of lies and deceit! Lawd have mercy! Did that hussy give you beer?"

"No, ma'am," Glory cried. "I don't have demons!" She tried to pull away, but her mother's grip was too strong.

"Satan! You took my husband, but you will not have this child!"

"Mama, please. I don't have any demons. Please, Mama, can I go to bed?"

"Child's daddy let them demons get all up in her. Now she got the Jezebel spirit in her too. Well, not today, Satan! I bind you in the name of Jesus!"

Glory's mother shoved her into the space between the kitchen table and the back door. When Mary reached for the extension cord that had hung undisturbed for the last three years, Glory remembered. She remembered the beatings and her daddy's tears when he found out and him yelling at her mother. She remembered her mother praying for protection from devils and demons. And Glory remembered the pain.

"Please, Mama, no! I'll be good! I'll be good! I'll be good! I'll be—"

The thick plastic cord bit into Glory's shoulder and snagged on the buttons on the front of her blouse. Glory sank to the floor in a tight ball, protecting her face and arms. The cord ripped through her shirt and burned into her back.

Glory screamed and cried and called on Jesus, just like she'd done when she was five and the demons got in her and she said a bad word and Mama had to get 'em out with the cord. And with every lash of the extension cord, Glory knew that her daddy was gone and never coming back.

Chapter 8
SPRING 1984

Glory tried to hold still while Mrs. Beyers made a few last-minute adjustments to the off-white dress Glory still wasn't quite sure was right for a church cotillion. Gold ribbons wrapped around her waist, crossed her chest, and ended in streamers attached to a flowing shawl that covered her arms and draped down her back. Only the barest amount of skin showed at her collarbone, through openings at the shoulders and side splits up to her knees. After more than a week of practice, Miss Anita had pronounced Glory hopeless in high heels and found the perfect pair of flat gold-ribbon sandals, and to complete the look, Herschel had braided thin gold ribbons through Glory's hair and wound the braids up like a crown.

"Those girls did a mighty fine job on this dress," Mrs. Beyers said. "You look like a Roman queen or something. The fabric looks sheer, but I can't see your scars at all."

"They did, didn't they?" Glory held her head up and looked in the mirror. She thought about smiling, but a serious face looked better with the dress. She felt a twinge of guilt, recognizing the vanity her mother fought so hard to keep out of her.

Waiting in the foyer for Dexter to finish whatever was taking him forever, she watched herself in the mirror, practicing the proper way to hold the gold clutch purse and the fur wrap borrowed from Miss Anita. The Porters had already left, and Malcolm would meet them at the country club. She tried to imagine the look on his face when he saw her. He'd have to smile and say something respectful. She'd smile back and try to flirt with just her eyes, that look she'd seen Tressa *accidentally* use to make boys stupid. Yeah, she'd look at Malcolm like that.

Glory was still smiling to herself when she noticed Dexter's reflection in the mirror. "What took you so long?"

"Well, I couldn't decide if I should wear this or go with a plain black suit and look like a real chauffeur," Dexter said. "You look nice."

Glory looked at him for a second. "I'm glad you picked the blue, 'cause you're not a real chauffeur. You're my guest. You look nice too." Glory remembered she was still practicing Tressa's flirty eyes and switched back to her serious face.

Dexter smiled. "Let's go. Can't be late. Don't wanna give your..." He coughed loudly. "A reason to try to kill me."

Glory hugged the stern housekeeper. "See you there, Mrs. Beyers. Thank you." Then she opened the front door, elbowing Dexter in the stomach. "Oops!"

"I'm serious." Dexter helped Glory into the passenger seat. "You're beautiful."

"Stop it," Glory said as he closed the door. "I don't think this dress is right." Dexter took his place in the driver's seat. "Miss Anita picked it, and everybody else will have on fluffy white prom dresses—"

"And you're walking in looking like, 'Damn!'"

"I like it, but I think it's too much for church and—"

"Nobody's gonna say anything. Watch. But, um... who's your date?"

"Andre, a boy from church. He thinks he can sing, but he really can't. It's not a date. He's just an escort. He walks me in, and we hafta sit together and dance together once. He's clumsy."

"Well, I hope he's gay." Dexter laughed. "'Cause your"—he coughed—"might make him disappear after he sees you."

"I really wish you'd stop saying that," Glory said. "It's not funny."

"Okay, okay." Dexter turned and looked at her. "Hey, that really bothers you, doesn't it? I'm sorry. You know I'm just joking, right? I won't say it again. I promise." He reached out and pushed a loose strand of hair back from her face. "Forgive me?"

"Fine. Just stop, okay?"

They rode in silence the rest of the way to the South Shore Country Club. Waiting in the short line of cars, Glory prayed and practiced breathing to fight the knot growing in her stomach. For some of the girls from church, this was as close to the prom as they were allowed to get, and Glory's mother hadn't even allowed her to consider this vain and prideful show, yet here she sat in a custom-designed gown, waiting to walk into a country club.

Entering the building, Glory was met in the foyer by Anita, who was pacing anxiously, draped in pink-and-purple silk. "There you are, Precious! My, don't you look lovely! I accidentally told you the wrong time, so now you're fashionably late. Everybody's seated, and the girls are all lined up, so you'll hafta go in last."

Moving through the ornate lobby with its gold-trimmed columns and gold-framed mirrors, Glory couldn't help but notice that her dress matched the decor—she glanced at the chattering woman beside her—almost as if it had been planned that way.

The Spring Cotillion, one of the church's biggest events of the year, featured not only girls from Lake Shore but girls from other churches as well. The *Chicago Defender* newspaper was there and even *Jet* magazine. Tables set up in the lobby manned by tuxedo-clad attendants offered gifts from the event's supporters. A couple at the alderman's voter-registration table played cards, and the stylist at the Herschel's Salon table gasped when Glory walked by.

Easels throughout the lobby displayed framed portraits of the debutantes. Glory recognized the poses from her friends' senior portrait packages—photos she hadn't been allowed to take at school because her mother saw them as vain and prideful. Of course, Anita assured Glory that the photographer she'd hired would hide any blemishes and make sure her portrait was just as beautiful as the others.

"Yours is coming up." Anita smiled. "It's a little different because you had a different artist."

Glory paused at an easel holding a gold-flecked frame a bit larger than all the others. Whereas all the other girls' photos were traditional portraits from the shoulders up, with white fur and red roses, this frame held a classical oil painting of the Porters' library. A serious Glory looked out from where she stood near an open window with the wind blowing and the light hitting her face just so.

"When it arrived today, it was too late to change it," Anita whispered. "I know it doesn't match the others, but then, you're nothing like them, either, are you, Precious?"

Glory just stared.

"Regal, isn't it?" Anita said quietly. "The other girls were jealous. I told them they coulda used any picture they wanted, but they all picked the same one. I picked this one of you because you look so young and innocent. Those other girls think showing skin makes them look sophisticated, but in this innocent painting, they can't hold a candle to you. Now, come on." She tugged on Glory's hand. "Since I'm the hostess, they can't start without me, but it's best not to keep 'em waiting too long."

Anita spoke rapidly, reminding Glory to walk on her toes and smile. Her heels clicked on the marble floor as she led Glory across the lobby toward a pair of gilded white doors marked Debutantes. "Okay, everybody," Anita announced, entering the crowded room, pulling Glory behind her. "I found her. She's a bit nervous."

"Daaayuuum!" a boy's voice called out from somewhere deep in the room.

"Now, gentlemen, don't be rude!" Anita dropped Glory's hand and moved into the center of the room. "You can hear them finishing up the welcome, so I'll get out there now. Stay in line, and when that door back there opens, Mrs. Washington and I'll be calling your names just like we rehearsed. Ladies, stay light on your feet. Gentlemen, don't let them trip!" She turned and floated out of the room, closing the door behind her.

"Oh my God, Glory! Where did you get that dress?"

Glory was immediately swarmed by a throng of squealing girls from her church, who were immediately shushed by annoyed girls from other churches. All of them, wearing some variation of fluffy white with flowers or beads, were oohing and aahing and demanding to know how and where she got that dress.

"I got it in Atlanta during spring break," Glory said, telling the lightest version of the truth she could.

"It matches the room! I love the bracelets! Those sandals are so—oh my God! Look at your hair!" The girls all spoke at once, and Glory laughed and giggled with them. Since she'd started seeing Malcolm, she hadn't really participated in the Mary and Martha Young Ladies' Circle, and seeing the girls she'd grown up with looking almost like women, Glory wondered how much she'd been missing.

A door near the back of the room opened, and Cheryl Cannon and little Vanessa rushed in. "Okay, kids, this is it!" Cheryl stage whispered. "Places, everybody! Where's Candice Marie? You're first!"

Glory felt sorry for Candice from South Shore Church as she and her escort walked toward the door. The poor girl had hated everything about what she called "this ridiculous patriarchal spectacle" and refused to wear her hair in anything other than braids.

She'd actually walked out of rehearsal at the suggestion that she get contact lenses and wear makeup. Her yellow pumps didn't quite match her white dress with long, flowing sleeves, but the flowered wristbands and anklets and the ring of yellow flowers in her hair reminded Glory of Mother Nature from the margarine commercial. When Candice's name was called, nobody was really surprised that she stepped out of her shoes and walked through the door in her bare feet. Anita read through the details of Candice's lineage, Mrs. Washington detailed her accomplishments and aspirations, and finally, Anita listed her college acceptances, scholarships, and awards. Then she coolly remarked on Candice's choice to go barefoot and be true to herself, no matter what.

Glory took a seat on an overstuffed couch. It would be a while before her turn came. "Pedigree," Candice had called it—Glory was the daughter of Mary and the late Paul Bishop III and granddaughter of the late Reverend Charles Johnson Sr., superintendent of the Central Mississippi Baptist Convention. Glory sighed. These were normal girls, and this cotillion was a big party for the church. None of the boys cared at all, but the girls were giggly and nervous, never having worn high heels and suddenly being forced into them. For many of them, this was the biggest party they would ever have. Their parents had bought three tables and page after page of ads in the program book.

Glory stood up and walked across the room to a small table and poured a glass of ice water. After weeks of parties on Miss Anita's social calendar, Glory's world was now so much bigger than church cotillions. This was nothing. She put the glass of water down, not daring to take a sip because her hands wouldn't stop shaking.

"So, Glory, what's up with you?" Andre Bradley stood a little too close beside her, his shoulder touching hers, his Polo cologne a little too strong.

"Just nervous, I guess," Glory said.

"Well, that's an offa dress."

Glory glared at him. "Gee. Thanks."

"Heh, heh. Yeah, you look so good I wanna rip that dress right offa you."

Glory gave a fake little smile and turned to face him. "Bless you, Andre," she gushed. "Bless yo' little heart." She lifted her chin and returned to her seat on the couch. There were still eight girls before her.

"Oh, so you think you Mother Porter now?" Andre asked, following her. "Too good for everybody?"

In church, Glory never referred to Miss Anita by name, and she sometimes forgot she was Mother Porter to everyone else.

"Yeah, that lady is so stuck-up, she cain't hardly walk." Andre laughed, taking the seat beside Glory and placing a hand on her knee. "But you spent the night with JT, so I know you ain't stuck-up at all."

"Have you really been waiting almost a year to bring that up, Andre?" Glory didn't even look at him. She just lifted his hand from her knee and dropped it back on his lap.

Andre laughed again. "I'm just saying. Everybody knows JT. They say he probably hit every girl on the West Side. Don't nobody believe you held out."

"So, everybody thinks he slept with every girl on the West Side and only me on the South Side?"

"Hey, I'm just sayin'... that's what they think. And then you start bustin' out like you a different person—no more old-lady clothes. Shakin' yo' ass. Yo' titties standin' up and stuff. And now you walking in here like the Queen of Sheba, like ain't nobody here good enough for you to—"

"Bless you, Andre." Glory stood up from the couch. "Bless you and every God-blessed one of you—"

Andre stood up nose to nose with her. "Damn. You sexy when you fake cuss," he mumbled in his deep singing voice. "I wanna push my tongue down your throat right now."

"Then I'd hafta have you killed," Glory whispered in her best imitation of Miss Anita. "I really have changed. A lot." She took a step back from him and went to wait with the other girls. She would hold his arm going through the door, but she didn't need to put up with Andre Bradley until then.

"Hey, gimme your stuff."

Glory looked down at the little girl tugging at her elbow.

"I need your stuff," Vanessa said again. "I hafta put it on your table."

"Oh." Glory handed the little girl her purse and fur wrap. When she removed her gloves, revealing rings on every finger, Vanessa gasped.

"Wow. Do you have 'em on your toes too?" Vanessa asked.

Glory lifted the hem of her dress, revealing the gold straps of her sandals and her painted-red toenails. "Almost."

"Oh my God. You're the prettiest one here."

Glory stood back and watched as her friend Dawn Tursten took her walk through the door and into the ballroom. Dawn went up three steps onto the stage then moved to the center and curtsied—which Candice Marie hadn't done—and proceeded to the other side of the stage to accept a flower from somebody then returned to the center, where Willie Clayton held her hand to help her down the three steps to the ballroom floor. After making another curtsy toward the head tables where pastors, aldermen, and bigwigs sat—Candice had merely waved—she finally went back to her own table, where she stood until Miss Anita and Mrs. Washington finished talking about her.

Glory placed her hand on Andre's elbow. He laid his hand over hers a little too tightly. "Time to shake your thang, your highness," Andre whispered.

"Bless your heart," Glory whispered back through clenched teeth.

"And now for our final debutante of the evening." Anita's voice rose a bit as the applause for Dawn died down. "The star of our program cover, Miss Glory Bishop!"

The what?

Andre stepped through the door, pulling Glory a millisecond behind him.

Star? Glory remembered to walk on her toes and smile. *What star?*

At the center of the stage, she dipped into her curtsy, straining to see out into the dimly lit ballroom, her view blocked by camera flashes. She tried to listen to the commentary as she took her walk, but the murmurs and applause of the crowd made it difficult. Facing the head tables, Glory curtsied and smiled at Malcolm, flashing her well-practiced flirty eyes. Malcolm's return smile was more of an impressed smirk. He blinked slowly and nodded. Satisfied, Glory continued her walk through the ballroom and finally arrived at her table, where she received a standing ovation from Herschel and her friends.

"Has received scholarships from Tuskegee University in Tuskegee, Alabama... Fisk University in Nashville, Tennessee... Howard University in Washington, DC... Spelman College in Atlanta, Georgia... Dillard University in New Orleans, Louisiana... and the University of Ghana in Greater Accra Region, Ghana. Glory has also been accepted at Jackson State, Michigan State, Grambling, Alabama State, Florida A&M, Cornell, and Brown Universities."

What the heck? Glory grabbed Herschel's hand to steady herself. This was the first she'd heard of the scholarships and acceptances. *Was this the reason for all those meetings with those uppity people?* She looked at the stage, where Miss Anita continued announcing the smaller scholarships she'd received, most of which Glory hadn't known she'd applied for. She tried to see across to the other side of the room, where Malcolm sat, but by that point, everyone was on their feet, applauding, with photographers blocking her view.

Herschel slipped a protective arm around her. "Smile and nod to your fans, darling," he whispered.

Glory smiled and nodded to her left and right.

"Okay, turn a little so you can nod behind you too," Herschel coached.

Glory turned to her right and nodded that way then back to the front. She caught a glimpse of an unsmiling Malcolm standing and clapping.

"That's a good girl. You're doing fine. Deep breath, now."

Glory stood smiling until the applause died down and then took her seat between Herschel and Andre. Again, Herschel placed an arm around her. "I am so proud of you, darling," he whispered.

Glory heard the catch in his throat and fought back her own tears. She looked around the table at the beaming faces of Christy, Tressa, Quentin, Dexter, Mrs. Beyers, Andre, and Mrs. Bradley. She tried not to notice her mother's empty seat.

On top of the place setting in front of her lay the program booklet with her black-and-white portrait on the cover. She looked around and realized that, of course, everybody had already seen it. In the packed room, people flipped through the booklet or looked up at the stage, where Anita and Mrs. Washington were still talking. Glory flipped through the pages of debutantes. Each two-page spread featured a young lady's portrait, her family information, and her accomplishments and honors, followed by five or six pages of paid ads and dedications.

She reached her page and gasped. Her spread looked like something out of a magazine, with eight large photos across the top of two pages and her accomplishments and honors in several neat columns across the bottom, punctuated by smaller photos. Glory looked around and saw a few unsmiling debutantes looking her way. She couldn't blame them. On the dedication pages, she was touched to find full-page ads from Herschel's Salon and O'Reilly's Restaurant. She couldn't help smiling at the ad from Mr. and Mrs. Harris at the Wolcott High School bookstore. Then came at least fifteen pages from Anita's friends.

Embarrassed and overwhelmed, Glory closed the book just as a perfectly folded paper airplane flew past her. She looked up to see Christy, Tressa, Dexter, and even Mrs. Beyers pointing at a shocked Quentin, who indignantly protested his innocence.

"ANDRE!" GLORY HISSED at her dance partner. "If you step on my foot or lower your hand on my back one more time, I will knee you in the privates and leave you crying on this dance floor." After a sumptuous dinner, the formal dancing had begun, and barely two minutes into the first dance, Glory's toes ached.

"Well," Andre leered, "if you mess with mine, I get to mess with yours."

Glory shifted her weight and was preparing to raise her knee when the music changed and the father-daughter dance was announced. This was when Glory would discreetly excuse herself. Her mother hadn't allowed her to invite family members, so she had nobody for this dance. Of course, men from church danced with other fatherless girls, but Glory didn't think anybody but her uncle Bobby should stand in for her daddy. She'd made it nearly back at her seat when she found herself caught in a perfect spin on Herschel's arm.

"C'mon, Glory-Glory," Herschel whispered. "Dance with your uncle sister."

Glory cleared her throat and blinked back tears. "Are you trying to make me laugh or cry?"

"Both! I'm a mad scientist, remember?" He laughed and twirled her around. "You're just the belle of the ball, aren't you, darling? I I see why you're hardly at work... busy applying for every college in the world and schmoozing with high society."

"Herschel," Glory said as they moved over the dance floor, "I never applied to any of those schools."

"What! None of 'em?"

"No, not a one. I only applied to schools in Chicago." Glory nodded toward the six or seven tables filled with ladies she recognized from Anita's sorority and social circle, way more than the few she'd been told were coming. "It's all from Miss Anita and all the sorority ladies over there."

"The pink-and-purple bunch?" Herschel scoffed. "Looks like the Easter Bunny threw up over there. Hmph." His voice turned pleasant again. "But we are very grateful for their favor, aren't we, darling? Aha ha ha!"

After the formal dances, the party picked up full swing, but Glory waltzed for every song, no matter the tempo, because it was the only dance she knew. She stumbled a bit when she saw Cheryl pulling Malcolm to the dance floor and felt a twinge of jealousy when she saw Dexter and Christy dancing close. But the highlight was Herschel down on one knee, proposing that Mrs. Beyers dance with him. After turning down everybody, including Malcolm, the Porters' housekeeper couldn't say no to Herschel, and the crowd cheered.

"THAT ANDRE GUY IS A real jerk," Quentin said as he and Glory strolled among the portraits in the lobby. "He asked Tressa if her boobs were real and then tried to check. She scratched him up real good."

Glory sighed. Maybe she should sic Malcolm on him.

"Me and Dexter wanna take him out back and throw him off the terrace," Quentin continued. "He's not bothering you, is he?"

"Of course he is, but I can handle—"

"You shouldn't have to. I'll deal with him."

"Quentin, no," Glory protested. "It's okay." She pulled her friend into a hug and kissed his cheek. "I love you for caring, but it's okay. He's just a stupid jerk. I'm a big girl. I handled it."

"Okay." Quentin relented. "If you need help, I'll be close by."

"I know you will, Q." Glory stepped back and saw Malcolm watching from a distance.

"I'M NOT HIDING." GLORY said, her voice muffled by bed covers. "I just don't want anybody to see me today."

"Well, I'm sorry, Precious. You're still going to church. At least, put in an appearance. Smile at people. Everybody's gon' want to congratulate you."

Glory sighed and pulled the covers from over her head. The previous night, at the cotillion, she'd been more than a princess—she'd been a queen. Everybody had called her glorious. But that morning, in the light of day with no makeup and no sparkly dresses and no accolades, Glory remembered people saying she was stuck-up, the other girls' dirty looks and whispers about her mother's absence, and Malcolm's anger. She got out of bed, wearing an old gray pleated skirt, white blouse, and beige sweater. She even had on brown nylon pantyhose.

"I beg your pardon," Anita stared her up and down. "You can't be serious."

Glory sighed again. "Can't I just wear this?"

Anita smiled and lifted Glory's chin. "Oh, no. It's much too late for that now, Precious. People have seen you as a queen in all your glory. They know you're not one of them now. You can't go back down to that level ever again. I'll set out the white with the polka dots and the red belt for you. It'll be on the chair."

Glory watched Malcolm's mother choose her outfit and then glide from the room. This woman was a million miles from Mary Bishop. She was married to an old preacher, but there was no godly submission in her. Vain and prideful, she lived for compliments. She served no one and expected service and obedience from everyone. She acted like she ruled the world, and it seemed like the world agreed. And God wasn't punishing her at all.

In her old world, the world of Godly purity with no light and no sin, Glory had known little joy and mostly sadness, loss, and pain—constant, relentless wars against demons and the torturous beatings to purge them. But in this new world of vanity, pride, secrets, manipulation, and outright lies, Glory found warmth, comfort, light and peace, love and joy, and no pain. She reveled in decadence by openly reading books and drinking wine coolers in the library. She wore perfume and silk undies. She'd embraced all the demons her mother fought against, yet God was not punishing her.

Maybe Miss Anita was her reward for her old life, God's way of making up for that empty chair the night before. Of course, she would always love her mother, but her mother obviously didn't know how God worked. Glory pulled the dress down over her head and tightened the wide belt around her waist. A bright-yellow jacket with puffy shoulder pads and bright red buttons and a pair of shiny red flats completed the outfit. And maybe Malcolm's temper was to keep her from being too much like Miss Anita and remind her that she was still his beloved.

CHURCH WAS JUST AS Glory had expected it would be. Elder Porter's message was on the virtues of the good wife, and Malcolm's selections railed against vanity and the Canaanite girls. The portraits of Glory and her friends, along with the leftover program booklets, were displayed in the Robinson Room after service, and Glory received hugs and congratulations from everybody she met and ignored the whispers when she moved past them.

At first, she tried to shield her mother from the compliments that came to her at every turn, but Mary brushed them off easily. "God knows how smart this child is. I don't need no fancy show to tell me. I had better things to do than go to that mess."

Then Glory would receive clucks of pity, and a few well-meaning saints stuffed ten-dollar bills in her hand. "Yo' mama, bless her heart," they'd say. "You gon' be leaving for school soon anyway."

Glory, of course, tried to return the gifts, and she eventually slipped away to the sanctuary so she could stuff the wads of crumpled bills into the benevolent-offering box. That day was one of the rare Sundays with only one service, so the sanctuary was empty. Most of the offices overlooking the sanctuary were dark, and the few men still around loudly debated the sermon behind closed doors. Standing near the treasury office door at the front of the sanctuary, Glory smoothed the four bills then slipped them into the slot on the box protruding from the door.

"Glory, glory, hallelujah..." a deep voice sang close behind her.

"Not now, Andre, okay?" Glory didn't turn around. She placed both hands on the donation box and said a prayer for patience.

"C'mon, Glory, sing with me." Andre placed his hands on Glory's hips, earning himself an elbow to the chest.

"Don't you ever touch me!" Glory snapped, spinning to face him. "Ever!"

"Ow!" Andre rubbed his chest, laughing, but didn't step back. "Why you so rough? You and JT wrestled in the car, too, huh? I can dig that."

"I hate you!" Glory spat, pushing past him. She barely got a step before his hand closed around her wrist, pressing her bracelets against the back of her hand. "I said, don't touch me!"

"Okay, okay." Andre shushed her. "Can I just talk to you a minute? Why you so uptight... playing so hard to get?"

"Get your hands off of me right now before only God—"

"Miss Bishop, are you all right?"

Too late. Glory and Andre turned to see Malcolm descending the staircase from the balcony. Andre let go of Glory's wrist and stepped back from her. "Yeah, she okay. We just talkin'." Andre laughed. "She likes to get attention."

"He that hideth hatred with lying lips, and he that uttereth a slander, is a fool." Malcolm laughed back at Andre. He turned to Glory, his smile gone. "Miss Bishop, are you all right?" he repeated.

"I'm fine, Malcolm," Glory kept her eyes down, rubbing her wrist. It would serve that jerk right if she did sic Malcolm on him right there in the sanctuary. "I'm just trying to get out of here."

"I'll walk you back upstairs," Malcolm said. "See you later, Andre."

"Later, Rev." Andre pushed past Malcolm. "Don't waste your time, though. You too old, and Miss Goody-Goody only likes to play in dirt!"

Glory grabbed the front of Malcolm's suit jacket before he could move. "Please, let it go." She held on with both hands, silently mouthing her plea, watching Malcolm's jaw clench. "He's just a stupid boy."

Malcolm stared at her. "I know he's a stupid boy. Why are you in here with him?"

What? Glory released Malcolm's jacket. "I'm not in here *with him*. I came in here by myself to make a donation. He just followed me. I was trying to leave."

"I watched you with him yesterday, and now today—"

"In church, Malcolm?" Glory wanted to walk away from him, but this was no place to start a fight. "Do you really think I'm like that?"

"Come on," he said, turning away from her. "You're going back upstairs, and you're gonna stay in the Robinson Room until it's time to go. Button up your jacket."

Glory followed Malcolm quietly without protest. There weren't many people around, but a long or loud conversation would be noticed by somebody, and after all these months, their relationship was still a secret. Maybe it would be better if she found a different church. Of course, Malcolm would never allow it, but maybe if she could discuss it with Anita. She could come up with a way to convince Elder Porter that it was a great idea, and Malcolm would have to go along with it.

Glory shook her head. Crazy thoughts. She could never be manipulative like that.

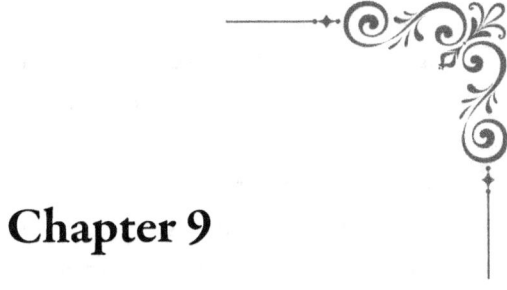

Chapter 9

Never in her wildest dreams had Glory imagined she'd be attending a prom, let alone needing a date. Not that she cared, but her night with JT had made her off-limits to the nice boys at church, and the boys in Anita's social circle were all just disgusting. Out of desperation, she considered abusing her powers and asking Quentin to take her. She was pretty sure he would do it, but that would be mean to his girlfriend, Paula.

Finally, a week before prom, Anita turned to Malcolm for help. "Maybe there's a nice young man at your mission that could serve as escort. I'm sure there's somebody there who'd love to take Cinderella to the ball."

Glory covered her face with her napkin, praying for the rapture to come that very second.

"So, I'm supposed to get a homeless man or an addict to take my lady to her prom because you think I'm too old?" Malcolm stopped pacing and looked at his mother. "You're actually serious, aren't you?"

"Oh, stop being dramatic. I know some of the volunteers are younger... and not addicts or homeless." Anita sipped her tea. "Please, sit down. Have some breakfast. Glory, take that napkin off your face. If you'd taken care of this—"

"Or if you'd just let it go, Mother," Malcolm interrupted, taking a seat as Mrs. Beyers placed a plate in front of him. "Thanks."

"Wait! I have the perfect solution!" Anita clapped her hands. "Of course! Dexter can take her! He's family, so you know he'll be a gentleman. He gets along with her friends. They're very cute together—she'll never regret the photos. You'll both just hafta agree!"

Glory looked from Anita's excited face to Malcolm's skeptical one. It really was a perfect solution. The previous weekend at the cotillion, he'd entertained her friends and twirled Tressa and Christy around the dance floor. He'd even asked Mrs. Beyers to dance. Twice. He was kind of perfect, so Glory knew where this was going.

"Fine," Malcolm said slowly.

Huh?

"If he's okay with it, my little cousin can do it. But how are you gonna have him ready by Friday? That's not much time."

"Don't you worry. Everything's gonna be perfect." Anita reached over and squeezed Glory's hand. "Now, you go on and have a good day, Precious." She looked up at Malcolm. "You know me, son. I'll make sure everything's ready. Y'all run along, now, before you're late."

Malcolm walked around the table and kissed his mother's cheek. "I do know you, Mother. I'm sure everything's been ready for a while."

"Malcolm, what just happened?" Glory asked as he opened the car's passenger door and took her backpack. "Why are you okay with this?"

Malcolm smiled. "Sometimes you hafta give her small victories." He closed the door. When he climbed into the driver's seat, Glory just stared at him. "Mother really wants this." Malcolm laughed a little. "Making you the queen of the church cotillion was only the first step in her plot for world domination. She's gonna raise up an army of debutantes and make you her second-in-command. I was gonna be her henchman, but I kept messin' around with her army."

"Malcolm!" Glory laughed. *I guess every boy has comic-book dreams.*

"Dexter is her new stooge. Somebody she can control. He'll have you home by midnight, completely un-messed-around-with. You'll have a good time, and Mother is happy."

"I don't get it, but okay. I just don't want you mad at me."

He reached over and squeezed her hand. "Don't worry. I promise I won't be. I'll stop by to see how you look and give you a kiss... remind li'l cuz whose *beloved* you are."

"LOOK TO YOUR RIGHT. More. More. Beautiful. You're doing great. Chin up. More. More. Eyes down. Perfect! Hold it!"

Glory held her breath and prayed that the photographer would drop his camera. Since the hoopla over her portraits at the church cotillion, Cooter Davis had been in high demand, and he wanted to make every shot of Glory worthy of a magazine cover. He had even brought a fan that sent her dress billowing up around her.

"You're beautiful, baby! A few more, then we'll take a break!"

Her long-sleeved Egyptian-style off-white gown had an ornate gold yoke that matched her jewelry. The bodice gathered at a broad gold belt then flowed to a sweeping, finely pleated skirt that fell to the floor. When she turned, and light touched the dress just right, tiny strands of gold in the fabric made her dress appear to glow, and Glory moved gracefully in the matching low-heeled slippers. To complete the look, Herschel had styled Glory's hair straight back with a simple gold headband.

"Okaaay... one mooore... got it! So, when does the date get here? We're losing this *très magnifique* light."

Turning this way and that, Glory tried not to giggle at Cooter's new French accent.

"Dexter should be here any minute," Anita said. "Mrs. Beyers, will you please take the *artiste* into the library and pour him a sherry? Dexter is running a bit late. Let us know when he arrives."

Mrs. Beyers nodded. "This way, Cooter." She led the photographer from the room without checking to see if he was following.

"Well, Precious..." Anita brushed Glory's hair back from her shoulders. "I remember my big dance. Seems so long ago. I was all decked out like a big ol' ball of taffeta and crinoline. I wish I'd had your curves." She smoothed Glory's sleeves. "Those girls did better than I thought possible on this dress."

"I really do like it." Glory turned slowly. "I don't know how to thank you. Ever." She felt familiar pressure and burning in her eyes. Anita had already chided her for ruining her makeup once that day.

"You just have a great time, and tell me all about it tomorrow. Your Dexter is a nice boy, just like my date was. Nice boy named Earl. My parents hated him, but I loved me some Earl. He was tall and strong on account of he worked on my daddy's land, trying to prove how good a provider he would be. And he was pretty and blacker than midnight. He'd smile and show his perfect white teeth... make all the girls swoon. He was tough, though, because he had to fight a lot. My daddy said it was because he was always looking above his station, and the only reason he wanted me was because I was so fair."

Glory watched the window as the reflection of her future mother-in-law adjusted her already perfectly adjusted dress.

"On the night of the big dance, my mother dear had arranged a date with a local boy, and I guess he was all right. He was from a good family, and he was headed to Morehouse College, but Earl and I had this plan that he would get there early all dressed up, and I'd just act like the other boy had canceled. Well, Daddy didn't buy it at all, and Mother dear sent somebody to the other boy's house to check."

Anita flicked more invisible dust from Glory's shoulders. "Daddy wouldn't let me off the porch, and Earl stood there with flowers for me. I begged Daddy, and he said I'd go with that dirt-poor darkie over his dead body. I cried and told Daddy how much I loved Earl, but he still wouldn't budge."

"That's so sad. What did your mom do?" Glory imagined young Anita St. Jacques looking like a movie star, crying on the steps of an old Southern mansion.

"Mother dear always did whatever Daddy said. And when that other boy—whatever his name was—drove up in his fancy car, he had his two brothers with him, and they said awful things to Earl. He didn't say anything back except to tell them not to speak that way in front of ladies. So I told them I wasn't going to the dance at all, and then my daddy told those stupid boys, 'Ya'll get this dirt nigger outta here.' Then Earl laid my flowers on the bottom step—I still have some of those petals—and my big black buck whipped them high-yella boys and rolled them in the mud until they were blacker than him, all three of 'em. Whipped them till they couldn't get up, and then I ran down the steps and kissed him full on the mouth right there in front of my daddy, just like in the movies. Then Daddy got his shotgun and gave Earl and his family till sunrise to get off our land."

"Did you ever see him again?" Glory asked. "Please tell me you... oh, wait. You're married to Elder Porter, aren't you?"

"Yes, Precious. I am. I am happily married to a very, very good man. Earl wound up in the navy. He married a nice dark-skinned girl, and they're happy."

"Miss Anita, this is the saddest story you've ever told me." Glory sighed. "Thanks a lot. I'll go have a *lot* of fun now."

"Precious, don't be like that." Anita laughed. "I want you to have fun for real. I missed my big dance on account of my daddy's foolishness. I want you and Dexter to go out tonight and have all the fun in the world for me. When a boy pays you a compliment—and they will—don't say, 'Thank you.' I want you to laugh and say, 'I know.' Ya hear me, Precious? I want you to live, laugh, love, and be fascinating tonight."

Glory blushed. "I'm not fascinating."

"Oh, yes, you are, Precious. You're just like I was. Reaching to get out of your plain little world. I want you to live it up tonight." Anita reached into her pocket and pulled out a small zippered pouch in the same fabric as Glory's dress. "I've got something for you. This is more discreet than a regular purse and can hang from your wrist. You can also tuck it into your belt. Open it."

Glory opened the pouch and gasped.

"It's called mad money, Precious. If you get mad and need to leave, you can. The keys are to your suite."

"But—"

"I know how kids are. Somebody is gonna have liquor. You can have a small get-together in your suite if anybody is too tipsy to go home, and y'all can stay until Sunday. I had them make it special and leave a few treats in the rooms. My Bonwit's card is in that side part so you can get fresh clothes for the weekend. If you call customer service and ask for Jewel, she'll send over outfits for everybody."

"But, Miss Anita—"

"No buts, Precious. This is your time." Anita pulled Glory into a hug. "When somebody spikes the punch, drink it. Do anything! Try everything! I want you to get drunk on life and love tonight!"

Glory held out her arms and twirled, sending her gown straight out in a sparkling spiral around her. Catching a glimpse of her reflection, Glory wished the world would stop so she could stay in this moment forever.

"Okay! Do that one more time." Cooter Davis rushed into the room, reaching for his camera. "A little slower. This is going on the cover of *Chicago* magazine!" She tried to imagine the look on Malcolm's face when he stopped by. He'd smile and say she was glorious. She'd smile back and flash her flirty eyes at him.

"Yes. Do it again," Malcolm said from the hallway, leaning against the doorframe. "I want a copy for the wall in front of my desk so I see it whenever I look up."

"Oh, son, you're here," Anita said.

Out of breath and smiling, Glory twirled for the photographer, practicing her flirty eyes on Malcolm, slowly realizing he was dressed in a black tuxedo and carrying a corsage. "Malcolm, you're taking me?" Glory asked. She kept moving, turning her head to look between him and Anita and catching glimpses of the amused grin on Mrs. Beyers's face.

"Yes," he said.

"Now, Malcolm, we discussed this," Anita snapped. "You're going to ruin her big night!"

"No, I won't, Mother." Malcolm didn't take his eyes off Glory.

"How are you going to sit in a hall full of teenagers and not stick out like one of the chaperones? Really, Malcolm, this is ridiculous!"

"No, it's not, Mother." Malcolm walked in front of the camera and took Glory's hand. "Mother, you once told me the story of missing your prom because your lover beat the tar out of your arranged date. That, Mother, is ridiculous. Those who forget their history are doomed to repeat it."

Glory's eyes went wide.

"Malcolm, what did you do?" Anita demanded. "Where's Dexter?"

"Mother, please. I bought him a case of beer and sent him and his friends to the show. He'll be here later tonight. There's no way I'm letting anybody else take my lady out on her big night. I'm surprised you thought I would." He slipped the corsage on Glory's left wrist, just above her bracelets. "The finest woman in the world belongs to me. Nobody but me gets to take her out, okay, Mother?"

The photographer snapped away, and Mrs. Beyers mumbled something about drama and popcorn.

"Well, her curfew is eleven, Malcolm." Anita pouted. "See that you have her home by then."

"I'll have her home by midnight." Malcolm kissed Glory lightly on the lips. "Whose beloved are you?"

"Yours," Glory answered, although she knew the question was more for his mother than anybody else.

"Glory, don't forget my fur wrap!" Anita said.

"It's warm out. You don't need a coat," Malcolm said. "Let's get going."

Glory felt his hand on the small of her back, lower than he'd ever touched her before. She heard Mrs. Beyers telling the photographer to put his camera away.

"Malcolm, don't you ruin her fun. You let her dance with every boy who asks, you hear me? She's gonna be wild and free tonight, understand?"

"Yes, Mother."

Anita pulled Glory into a tight hug. "I'll be up when you get home, Precious. You tell me if he gets in your way. Don't you let him boss you around. He doesn't own you!"

"It'll be fine." Glory returned the hug. "Everything will be just fine."

Chapter 10

The Red Lacquer Ballroom at the Palmer House Hotel reminded Glory of every other fancy ballroom she'd seen lately, except this one was mostly full of people she knew, some of whom she was actually glad to see. Loud music filled the air, and chaperones separated couples on the dance floor. Some girls teetered on heels too high, while others stood in bare feet, having given up on heels seconds after taking the obligatory photo. Their prom dresses were in every shade and style, from fluffy wedding cakes to sexy lingerie. The boys wore every imaginable tuxedo with cummerbunds, tails, top hats, and canes, and the coolest boys wore gym shoes that matched their clothes or even matched their dates' dresses.

Glory and Malcolm made their way through the milling crowd to their table. Christy was already there, holding court and reserving seats, looking like royalty in rich purple, a young man beside her laughing and talking sports with a boy Glory didn't recognize.

"What the hell?" Christy said. "I didn't think you could outdo the cotillion dress, but wow!"

Glory felt Malcolm's hand on her shoulder as she took a seat in the chair he held for her.

"Hi, Dexter." Christy laughed. "That's an awesome Malcolm costume."

"Shhh! Don't blow my cover. Malcolm doesn't know," Malcolm joked. He bowed over Christy's outstretched hand. "You look great, Your Highness."

"Why, thank you, good sir." Christy smiled, unflustered. She never blushed. "So, did you ambush Dexter, leave him tied up somewhere? Glory, don't you kick me!"

Malcolm laughed again. "No, he's fine. I just wanted to bring her myself." He placed a hand on Glory's shoulder. "Isn't she glorious? Taking my breath away. Can't even look directly at her. Like looking at the sun—"

"You can stop now," Glory said from behind her hands.

"Oh," Christy said. "Now you wanna hide? Too late, princess. Everybody in this ballroom saw you come in. They're still looking."

Malcolm leaned in close to Glory. "Sit up straight and take it like a woman right now," he whispered. "You've walked through better crowds than this for months—"

"I'd be fine if you two would just stop," Glory groaned.

"Ooo," Christy said. "Malcolm, I think we've overcomplimented the princess."

"Okay, okay. But relax. You look beautiful. People are gonna compliment you tonight." Malcolm stroked her cheek, leaned back in his chair, and looked around. "Look, here comes the third musketeer."

Glory stood up to hug her calm, rational friend, who immediately started squealing and bouncing. "Et tu, Tressa?" Glory sighed.

"Oh my God, Glory—"

"Don't say it," Christy said a bit louder than necessary. "She's trying to be invisible."

"Oh, okay." Tressa giggled. "Hi, Malcolm. What did you do to Dexter?" she asked, taking her seat, motioning for the silent boy beside her to sit down.

"Glory," Malcolm asked, "should I just start telling people he's in the trunk?"

"Sure, why not? One more crazy rumor can't hurt." Glory looked around and saw another friend approaching. "Hi,

Quentin!" He looked adorable in his white tuxedo and black ruf-
fled shirt. "Where's Paula?"

Quentin paused, looking around. "She's in the bathroom." He
looked at Malcolm. "Hi."

"Oh, Malcolm, this is Quentin, my friend since freshman year."
Glory made introductions. "Quentin, this is Malcolm Porter."

"Nice to meet you, Quentin." Malcolm rose slightly to shake
Quentin's hand.

"Yeah," Quentin shook Malcolm's hand. "Likewise. Can I borrow her for a minute?" He pointed his thumb to the dance floor.

"Uh, no!" Glory said. "You know I only know how to waltz.
I'm not embarrassing myself by dancing to fast music—"

"So waltz." Malcolm patted her shoulder. "Go on, have fun."

Quentin grabbed Glory's hand and practically pulled her from
her seat. The route to the dance floor was long, and so many people
she had never spoken to seemed to know her and wanted her to
stop and take pictures with them. They reached the dance floor just
as the music changed to something slower.

"So, while you were being mobbed, I was gonna fight 'em off,
but this tux is pretty low-level armor. Then I tried an invisibility
spell, but I didn't have the right dice," Quentin said. "Best I could
do was give the DJ two bucks to change the music."

"My hero!" Glory laughed. "Whatever would I do without
you?"

"You'd be swallowed by a sea of popularity, and your bodyguard
would hafta go in after you—"

"Okay, okay... you're probably right." Glory looked around
again, noticing people still whispering and glancing in their direction. "People are staring at you."

"Ha! Nope!" He tried to spin her around, resulting in an awk-
ward trip that set Glory's dress swirling around her, drawing gasps

from those nearby. "It's all you. It's like watching evolution or meta-morphosis or emergence or something."

"Quentin, what are you talking about?"

"Glory, you've been this quiet, invisible, mousy thing for years. Then lightning struck, and you went from Church Girl to Mob Princess to Supervillainess. Last week, you walked into the cotillion like a queen. Now you float in here like a goddess. I'm waiting for you to turn into pure light next and destroy all darkness in the uni-verse."

"Wow." Glory blushed at the strangest compliment she'd ever received. "That tuxedo magnifies your nerd to the tenth power, huh?"

"So, why did you bring your bodyguard to the prom?" Quentin asked seriously. "Lots of other guys woulda taken you."

"Your rumors about me having scary connections worked too well." Glory shrugged. "Nobody asked me."

"Geez, Glory, really?" Quentin hung his head, turning bright red again. "I didn't mean to scare people off. Oh my God, I'm so sorry." He pulled Glory into a hug. "I promise I'll keep you compa-ny all night—"

"Whoa!" Glory pulled away. "It's okay. I'm fine. Malcolm is a great guy, and he's going to make sure I have a great time—"

"But you shouldn't hafta be here tonight, looking like this, with some old guy—"

"Quentin, stop! It's fine. Malcolm isn't some old guy. And be-sides, I don't think Paula will like it if you ruin her prom night try-ing to fix mine, especially since mine is going just fine."

"But—"

"No buts, Quentin."

"I would've brought you."

"Stop it."

"Okay, fine," Quentin said. "It's just that... never mind." As the music ended and dinner was announced, Glory hugged her friend, pretending he wasn't hugging her a little too long and that the hug didn't feel a little too good.

After dinner, the dance floor filled up, and to Glory's great consternation, she found herself counting steps, trying to keep up with Malcolm, while her friends danced nearby.

"Malcolm, why would you think she could step?" Christy asked. "When was she gonna learn—in cotillion school?"

"Bless you, Christy," Glory muttered. "You're lucky I can't kick you right now."

Holding both of Glory's hands, Malcolm slowly turned her around. "You're doing fine. Just keep counting." He laughed.

"Pardon me. I can't watch this any longer." Christy stepped in front of Glory and took Malcolm's hand, and just like that, the crowd opened up, and Malcolm and Christy took the center of the dance floor. They stepped and moved to the fast song, spinning and dipping, the people clapping along to the beat. When the song ended, Christy curtsied to the onlookers, and Malcolm wiped his brow and winked at Glory who, just when she'd felt like the luckiest girl in the world, suddenly found herself pulled back onto the dance floor by Steven from her social studies class.

"Hey, Bishop, if you keep this up, people are gonna start thinking you're a real girl," he said. "You look awesome. I didn't recognize you."

"Gee, thanks." Glory rolled her eyes.

"You wanna ditch your bodyguard and go out sometime?"

"That sounds nice, but I don't want to ditch him. I actually like him." Glory heard herself not denying Malcolm yet not claiming him either. *But it really isn't anybody's business, is it?*

"Well, I'm gonna step out of here for some air in a second. If I see you outside, we'll take a walk, okay?"

"Sure, if I can get away." Glory looked toward her table, where Malcolm stood talking to a teacher and another chaperone while Tressa pulled her date from his seat.

"My turn!"

"Huh?" Glory turned and faced Gary Clark, a secret crush she'd had for at least two years

"You're gonna hafta turn in your nerd card. The other girls are jealous."

"Hi, Gary. I was just going to sit down. I'm kinda tired." The last thing Glory wanted to do was trip in front of this boy.

"Don't worry." Gary wrapped his arms around her waist and pulled her close. "I'll hold you up."

"No." Glory pushed herself away from the boy she'd have once welcomed. "That's not a good idea." She looked around to see Malcolm still talking to other adults.

"Oh crap! I forgot!" Gary stepped back. "Damn. Well, you come in here looking like Cleopatra, I guess you do need a bodyguard." Gary looked around the room. "A whole lotta guys here wishing they'da looked at you more. So, is his name really Bruno?"

"No." Glory giggled. "His name is Malcolm."

"So, why is he here? What's he guarding you from?"

Tressa and Christy appeared. "He's guarding her from all sorts of things. Bye, Gary," Christy said as, one on each side, the girls slipped their arms through Glory's and led her from the dance floor toward their table, where Malcolm stood watching.

THE LINE FOR THE LADIES' room stretched down the hall and around the corner. A group of girls walking past them whispered and pointed.

"Welcome to the world of jealous bi—"

"Witches!" Tressa said. "Jealous witches, Christy. We don't stoop to their level."

"Oh, please," Christy snapped. "Imma stomp all over their level... ignorant heffas!"

"Maybe there's another bathroom somewhere else?" Tressa suggested.

"Or we could just bust up in the men's room. That line is probably a lot shorter," Christy muttered. "I bet it moves a lot faster."

Chaperones tried to keep the girls from wandering, though a few girls did manage to sneak off and report back that the restrooms were just as crowded at other events. The girls in the long line laughed and gossiped and freshened their makeup in the mirrors that decorated the hallway.

"Hey, let's go for a walk." Glory leaned in close to her friends. "I know where there's a bathroom with no line."

"Where?" Tressa looked around. "Everybody said the others are all full too."

"I've been in this line for ten minutes already." Christy pouted. "I'm not walking a mile to wait in another thirty-minute line."

"Suit yourself." Glory stepped out of the line. "I'm not waiting." She turned with a dramatic flounce, sending her dress in a wide flourish around her.

"Can you believe this girl?" Christy grabbed Tressa's arm. "Come on. This better not be far."

The girls slipped past a chaperone and around a corner to the elevators.

"Glory, why are we up here?" Christy asked as they stepped out of the elevator onto the hotel's executive floor.

"I told you," Glory answered. "We're going to the bathroom."

Outside of a room on the eighteenth floor, Glory dug into her purse and pulled out the key Anita had given her. "It's in here."

"Glory, whose room is this?" Tressa asked. "Are we gonna get in trouble?"

Glory pushed the door open and bowed dramatically. "Welcome to our suite. The bathroom with no waiting should be right through the bedroom, but there's probably a powder room out here somewhere, too, in this foyer."

"Giirrrl!" Christy leaned against the doorframe. "If them heffas could see this!"

"Well, they can't." Tressa prodded her friend through the door. "I thought you had to go so bad."

"I'm going!" Christy hurried through the parlor into the bedroom "Oh my God, it gets better!" she said, slamming the bathroom door.

"Glory, this is nice." Tressa said. "But why do you have this huge suite?"

"Oh, this isn't huge." Glory walked into the parlor and flopped down on a red leather couch. "This is small. You should see the ones I usually get." She stretched out and took a chocolate from a tray on an end table. "These aren't even imported. I bet the water's domestic too."

Tressa raised an eyebrow. "Glory Bishop, are you kidding me?"

"Oh my God! Yes! I'm totally kidding!" Glory squealed, jumping up from the couch. "Can you believe this place?" She spun around the room. "Look how big it is—look at the view! Look at all the stuff! Lounges and pillows. Chocolates and roses and hors d'oeuvres and a wet bar and a stereo! Oh my God! Miss Anita got us this suite and said live it up! And we coulda had it for the whole weekend if Malcolm hadn't showed up! Arrrgh!" She groaned, collapsing back on the couch again, an arm draped across her eyes.

"Is she done yet?" Christy asked, emerging from the bedroom.

"I think so," Tressa said. "Shouldn't we fan her or something?"

"Maybe we should throw a glass of water in her face," Christy suggested. "That's what they do to the drama queens in the movies."

"Slap her?"

"Oh... I know!" Christy headed back into the bedroom. "I saw just the thing. You said this is for us, right?"

"Yes, all ours! The rooms, the walls, the floors, the cute little soaps, all of it!" Glory moaned. "What fun we would've had! The room service, the shopping..."

"Hurry, Christy," Tressa deadpanned. "I think Her Highness has the vapors."

"Yes, dear sister, hurry." Glory moaned. "I have the vapors!"

"Just a minute," Christy called from the bedroom. A muffled pop, a clink of glasses, and an expletive later, Christy emerged from the bedroom, holding an open wine bottle and a tray with chocolate-covered strawberries and three glasses. "Don't the Bible say something about 'refresh me with champagne and sexy fruit?'"

Tressa gasped. "No, it does not! Where did you get that?"

Christy looked back over her shoulder. "Didn't you just see me come out of that bedroom? Where do you think I got it?" She placed the bottle and tray on the coffee table and took a glass.

"This can't be real. We're kids." Tressa picked up a glass and sniffed it.

"Nope, it's real champagne!" Christy took a swallow. "Nothing fake for the princess."

Glory sat up and took a sip from the remaining glass. "Well, actually, it's not champagne. It's Spumante—sweet sparkling wine from Italy, much better than champagne."

"So, let me get this straight," Christy said, taking a seat in a red tartan armchair. "The first lady of your church got us a fancy hotel suite for prom night, and she bought us liquor?"

"Not exactly." Glory sipped her drink, feeling sophisticated. "Actually, she got it for the whole weekend. She said somebody down there would probably spike the punch, and if we got too tipsy to drive home, we could stay here—"

"So, if we got drunk, she got us more liquor?" Christy asked, draining her glass.

"No." Glory laughed, draining her glass, also. "She told the hotel it was an important night and to leave some treats." Glory giggled as Christy refilled their empty glasses and topped off Tressa's. "I guess the staff misunderstood."

The girls sipped their drinks while Glory told the story of Anita's missed prom and her own promise to have fun. They sighed wistfully at the thought of ordering clothes from Bonwit's and spending the weekend in the luxury suite.

"Um, Glory," Tressa asked carefully, finally emptying her glass and holding it out for more. "Why can't we still stay? That would be so awesome."

"Well, when Malcolm showed up instead of Dexter, Miss Anita said I had to come home—"

"Hold up!" Christy divided the last of a bottle between their three glasses. "Malcolm doesn't know about this suite?"

"I don't know," Glory admitted. "I never mentioned it. I didn't really think about it."

"But, Glory, what if me and Christy had to go home?" Tressa looked over her glass. "You would have been here with Dexter—"

"No," Glory said. "Only if somebody got too drunk to go home—"

Christy held up a hand. "Your fiancé's mother got you a room with champagne and chocolates for a whole weekend with Dexter?"

"There's only one bed," Tressa said.

"There's couches and loveseats too," Glory said. "That's plenty of sleeping space. And it's for all of us—"

"And she tells you to get drunk on life and love with Dexter and then cancels it when Malcolm shows up?" Christy asked. "Girl, this is some crazy soap-opera mess—"

"It's not like that!" Glory protested.

"But, Glory," Tressa said gently, "why doesn't Malcolm know about this?"

Glory looked away from her friends. They had no idea what they were talking about. There was no way they could understand how much Miss Anita did for her... how ridiculous they sounded.

"I bet Malcolm does know," Glory said finally. "I'll bet Miss Anita told him. That's why he decided to bring me himself." She stared into her drink, watching the bubbles rise to the top. *This whole discussion is silly.*

"You're right," Tressa said, rising. "I'm sure Malcolm and his mother arranged this together. And I bet Malcolm is wondering where you are. We should get back."

"First, I'd like to propose a toast." Christy raised her glass. "To those heffas down there, standing in line for an hour to share a wine cooler in the bathroom and bettin' on whose back seat they gon' land in, while we up here drinking champagne in the executive suite." The girls clinked glasses. "Can we call somebody to come up to take a picture?"

"It's not champagne," Tressa corrected. "It's spumoni."

"Spumante." Glory raised her glass. "It's Spumante."

GLORY WOULDN'T SAY she was drunk, but a few glasses of sparkling wine definitely felt better than wine cooler. Finding their way back to the ballroom, Glory and her friends laughed at the "heffas" still lined up outside the ladies' room. With photo evidence of their executive-suite adventure hidden in Christy's purse, the girls tried to quiet their giggles while walking past curious class-mates and suspicious chaperones.

Back at their table, Christy's and Tressa's dates sat talking, but Malcolm was nowhere in sight. "I think he went looking for you," one of the boys said.

"Where did you run off to?" Quentin asked, pushing his way between the girls. "Did you hear some girls got caught drinking in the bathroom?"

Glory, Christy, and Tressa looked at each other and then howled with laughter, driving Christy to a coughing fit.

"It's not that funny." Quentin said.

"Okay, okay, okay..." Christy said, catching her breath. "You're right. Drinking in the *bathroom* is for stupid, jealous heffas!" The girls collapsed in another fit of giggles.

Christy pointed at her date and then at the dance floor. "You. Let's go."

The young man followed her dutifully. Tressa dabbed her eyes then whispered something in her date's ear that made him blush.

The music changed to something slow, and Glory grabbed Quentin's hand. "Dance with me," she said.

"Shouldn't you wait here?" Quentin looked around. "Malcolm's looking for you."

Glory moved in close to her friend, flashing her flirty eyes. "You smell really good. Please dance with me," she whispered.

"Holy crap, Glory! Were you drinking in the bathroom too?"

Glory giggled. "I promise you, Quentin, I have absolutely not been drinking in any bathrooms." She took both of his hands. "Now, c'mon, dance with me." She blinked slowly, flashing her best flirty eyes again as she pulled him toward the dance floor. "You know you want to. Maybe you should roll for initiative and take the lead." *Spirit of Jezebel!*

Quentin stopped walking, causing Glory to stumble. He pulled his hands away and stepped in close. "Listen, *friend*," he hissed. "Don't talk *Dungeons & Dragons* to me unless you really mean it."

"Aww, Quentin, you know I'm just playing."

"Yeah. I know." He walked away from her.

Glory stood at the edge of the dance floor and watched her friend walk back toward his table. She started to call out to him, but two boys she didn't know pulled her out onto the dance floor, and it didn't really matter because at that moment, swaying between them, moving to the music with her eyes closed and her mind and spirit drunk with life, Glory was having the best time ever, and all boys were mostly the same anyway.

The moment Glory felt a hand on her shoulder, the boys around her nodded and walked away.

"Hi, Malcolm," she turned and looked up at him. "Where've you been?"

"Looking for you. Where were you?"

"Having fun." Breaking all protocol, Glory wrapped her arms around his waist and hugged him, pretending not to notice his irritation. "I'm so glad you brought me."

Malcolm pulled away, no hint of a smile on his face. "Answer my question. Where were you?"

"We went to the bathroom," Glory laughed. "Where do you think? You know how long girls take."

Malcolm leaned closer. "You should really start telling me the truth. Some girls got caught drinking—"

"C'mon, Malcolm, you know that wasn't us. They probably got sent home."

"Woman, it cost me a C-note to find out that somebody looking like you paid fifty bucks to party with some bellhops, and they took pictures."

"Geez, Malcolm." Glory sighed. "We did go to the bathroom... the line was too long, so we went up to the suite your mother got us for the weekend."

"The suite my mother got you for the weekend..." Malcolm repeated slowly.

"Well, those stupid girls who got caught drinking wine coolers were down here, making fun of me, so we went upstairs, and the concierge sent somebody up to take pictures of us with real champagne. Well, not champagne. Spumante." Glory couldn't help giggling again.

"I see. Drinking in the penthouse makes you better than the girls drinking in the bathroom."

"Yes." Glory pouted. She now understood the meaning of *buzzkill* and *party pooper* because Malcolm was being both. "Malcolm, it was only a little. And Miss Anita said for me to drink the spiked punch—"

"Stop." Malcolm placed a hand on her shoulder and ushered her from the dance floor. "It's time to go."

"Malcolm, no," Glory protested. "I'm not ready to go—"

"Listen," Malcolm whispered. "It's time for you to go, and it's gonna get real embarrassing if you and your friends get busted for drinking, won't it?"

"But there's an after-party—"

"That you're not going to. Now. Let's. Go."

Back at the table, Malcolm made sure Christy and Tressa knew he was on to them. Glory said goodbye to her surprised friends and begged them to finish the party for her. Heading past the bell desk, Glory smiled but didn't return the waves from the bellhops, and at the valet stand, while Malcolm went to get the car, Glory moved away from the other girls whispering loudly about Cinderella getting home before it was too late. Waiting alone in the lobby, Glory was happy to see Quentin and Paula walking hand in hand. He'd tried so hard to make Glory's night special, even though he had his own date to think about. She followed the couple outside but quickly turned her head when she saw them pause for a long kiss. Having been close to Quentin twice that day, Glory felt a twinge of something at the sight of his arms wrapped around Paula. She turned her back and looked toward where she hoped Malcolm would appear.

"Hi, Glory! I love your dress!"

Glory turned around. A giggly Paula stood wrapped in Quentin's arms. Quentin, for his part, seemed too intent on nuzzling Paula's neck to look up. "Hi, Paula. Thanks. I like yours too. You look great."

"Thanks! What after-party are you going to? We're going to Sauer's."

"I'm not going to one." Glory sighed. "My ride's turning into a pumpkin." She giggled.

A few more classmates appeared and offered her rides and help ditching her boring old bodyguard. Glory laughed and actually thought about disappearing into the growing crowd of people waiting for cars, maybe calling Dexter to come and get her or sneaking back up to the suite and having her own after-party. Malcolm would go crazy, but the thought was amusing. But the sudden silence and a hand on her shoulder told Glory the party was truly over, and it was time to go.

"MALCOLM, IT'S ONLY ten o'clock," Glory whined as he pulled the car away from the curb. "It's too early to go in. I'm supposed to be out—"

"Bodyguard?"

"Huh?"

"You've been telling people I'm your bodyguard. I've been hearing it all night. I'm some old guy from your church. Hired escort. Uncle. And yeah, bodyguard."

Glory looked over at him and took a deep breath. He was seething, and having him angry was the last thing she wanted, especially that night. "Malcolm, I never said any of that. People just assumed that—"

"And you didn't correct it!" Malcolm snapped.

"What was I supposed to do? We can't tell anybody, remember?"

"Then you disappear and come back drunk. Messing around with bellboys!"

"You know that's not true! We weren't doing anything. We had a few drinks from *your* mother and took a picture—that's all."

"And then I find you out there on the floor moving around like a stripper with every boy in the place—"

"Malcolm, I was dancing!" Glory heard her tone rising. "Just like your mother and you said I could! Just like people my age dance!" The Spumante had relaxed her, and he was being unreasonable and unfair. "You don't own me, Malcolm Porter! This was my night to be young and wild and free. You are only a man! You don't run my life! You don't have power over me!"

When the car screeched to a halt at a red light, Glory raised her left arm, barely shielding her face from the blow she knew was coming. She would have apologized, but the words she'd learned from Miss Anita came out before she could stop them, and when the back of his hand hit her a second time, it was too late to take anything back.

"Whoredom and wine take away the heart!"

Glory stayed silent, protecting her face. More blows came.

"There shall be no whores among the daughters of Israel!"

Glory curled into a ball against the passenger door. Keeping one hand on the steering wheel, Malcolm had to stretch to reach her, and most of his blows, barely grazing her arm, landed with loud thuds against the leather seat.

When Glory felt the familiar lurch of the car going into park, she pulled up on the door handle.

"You are not Anita Porter! Don't you ever—"

"Malcom, *stop*!" Glory screamed. She managed to get the door open, only to be yanked back in as the light turned green and other drivers began honking. "Malcolm, please!" She heard car doors slamming, voices, and more honking. Then, with his grip on her wrist, pressing the bracelets against bone, Malcolm put the car in gear and peeled off toward Lake Shore Drive.

The rest of the drive home, Glory watched Malcolm from the corner of her eye. He kept his eyes forward and seemed to bow his head in prayer at red lights. Glory didn't move when he shut off the engine in front of the Porters' building—she wouldn't risk further provoking him. She sat still until he opened the passenger door and let her out.

"You know," Malcolm said quietly, "my mother wants you to be like her."

Glory wanted to disagree, but she held her tongue.

"She thinks a woman's job is to silently dominate her man. Trick him. Control things that he won't notice."

Again, Glory wanted to disagree, but she remained silent.

"When I heard her words coming out of you, it got to me. You can't be her."

"Malcolm," Glory said softly, not trusting her voice to speak too much above a whisper. "Your mother is the best woman I know. She's beautiful and powerful, and everybody loves her. And she wants me to be happy, too, just like you do. She gives me the world, and I wouldn't be anything without her."

Malcolm bowed his head again and stood quietly for a minute. "I see more than you think." He reached out and touched her arm through the torn spot on her sleeve. "You looked so beautiful tonight. I'm sorry I lost it."

"I know." Glory sighed. "I felt beautiful."

"Your friend Quentin really likes you."

"Nah," Glory said. "He has a girlfriend."

"Trust me, his girlfriend is the consolation prize." Malcolm squeezed her hand. "I'm sorry I got so mad. I don't know what comes over me."

"I don't know either."

"I'm gonna talk to somebody, okay?" Malcolm said. "I'm not gonna keep hurting you."

Glory squeezed his hand back, feeling a tear coming. "Can I go in now?"

"Yeah. Forgive me?"

"You know I do," Glory said.

Inside, Glory found the foyer lights dimmed. She tiptoed through the quiet apartment to see if Anita had waited up. She followed the muffled sounds of music to the library. By the light of the muted TV, Glory could make out a sleeping Dexter, a paused video game, and a half-eaten pizza—things Glory always felt didn't belong in this elegant room.

"Hey." Glory shook him awake. "It's Friday night. Why aren't you out on a date or something?"

Dexter sat up on the couch and smiled. "My cousin stole my date."

Glory smiled back. "I'm sure you coulda got another one. I'm gonna raid your pizza, okay?" She sat down and dug into the pizza, not waiting for permission.

"So, how was your night?" Dexter opened a wine cooler, filled a glass, and passed it to her.

"Well, it all started with a wine cooler..." Glory raised her glass in a mock toast and launched into the details of the entire night.

"Wow!" Dexter said as Glory finished her story. "Executive suite, huh?"

"Yup. Asti Spumante, chocolate-covered strawberries—coulda had it all weekend." Glory drained her glass and allowed Dexter to refill it yet again. *Because it's still prom night, right?*

"I'm sorry he made you leave early. You missed the last dance and the balloon drop and stuff."

"Yeah, but I kinda brought it on myself. I did get a little wild—"

"No." Dexter laughed. "You got noticed and appreciated, and he's not used to that. Go stand over by the windows. I wanna see your dress."

"It's torn on the shoulder," Glory brushed a string away. "I snagged it."

"I still wanna see."

Glory walked around the coffee table to stand in front of the windows. She held out her arms and turned in the light of the TV. Everything in her told her it was time to say good night, but...

"Damn," he said. "I see why he wouldn't let me take you."

"But I bet you woulda let me stay till the end..."

"Well, yeah," Dexter admitted.

"And spend the weekend?"

"Um... I don't know about all that..."

Glory smiled a little, flashing her flirty eyes at him, holding out her hands. "How 'bout that last dance?" *One last bit of attention on prom night... feel glorious one last time...*

Dexter looked at her for a minute then went to the TV and turned it off, plunging the library into semidarkness. He went to the stereo and changed the music to "Hold Me," by Whitney Houston, and when he pulled her into his arms, it wasn't like the respectable waltz at the cotillion. He didn't hold one hand and turn her slowly. He held her whole body against his and swayed. He held her not like she belonged to his cousin but like she belonged to him, the way boys always held normal girls when they danced—bodies touching, grinding to the music, faces close, lips accidentally brushing cheeks when they moved their heads. As they neared the end of the song, she realized Dexter was running out of time to try for a kiss and wondered if he knew he could have a kiss if he wanted one.

But the song wasn't almost over when they both moved, and their lips touched. Maybe it was the music and the wine coolers. Maybe this was being drunk on life and love. Glory just knew it was time to be kissed, and the kiss lasted until long after the end of the song, and a boy's warm, hungry kiss over the city lights under the stars was the perfect ending to a normal girl's prom night.

Then he reached up, touched her face, his finger lightly brushing the sore spot on her cheek, and the spell broke. And Glory remembered that she wasn't a normal girl. She was a godly young lady behaving very badly. A rebellious and sinful girl. Malcolm's *beloved* who he'd do anything for, betraying him with his own cousin. A filthy Jezebel tempting a nice boy to certain danger if Malcolm found out.

"I hafta go," Glory whispered. "I can't do this. I hafta go." She pulled away from him.

"Glory, wait. What else happened to you?" Dexter called as she practically ran from the library.

BY THE DIMMED VANITY light, she wiped away her makeup and prayed there would be no mark on her face. Malcolm had apologized, and she'd forgiven him. But Dexter and those boys from school and even Quentin... all the boys who treated her like a normal girl, they didn't matter. Malcolm had saved her and freed her and changed her life, and he loved her. She was his.

Her bracelets clinked as she climbed into bed and slid under the covers, and Glory prayed for forgiveness. Before Malcolm, her world had been church, the salon, and JT. She'd been Church Girl with a secret life of books. With Malcolm, she had the life she'd dreamed about, and when he was happy, even if she only loved him a little, she loved being Malcolm's beloved.

INTERLUDE
MAY 1976

The Saturday morning after her father had died, Glory woke up and tried to stretch. She still felt the sting of welts, and her arms and throat were sore. Sitting up, she found that her undershirt had stuck to places on her body where the lashes had broken her skin. Looking around the room, Glory fought the urge to scream and cry. Her daddy was supposed to be home. He was supposed to be singing their song.

Our song?

Glory couldn't believe the music she was hearing. Maybe her daddy was just sick and had come home and was playing their song on the stereo. She tried to jump up from the bed, but aches and pains made her move slowly. She slipped a nightgown over her tattered undershirt—she didn't want her daddy to yell at Mama again—and ventured out of her room, following the music to the living room.

"Good morning, baby!" Mary called from the kitchen.

Glory looked around the living room. There was no sign of her daddy. No sign at all. The pictures on the walls were gone. The photo album open on the coffee table had light-colored squares where photos used to be. The black velvet painting of their little family lay on the floor, its carved wooden frame twisted and mangled, smashed.

"Mama? How did the picture get broke?" Glory tried to keep her voice from sounding too funny, but her throat was raw from screaming and crying the night before.

"It broke when I took it off the wall. That frame was cheap anyway. Come in here. Lemme look at you."

Glory padded into the kitchen, her bare feet slapping against the hardwood floor. The first things Glory noticed were the pieces of cardboard taped over the windows—one over the sink and one over the glass in the back door. The flowered curtains were still in place, but no daylight came into the kitchen. On the back door hung the picture of blond, blue-eyed Jesus that her daddy had hated.

"How you feel this morning, baby?" Mary stood at the counter sorting silverware and dropping certain pieces into a mug imprinted with her daddy's truck logo.

"Good." Glory didn't feel like it was a real lie because she didn't feel all bad... just a little good.

Mary looked over at her daughter. "Demons all gone, baby?"

Glory hung her head. "Yes, ma'am. Demons all gone."

"Don't hang your head. Look in my eyes. Demons cain't look you in the eyes and lie."

Glory snapped her head up and looked into her mother's eyes, praying she saw no more demons.

"Any demons still in you?"

"No, ma'am. Demons all gone," Glory repeated, with her eyes open as wide as she could.

Her mother stared at her for a minute. Glory didn't move, didn't blink, didn't even exhale.

Finally, Mary turned back to the silverware. "Praise the Lord, baby. We got 'em all outta you."

Glory stifled a sigh of relief and took a seat at the kitchen table. She didn't go to her usual seat—she took the seat at the end by the wall where her daddy usually sat... used to sit. His worn red cushion was gone, as was the pile of newspaper funnies she'd collected for him to read out loud.

Mary poured frosted rice cereal into a bowl and placed it and a glass of milk in front of Glory then kissed her on her forehead. "You hurry up and eat. We got a lotta work to do today."

While she ate her breakfast, Glory watched her mother moving around the kitchen, opening and closing cabinets, whispering a prayer each time. When she opened the spice cabinet, Mary took out a red-and-white can. Glory watched her spoon some green stuff into a teacup and then add water from the kettle simmering on the stove, sending the strong fragrance wafting through the kitchen. It smelled like Thanksgiving and chicken soup.

"Mama, what's that?"

"No talking with food in your mouth!"

Glory quickly closed her mouth and swallowed.

"Since you gotta know everything," Mary said, "I'm making sage tea. Ain't drinkin' no mo' coffee. That's Satan's brew. Get you all addicted—hurt you, make you mean as the devil when you cain't get it. It's a sin to get addicted." She turned and shook her finger at Glory. "Yo' body is a temple. Don't put nothin' sinful in yo' body." She carried the steaming cup to the table and took her usual seat at the end by the back door. "I threw out the coffee and dumped out all the liquor. Crazy man talkin' 'bout Jesus had libations. Bible say Jesus turned water into wine. It don't say he drunk it."

Glory watched her mother reach into her bosom and pull out a tightly rolled piece of brown paper. Mary picked up the electric lighter and placed the small flame to the end of the paper roll.

"What about cigarettes?" Glory asked, careful to keep her eyes down. "Some people get addicted—"

"And that's a sin too." Mary inhaled deeply. "Got folks beggin' on the street for butts."

Glory cleared her throat to keep from giggling when her mother said "butts."

"This here?" Mary continued puffing away. "Ain't nothin' but a rolled-up piece of paper. Ain't no tobacco, so it ain't a sin. Been too much sin in this house. Demons all through this house. Yo' daddy gone 'cause of sin." Mary sat up straight and crushed out her pretend cigarette. "Well, ain't gon' be no more sin in this house, hear me, girl?"

"Yes, ma'am." Glory turned up her cereal bowl to finish the milk. The green plastic bowl nearly covered her whole face, and Glory tried to cross her eyes and watch the last drops of milk run down to her lips.

She gripped the rim of the bowl in her teeth and counted to see how long she could hold it. The loud smack of her mother's hand hitting the green-flecked table shocked her into dropping the bowl. The bowl bounced on the table, and then Glory watched in terror as the bowl spun over the edge and landed on the floor.

"What I tell you about playin' at the table!" Mary snapped. "You lettin' demons in you again?"

"No, ma'am." Glory's voice trembled almost as much as her body. "You said not to play. I'm sorry, Mama." Glory hoped her tears would show how truly sorry she was.

"You know it's a sin to play with your food, and then you disobey too? Maybe some demons got back in you already." Mary pulled another paper cigarette from her bosom and lit it. She sat back and leaned her head against the wall, blowing perfect smoke rings into the air. "Today, we gon' purge this house. Gettin' rid of everything sinful. All Paul's stuff gotta go. Cleanin' it all out. Everything! We gon' make a lotta trips out to the garbage today."

Glory listened in horror as her mother described the purge. Everything of her daddy's was going in the garbage. Glory had cried when Uncle Bobby took most of his clothes and shoes, but that was better than throwing everything in the alley.

"Mama, why do we hafta throw Daddy's stuff out?" Glory whispered. The lump in her throat didn't allow her to speak any louder.

"Come here, baby." Mary summoned her daughter with a wave.

Glory got up from the table, each breath trembling with suppressed sobs. She stood in front of her mother.

"Listen, baby." Mary took both of Glory's hands in hers. "A long time ago, I sinned real bad. I sinned so bad that God took my four babies to heaven with him. And I still didn't repent. I just kept on' doin' wrong. When me and Paul got married, I was still deep in sin. I had a long time to get myself together, but I didn't, so God took him from me."

"Did I sin bad too?" Glory knew she sinned, but she didn't think it was bad enough for God to take her daddy away.

"Yes, baby, we both sinners, but it's my sins that got yo' daddy took away. You ain't gon' be a sinner like I was. Imma make sure of that. God ain't gon' never hafta punish you like he punishing me."

"But can we just keep the pictures? Pleeease?" Glory knew she was whining, but they couldn't get rid of every trace of Daddy, could they?

Mary pulled Glory into her arms. "No, baby. God took him away. He ain't mine, so all his stuff gotta go. I 'a be sinnin' just like them Israelites that kept the treasure when God said burn it."

On her first few trips to the trash cans out by the alley, Glory threw out just papers. When she had to throw out the *Ebony, Jet,* and *Ebony Jr.* magazines, she gritted her teeth and straightened her back and held her breath to keep from crying. Her daddy used to read to her the whole *Ebony Jr.* until she learned to read, and then she would read it to him.

"Hey! Whatcha doin'?"

Glory wiped her almost tears and tried to ignore the boy tossing a rubber ball so that it bounced right beside her. The back door to Josiah Jackson's house was right across the alley from the back of the Bishops' apartment building. It seemed like whenever Glory went to the garbage, the boy was always there.

"Wanna play?" Josiah tossed the ball again and made a great show of catching it with one hand.

Glory was just a bit taller than the trash barrel, so she had to lift the brown paper bag of magazines over her head. They landed with a soft thump on the pile of clothes already in there. Glory looked down at the spilled magazines. She could see the brown sleeve of her daddy's worn leather jacket—the jacked she'd snuggled under whenever she rode in his truck.

"Whatcha looking at?" Josiah came and stood next to Glory so their arms almost touched. "What's in there?" he asked, looking down into the trash can.

"None of your beeswax, Josiah!" Glory snapped. "Leave me alone!"

"Fine, Mrs. Glory!" Josiah laughed. He turned away from her and tossed the ball in the air. "I'll just look when you go in, so ha!" He caught the ball and tossed it up again.

"Well, you a... a..." Glory stuttered. She couldn't say what she really wanted to say because it was a sin, and her mom said there would be no more sinning. "Well, you don't have no friends! That's why you stay in the alley, playing with yourself!" There. She'd won the battle of words by telling the truth.

Glory turned and headed back inside, ignoring Josiah's laughing pleas of "Come back, Mrs. Glory!"

Her next few trips to the garbage, she brought books. All kinds of books. Her mother said the only book they needed was the Bible, so everything that wasn't a Bible had to go. She made four trips, carrying books, walking slower and slower each time. *Why is it a sin to have books?* Glory had begged her mother to at least keep the monster book her daddy had been reading to her since she was three. Mary just ripped the Golden Book in half. The monster in the book was of the devil.

Glory stood at the garbage can and let herself cry just a little bit. She carefully laid each book atop the growing pile of precious things in the nearly full garbage can. She hugged the torn monster book to her chest then carefully hid it behind the garbage can. She'd get it on her way to school Monday. She was only being a little sneaky, so it wasn't a real sin.

"I saaaw what yooou did!"

Glory turned to see the annoying boy peeking through a bush in his backyard. "Josiah Jackson, you leave me alone right now!" She picked up a rock, threw it into the bush, and ran back to her porch. She wanted to yell that she hated him, but that would be a bad sin, and besides, her mother might hear.

Back inside the apartment, Glory found her mother sitting in the kitchen with a cup of sage tea. "Baby, we almost done. I been praying and asking the Lord for guidance." She took a long drag on her paper cigarette. "Lord say we can be in the world but not of it. We gon' get rid of all the worldly mess in this house."

Glory looked around the kitchen. The cat clock with the moving eyes and tail was gone. "Mama, are clocks worldly?"

"Not all of 'em, but that black cat was. Had that diamond necklace on." Mary took another puff. "Besides, black cats is for witches." She crushed out the paper cigarette. "You take out that last bag in the front room. I'll get us some lunch together."

Glory grabbed the brown paper bag. It wasn't heavy at all, so it couldn't have been books. When she got to the back porch, she opened the bag. The first thing she saw was her daddy's smiling face. Well, half of it, at least. Glory reached into the bag and pulled out a handful of paper scraps, all pictures of her daddy—some cut up, others scribbled with black marker. Glory hurried to the alley. She placed the monster book in the bag with the photos and hid it behind the garbage can. Monday morning, she'd take them to school and try to put the cut ones back together during recess. She looked around. No sign of nosy Josiah spying on her.

Back inside, lunch was a bologna sandwich with lettuce and a lot of mayonnaise, just like Glory liked it. She enjoyed it with chocolate milk and a cookie. It almost felt like normal. Almost. Sitting at the kitchen table was fine, but her daddy always let her sit in the front room and watch cartoons. She knew better than to ask her mother to let her eat in the front room, so she finished her lunch quickly and ran to turn the TV on.

When she pushed the on button, nothing happened. Glory pushed the button a few more times. She reached for the cord and gave it a slight tug to see if the TV was plugged in. Pulling the cord, Glory immediately saw the problem. The TV cord had been cut. The other end lay on top of the polished brown wood television set.

"Ma, what happened to the TV?" Glory went back into the kitchen, where Mary sat finishing her own lunch. "The cord is broke."

"No more TV in this house, baby." Mary stood up and took her dishes to the sink. "Too much worldliness on TV. Shows got nothin' but liars and cheats. Ain't no demons gettin' in this house through that thing."

No more TV? Glory gaped at her mother. But her favorite shows weren't bad. *Sesame Street*, *Electric Company*, *Mr. Rogers*, and *Zoom*. There wasn't anything bad about any of those shows. And the monsters were all good guys.

After lunch, Glory leaned against the doorframe of her bedroom, watching her mother tape layers of black plastic bags to her bedroom windows, blocking out the bright sunny day, making the cheerful room almost as dark as nighttime.

"See, baby, this gon' keep any evil from looking in and getting to you while you sleep." Mary walked over to the light in the middle of the ceiling and pulled the string, bathing the room in a yellowish glow from two bulbs in the ornate but uncovered ceiling fixture.

"Ma, you taped it to the frame. How can I open the window?"

"Ain't gon' be no mo' opening windows in this house... let evil in that way. Then I'll hafta get 'em outta you all the time. You don't want that, now, do you?"

Glory shook her head. "No, ma'am. I'm just gonna miss the stars and the moon at night, that's all."

"Well, you can read about the moon and stars in the Bible. God don't like you looking too much at stuff like you worshippin' it. Our God is a jealous god." Mary went to Glory's chest of drawers. "Where yo' pants at?"

"In the bottom drawer," Glory answered, and her mother bent down and opened the drawer. She watched her mother pull out every pair of pants.

"You gon' dress like a lady from now on." Mary declared. "No mo' worldly ways, running around in pants and stuff. Take off them what you got on."

Glory sat on her small bed and slowly removed her favorite pair of jeans, the ones with the flare legs, made of big squares of blue jean material—the ones that were just a little too short, so she couldn't wear them to school anymore. Her daddy had said she could cut them off and make some shorts for the summer. With a heavy heart, she handed the jeans to her mother.

"Put some clothes on, and get me a garbage bag." Mary tossed the jeans into a pile on the floor and opened another drawer.

Glory walked down the hallway, trying not to look at the light spots where pictures had once hung and trying not to hear her mother's nonstop fussing about worldly clothes. Most of her couldn't believe what was happening. She'd always felt their house was no fun when Daddy wasn't home, but with him never coming back, she wondered if her mother was taking away all the fun forever. And her clothes...

How can I play in a skirt? My jeans have holey knees already. What will happen to my real knees? And what about the stupid boys who like to lift girls' skirts? And I won't be able to turn cartwheels or jump rope. The more Glory thought about it, the more she wanted to cry again, but her mother had said that was enough crying and hinted that she might have the demon of sadness in her.

Back in her bedroom, Glory looked at the pile of worldly clothes. "Ma, how come the T-shirts are worldly? They just have states on 'em." The pile of T-shirts had come from her daddy's travels around the country. She had T-shirts from almost every state.

"They got words on the front." Mary tossed another shirt on the pile. "Got folks lookin' at your chest all the time. That ain't godly." She held open the trash bag. "Put them clothes in here."

"Can we give them to the poor? Maybe help other kids?" Glory moved as slowly as she could without raising her mother's ire.

"Oh no, baby! It's a sin to give out ungodly stuff. That's enough—not too heavy, now. Go get a couple more bags."

Glory dragged a bag through the kitchen and out the back door. At the top of the stairs, she dropped it and let it fall. She watched the bag of clothes—her favorite clothes—tumble down the short flight and snag on a splinter. It ripped, and she could see her favorite jeans pushing out of the bag like they were trying to escape their fate.

"I wish I could keep you, box pants, but I can't fit you anymore, and I got nowhere to hide you." Glory whispered her wish to all the clothes in the bag and then dragged the bag out to the alley, too sad to care that the plastic was ripping more and more.

"Why you keep coming out to the garbage?" Josiah launched a rubber-band-powered airplane toward the sky. The plane made a perfect arc and crashed dangerously close to a pile of dog doo. "Is your house *that* dirty?" He didn't go pick up the plane—he bent down and grabbed a bundle of clothes that had fallen out of the bag.

"Why you keep coming out and bothering me?" Glory heaved the now-lighter bag over the edge of the garbage can. "Leave me alone!" she snapped.

Josiah pulled out the rubber ball he'd had earlier and started bouncing it. "Why are you so mad today?"

"Leave me alone! I'm not mad! I'm just... just..." Glory's voice broke. "I'm just really, really sad. My mother is making me throw everything away." She felt tears coming and took off running back to the house. The last thing she wanted was for that boy to see her crying.

"I'm sorry you're sad!" Josiah called after her.

Glory wiped her eyes as she went back inside. "What took you so long?" Mary asked her daughter when she turned and saw her.

"The bag tore." Glory didn't try to hide the sadness in her voice. "And Josiah wouldn't leave me alone."

"You know that boy is trouble, don't you?" Mary laughed. "He probably likes you and don't know how to act. Boys be so silly sometimes."

"Yeah." Glory thought about that day in church when Josiah had tricked her into marrying him. Then she thought about the stupid teenager. She was glad the teenager didn't come to church anymore. Then her thoughts went to her daddy and him assuring her that she wasn't married. *And now he's dead. Why couldn't God take somebody else?*

"Quit daydreaming, and get over here, I said!"

Mary's voice pulled Glory from her thoughts. "Yes, ma'am." Glory rushed to the garbage bag at her mother's feet.

"This the last bag, and we all done. I tell you, I'm tired." Mary wiped her brow with her sleeve. "I looked at your toys. Most of 'em are just fine..."

Glory quickly scanned her room. There was her toy oven that really cooked... and the toy popcorn popper and hamburger grill. Her stuffed animals were mostly there except the snake and the colorful furry rectangle with eyes. She didn't see her stuffed sun, moon, and stars pillow either. And she didn't see...

"But all that Barbie mess got to go."

Glory looked in the bag she was holding. Sure enough, there were her stuffed toys, Barbie's camper and airplane, and right on top, the big pink wardrobe case.

"Mama, pleeease," Glory whispered, her voice choked with grief. "Barbies the last toys Daddy gave me. Please!"

"Oh no, baby. That doll is of the devil. Got girls thinkin' tha's how they supposed to look. Enough devilment in you as it is—"

"Oh God, Mama, please." Glory went down on her knees and clasped her hands in front of her chest. "Please, please, please!" she begged. "I promise I'll be good. I promise to God—"

The blow to the side of her head knocked her over, and Glory lay on the floor, sobbing. "Please, God, don't take my dolls. You can take all my other toys. Please, Jesus." Eyes closed, hands still clasped, Glory prayed. She begged God and called on Jesus. The kick to her leg didn't even bother her.

"Giiirl... you takin' the Lord's name in vain and worshiping idols, cryin' and prayin' for worldly toys! You got the demons of greed and idolatry, don't you!"

"No, Mama! No demons!" Glory got up from the floor. Keeping her eyes wide open, she looked into her mother's eyes. "See, Mama... no demons." She tried to smile, even though barely suppressed sobs pushed against her chest and throat. Her eyes and nose burned from unshed tears forcing their way out.

"Then you better hush up all that noise and get this here last bag to the garbage. Then we gon' pray for God to fix your heart so you won't want no worldly toys."

Glory grabbed the bag and dragged it behind her. She was just a few steps out of the room when the pent-up grief forced its way out in the form of deep, choking sobs. The tears she'd tried to hold back overflowed and ran down her cheeks. Glory cried as quietly as she could, lest her mother suspect more demons.

"GLORY, WHY YOU CRYING?"

"Leave me alone, Josiah." Glory hauled the bag of her precious toys through the brown backyard grass to the back gate.

"What's the matter? Something else bad happen?" He stood blocking Glory's path at the gate. "Tell me, pleeease."

Glory bent down, picked up a fallen stick, and swung it. Josiah took a step back from the gate. "Josiah, if you don't leave me alone," she snarled, "I promise to God I'm gonna beat you up again!"

"You never beat me up, before, Mrs. Glory! Ha ha!" Josiah took another step back. "And you couldn't catch me anyway!" He took another step back and slipped, and his arms whirled like windmills as he tried to keep his balance.

"Ha ha!" Glory yelled. "You stepped in—"

"Shit!" Josiah finished her sentence. "And I'm gonna wipe it on you."

Glory screamed and waved the stick even harder. She tried not to laugh at the boy hopping toward her on one foot, but she couldn't help letting a smile escape.

"Jaaay Teee!" a voice called from across the alley. "Jaaay Teee!"

Josiah stopped hopping. "Coming!" he called back. He turned to Glory. "I gotta go. I'm sorry you're sad, and I'm sorry about your toys." He headed home, dragging his left foot behind him, scraping the mess from his shoe. "Bye, Mrs. Glory!"

Glory started to wave at his back. That boy was the most annoying person in the world, but despite her misery, he'd made her smile a little bit, even if the alley was suddenly stinky. She tried to lift the bulky bag into the trash can, but the toys inside moved around too much. She opened the bag, reached inside, and grabbed the bed pillow she'd had ever since she could remember. On the light-blue side were the sun and clouds. On the dark-blue side were the moon and stars. Glory hugged the pillow to her chest, kissed it goodbye, and dropped it into the trash can. She pulled out her Bippy, a stiff pillow that was yellow on one side and furry psychedelic on the other. He had big googly eyes and a necktie with his name on it. She would hold Bippy when she and her dad watched *Creature Features* on Saturday nights. She hugged and kissed Bippy and whispered goodbye then dropped him in the trash can too.

With an aching heart, she pulled out the six-foot pink plaid snake. "Bye, Sakey," she whispered. "I'll never forget you." She'd had that snake since she first started talking and couldn't say "snake." Tears started falling when she took out Barbie's motor home. The bright-yellow bus had taken her and Barbie camping in every corner of the house. And the airplane—*Barbie's Friendship*—had taken Barbie on trips to the lands Glory had read about in her now-discarded *World Book Encyclopedia*. She sobbed openly as she held the two toys. Maybe if she left them on top of the garbage can, somebody would come down the alley and take them. She looked around then walked over to the next gate and placed her two favorite toys on the garbage-can lids. She touched them one last time and wished them luck.

The last thing in the bag was the pink case. Glory threw her head back and begged God one more time. Barbie, Midge, and Ken all huddled in that case along with their fabulous wardrobe... the clothes Glory had sewn from scraps of fabric and old socks. This day was almost as bad as the day she'd found out about her daddy.

No. There's gotta be a way.

Glory looked around. In her heart of hearts, she knew what she was about to do was wrong. God was watching her, but so was her daddy, and her daddy would tell God that having Barbies wasn't sinful and worldly. It took more strength than she expected to widen the space behind another garbage can. She wrapped the plastic bag tightly around the doll case and then squeezed it in behind the garbage can. She could get them Monday morning and give them to Miss Joyce as a gift. That way, even though she'd disobeyed, she'd have done something good too. And Miss Joyce would surely let Glory play with *her* new Barbie dolls.

GLORY AWOKE MONDAY morning in the dark bedroom. It was a little scary, so she said a quick prayer and briefly wondered again if Jesus was scared of the dark when he was a kid. Then she heard the rumble of garbage cans being tossed around. She jumped out of bed and ran to the kitchen to look out of the back door, but the glass was covered, as was the window over the sink. In the dining room, the windows had been covered as well, but Glory desperately needed to see what the garbage men were doing and find out whether her treasured things were still there. She tried listening at the back door, but she didn't dare open it. Then came the telltale sound of the truck moving on farther down the alley. Glory said another prayer, and at seven thirty, she kissed her mother's cheek and ran up to Miss Joyce's.

The first thing Glory did was sit down on the floor in front of the TV. Ray Rayner was talking to his stuffed dog Cuddly Duddly. She switched to channel eleven and watched a little of *Sesame Street*, and next, *Magilla Gorilla* on Channel 32. Living without

TV at home wouldn't be so bad as long as she could still come to Miss Joyce's and watch TV there. Her mother never said she couldn't watch TV... just not at home. She reached out and turned to Channel 44 and watched the giant gold robot fighting a monster.

At eight o'clock, when she was sure her mother had already left for work, Glory went to Miss Joyce's kitchen and looked out the backdoor window. She could see as far as the back gate, but the high wooden fence hid the garbage cans from view. "Miss Joyce, can I go look for something I left in the backyard?"

The babysitter looked up from the magazine she was reading. "Sho, just make sure you pull that door up. Don't let no flies in."

"Yes, ma'am."

Glory went out the back door, and as soon as she was sure it was closed, she ran down the back stairs and out to the yard and to the back gate. Out in the alley, she first noticed that Barbie's motor home and airplane were gone. She smiled a little. Maybe somebody had come by and taken them to another girl who liked Barbie. *But... wait...* Glory's face fell, and she got the familiar knot in her stomach. She hadn't done exactly as she was told. *Do I have demons of sneakiness and disobedience? Will it make God punish me?* Glory pushed the thoughts away and looked next to the garbage at... nothing. *Did I put it behind the can?* She checked back there. Nothing.

No. The knot in her stomach grew tighter.

No, no, no. Glory ran checking behind cans on both sides of the alley.

Please, God, no. Back at her gate, Glory stared at the empty hiding place, and her heart broke all over again. Her book and the pictures and her precious Barbie dolls were gone. Her mother was right. She was sneaky, and God had punished her.

———— ⁑ ————

"HEY, GLORY!"

Glory kept walking across the school playground. If she ignored him, maybe he'd go away.

"Glooorry!"

She picked up her pace. Her day was miserable enough without *that boy* adding to it.

"Glory, glory, halleluuujah!"

"Josiah, what do you want!" She stopped walking and turned to face the boy jogging to catch up with her. He dodged a ball rolling toward him and deliberately stuck his hand in the rope where a girl was jumping double Dutch. "Why are you bothering me!"

"I wanna show you something." He was practically out of breath.

Glory turned and kept walking. "I don't wanna see nothing you have."

"C'mon. I can't show you here... come over by the bushes."

Glory's eyes narrowed. "I am not going near any bushes with you, Josiah Jackson. I'd rather eat a worm!"

"Please, Miss Glory. You really wanna see this." Josiah smiled at her. "Trust me."

Glory stared at him for a minute. "Fine! But don't make me hafta beat you up again."

As they wound their way through the crowds in the playground, Glory tried to look like she wasn't walking with the loud, bouncy boy. The last time he'd said, "Trust me," Glory had had to beat him up for tricking her. Even though it made her smile a little to think about, she still didn't trust him.

As they got to the edge of the playground, Josiah ran behind the lilac bushes and motioned for Glory to follow. She folded her arms and followed him as far as the edge of the neatly trimmed bushes. "I'm not comin' back there with you!"

"Okay, fine. You can see from there." Josiah took off his backpack and went down on one knee while opening it. The zipper snagged on something, and he cussed just loud enough for Glory to hear.

"Stop cussin' and hurry up! The bell is gonna ring!"

"Gimme just a second..." Josiah struggled with the zipper a bit then pulled a crumpled brown paper bag from his backpack. "You hafta come closer if you wanna see!"

"I'm not coming behind the bushes with you..." Glory's protesting trailed off as she looked at what Josiah pulled from the brown paper bag.

Josiah smiled. "I got 'em from the garbage man this morning."

"Josiah, you saved my Barbies?" Glory felt her eyes watering with tears she didn't understand.

"Yeah, I guess." Blushing, Josiah pushed the dolls back down into the paper bag and held it out to Glory. "Are you gonna start crying again?"

"No," Glory said as a tear escaped down her cheek. "I think I hafta give you a hug or something."

"Nah. You don't have to." He stood and dusted debris from his pants. "I mean, you can if you want to..."

Just then, the bell rang, and children rushed to line up behind their room numbers painted on the asphalt. Glory took the bag from Josiah and stepped closer to him. She wrapped her arms around his neck and squeezed. Josiah stood stiff as a board then wrapped his arms around her back, returning the hug.

"I gotta go," he said quietly.

"Me too." Glory broke the hug. "But I can't take these home."

"Keep 'em here. I'll take 'em home on the weekend. Like joint custody, okay?"

"Okay." Glory nodded. She watched Josiah pick up his backpack and jog across the playground to line up with his fifth-grade class. He really wasn't that annoying. And that day, he actually looked kind of nice. Glory went to line up with her class, wondering if she should have kissed him on the cheek too.

Chapter 11

Glory spent Saturday and Sunday regaling Anita with tales of her prom night, repeating over and over again her grand entrance and the reactions of the jealous "heffas." She told her about the boys who spoke to her for the first time in four years and about her friend's suspected crush and about how she twirled around the floor with two boys at once. They both laughed when she described the girls sharing bottles of wine cooler in the bathroom while Glory and her friends drank the real thing from crystal flutes in the executive suite.

"And that, Precious, will always be what separates you from them," Anita said. "Even before you ever touched fine crystal, you wouldn'ta been caught dead drinking from a bottle in a bathroom."

"No, ma'am," Glory said. "Never."

"That's right. I always knew you were different from everybody else."

Glory tried to push those conversations out of her thoughts. "Stuck-uppetry," Herschel called it, saying Anita was trying to change Glory—the same thing Malcolm said. Glory didn't really think that was a bad thing. There were worse people she could be than Anita D. S. Porter.

When Glory came out to breakfast Monday morning, Malcolm was waiting for her. "Don't sit down. We're going out for breakfast."

"But, Malcolm, we always breakfast together," Anita protested. "You can't just—"

"Not this morning, Mother, I need some time with my lady." He kissed his mother's cheek. "I love you, Mother. We'll see you later." He placed a hand on Glory's shoulder and steered her toward the door.

"Malcolm!" Anita called after them. "You make sure she gets a good breakfast. She's still a young girl!"

"Malcolm, that wasn't nice," Glory said when he got into the driver's seat. "What's going on?"

"We need to talk." Malcolm started the car and pulled off.

"Oh?" Glory looked over at him. He didn't look especially serious or happy. She looked out of the window. "Did you miss your turn? We're not going to Red Apple?"

"Nope, we're going to my place."

"Really? But, Malcolm, I can't be seen—"

"Woman, it's six o'clock in the morning. Nobody's gonna see you." He placed a hand over hers. "Relax."

Glory couldn't, though, as he ushered her through the steel door on the side of the church building or as they stepped into the tiny elevator and rode to the fourth floor.

"I've done a bit of redecorating," Malcolm said. "Got some furniture and some new paint. Made it more hip." He pushed open the door with a flourish. "Welcome to my bachelor pad."

"Wow, Malcolm. This is really nice." Glory meant it. The apartment still had the same gleaming hardwood floors, but he'd added a semisheer curtain to the giant half-circle windows that turned the view of the city street into a sparkling mountain stream. The overstuffed couch and chairs had been replaced by a dark-brown sectional conversation pit.

"Take a look around," Malcolm headed to the kitchen. "Breakfast will be ready in a minute."

Glory wandered down the hall, where flowered wallpaper had been replaced by mirrored panels and black-and-white photos with spots of color. She stood at the door but didn't enter Malcolm's bedroom. His king-sized bed rested on a wooden platform with the nightstands sticking out from the sides. The tall, curved headboard was the same color and shape as the window frames, making it look like the room had giant windows on three walls. White globe lamps on wooden blocks stood on the nightstands, and his worn Bible rested on the right side near the phone. The rumpled satin bedding made Glory smile. Of course, Malcolm would choose a shiny chocolate brown just like his Cadillac.

Malcolm had moved the old furniture into the other two bedrooms. Both smelled of fresh paint. One room had an armchair and a bed. The other held the couch and another armchair. In the second room, the walls were lined with white bookshelves, and the panels in the door had been replaced with glass. Glory smiled again—Malcolm was building a library. Beyond the living room, what used to be the pastor's study now served as a den with recliners and the biggest TV Glory had ever seen.

"So, what do you think?" Malcolm asked when Glory joined him in the kitchen.

"It's like a small version of your parents' house. The only things missing are the conservatory and another bedroom."

"And about twenty more feet in each room and another couple of bathrooms." Malcolm laughed. "I haven't gotten to the dining room yet, and the china cabinet is still full of dishes from the church kitchen. The laundry room and housekeeper's rooms still needed some attention too. Probably just gonna paint back there." He flipped the switch on the coffee maker, put bacon on a plate, and dropped frozen French toast into the toaster.

"Well, everything looks great. So, what do you need to talk to me about?" she asked.

"Breakfast first. We'll talk after you're done. It's really important."

During breakfast, Glory noticed that she was the only one eating. After she finished, when she moved her dishes to the sink and started to wash them, Malcolm placed a hand on hers. "Not now. Let's sit down." He led her to the living room couch. He sat with his arms folded for a minute and then took a deep breath. "Glory, I've been fasting and praying about this for a few days... since the cotillion actually. We hafta—"

"Malcolm, are you breaking up with me?" Glory asked. "Was I that bad at prom?"

Malcolm's eyes went wide. "What? Oh, God, woman, no!" He pulled her into his arms. "God, no. Never!" He buried his face in her hair. "Jesus, no."

"Then what, Malcolm? You're scaring me."

He took another deep breath and stood up. "Glory, we hafta get married now. Today. I hafta get you out of my mother's house right now."

"Malcolm, no! That's sil—crazy. It was just one little—"

"Glory, please. Trust me on this. My mother is not what you think she is."

Glory folded her arms and looked up at him. "You keep saying that."

"My mother is controlling and manipulative, and she'll do anything to get what she wants—"

"Malcolm, I love you, but I'm not gonna sit here and listen to you talk that way about Miss Anita." Glory stood up and went to the kitchen to finish washing dishes. "Your mother is an awesome woman. Everybody loves her."

"No, Glory." Malcolm followed her to the kitchen. "She has connections, not friends. And everybody respects and fears her.

Nobody loves her. Nobody can stand her. My dad can't even stand her. Hell, I love her, and I can't stand her."

"I can't believe how hateful you're being right now, Malcolm." Glory glanced at the wall clock. "Shouldn't we be leaving?"

"No." Malcolm ran his hands through his hair. "You're not going to school today. I told you, we hafta get married so you can move in here."

Glory turned and stared at him. "Malcolm," she said slowly, "we can't get married. I'm only seventeen."

Malcolm sighed. "I know how old you are. Your mother is gonna sign for you. I already talked to her—"

"You what? Behind my back? And you say your mother is manipulative?" Glory paused, quickly lowering her voice to a more respectful hiss. "Malcolm, I'm not marrying you today or any time before I'm twenty-one." She pushed past him and went back to the living room. *How dare he think he can just rearrange my life like that?*

Glory stood facing the window, looking down on the morning traffic on Seventy-Fifth Street. This had to be the most ridiculous argument she'd ever had. Whatever mother issues Malcolm had weren't her problem, and she was not about to let him ruin her life over it.

Malcolm came up behind her and wrapped an arm around her waist. "I'm sorry. I'm doing this wrong." He pushed her hair aside and kissed her neck. "I love you so much and—"

"Malcolm, is this about sex? Because, if it is, I've been ready for a long time. We don't hafta get married." Glory turned around and kissed him seriously hard, like a woman, until she felt him relax and respond, pulling her closer.

Malcolm broke the kiss and sighed. "No, it's not about sex. I promise, I do want you, and we will have sex, but this ain't about that."

"You know what, Malcolm?" Glory pushed past him. "You're making me crazy right now. You're talking bad about your mother for no reason and trying to mess up my life—"

"No, wait... okay... okay. Let's sit down." He led her to the couch again. "Let me try another way. How many schools did you apply to?"

"Three, I don't know, maybe four."

"Which ones? The schools I took you to—which ones did you actually send in applications to?"

"Well..." Glory thought for a few seconds. "Chicago State, Loyola, University of Chicago, and Kendall."

"All around Chicago, right?"

"Yeah, but I didn't get into any of those."

"C'mon, Glory, think. My mother got you into Brown, Cornell, and Spelman but not Chicago State?"

"Well, maybe she doesn't have connections there."

"Dammit, Glory, it's a public college! They hafta accept everybody. She doesn't need connections to get you in there, but her connections could easily keep you out. You didn't get into a single school in Chicago."

"Malcolm, what are you trying to say?"

"Baby, my mother is trying to send you away. She's trying to get you away from me."

"No, Malcolm. That's crazy." Glory stood up. "Your mother treats me like family. Like a daughter. She calls me *Precious*."

"You got into schools you didn't apply to and got scholarships you didn't ask for, all hundreds... even thousands... of miles away. The University of Ghana, in Africa? Come on!"

"She cares about my future, Malcolm, our future. She got me into the best schools so *your* wife would have the best education!"

"Glory, please. She's controlling you and twisting your mind into thinking she's doing you favors—"

No.

"She's not controlling me!" Glory snapped. "She's not twisting my mind, and she *is* doing me favors! She's giving me *everything* and letting me be normal—"

"By telling you you're different from everybody? By parading you around like a queen in fancy stuff that no *normal* girl has and telling you you're so much better than everybody and that you need to go away and be with 'your own kind'?"

"Malcolm, you're wrong. She's not doing that! She's teaching me how to hold my head up!"

No, no, no.

Malcolm stood up behind Glory, again taking her in his arms. "She got you a hotel suite to spend the weekend with Dexter," he said quietly.

"No! It was for me and my friends—" Glory tried to pull away, but Malcolm held her fast.

"Why did she change her mind when I showed up?" Malcolm asked.

"You don't know what you're talking about!" Glory struggled against Malcolm's embrace.

"What kind of mother does that for teenagers with alcohol?" Malcolm asked. "She didn't want me to know because she wanted you there with Dexter."

"Malcolm, let me go!" Glory screamed. "You're mad because she's letting me grow up and be a woman! I'm not being Church Girl anymore! The hotel just left stuff there 'cause she said to leave something nice." *Please, no.*

"Glory, hotels don't leave champagne and roses on the bed unless you ask. She's been pushing you on Dexter since you moved in. I wouldn't be surprised if she's hoping he'll get you pregnant... anything to get rid of you."

"Shut up!" Glory struggled against Malcolm and against the truth of his words. "Why are you doing this?"

"Because I love you, and I don't want to lose you. She's changing you! You talk like her, you act like her, you're even thinking like her now, but she hates you and wants you to go away!"

"Why?"

"Because you're a young girl from plain old regular people. She thinks you're too young for me and not good enough to be in her family—that you're weak and low-class."

Glory stopped struggling, feeling the weight of Malcolm's words crushing her, pushing her down to the floor. She thought of all the encouragement to ignore Malcolm's wishes, keep secrets from him, lie to him. Every pretty dress to show off her figure. Every reminder to sit up straight, shoulders back, chest out to look nice for the boys. Every suggestion to sit in the darkened library and watch a movie with Dexter. Every instruction to sit closer or give him a big hug. Every evening she'd been left home alone with Dexter and told to have fun.

"When I took you to her," Malcolm said quietly, "it was to protect you, but I made a mistake. Now I'm getting you out of there. I can't take you back to your mother's, so we're getting married, and you're moving in here."

Malcolm went down on one knee and lifted Glory's chin. "I know this is sooner than we planned, but in her house, she controls you, and I know you don't want to go back to your old life, but, Glory"—Malcolm took both of her hands in his— "you know I'm right."

Glory sat staring at the floor. In her new life, she'd been beautiful and powerful. They were the best days and nights of her life—waking up in a world of books and music and light, being *Precious* and treated like a princess and a queen, being glorious...

"When we get married, you'll be the woman of this house right here, and you won't be controlled by anybody. You'll still have—"

Glory pressed her hands over her ears.

She's sitting back, waiting for you to look stupid 'cause you have no idea.

Dumb, mama-fearing little girl who hasn't read The Cat in the Hat *and is not woman enough for my son. Hell, she cain't even stand up and say her own name.*

Weak and dependent.

Low-class. Not good enough.

Lettin' them worldly ways turn yo' head. Lettin' demons rule you! Ugly things in yo' heart.

You ain't that fancy.

Not precious.

Not glorious.

Not beautiful.

Demons of vanity and pride.

Demons of ungodly rebellion.

Filthy Jezebel.

"*Daemones de fraude et mendacio.*" Glory picked herself up from the floor, took a deep breath, and wiped a tear. "*Gloria est nomen meum. Et ego non uror.*"

Malcolm stood up and grabbed Glory by the shoulders. "What?"

"It's Latin," Glory said quietly. "Demons of lies and deceit. My name is Glory. I am not weak." She folded her arms, still looking at the floor. "Your mother called me dumb once and illiterate. I told her in Latin that I'd read a lot of books. I told her to say my name right. She was shocked." She looked up at Malcolm. "*Gloria est nomen meum. Et ego non uror.*"

Malcolm reached out and brushed her hair back from her face. "No, Glory, you're not weak."

"So, now what?"

"Well," Malcolm said, "while I call your mother at work and let her know we'll be there in an hour, you go look in the big closet in my... I mean, our room. I picked up a little something for you. Then we drive to Indiana."

"Okay." Glory heard the tremor in her voice. "Malcolm?" Her world was upside down, and Malcolm was rescuing her. Again.

Malcolm pulled her into his arms. "In a few hours, we're gonna come back here and be home," he said gently. "Me, you, and God against the world."

Glory just held on.

Chapter 12

Glory hadn't really considered her wedding day since that day when she was five and she beat up JT for tricking her into saying, "I do," and becoming his bride. Then, less than a year earlier, she'd agreed to marry him for real, kissed him goodbye, and he'd just walked out of her life. She'd never given much thought to wedding dresses either. Even though Glory had spent much of the past three months draped in some form of ball gown or cocktail dress, the activities never led to imagining her own wedding attire. Even when there were weddings at church, she never gave such things much thought, and even though her own life had been in preparation for being a good, proper, godly wife, nowhere in her wildest imagination had Glory ever pictured herself being *Mrs.* anybody.

But three days after her senior prom, dressed like a little girl on Easter Sunday—white straw hat and all—in an outfit Malcolm had chosen, Glory held in her white-gloved hands a sheet of paper that said she was Glory Hallelujah Bishop-Porter, wife of Malcolm Devereaux-St. Jacques Porter. Looking out the window at the factories and steel mills whizzing by, Glory knew this was supposed to be the happiest day of her life, but all she felt was something like a giant, wet, twisted towel stuck in her throat and her chest and her stomach. She pulled down the visor and looked at the mirror strapped there. The face in the white-trimmed shades staring back at her looked exactly like the *glorious princess* who'd walked with Anita through airports all over the country and nothing like the classless weakling who couldn't even say her own name... who Malcolm needed to rescue yet again.

She glanced at her mother dozing in the back seat, the picture of contentment. This was truly the happiest day of her mother's life. Mary had practically trembled with excitement when she signed the consent papers, and when the judge had pronounced Malcolm and Glory husband and wife, Glory thought her mother would get the Holy Ghost right there in the office.

Husband. Malcolm was now her husband. Not just *Superman* or *knight in shining armor*, but protector, provider, lord, and master... and a man who sometimes lost his temper. The knot in Glory's stomach grew tighter. Malcolm gave her the world and fought for her and had almost killed for her. All she had to do now was love, cherish, honor, and obey him.

But Anita did none of that and lived happily ever after, while her mother had done all of that and had been forced to take cotton root to abort her babies.

Babies. Malcolm promised they wouldn't have kids until after she finished college, but anything could happen. Glory thought about the pills and condoms in the lining of her purse. After she'd moved out of her mother's house, she'd made sure to get more from Herschel. Getting married at seventeen was one thing. Becoming a mother was something else entirely.

"Hey."

Glory looked over at Malcolm.

"We're almost to my parents," he said. "What's on your mind, Mrs. Porter?" He smiled.

Glory tried to smile back. *He really is kinda cute.* "Nothing, really."

"You haven't said a word this whole ride."

"I guess I'm a little tired. It's been a busy day."

"Yeah, it has." Malcolm reached over and squeezed her hand. "But it's something else on your mind. Talk to me."

"I'm scared," Glory admitted. "I don't wanna go home... to your mother's house. I don't want to see her."

"Woman, you have nothing to be scared of. You don't hafta say a word if you don't want to. I'll do all the talking. We're just gonna get your things, and that's it, okay?" He squeezed her hand again.

"Okay," Glory said. The closer they got to home, the tighter the knots in her stomach grew until she could barely hold down the gas station lunch of chips and ginger ale Malcolm had bought.

STANDING AT THE DOOR to the Porters' apartment, a door she'd unlocked on her own every day for the past three months, Glory felt like an unwelcome intruder. The gold key on the beaded unicorn keychain felt foreign, like something she shouldn't be touching. Malcolm took out his key and opened the door, stepping back to allow Glory and Mary to enter first.

Glory breathed a sigh of relief. The deep, hearty laughter coming from the direction of Elder Porter's study meant guests and that their announcement would have to wait a little longer.

"Let's go find Mother," Malcolm said. "She can tell Dad—"

"Malcolm, just the man I need to see." Elder Porter, Deacon Strahan, and Pastor Langdon from Beverly Hills Methodist Church came into the foyer. "Help us settle a small wager, son. It'll only take a second." He placed a hand on Malcolm's shoulder. "Excuse us, ladies. This won't take a minute."

"Okay, Dad. I'll be in there in just a bit." Malcolm turned to Glory. "Go get packed," he whispered as the men walked away, laughing. "I'll be right back."

Glory nodded and headed for her room. She'd only pack the things she'd brought with her, not even the underwear Anita had bought. Headed down the marble hallway, she tried to get angry to keep herself from crying.

"Precious? Is that you? Good! You're home early!" Anita stepped out of the conservatory. "Mary! Welcome! To what do we owe the pleasure?" She turned back to Glory without waiting for Mary to answer. "Precious, I have the most wonderful news." She grabbed Glory's hand and pulled her into the room.

"Hello, Anita. It's good to see you too," Mary said.

"That's a lovely ensemble, Precious." Anita pulled Glory behind her. "But it's much too soon for all white. Please leave picking clothes and such to me until you know better. Can't be embarrassing ourselves, now, can we?"

Glory pulled her hand away. *Why didn't I hear this tone before?*

"Do make yourself comfortable, Mary. I'll call Mrs. Beyers to bring a tray in. Oh, Precious, we have done it! Your perfect wit and charm and excellent grades have earned you a full ride to Jackson State University! Isn't that wonderful, Mary? That's where your whole family went—all except you, that is—right? Right down in Jackson, not far from your family home. You won't even need to travel for holidays. Isn't that wonderful?"

Glory just stared. She could almost see the horns sticking out of Anita's head.

"And that's not all," Anita continued. "The scholarship includes a monthly stipend, so you'll have spending money and not need to work. Isn't that marvelous?"

Glory nodded, watching Anita's tongue slip in and out of her mouth like a snake's.

"And when we head down for your eighteenth birthday, we'll get your apartment all set up." Anita reached out and brushed Glory's hair back from her face. "As long as our Precious is down there, we're gonna see that she lives in the manner she deserves. After all, you are gonna be a Porter woman, right?"

"You're too late, Mother. My wife isn't going anywhere."

"Oh, son, you're here!" Anita said. "We've got wonderful news. I know you're not gonna like it, but it really is the best thing for Precious—"

"Mother, you're not listening," Malcolm came into the room and stood beside Glory, placing a hand on her shoulder. "*My wife* is not going anywhere."

Anita snatched her hand back from Glory's face. "Your what?" she asked, her voice still as pleasant as the afternoon sun.

"My wife, Mother." Malcolm handed her the white envelope with the State of Indiana seal. "We got married this afternoon."

Anita ripped open the envelope, letting it fall to the floor. She stared at the official document, her face going nearly white. "Glory, *Precious*! This is what you wanted?"

Glory nodded.

Anita lifted Glory's chin. "Look at me. I can get this annulled by morning. Is this really what you want? Your own free will?"

The clerk at the office had asked her that same question, except Glory trusted the clerk more than this piece of work in front of her.

"Yes, ma'am," Glory said.

"Mary?" Anita's voice rose, no more pleasant lilt. "You approved of this? You signed your daughter away?"

"I most certainly did," Mary said. Glory didn't turn to look at her mother, but she could hear Mary, for once, giving in and feeling pride.

"You crazy old fool!" Anita snarled. "You have no idea what you've done—"

"My daughter has a good, godly husband to take care of her, and she'll be a good wife—"

"Argh!" Anita growled her frustration, tearing the marriage license in half, throwing it to the floor.

"Mother." Malcolm smirked. "There are other copies. I've got one right here—"

The slap echoed like a gunshot.

Glory held her breath.

Malcolm remained frozen, his hand still reaching for his inside pocket.

"How could you?" Anita hissed, her hand still raised, ready to strike her son again. "How could you with this... this—"

"This what, Mother?"

Glory flinched at the darkness in Malcolm's voice.

"This poor ignorant child!" Anita practically screamed at her son. "Malcolm, how could you? This is low even for you!"

"Anita, I can hear you screaming all through the house. What's all the commotion?" Elder Porter walked into the conservatory, swirling his glass of port wine. The old minister lived well in his eighth decade and didn't take kindly to angry outbursts in his home.

"Elder," Anita said, her voice a shrill snap. "Our son and this... this child were married today."

Elder Porter looked from Anita to Malcolm and then sipped his wine. "Is this true, son?"

"Yes, sir," Malcolm said.

"And you signed for this, Mary?" Elder Porter asked.

"Yes, Pastor, I did," Mary said.

"I see." Elder Porter sipped his wine again. "Son. Come to my study. We need to talk."

Malcolm stepped closer to Glory. "Dad, I know what you're gonna say—"

"Boy." The old man looked over his glasses. "I can assure you, you have no idea what I'm *gonna* say."

"I'm sorry, Dad." Malcolm reached down and squeezed Glory's hand. "Whatever you need to say, you'll hafta say in front of my wife."

The madness swirling around Glory didn't belong in this beautiful room filled with music and hung with flowing white drapes. The false angel in front of her, wrapped in purple-and-pink silk, walked on cloven hooves and spoke with a serpent's tongue. Her mother stood there, beaming with pride as if she herself had just married Malcolm. And Malcolm beside her had the imprint of his mother's rage glowing on his face, his own darkness burning in his eyes.

"Okay, fine." Elder Porter looked at Glory. "Young lady, are you pregnant?"

Glory hung her head. She hadn't expected that question. She wanted to run back and hide in her bright-yellow bedroom and start the day all over—no, start the month over. She wanted to go all the way back to before the prom, before the stupid cotillion, before Malcolm saw her giggling with Dexter.

Mary spoke up. "Pastor, my daughter is a good girl."

"Oh, Mary, shut up!" Anita snapped. "You've been throwing her at—"

"Woman, that's enough!" Elder Porter's words silenced his wife. "Answer me, young lady."

"No, sir. I'm not pregnant," Glory said.

"Good. When will you turn eighteen?" He sipped his wine again and paced.

"In two months," Glory said. "July."

"Then this is manageable. Three months after her eighteenth birthday, in October, you two will have a small, private wedding at church. Nothing big and no announcements. Until then, this is to be kept secret. Malcolm, a man in your position cannot be associated with a child—"

"My wife is not a child, Dad."

"Boy, stop being foolish. Yes, she is, and I will not have the fire in your loins burning a scandal in my church. You will no longer be associated with any youth activities whatsoever. You're doing the sick and shut-ins, and you can do prison ministry and work with seniors but nothing that will put you near anybody's daughters. Understand?"

"What does that have to do with anything?"

"Son, right after the wedding, everybody's gonna wonder when an almost-thirty-year-old had time to fall for an eighteen-year-old. It will not be because he met her in the church youth group! And whatever you do, don't conceive a child until six months after the wedding—not a day sooner. There can be no question of legitimacy. Do you understand?"

"C'mon, Dad—"

"Don't 'C'mon, Dad' me. I've worked too hard building this ministry to have your foolishness destroy it with a scandal. You will not touch her in public before the wedding. And don't you dare let yourselves be seen near the parsonage together."

"Fine," Malcolm said. "Anything else?"

"Yes," said Elder Porter. "As a married man, you don't get to live in the parsonage anymore as our son, only as a full-time assistant pastor. That means starting Sunday, you'll put in forty hours a week at church—"

"But, Dad, I've got school and the mission!"

"As of now, you're done with that mission. You've got a wife to look after. After graduation, you'll be expected at church fifty hours and on-call an additional ten hours on weekends."

Malcolm let go of Glory and ran his hands through his hair.

"Son," his father continued, "you've got responsibility now. You can't be taking your wife down to hang out with that riffraff. As an assistant pastor, you'll have a home and a salary so you can keep her like she should be kept. Your little trust fund won't do that."

"What if I say no?" Malcolm asked.

"Then you have a week to find a place for you and your wife to live, but this church saved your life and put you through school. You owe it to us... seven years."

"But, Dad, you're taking my ministry. I help people there," Malcolm said.

Glory heard the pleading in Malcolm's voice. She wanted to reach out to him and tell him everything would be okay. She wanted to be the good wife and support him and tell him they would make it no matter what. But the truth was, she didn't like going to the mission, and if she could undo the whole day, she would. She would give anything to go back to believing what she'd believed not even eight hours earlier.

"Stop being so dramatic, boy," Elder Porter said. "I'm doing nothing of the sort. If anything, I'm helping your little mission. If you wanna help those people, bring 'em to the real church. Get 'em off the streets and into a real Christian fellowship. It's time for you to stop wallowing in the gutters." He nodded at Glory. "My new daughter deserves better than that."

Glory blushed at being called "daughter," feeling stirrings of happiness even as she watched Malcolm's surrender.

"Okay." Malcolm sighed. "Fine."

"You're a good man, son." Elder Porter reached out to shake Malcolm's hand and pulled him into a hug. "I knew you'd do the right thing."

"Elder, you're just going to accept this?" Anita asked.

"Woman, it's done. Now you've got five months to plan a proper wedding. Nothing big. Just family and local ministers. None of your friends. Understand? This is not for the society pages." Elder Porter pulled out his money clip and peeled off several large bills.

"I wish I'd had time to get a decent gift," he said, pushing the money into Malcolm's hand. "We'll see that Mary gets home. You take your wife someplace nice—"

"But, Elder—" Anita interrupted.

"Wife, I expect nothing less than your usual perfection. Is that clear?"

"Of course, dear," Anita said, cowed. "But—"

Elder Porter leaned down and kissed his wife on the forehead. "I know it feels like you're losing your baby, but he's a grown man, and he's got a wife now. Give him a hug, tell him you love him, and welcome our daughter into the family."

"He knows how I feel, Elder." Anita pouted.

Malcolm reached out and yanked his mother into a hug. "Yes, Dad, I know exactly how she feels, and I love her anyway."

Anita pulled away from Malcolm and turned to Glory. "So, you think you're up to being a Porter woman?" She placed her hands on Glory's shoulders, leaning in for a formal hug. "Welcome to the family, Gloria."

"*Gloria est nomen meum. Et ego non uror,*" Glory said with the confidence she'd learned from the woman facing her.

"No, little Glory," Anita whispered, leaning in closely. She reached up to brush the hair from Glory's face, her hand lingering on Glory's cheek. "You might not be weak, but I'd hoped you were smart. He always aims for the left side." She looked into Glory's eyes. "But I bet you know that already, don't you?"

Staring at her mother-in-law, Glory imagined tossing a bucket of water on her and watching her melt into the floor. "Bless you, Mother Porter," Glory whispered back.

Chapter 13

"Mother's probably gonna stay in bed for the rest of the week," Malcolm said as they drove up Lake Shore Drive an hour later.

They'd stayed at the Porters' awhile longer, for Glory to change clothes and grab her jewelry box, blanket, and grandmother's rug. Then they drank a champagne toast and watched Mary's shock at seeing the pastor consuming alcohol. Glory got some satisfaction when Mother Porter blanched as Elder Porter ordered her to have all of Glory's old and new things delivered to the parsonage.

"I'm sorry she slapped you," Glory said.

"It's not the first time. I shoulda saw it coming." Malcolm laughed. "She always aims for the left side." He reached up and rubbed his still-reddened cheek. "You know Mother was down South on Valentine's Day?" Malcolm continued. "When I called and told her you were hurt, she dropped everything and flew home... and she really hates flying. This was her first winter here in more than ten years. I told her what I wanted, and she came home and made it happen. She acts like she'll do anything for me."

"I didn't know she hated flying. We flew everywhere," Glory said, remembering the recent first-class trips.

"Yeah, she hates it, but she was on a mission, and she had to get to work on you." Malcolm stared straight ahead. "I wasn't playing about her world-domination kick. She wants me to be this big, important somebody or at least inherit Dad's pulpit. And she wants me to have a wife like her to pull strings in the background... like she does for Dad." Malcolm sighed. "That's not you."

"Oh," Glory said. "I guess not."

"Did you know Cheryl Cannon has three degrees, and Mother has been throwing her at me practically since we were kids, especially since I came back to Chicago? Cheryl's been to every Friday Bible study, and now she's trying to start a women's business institute at the mission."

"I didn't know that," Glory said. *How could I know? You never told me how many other girls were after you.* "I wonder what Cheryl's gonna do when she finds out we're married."

"I don't know. Don't really care. I'm not trying to take over the world. Back when I was little, watching people kiss Mother's rings, that was cool. I don't need that mess now." Malcolm reached across the seat and squeezed Glory's hand. "And you don't need it either."

Glory squeezed his hand back. No, she didn't need it, but Miss Anita—Mother Porter—wasn't afraid of anything, and Glory had spent the last three months living in freedom and without fear. She didn't need Anita's idea of power, but Glory could admit that she desperately wanted it.

MALCOLM MIGHT NOT HAVE wanted his mother's power and influence, but asking the manager of Orly's open the small, private banquet room and personally serve just the two of them was what Anita would have done, and that was exactly what Malcolm did. Their secret wedding reception was attended only by the manager and her assistant, and a reasonably talented waitress was tapped to sing for their first dance. The wedding cake, an extra-wide slice of cheesecake, had a bridal couple carefully drawn in chocolate. The manager even took pictures and gave them the film. As they left the restaurant, the staff showered them in fistfuls of rice and gifted them with two complete place settings of Orly's green-trimmed dinnerware and a set of engraved glasses.

Finally arriving home, Glory waited in the car while Malcolm made sure the church was empty. This would be their routine for the next five months. The thought of sneaking around with her husband made her giggle... or maybe it was the champagne. Glory put on her white-trimmed shades and scooched down in the seat and giggled some more. She jumped when Malcolm opened her door and extended his hand.

"This way, Mrs. Porter," Malcolm said. Glory giggled again and allowed him to help her from the car.

On the tight elevator ride to the fourth floor, Glory tried to accept that she was going home. *Her* apartment. *Her* place. She got off the elevator with *her* husband and walked down the hall to *her* front door... then laughed hysterically. As ordered, *her* mother-in-law had had all *her* belongings boxed and delivered. Eight boxes were stacked neatly, nearly to the ceiling, completely blocking the door.

"I see Mother was here," Malcolm groaned.

"Will she melt if I throw water on her?" Glory asked.

"Nope," Malcolm said. "She's only afraid of falling houses."

Glory leaned against a wall and tried to look appropriately sympathetic while Malcolm moved enough boxes to the side to open the door. Then he pushed all the boxes into the foyer. When Glory picked up her suitcase, he held up a hand. "Mrs. Porter, would you please wait—let me do my job?"

"Okay." Handing him her suitcase, Glory placed a hand over her mouth, holding back more giggles. She was about to follow him in when he stopped her again and took the doggie bag from her.

"Wait right here. I'll be right back."

"Okay." Glory laughed. She had to admit, watching Malcolm run back and forth being uncool was adorable.

He came back, still pushing boxes around, and opened the door as wide as it would go. He stepped out into the hall, and in a move Glory totally expected but pretended to be surprised about anyway, Malcolm scooped her up into his arms and carried her over the threshold. "Okay, Mrs. Porter. Welcome home."

When he kicked the door closed behind him and gently lowered her to the floor, he held her close and looked into her eyes, being cool Malcolm again.

"Hi, Glory."

"Hi, Malcolm."

"You okay?"

"Yes," Glory lied. Alone in her own home with her new husband, she hadn't been less okay in a long time. *Any minute now, he'll want to make love to me... and...*

"Hey, let's get the food in the fridge," Malcolm said.

"Okay." Glory grabbed the doggie bag off the nearby box and headed to the kitchen. *Her* kitchen. She paused for a second in the dark before shaking her head and going to the refrigerator. *What woman can't find her way around her own kitchen?* She would look for the light switches in the morning.

Leaving the kitchen, she paused in the dining room and looked at the huge dark wood table with chairs for twelve people. She'd learned enough from Miss Anita—Mother Porter—to throw the perfect fancy dinner party but wondered if her plain old family could sit at this table. *And where? Malcolm would sit at the head, but would I really hafta sit so far away?*

Glory smiled a little. Of course not. This was *her house.* She'd sit wherever she wanted.

Moving on, she followed sounds of music to the den and found Malcolm crouched low, adjusting the stereo.

"Hi," Glory said.

"Hey." Malcolm looked up. "What do you think? Not big enough for a conservatory, but it's a pretty good home theater, huh?" He pointed at the bar in the corner with the popcorn machine. "Cool, huh?"

"Oh, yeah." Glory grinned. "Way cooler than a conservatory. Can we get movie posters?"

"Of course! And some cardboard people too!" Malcolm stood up and grabbed Glory's hand. "C'mon. I wanna show you something else." He pulled her to the room with the bookshelves and glass-paneled door. "This room is for you. What should we do with your library?"

"Wow, I don't know," Glory said. "Definitely keep the couch in the middle facing the window and then the chair by the window, facing this way. Maybe a coffee table and some end tables... and of course reading lamps. Oh, and pillows! Yeah, and curtains. But not heavy ones—layers of sheers to adjust the light a little at a time. Oh my God, Malcolm!" Glory threw her arms around him. "This is gonna be so awesome!"

"I told you. This is your house. You're the woman of the house here. It'll be whatever you want." He took her hand again and led her to the next bedroom. "I think we should decorate this one in wild bright colors for Supergirl."

"Huh? Who?"

"For your cousin Jillian when she visits." Malcolm pulled Glory into his arms. "I say we cover the walls with posters of gloriously strong superhero women—"

Glory kissed her husband. She felt him freeze then yield then pull her close... then stop. "Wait." Malcolm took a deep breath. "There's no rush. We have time."

"I know." Glory laid her head against his chest. "What you said was so awesome I just needed to kiss you."

"Okay."

"Malcolm?"

"Yeah, Glory?"

"We should go to our bedroom now."

Malcolm cleared his throat. "Are you sure?"

"Yes." She looked up at him and took his hand, surprised to find it moist. "You know, Malcolm, I thought I was supposed to be the nervous one."

"Yeah." Malcolm followed her down the hall. "That's what I thought too."

In the dimly lit bedroom, Glory stood with her back to her husband and let her dress fall from her shoulders. She hoped she looked right stepping out of it, like the ladies in the movies. The silk slip she wore made her feel beautiful, but the thin straps did nothing to hide her scars. She felt Malcolm's hands on her shoulders and his bare chest warm against her back.

"You, my love, excite men as a mare excites the stallions of Pharaoh's chariots. Your hair is beautiful upon your cheeks and falls along your neck like jewels." He laughed a little. "Look who's nervous now." He pushed her hair aside and kissed her neck.

"Yeah, kinda," Glory said. "Can we turn the lights out?"

"No." He pushed her slip off her shoulders and down her arms and hips.

As her last bit of covering fell away, leaving her naked with every scar exposed, Glory held her breath, feeling her husband's hands moving over her body for the first time.

"How beautiful you are, my love. How perfect you are," Malcolm whispered.

Glory crossed her arms, her bracelets offering pitiful cover. "Malcolm, my scars..." All confidence gone, she heard herself trying not to cry. *Please stop quoting the Bible. Please.*

Malcolm turned her to face him. "My love, you are as beautiful as Jerusalem, as lovely as the city of Tirzah, as breathtaking as all the great cities." His kiss was hungry, eager, almost like a boy's kiss, full of pent-up energy, like he'd been waiting for this moment his whole life. "I am trembling. You have made me as eager for love as a chariot driver is for battle."

He kissed her until Glory finally relaxed and returned his kisses. And when he picked her up and laid her down on their bed, his touch was gentle...

"Malcolm, wait," Glory said, catching her breath. "Your dad said we hafta be careful, remember?"

"Woman, wife, Mrs. Porter..." Malcolm punctuated his words with kisses as he moved into her arms. "If he thinks I'm not gonna fully know my wife on our wedding night, he's crazy."

Glory gasped.

"We'll be careful tomorrow and every day after that, okay?" he whispered.

"Okay... husband," Glory returned his kiss.

Let him have his small victory. Tomorrow, I'll take ten birth control pills and get a new pack to take regularly. Sometimes a wife needs to rebel to protect a man from his own bad decisions.

PEEING BURNED A LITTLE, just like last time... her first time. Malcolm was so different from JT. He was so serious, moved more slowly, and took a lot longer, and there was no tingle this time. Maybe because she was so nervous. *Or maybe because Malcolm is... so much?*

Glory shook her head. *Why would JT be on my mind now?* As she pressed a warm washcloth to her sore parts, she tried to imagine her husband and to see if she could cause her own tingle. Maybe in time, Malcolm's touch would cause tremors and tingles and all those feelings that a good wife should feel. Maybe one day, her desire would be toward him like the Bible said. Her bracelets clinked softly when she moved her hand. After all, she was his beloved, and his desire was toward her.

Hidden by the shadows of the darkened bedroom, Glory Bishop Porter leaned against the window, looking down on Seventy-Fifth Street, and wiped a tear. This life—this minute—was all she'd ever wanted. No angry God punishing her for wanting to know the world. Nobody controlling her. Nobody leaving her. In a few months, she'd be a college student by day and working in the salon in the evenings and then coming home to *her apartment* to look down on the streetlights or up at the stars. And now, with her husband snoring softly in the bed behind her, Glory prayed that streetlights and stars and Seventy-Fifth Street would always be enough.

Part 2

INTERLUDE
FEBRUARY 1978

Catch a Girl, Kiss a Girl was always a stupid game, but for the third Thursday in a row, eleven-year-old Glory found herself hiding in the hallway behind the sanctuary. The haunted hallway, they called it. The long, narrow, dark-paneled space had locked doors on both sides. The only unlocked room had a giant safe. All the kids knew to stay away from that room. Once, a kid had gotten locked in the safe and starved to death before they could get him out. Now his skeleton walked around the hallway, looking for food. All the kids claimed to have seen him, and Lori Foster said he'd actually talked to her. The kids held séance after séance, begging his spirit to speak. When Mr. Nick caught them sitting on the floor in a circle holding hands, Josiah easily convinced him they were reciting something from the Bible. Of course, the old church custodian took the opportunity to sit with them and share his biblical knowledge. Willie Clayton had joked that the old man knew so much about the Bible because he was probably there when it was written.

Seated in the dark at the top of a polished wooden staircase, Glory listened to the running, bumping, and occasional screams and shook her head at Trina's feigned helplessness. That girl always hid where she could be easily found, and Johnny Turner always seemed to find her, but everybody knew he was scared of girls. Glory had only ever been caught once, and when Andre Bradley had tried to kiss her, he got a fat lip for his trouble. Of course, An-

182

dre had wanted to fight, but Josiah stepped in, and Andre backed down. That was when Glory ran and hid at the top of the stairway in the haunted hallway. It had felt funny to have Josiah protecting her, but it felt even funnier to admit that if Josiah found her, he could have a kiss.

Women's choir rehearsal would be over soon, so Glory made plans to creep down the staircase when mothers started calling for their children. She froze when all twelve kids poured into the hallway.

"She probably went home," a girl's voice said. "You know she's scared of boys."

"She's not scared." Glory recognized Josiah's voice. "She's just good at hiding."

"I gotta go pee." Trina's voice. "I'm gonna look for her at the back stairs."

Glory shook her head and tried to guess who would follow.

"Hey, did anybody look up the stairs? What if—"

"She wouldn't go up there," Josiah said. "She's afraid of the dark. Go check the Robinson Room and the basement again. She's probably moving from place to place, so we hafta look everywhere at the same time."

Glory listened to the throng of children running toward other parts of the giant old building then took a few steps down. When her foot landed on a creaky stair, she froze.

"Glory, are you up there?" Josiah's whispered voice. "I bet you are! I'm coming up."

Glory backed up the stairs to the landing and crouched in the shadows.

"Glooory, I know you're uuup heeere."

From her hiding space, Glory watched Josiah creep up the stairs. She tiptoed across the landing and moved up a few steps, farther into the darkness. Another stair creaked. She wasn't sure if it was her or Josiah.

"Miss Glory, you can come out." Josiah reached the landing. "I won't tell anybody your hiding place."

Seated in near pitch blackness, Glory could barely see her hand in front of her face. She moved up two more steps.

"I know you're here." Josiah said. "I can smell your hair grease."

Glory giggled then quickly placed a hand over her mouth.

"Aha! I knew it!" he whispered. "Give up—you're busted."

Glory remained silent and crept up another stair.

Josiah moved a few steps up the second staircase. "I can see your shadow, you know. That window lets in some light."

Glory moved up even farther.

"I'm not playing the game anymore. Really." Josiah reached his hand out into the darkness. "You can come out. Trust me."

At the second landing, Glory didn't dare go any higher. Though she didn't believe in ghosts, she knew there was something at the top of the third staircase. She'd heard things moving behind the door.

Josiah reached the second landing and sat down on the top step. "You hide really good. Nobody is gonna come up here looking for you."

"Well, you came up here."

"Aha! I knew it." Josiah felt around until his hand found Glory's leg. "I caught you!"

Glory tried to snatch away but lost her balance and landed on her bottom. Only the boy's hands holding her leg kept her from tumbling down the stairs.

"Shhh!" Josiah hissed. "Do you want them to find us?"

"Us?" Glory took a seat beside him on the top step. "This is my hiding place."

"It's mine now too." He yawned and stretched his arms out to his sides. He slipped his right arm around Glory. "Yup... mine too."

Glory didn't know how to feel, sitting in the dark with Josiah. He'd gotten a lot cuter since he was in fifth grade, but he was a friend, and this just felt funny. "Are you gonna kiss me?" she asked.

Josiah sat quietly for a minute. "Only if you ask me to, Miss Glory." He draped his arm over her shoulder. "I don't hafta steal kisses. A lot of girls will kiss anybody."

Glory gasped. "Josiah, did you kiss Trina?"

He laughed quietly. "Nah. *She* tried to kiss *me*. You know how she always tells where she's hiding. I keep sending Johnny to find her."

"Oh. Okay." Glory didn't know why, but she breathed a sigh of relief. "Why don't you wanna kiss her?"

"'Cause she's a hoe."

Glory gasped again. "You can't say that in church."

"Fine. I just don't like her. She probably lets Johnny get her—"

Glory shrugged Josiah's arm from her shoulder. "Stop saying stuff like that," she whispered as loudly as she dared. "She's not that bad."

"Oh, really? Ask Johnny what color her panties are. I bet he knows. So, do you want me to kiss you or not?"

Glory stood up. "There's no way I'm kissing a rude boy like you!" she hissed.

"Okay, fine." He stood up, climbed on the banister, and slid down to the first landing. "I'm tired of playing this game anyway."

Glory crept down the stairs to the landing and listened to him slide down the banister to the first floor. The other kids were coming back.

"I looked up there. And didn't see her," Josiah said. "I'm tired of playin' this. Let's go downstairs and play spin the bottle. If Glory wants to play, she'll find us."

Glory sat frowning in the darkness. She didn't like thinking of Josiah playing spin the bottle with a bunch of other girls. She buried her face in her hands. Boys were so stupid. *But why does Josiah make me happy and mad at the same time?*

GLORY LIKED SATURDAY mornings at the beauty salon, even though she struggled to find a comfortable position on the hard, plastic chairs while she read the only book she was allowed to read. The gospel music blaring from the boom box, the news on TV with no sound, and the nonstop chatter of the stylists and their early-morning clients was more life than she ever saw at home. The giant front window with the green curtains pulled back and winter morning sunlight streaming in reminded Glory of times before, when there was music and light in their apartment. It had been two years, but for Glory, her daddy's death seemed like forever ago. She had only cloudy recollections of the time before she had demons, before she needed purging, before she became a godly young lady.

"Glory, get up from there! Let the lady sit down!" Mary yelled at Glory from under the hair dryer. She really hadn't needed to yell, but Glory knew her mother couldn't really hear herself under the dryer.

Glory moved from the last chair and took a seat on the floor in front of a tall plastic tree, out of everybody's way. Her new blue-jean-covered Bible, the Good News, was the only new book allowed in their apartment, and that was because it was a gift from Greg Jones, the new youth pastor at church. Rev. Greg said the new Bible was easier for kids to understand. He was right. Much to her mother's delight, Glory was enthralled by the Old Testament. They often made a game of comparing the King James and the Good News versions. In plain English, the stories were as exciting as any book she secretly read in school. But Glory was careful not to show too much interest, lest her mother find out she read Judges 19 or the Song of Solomon.

"Mary... let her go sit on the couch in the back room!" Mrs. Morris, one of the stylists, gestured as she talked, pointing from Glory to the beaded curtain that covered the doorway to the back rooms.

"What?" Mary lifted the dryer from her head and adjusted the foam pads protecting her ears.

"I said, she can go sit in the back. Ain't nothin' back there to get into. You got at least another hour."

"Glory, ya hear that?" Mary pulled the dryer back down. "Get up off that floor! Go sit in the back room!"

Glory folded down the corner of the page she was reading and headed for the back rooms. Through the beaded curtain and to her left was the washroom. It had fancy little soaps and usually smelled really nice on Saturday mornings. In front of her was a door labeled Employees Only, obviously the way to the back room. Through the heavy, squeaky door, the first thing Glory noticed was the strong scent of mint and vanilla. Then she saw that she was in a kitchen. *A kitchen?* Refrigerator, white metal cabinets, and a sink on the left. Barred windows and a backdoor straight ahead. On the right was a stove with shelves beside it and a mad scientist stirring a huge pot. *A mad scientist?*

At least, that was the first thought that came to Glory's mind. The person at the stove wore a lime-green lab coat with orange and brown swirls, an orange scarf tied over their hair, some goggles, and bright-yellow rubber gloves. "Darlin', either in or out, but close that door!"

Glory took a step farther into the room and closed the door behind her. The scientist lifted a wooden spoon and poured a strand of thick white liquid back into the pot then turned and faced Glory. "What can I do for you, darling? You come back here to help?"

Glory couldn't tell whether the tall dark-skinned scientist was a man or a lady. She didn't dare say "No, sir" or "No, ma'am," so she just shook her head.

"They ran outta room out there, huh? Well, the couch is in there." The scientist pointed with the spoon toward another room on Glory's right. "You can turn the TV on, but keep it down, okay?"

"Yes, mmm... sir?" Glory took a chance.

The scientist turned and walked—not walked, more like glided—toward Glory while removing the yellow gloves. "Hello, darling. I'm Herschel." He extended his hand. "What should I call you?"

"Um, Glory?"

"Um? You asking me? You're not sure? What did your mama name you?" Herschel spoke slowly, enunciating each word with his whole mouth.

"Yeah, my name is Glory." She laughed a little.

The man in front of her had a voice kind of like a lady, and he walked like he was in a fashion show. Glory had seen them on the street, and people said the choir director was one, but Glory had never met a real live out-in-the-open *sissy*. She wasn't sure what she should say.

He reached out and took Glory's right hand. "Glory? Like glory-glory-hallelujah Glory? Oh, I'll bet you get that a lot."

"Yeah, kinda," Glory admitted. Herschel's hands were as soft as a woman's—softer than any hands Glory had ever felt. She pulled her hand away.

"Oh, where are my manners?" Herschel lifted his goggles up and over his head, snagging the orange scarf and pulling that along. The tall, clean-shaven man wore his hair in cornrows and sported a sparkly earring in his left ear. "Please to meet you, Miss Glory-Glory." He walked back over to the pot and stirred it again. "So what are we reading?"

"Just the Bible." Glory hoped she didn't look too embarrassed.

"Just the Bible? Did you say, 'Just the Bible'?"

Glory shrugged. "Yeah."

"Obviously, you're not reading it right. Hand me one of them jars on that shelf."

Glory laid her Bible on the white kitchen table—it seemed everybody had that same table—grabbed a small plastic jar from the shelf near the stove, and passed it to Herschel, who took a ladle and filled the jar with some of the wonderful-smelling vanilla-mint whatever-it-was from the pot. Glory handed him another jar.

"You reading the Old Testament?" Herschel asked.

"Yeah." Glory picked up her pace, handing Herschel the jars as fast as he filled them.

"Well, that's the best part. All that drama and intrigue... love and lust... loyalty and betrayal. The whole thing is like a soap opera. Help me move these to the table. Careful, now. They a little warm."

"Uh-huh" Glory held two jars by the rim and carried them over to the table. "What is this stuff? It smells nice."

"It's hair conditioner. A little this, a little that, some good-smellin' oils, and you got a wonderful, all-natural hair conditioner. This one will make your hair nice and shiny and soft as baby butt."

Glory giggled as she carried warm jars over to the table. "Are you a scientist?"

"Ah ha ha ha!" Herschel threw his head back, laughing. "A scientist? Well, hmmm. I guess I might be. I make hair lotions and tonics, and sometimes I even invent my own scents, so I guess I am a scientist, Glory-Glory. Ah ha ha ha!"

Herschel's laugh made Glory smile. He sounded just like the man on the old 7-Up commercials.

"Yeah, I make a lotta the hair stuff they use out there in the shop. I'm gonna start making skincare stuff in the spring—you know, soaps, lotions, creams, all that stuff. But your skin is so nice you won't need any of it."

Glory smiled some more. She really liked the strange man and his pretty lab coat.

"SO, GLORY-GLORY." HERSCHEL tightened the last jar. "What did she say?"

"She said yeah, I can help till it's time to go."

"And did you tell her I was paying you five dollars?"

Glory hung her head. "No. I left that part out. She mighta said no."

"Hmmm..." Herschel carried the big pot over to the sink. "Do you always tell your dear mother only half the truth?"

"Not always," Glory mumbled.

"What's that?" Herschel cupped his hand around his ear. "I didn't quite get that!"

Glory spoke up. "I said, not always. But sometimes, I wanna do stuff, and she says doing stuff—anything—is sinful, so I don't tell her everything."

"I see. Well, Miss Lady, what do you think you should do now? I know if you were mine, I'd make sure I knew who you workin' for."

"Fine." Glory headed for the door back out to the salon. Her deep sigh sounded almost like a long grunt.

"Gee, that's so ladylike. Your mother must be real proud."

A minute later, Glory burst back into the kitchen. "She said I could get paid!"

"So, your mother is a reasonable woman after all, huh?" Herschel poured clear liquid from a jug into the pot. "This is for the shampoo. Imma add some witch hazel before I add the scents. It goes with the conditioner."

Glory stood on tiptoe to look over the rim of the pot as Herschel added different ingredients. "So, what's this part?" She picked up the empty white jug.

"That's the detergent. This is the shampoo you use when you wanna strip out all the old grease and conditioner. *Clarifying*, it's called." He carried the pot from the table to the stove. "We're gonna warm this up just a little... just enough for it to pour easily. See those plastic bottles on the shelf? Yeah, the ones with the label. Start handing those to me while I pour."

Glory pushed the bottles from the right side to the left side of the shelf, knocking several to the floor.

"Don't pick 'em up," Herschel said. "They contaminated now. I'll use those for cleaning stuff. They won't go to waste."

Glory and her new friend chatted while they filled the shampoo bottles, Herschel telling of his adventures at the salon and Glory sharing the intrigues of sixth grade and church.

"You know, your face just lights up when you talk about that boy, Josiah. Is he cute?"

"I guess," Glory answered, willing a blush not to rise in her face. "He's okay."

"Sounds to me like he pays a lotta attention to you. He sounds like a nice boy."

Glory laughed. "Ha! He's always been bad."

"How so?" Herschel wiped spilled shampoo from the bottle in his hand. "Is he mean? Does he kick puppies or something?"

"No, not like that. He's not mean. He just gets in trouble a lot for acting up. And he wants people to call him JT instead of his name. JT sounds like a gangbanger name." Glory began placing caps on the shampoo, stopping to smell each bottle. "I mean, he's nice to me... just rude and annoying sometimes."

Herschel laughed at Glory's tale of her *marriage* to Josiah when she was five. "Well, darlin', I don't care what you say—I like this JT fella. Now run in the other room and fold those towels on the table."

When Glory and Mary left the salon, Glory was five dollars richer and had an invitation to come back to work any Saturday her mom got her hair done. Glory was somewhat glad her mother hadn't gotten to meet Herschel. There was no way she would have understood or let Glory work for him. They walked the few blocks to their apartment, stopping at the store for a loaf of bread and a few snacks. Glory would never say anything, but she suspected these convenience-store stops were just excuses to get more brown paper bags.

CHAPTER 14
May 1984

The morning sounds weren't quite right, and that made Glory open her eyes. She stared at the slowly spinning brown wooden blades of a gold ceiling fan. That was wrong too. She should have been looking at a yellow canopy dotted with small green-and-white flowers. When she moved to sit up, the smooth brown satin sheets felt good moving against her bare skin.

Bare skin...?

Before Glory could finish the thought, a slender muscular arm snaked across her belly, and a warm naked body pressed against her side, and she remembered. She was at Malcolm's apartment in his bed—no, she was in *her* apartment in *her* bed, and the slender muscular arm and warm naked body belonged to Malcolm... her husband. She tried to sit up, but Malcolm's arm held her in place.

"Malcolm." Glory sighed and tried using both hands to move his arm. "It's time to get up. I hafta get to school. I can't be late for first period." She giggled a little when Malcolm held her even tighter, pinning her arms to her sides. "Come on... I'm serious." She laughed as he moved on top of her. "We don't have time for this, and besides—"

"Oh no, Mrs. Porter." Malcolm grabbed Glory's wrists and pulled them up over her head. "Today is a holiday. There's no school for you today." He kissed her neck and breasts.

"Yeah, right. What holiday is it?" Glory turned her head when he went to kiss her on the mouth. Though she felt like she was playing a scene from a romance novel, none of the novels ever said anything about morning breath.

"It's Newlywed Day. No school or work for any newlyweds today."

To keep a straight face, Glory narrowed her eyes. "Oh, really? How come I've never heard of it before?"

"I don't know, Mrs. Porter. How many times have you been a newlywed?"

Looking up at her husband's light-brown eyes crinkled at the corner and the smile on his lips that lit up his whole face, Glory suppressed a laugh. It didn't seem like the right time to mention her wedding to JT way back when she was five.

"So, Mr. Porter, what are we gonna do today?" Glory tried to move her arms, but he held them fast in one hand, pinned above her head. With the other hand, he held her face and kissed her on the mouth.

"Well, first," Malcolm said between long, slow kisses, "we're gonna make love some more, and then—"

"Malcolm, wait... stop." Glory protested. "I'm really sore, and we hafta use protection, remember?"

Malcolm began moving as if she hadn't spoken. "Then we're gonna hop in the shower and make love there—"

"Please, Malcolm, this really hurts."

"Shhh, it's okay," he whispered. "Do you know how much I love you, woman?"

"Malcolm, stop! Are you even listening to me?"

Malcolm slowed down but didn't pause. "Yes, I hear you," he said, kissing her again. "Now, whose beloved are you?"

"Yours." Glory groaned into her husband's kiss, not keeping the pain out of her voice.

"And my desire is toward you, so why would I want to stop?"

Glory lay still beneath her husband, bearing the pain, accepting his kisses. And when he was spent, she turned on her side with her back to him and pretended to sleep until she felt his arms around her and his lips on the back of her neck.

"I'm sorry," Malcolm said. "That was selfish of me, but it's all your fault for being so beautiful..." He ended his sentence by kissing the scars on her shoulder blade, reminding Glory of how totally *not beautiful* her back was. "We don't hafta make love in the shower this morning if you don't want to. We can do that tonight. Right now, we'll just hop in and wash up... then have breakfast and go do some shopping. Okay?"

"Yeah." Glory pouted.

"Then we'll come home, make love some more, have dinner, and then make love one more time. Sound good?"

"No, Malcolm, it sounds painful."

"Okay, okay, okay... we'll see how we feel when we get home. Okay?" He kissed her back again. "It's seven o'clock. Let's get going. You take this bathroom. I'll go make coffee."

Glory watched her husband get out of bed, slip on a pair of boxers, and head out of the bedroom. He really did have a nice body despite the fuzzy green dollar signs tattooed on his left shoulder and on the left side of his chest.

Sitting up in bed, Glory pulled the sheet to her chest, wrapped it around herself, then stood up. The curtains were drawn over the bottom portion of the giant half-circle windows on two walls, but still, Glory's modesty wouldn't let her walk around the bedroom—her bedroom—naked. She dragged the sheet with her to the bathroom and quickly slipped inside, dropping the sheet at the door. The girl in the mirror looked nothing like a recently married woman. Nothing like a woman who less than an hour before had been bathed in her new husband's sweat.

AFTER THE MORNING'S tiff, the day got better. They lunched on pizza at Ronnie's Steakhouse and then drove up North Michigan Avenue to get Garrett's popcorn and then to get the best cookies ever from the Original Cookie Company. As they sped down the Dan Ryan Expressway, Glory looked over at her husband. She wasn't sure what she felt. Of course, she loved him, but how much and why? She closed her eyes and rested her head against the seat. She definitely felt gratitude for everything he did for her, but what about the things he did *to* her? *Did he really try to hit me with his fist only four days ago?* Maybe that didn't really matter when weighed against his love and protection. He could be bossy and pushy... *But that's how boys—men—are, right?*

"Hey." Malcolm tapped her hand. "No sleeping. We still hafta shop for the house."

Glory opened her eyes. "I'm not asleep. Just resting my eyes and thinking, that's all."

"Whatcha thinking about?"

"School," Glory lied. "What I've missed in two days, and now my life is totally different, and I hafta go to school tomorrow like nothing's happened, and I can't even tell my best friends."

"Yeah." He patted her hand. "I'm sorry my dad is so uptight about that, but I kinda see his point. Woman, if I could've waited till your birthday, I would've, but I had to get you outta there. My mother was changing you... and not in a good way. That eyeblinking, lip-licking thing you been doing lately—yeah, I noticed—that's one of Mother's moves. She controls every man in that church by doing that."

"Malcolm, she's not that bad, and I don't do that."

"Hmph! You did it to me at the cotillion... right in front of people. Alderman Reynolds called you dangerous." Malcolm chuckled.

"Thought I was gon' hafta fight 'im. And then when I picked you up on prom night, you did it again. That's probably why—"

"Can we not talk about that?" Glory interrupted.

Malcolm squeezed her hand.

"So can I at least tell Herschel?" Glory asked. "His feelings are gonna be hurt if I keep this big a secret from him."

"Nah. My dad said nobody can know until after our *real* wedding. Listen, I don't like it either. I wanna tell everybody you officially belong to me, but we gotta wait till October. Think of it this way—Mother's gonna throw us the biggest, fanciest little wedding Chicago's ever seen. It'll be fun."

Glory looked out of the side window as the car moved up the exit ramp at Seventy-Ninth Street.

"And besides," Malcolm continued, "you're not gonna be spending that much time with Herschel anyway."

Glory looked over at her husband. "What do you mean? He's my best friend, and I still hafta go to work."

"Woman, you know it don't look right for you to have a forty-year-old man for a best friend, even if he is a little funny, especially since you're married. I can't have people gossiping about you."

"Malcolm, nobody gossips about me now. And I like working at the salon."

"You don't need to work anywhere. I take you everywhere, and I'll make sure you have all the pocket money you need."

"But a woman should have her own money, and—"

"That sounds like something my mother says," Malcolm scolded her.

"Yes!" Glory shot back but softened her tone at Malcolm's scowl. "Your mother and Herschel and my aunts—every smart woman I know says it."

"I bet your mother doesn't say it, and besides, you won't have time to work what with school and now a man and a house and maybe kids to take care of."

Glory stared at Malcolm. He was serious. "Malcolm, I don't want kids for at least ten years, and your dad said we hafta be careful."

"I know, I know." Malcolm patted her hand, but Glory was not reassured. "We're gonna be careful, but who knows? Between last night and this morning, maybe God decided it's time for kids now. Wouldn't that be funny?"

Glory laughed a little with her husband. She thought about the five emergency birth control pills she'd taken just after eight o'clock that morning and about the five more pills she would take that night. There would be no babies now or any time before she decided she was ready... no matter how careless Malcolm wanted to be.

CROUCHED DOWN BEHIND piles of black-and-white-striped bags from Venture and grocery bags from Jewel, Glory felt like she was playing the worst game of hide-and-seek ever. Her nose itched, and her knees ached, and nothing Malcolm said could get Mr. Nick, the church custodian, to stop helping bring bags from the car to the tiny elevator that would take them to their fourth-floor apartment—*penthouse*, Malcolm called it—in the Lake Shore Christian Fellowship Church building. *Is this my life now—hiding in the elevator, sneaking into my own home?* Glory tried not to sigh, but it was hard not to be irritated.

"So how you gon' get all this stuff into yo' place?" Mr. Nick dropped a grocery bag onto the floor of the crowded elevator. Glory prayed it wasn't the bag with the eggs. "Looks like you gon' need my help some mo.'"

"Naah, Mr. Nick," Malcolm said. "I can handle it. Besides, I need the workout." Malcolm placed another bag atop the pile hiding Glory. "That's the last one. I can take it from here. I appreciate the help."

"Boy, I don't want yo' money. 'Whatsoever ye do, do it heartily, as to the Lord, and not unto men.' I'm glad to help. Heh… I need the workout too. Sure you don't want me to come up and help you unload?"

"Naah, I'm straight. 'Man goeth forth unto his work and to his labor until the evening.' I'm not in a rush."

Glory listened to the men's conversation and rolled her eyes. Malcolm was trying to out-quote the old man. He'd been in a terrible accident as a teenager and had learned the Bible by heart during his recovery. He called it a blessing and a curse. Glory knew well the curse part. Malcolm had a verse for everything and might slip into King James Bible verses midsentence.

She heard Malcolm closing the elevator door and felt the car begin to move. Up, up, up to the fourth floor of the church building. The old elevator stopped with a lurch, and Glory stood, sending plastic bags of housewares tumbling to land on the paper grocery bags.

"Oh my God, Malcolm! I thought he'd never leave."

Malcolm pressed the hold button. "There. Now he can't come up and surprise us. Let's get these things inside." They made two or three trips between the elevator and their apartment, and the foyer was soon full of paper and plastic bags.

"You go unpack the other stuff while I put the groceries away," Glory instructed. If she was going to be the woman of the house, she might as well get started.

"GLORY BISHOP, WHERE the heck have you been!"

Glory smiled and slid out from her seat in their usual booth just as Mr. Harris placed their order on the table. He'd been doing that since February—waiting on them personally, making the other kids who came into the tiny diner and bookstore wonder why Glory and her friends got special treatment. Harris walked away, tipping an invisible hat to Tressa and Christy as they approached the booth.

"Girl. Where have you been?" Christy repeated, taking her usual seat and reaching for a french fry.

"Yeah, we were gettin' really worried." Tressa slid into her regular spot, and Glory took the seat beside her. "You left prom," Tressa continued, "and we tried to call you all weekend—"

"And then you're outta school for two days, and there's rumors—ouch! Okay! Dang!" Christy took a sip of her drink and mumbled something about pinching and kicking. "Well? What's up with you?"

Glory looked at her friends and made a decision. "I'll tell you, but you hafta swear not to tell anybody. I mean really, super swear."

"Well, I'll be damned," Christy took a sip of her pop and smirked. "You and Malcolm *did it*, didn't you?"

"I bet he took her for a romantic getaway," Tressa said. "That's why she was gone so long."

"But four days? If she's been doin' it for four days, she wouldn't be able—"

"Maybe they went back to that hotel suite for the weekend and kept it an extra day or two."

Laughing, Glory listened to her friends imagine her long weekend. Tressa's thoughts were always romantic, and Christy's ideas got progressively acrobatic.

"Okaaay," Glory finally interrupted them. "Just swear so I can tell you."

Tressa gasped. "You mean you really did do it? Oh my God, Glory! For real?"

"Shh, yes. Now, keep it down." She leaned into the table, whispering, "It's not everybody's business. And yes, I have pills."

"I knew it," Christy said. "Y'all did it all weekend, right?"

"I'm not saying anything else until you swear not to tell," Glory answered. "I'm serious."

"Okay. I swear to Michael Jackson, I won't tell." Tressa tried to stifle a giggle.

"I swear on Prince with his li'l sexy—"

"That's good enough," Glory interrupted before Christy got too excited. She took a deep breath. "Yes, me and Malcolm did it... but that's not the secret. Well, it is a secret 'cause it's nobody's business, and people would say he's too old, but—"

"Glory," Christy said, "You're babbling."

"Okay, okay." Glory was suddenly nervous. She reached into her blouse and pulled out the end of the silver chain, surprised at how easily she disobeyed her husband and father-in-law. She held the end of the chain letting the two rings rest in her open palm.

"Glory, did we just swear not to tell you're keeping your engagement ring on a chain now?" Tressa asked.

"No." Christy sat back in her seat and folded her arms. "Look closer."

Glory watched as the truth dawned on her friend. Tressa brought a hand to her mouth and then looked around the table and grabbed a napkin and brought it to her eyes.

"Jesus, Glory, no," Tressa whispered.

Glory dropped the rings back into her blouse and looked at her friends. She didn't know what she'd expected, but she hadn't expected Christy's coldness or Tressa's mourning. "C'mon, it's not that bad. I'm still the same person." Glory placed a hand on Tressa's shoulder. "This isn't gonna change anything. I promise." Glory gave what she thought was a reassuring smile, but her friends' expressions never changed.

"Glory, we were just joking about the sex part," Tressa began, gently. "But you actually married Malcolm?"

"Yes," Glory said. "Why are you acting like it's the end of the world?"

"Because," Tressa continued, "Quentin said Malcolm beat you up on prom night—"

"Other people said so too," Christy added.

Glory's eyes went wide. She'd tried to put the incident behind her—to forget about it. "We had an argument. It was nothing."

"They said you were screaming," Tressa whispered.

"It was a loud argument."

"And you tried to jump outta the car, but—"

"I wanted to go back to the prom." Glory felt defensive. "I was mostly drunk anyway."

Christy finally spoke up. "Did Malcolm hit you, Glory?"

The question was so simple and so complicated. Glory had never really asked or answered it herself. If she said yes, they'd call her a fool. If she said no, she was a liar. She could either worry or reassure her friends. The fight hadn't been that bad, really. He'd only hit her face once and mostly just hit her arm and the seat. It didn't even hurt that much. And Malcolm loved her. He'd proven that over and over again. He wouldn't have gotten so upset if he didn't.

"No," Glory lied. "He kept me from jumping outta the car when I was mad—that's all." She took three lukewarm french fries from the basket and looked both of her friends in the eye. The lie had come so easily that Glory almost believed it herself. Almost.

A WEEK LATER, ON THE last day of school for seniors, Glory made her way through halls crowded with students busy cleaning lockers and signing yearbooks. Arriving at her locker, Glory nearly choked herself laughing. The door was covered in artfully arranged toilet-paper flowers and streamers and a handwritten sign that said, "Yay, Glory!" A few people had already added messages to the sign, most about her scholarships, although one asked her *due date*. The decorations could only be the work of Tressa and Christy. Glory tore off a piece of one of the flowers and wiped a tear.

At the end of fourth period, when Glory arrived in the bookstore, Tressa and Christy were already in their usual spot. Sliding into her seat in their booth, Glory laughed at the pyramid of snack cakes decorated with whipped cream. "What's the occasion?" she asked, even though she already knew.

"It's your wedding reception," Tressa whispered. "The locker is your bridal shower."

Christy raised her drink. "A toast."

Glory and Tressa picked up their drinks.

"Keep the fights clean and the sex dirty and—ouch!"

"And that's enough," Tressa interrupted. "We love you, Glory."

"Seriously, though." Christy leaned into the table. "I know a lotta plants that can kill a man. Don't let me need to use 'em... and don't you dare kick me. I'm not even playing. I love you, and I want you to be happy—with or without Malcolm." Christy took a swallow of her drink and sat back in her seat.

Glory sipped her drink slowly and struggled not to hang her head. She'd lied to her best friends, and they were celebrating based on that lie. "Oh my God, Christy, lighten up. Malcolm *saved* me, remember? Why would he ever hurt me?"

"Ain't y'all leavin' kinda late?" Mr. Harris asked when the period ended and the girls filed past the school-supply counter. "Hey, Glory, lemme talk to you for a minute."

Christy and Tressa scowled, but Glory sighed and went over to the counter. "Hi, Mr. Harris."

The grungy old owner of the bookstore leaned against the counter, keeping his voice low. "Yo' friends was making you a weddin' cake, huh?"

Glory didn't answer.

"It's okay. I ain't gon' tell. I got a present for you." He handed Glory a tiny manila envelope the size of a business card. On the outside, he'd written his initials and a phone number.

Looking inside the envelope, Glory saw a folded fifty-dollar bill. She dropped the envelope back on the counter and turned to walk away.

"Now, wait a minute," Harris said quickly. "It ain't nothin' bad, I promise you."

Glory turned back to the counter. "What?"

"Tha's what you call mad money. You keep it in your purse for emergencies."

"Why do you think I need that?" Glory knew the answer, but still she asked.

"Girl, you ain't dumb." Harris scoffed. "We both know he ain't nice, and if you don't know yet, you gon' find out. That there money is f' when you need it f' emergency. I put my number on it 'cause... 'cause you a good girl, and maybe I might can help you one day. Tha's all. Okay?"

Glory looked from the old man whom her husband once threatened to beat to death to the envelope on the counter. Cal Harris knew Malcolm from his wild teenage years. He knew more about Malcolm than she did. *What's he trying to tell me? Did he hear the rumors too?* Malcolm had said she didn't need her own money. *Will I really need mad money?*

Glory picked up the envelope and tucked it into the lining of her purse. "Thank you."

Back at school, the generally festive mood, occasionally punctuated by tears, seemed to last the whole day. In the classrooms, teachers played music and collected books. Some passed out snacks or hall passes. Desperate students turned in those last missing assignments, begging to be allowed to graduate. In the halls, students hugged, saying their official goodbyes. Trash cans overflowed with the discarded artifacts of 412 high school seniors. Hall monitors didn't even try to keep the noise down.

Arriving at her locker, Glory saw that another sheet of paper had been taped below the first one, and it, too, was nearly full of more well wishes and speculation.

"Glory, where've you been?" Quentin pulled her into a hug before she could answer. "I was so worried. I tried to call, and you didn't answer, and then you were MIA for two days. I thought you were really hurt—"

"Whoa, Q, slow down. I'm fine." Glory freed herself from the lanky redhead's arms. "I just had to take care of something, and it took a couple of days. I'm okay, though." She felt her friend staring at her when she opened her locker and started collecting books from the top shelf.

"I'm not so sure," Quentin said from behind the open locker door. "According to the notes on these signs, besides congrats on the scholarships, there's 'Best wishes for a healthy baby,' 'Glad you're outta the hospital,' and 'Hope the police got the m-f.'" He opened his own locker. "Nobody knows what you're celebrating, do they?"

"Tressa and Christy know." Glory took a couple of steps to a nearby trash can to drop a stack of papers. Turning back around, she noticed Quentin staring at her locker door.

"Glory, why did they decorate your door with white streamers and flowers?" he asked slowly.

"'Cause that's the color of toilet paper? I don't know." She bent down to clean the pile of papers on the floor of her locker. When Quentin didn't ask her anything else, Glory looked up at him. He looked thunderstruck. "Oh, right. Besides the scholarship, everything else up there is wrong. Not pregnant, no hospital, no police. You can stop worrying." She flashed him a smile, but his expression didn't change.

"Are you getting married after graduation?"

Glory froze. Of course Quentin would get close to the truth. She stood up and faced him. "Yes. I am. In October." She easily told the half-truth.

Quentin stood with his arms folded, leaning back on his heels. Glory couldn't read his expression. "Do I know him? Does he go to this school?"

"You've met him, but he doesn't go here."

Quentin turned back to his locker and removed his backpack. "So, who is he? What's his name?"

"It's Malcolm," Glory said. "He's not really a bodyguard—"

"No shit." Quentin threw his backpack into his locker. "I saw him hit you."

"What?"

"Prom night. I saw him hit you."

"Quentin." Glory placed a hand on his arm. "It's not what you think—"

He brushed her hand away "I know what I saw. Other people saw too."

"You don't understand. I embarrassed him, and he was upset."

"So what? He's a grown man. You're a kid. You're a girl!"

"But—"

"He's driving down the street, kickin' your ass in the car!" Quentin growled through clenched teeth. "I saw him. I was in the next car to you when you tried to get away. He was swinging at you, and you were screaming for him to stop. That's what pimps do! And you're gonna marry him?"

"Quentin, would you listen to me, please?"

"What?" He folded his arms.

"He apologized. He made it up to me, and I know it won't happen again. And, Quentin..." She laid a hand on his wrist. "He saved my life. He almost killed somebody for me. I can't just ignore that. I know he loves me. God sent him to save me—"

Quentin threw up his hands. "What? Are you kidding me? Hephaestus never hit Aphrodite! Arthur never hit Guinevere! Neither Zaphod nor Arthur Dent ever hit Trillian! Princess Leia embarrassed Han Solo through two movies. He rescued her and killed for her, and he never hit her!" He counted off the examples on his fingers. "Men don't do that! And what the hell kind of God wants a girl to marry a grown man who beats her!" Quentin slammed his locker shut. "You know what? I hope you live happily ever after, princess, but I'm not watchin' this."

Glory watched her friend walk away. "Quentin, Arthur tried to kill Guinevere, but Lancelot saved her!"

CHAPTER 15
June 1984

"You know, Malcolm, I don't totally hafta go to graduation." Glory reached up, straightened her husband's tie, and ran a finger down his chest. "We could just stay here."

"Okay." Malcolm brushed her hand away. "This is the third time you've talked about skipping graduation. What's really goin' on?"

"Nothing." Glory averted her eyes and brushed invisible dust from her dressing gown. "I just thought we could spend some extra time together. You're always so busy." She turned away and went to the dresser mirror to finish pinning her hair up.

"Glory." Malcolm sounded more than a little irritated. "What. Is. Going. On."

She looked at him in the mirror and sighed. His face and tone left her no room for more playful banter. "Malcolm, I don't think you should come."

"Why not? They think I'm your bodyguard, remember?"

Glory turned to face him. "No, they don't. Not anymore."

"Okay. So?"

"Malcolm, too many people saw what happened on prom night."

"What, you dancing around drunk?"

"No, in the car. People saw the..." Glory searched for a word. "Incident."

"Oh." Malcolm hung his head and shoved his hands into his pockets. "I see."

Glory hated bringing it up again—the *incident*. Malcolm had apologized, and she'd only had a few bruises, and the torn sleeve on her dress had been easily repaired. But she could tell he was still embarrassed about losing his temper so violently. "So, staying home isn't a bad idea now, is it?" She turned back to the mirror.

Malcolm came up behind her and wrapped his arms around her waist. "Listen, I'm a grown man. Anybody have a problem with me, let 'em step up." He reached out and pulled the combs out of Glory's neat up-do. "Now, let your hair down. You know I don't like it pinned up like that."

THE CEREMONY AT THE Arie Crown theater lasted almost two hours. The covaledictorians gave moving speeches, and while a slideshow played, the senior class choir sang a song that made everybody cry. Glory found herself uncharacteristically emotional crossing the stage to get her diploma cover. High school was officially over. Though she hadn't felt like a child since getting married three weeks before, Glory would have sworn she felt herself walking into adulthood. When the class switched their tassels, she didn't try to stop the tears from falling.

In the packed theater lobby, she stood with her best friends, waiting by a pillar in front of the box office. The three girls—Glory, Tressa, and Christy—got in a long group hug before their families found them.

"Tee... damn, girl, quit it. It's not like we're never gonna see each other again." Christy rubbed her friend's back.

"Chicago won't be the same without y'all." Glory dabbed at her eyes too.

"We're not going that far away. I'll only be in Alabama," Christy said. "And Tee is just down the road in Champagne. And you'll be holding down the fort here. Tee'll be home for Thanksgiving, right?"

"Yeah." Tressa sniffed. "But it's just so sad... all the memories—"

"Come on! Don't start singing *that* song."

Somebody tapped Glory's left shoulder. "Huh?" She automatically looked to her right. She hadn't fallen for that old trick since grammar school.

"Hi." Quentin stood bouncing on his toes, looking adorable as ever in his light-gray suit and black shirt. The tall, gangly red-haired boy slipped an arm around Glory's shoulder. "Hi, y'all," he said to Tressa and Christy. "I'm gonna borrow this lady for a minute, capisce?" He steered Glory away from her friends without waiting for an answer.

When they'd walked a few steps, Glory found herself wrapped in Quentin's embrace. "Q? I thought you weren't speaking to me!"

"I'm sorry." He squeezed her a little tighter. "I didn't mean it. I just lost my temper."

Glory pulled herself from the hug and looked around. "That's okay. I hated the thought of losing you as a friend." *Good, Malcolm didn't see.*

"You're not gonna lose me." Quentin hugged her again. "I just couldn't stand the thought of you walking into a dangerous situation."

"Quentin." Glory pulled his arms from around her. "I'm gonna be fine." She felt a hand on her shoulder and took a step back from her friend.

"Hello," Malcolm said.

"I'm gonna be there for you, no matter what, okay?" Quentin continued speaking as if Malcolm wasn't there. "If you ever need help, call me, and I'll be there." He kissed Glory's forehead and pulled her into another hug.

Glory stiffly returned the hug, giving him a friendly pat on the back.

"Hi. I remember you. You're Glory's little friend... Quincy?" Malcolm offered his hand.

Quentin drew himself up to his full six feet, two inches and looked Malcolm in the eye. He placed a hand on Glory's shoulder and squeezed. "*I* love you, Glory." He faced Malcolm when he spoke, no warmth in his voice at all.

Malcolm withdrew his hand. Quentin squeezed Glory's shoulder again and walked away. Glory wanted to turn and watch him go, but she could feel Malcolm seething.

"I guess I know what that was about," Malcolm said.

Glory knew his casual tone was only because they were out in public. She tried to keep the mood light. "He gets so dramatic sometimes."

"They're over here." Herschel's voice carried over the crowd as he pushed his way through, closely followed by Glory's mother and Anita.

"This ain't over," Malcolm whispered.

Herschel draped an arm over Glory's shoulder and gave her a squeeze. "Glory-Glory, I am so proud of you." He looked dapper in his black suit and purple shirt. He even had a purple boutonniere.

"Thank you." Glory returned the hug and smiled up at her best friend. No matter what Malcolm said, she was not giving up the tall dark man as a friend, mentor, and uncle sister

Mother Porter stepped forward and air-kissed Glory on both cheeks. "Congratulations, Precious." She flicked Glory's tassel. "You look so smart in that outfit. I do hope your college graduation is conducted just as well."

"Congratulations, baby." Mary gave her daughter's shoulder a pat. "I'm real happy for you."

Glory didn't expect more of a reaction from her mother. Mary Bishop denounced pride as a sin and saw no practical reason for a married woman to care about educational pursuits.

"Oh, come now, Mary!" Anita gave Mary a pat on the back, pushing her forward slightly. "We're all so proud of Precious. Aren't you too? This is the time to tell her. Soon she'll be struggling in college—"

"Mother, Glory won't ever struggle. She's very smart." Malcolm's tone was polite and deferential, but he was definitely scolding his mother. "She'll be just fine."

Glory only partially listened to her family's pretend cordiality. She exchanged waves with some of her classmates and hugs with others, and as the crowd started thinning, she and her family headed to Orly's restaurant in Hyde Park for lunch.

THE STIFF WINGBACK chair was surprisingly comfortable, but then, Glory expected to find nothing less in Anita Porter's church office. Aside from the small antique writing desk, there was no other normal office furniture. Glory got up from the chair and looked around the room, which had dark wood bookcases and an explosion of lavender and pink accents—pillows, soft flowing curtains, pink desk accessories, and pink-and-lavender-flowered wallpaper. Walking around the small office with its uptight Victorian look, Glory smiled, remembering how impressive she'd once found this space. But after living three months with the Porters, she was quite used to the trappings of luxury and to Anita's style in general.

The older woman sat at her desk, taking a call on an antique-style telephone. She laughed and joked as if Glory were not standing there at her behest. As she finally said goodbye and ended the conversation, she motioned for Glory to sit down. Then she poured two cups of tea from a carafe on her desk and nodded to Glory.

Glory waited until Anita had sipped her tea before taking her cup. She couldn't help smiling. Vanilla, her favorite. She accepted her mother-in-law's offering and relaxed... a little.

"Thank you for coming, Glory. I hope I didn't take you away from anything important."

"Nothing important, really." Glory would not be drawn into small talk. "But I can't stay long. What did you want to talk to me about?"

Anita cleared her throat. "Right to the point, I see." She folded her hands on the desk. "Very well, then."

Glory sat back in the chair and tried to cross her legs like Anita had taught her, careful to keep from showing the bottoms of her pumps to the elegant lady.

"I must apologize for my behavior on your wedding day. It *was* an unexpected event, and I was in shock."

"Mother Porter, you called me an ignorant child." Glory drank her tea. Even though she kept her eyes down, she tried to sound confident. "You told Malcolm that marrying me was the lowest thing he ever did."

Anita blushed slightly but didn't hang her head. "I did, didn't I?" She sat back in her chair. "Well, I apologize for that, and when we're alone, you can still call me Miss Anita. Malcolm and I share a temperament. I'm sure you understand."

Though Glory sipped her tea and nodded, her stomach was in knots. Mother Porter—Miss Anita—had been her mentor, sponsor, and fairy godmother. The petite woman was the most intimidating person Glory knew. Her genteel Southern accent belied a spine of steel and a heart of stone. Glory kept her head up and carefully avoided direct eye contact. She knew her mother-in-law would easily defeat her in a staring contest.

"I asked you to visit because I need some answers, if you'll indulge an old woman for a few minutes."

Old woman? Glory fought an urge to laugh. At barely fifty, Anita Porter could easily pass for thirty. Glory just nodded.

Anita picked up her cup and saucer and sat back in her chair. She quietly sipped her tea just long enough for Glory's little confidence to wane. "What I want to know, Glory, is what Malcolm said to you to get you to throw away everything. I thought you enjoyed life with us. You seemed so happy. What happened, Precious?"

Glory hadn't been expecting that question. She drank her tea for a second. It was getting cold. *Tell the truth.* That was what Herschel always told her.

"Malcolm told me that you thought I was weak and low-class and that you were doing everything to get me away from him. He said you didn't think I was good enough to be in your family."

"I see." Anita sipped her tea. "And you believed him." It wasn't a question.

"Why did you book a romantic prom weekend for me and Dexter, Malcolm's own cousin?"

"Precious, I got that suite for you and your friends. The romance was just a mix-up with the hotel—"

"Miss Anita, you've taken me to enough hotels to know that they don't *accidentally* leave wine, chocolates, and roses."

"Well, that's all in the past. I'm sorry Malcolm said those things to you." She waved her hand dismissively. "He completely misread my intentions, and now you've gone and ruined all our fun by getting married."

"You mean your fun?" Glory mumbled just loud enough for Anita to hear.

"Well, yes, I admit I was having the time of my life. I loved watching you blossom into the beautiful, confident, sophisticated, and worldly young woman you've become."

Worldly. Just like her mother warned against. Mary Bishop had tried to beat demons of worldliness out of Glory, which was why Malcolm had moved her in with the Porters. Glory didn't like being called worldly.

"You can't tell me you didn't enjoy our time together." Anita poured more hot tea into her cup. She held the carafe up, but Glory declined.

"Yes, ma'am, I had fun," Glory said carefully. "But you were manipulating me. Pulling me away from Malcolm—"

"By steering you to college and a future as something more than a preacher's wife."

"I'm still going to college—"

Anita excitedly clapped her hands. "Why, yes you are. I've secured admission for you to DePaul University."

"What? Here in Chicago?" Glory's eyes narrowed. "Why?"

"Well..." Anita stood up and walked around the desk. "I like to finish what I start."

"Okay?"

"I mean, it won't be as much fun, what with no parties to plan—except the wedding, but that's small—and not as much travel, but you're my daughter-in-law, and you'll be the mother of my grandchildren, so you can still be my personal project. Oh, Precious, you just hafta agree!"

"'Personal project.' Hmmm." Glory drank her cold tea and looked up at her mother-in-law. Admission to a university... something she had stopped considering after marrying Malcolm. *But being Miss Anita's "personal project." Is college worth it?*

"Think about it, Precious. You know how much you liked traveling. And you loved being the center of attention at the cotillion and the prom. What was it your friend called you... a goddess? You know you want that again."

For the past three weeks, Glory had tried not to miss her life with the Porters. She'd tried not to miss her yellow bedroom or the grand library or the elegant conservatory... and she tried not to miss Cousin Dexter. She wondered if she could really have that life again—minus Dexter, of course.

"Honestly, Mother Porter—Miss Anita—Malcolm says I shouldn't trust you—"

"Oh, he's just silly. We don't need to tell him—"

"So you want me to lie to Malcolm?" Glory stood to leave. "It was nice visiting you, Miss Anita. Thank you for the tea."

"Glory... Precious. Wait."

Glory paused halfway to the door. She kept her head down but didn't turn around.

"My son sometimes loses his temper. I'm sure you know what I'm talking about."

Glory suppressed a sigh.

"What if one day you're without Malcolm and need to support yourself—or yourself and a child?"

"Miss Anita, I'll think about it, but I hafta discuss it with Malcolm."

"Very well." Anita stepped in front of Glory and placed a hand against the younger woman's cheek. "One last thing—your eighteenth birthday is coming up, and I'd like to be able to celebrate in the manner to which *you've* become accustomed. I've already started planning your party, okay, Precious?"

Leaving the room, Glory looked across the balcony to the open door of Malcolm's office. Cheryl Cannon stood shaking her finger at Malcolm. He remained seated, but even from a distance, Glory could tell that her husband wasn't taking the tongue-lashing very well. Making her way around the balcony, Glory caught bits of Cheryl's tirade.

"People need you... walk away... selfish... what kind of... abandons his flock..."

Glory stayed close to the wall and coughed before stepping into the office doorway. "Hi."

"Hi. What do you want?" Cheryl huffed, folding her arms. "Can't you see we're talking?"

"Oh. Sorry," Glory said in her least apologetic tone, turning to face Malcolm. She clasped her hands behind her back and twisted from side to side the way Tressa sometimes did to get boys to give her what she wanted. "Malcolm, are you still coming over for dinner today?" Glory spoke with wide-eyed innocence and was rewarded with Malcolm's indulgent smirk.

"He's got plans for dinner," Cheryl snapped.

Glory rolled her eyes at the woman in the fitted red dress with white buttons down the back and giant shoulder pads. She cleared her throat and turned back to face Malcolm. "Well?" She watched Malcolm struggle to keep a straight face and maintain control of the situation. She batted her eyelashes for good measure, prompting him to hide a smile by swiveling his chair and standing up.

"Cheryl, we'll finish this later." He motioned to the empty chair across from his desk. "Sit down, Miss Bishop. We need to have a talk about barging in."

"Oh, we will definitely finish this later, Malcolm." Cheryl turned to Glory. "Little Glory, you're becoming such a cute young lady. You're in what, ninth grade now—thirteen, fourteen?"

Glory giggled "Actually, I finished high school. I'll be eighteen in a couple of weeks. That makes you—what, forty?"

Malcolm cleared his throat before Cheryl could respond. "Uh, Cheryl, I'll be in touch this week. Glory, have a seat, please."

Glory watched Cheryl leave in a huff, the telltale swish of nylon hosiery announcing her departure. Glory giggled then looked up into Malcolm's scowling face.

"That was totally uncalled-for." He sat down again and leaned forward, his elbows on his desk. "Are you trying to cause trouble?"

"Well..." Glory pouted. "She started it. Shaking her finger like you're a kid or something."

Malcolm massaged his temples with his right hand.

Glory noticed that his normally manicured fingernails looked rough, almost like he'd been picking at them. "Why was she fussing at you?"

"I told her I'm leaving the mission and encouraged her to keep working there. She's really mad at me."

"Boo-hoo, poor baby."

"See, this is the attitude I've been talking about. My mother's turned you into such a brat. This is important to Cheryl, and it's really hard for me."

"But—"

"But nothing! Woman, do you know what it's like to be forced to give up something you love?"

"Well, actually—"

"Of course you don't." Malcolm stood and began pacing in the small space behind his desk. "You know, before me, there was no night ministry. I've seen people turn their lives completely around coming to the mission. It was my idea to go back into messed-up neighborhoods and minister to the people on the street, and now my dad wants me to just quit. He wants me to turn my ministry over to just anybody. He thinks they'll follow me to Lake Shore, but the people that come to the late-night services... they're not comin' out on a Sunday morning." Malcolm stuffed his hands into his pockets and kicked the back of his rolling desk chair, sending it crashing into the desk.

"Malcolm, why can't you have night services here? Would the people from the mission come out this far?"

"Nah, they all walk or take the bus." Malcolm pulled his chair out and sat back down. "And there's no way my dad would let a bunch of 'that riffraff' dirty up his beautiful building."

Glory thought about reaching across the desk to take his hand, but they couldn't touch in public until after their official wedding in four months. "Well, I know there's a—"

"Now, about your little performance, woman." Malcolm leaned back in the chair and folded his arms. "Don't do that again. When she gets the wedding announcement, she's gonna be hurt enough. You don't need to be barging in here with your big puppy dog eyes, rubbing her face in it. Understand?"

"But, Malcolm, she—"

"Glory, do you understand me?"

"Yeah, fine." Glory pouted.

"Glory." He spoke in that tone, the one that always got her attention, forcing her name out through clenched teeth.

Glory sat up straight in her chair. "Yes, Malcolm. I understand." She stifled a sigh. "Well, I just had a talk with your mother—"

"Save it." Malcolm stood up from his seat. "As soon as it's clear, get home. I don't want you hanging around here after service, understand?"

"But, Malcolm, it's really important—"

"Woman, I got enough stuff goin' wrong without having to deal with you."

"I'll go wait in the Robinson Room—"

Malcolm lowered his voice to just above a whisper. "Wives, submit yourselves unto your own husbands, as unto the Lord."

Glory stared at him for a few seconds. "Good day, Minister Porter." She stood up and left the office, walking slowly enough to show that she was leaving because *she* wanted to.

Glory decided to take the long way through the church to the *haunted hallway* that led to their apartment. She stopped in the

Robinson Room for a cup of tea, lingering a bit with her old friends to hear the latest gossip. Trina Toliver was pregnant again and trying to blame Johnny Turner, but after she'd lied about JT, nobody believed her, and everybody knew Johnny was kind of funny. Some of the kids who'd gone away to college the previous fall had come back acting like they were too good to speak to anybody. And Malcolm Porter wasn't the youth pastor anymore. Glory giggled a little at this last bit of gossip and moved on.

In the ladies' room, washing her hands with pound-cake-scented soap courtesy of Herschel's salon, Glory tried to keep her head down when Cheryl Cannon walked in. She busied herself with drying her hands and applying lip gloss when she heard Cheryl's high heels stop right behind her.

"You thought that was funny, didn't you?"

Glory shrugged. "Um... a little?" she said to Cheryl's reflection in the mirror.

The older woman moved to the next mirror, primping her hair. "So I guess you think spending the night with a boy means you can throw yourself at a grown man. Does your mother know?"

"I'm sorry." Glory sighed. "I shouldn'ta said you were forty."

"Listen, little girl..." Cheryl turned to face her, drumming her brown-polished fingernails on the counter. "I'm only gonna tell you one time, then I'm tellin' your mother."

"But—"

"Go back to the playground with boys your own age. Malcolm is more man than a kid like you could ever handle. He's a busy man, and he don't have time for Little Miss Hot-to-Trot flinging herself at him."

Glory avoided looking directly at Cheryl lest she laugh at the woman's sassy head rocking.

"Consider yourself warned." Cheryl turned on her heel and sauntered out of the ladies' room.

"Consider yourself warned," Glory mimicked under her breath. She fingered the silver beaded chain that bore her wedding and engagement rings. *I'll remember that tonight in bed with Malcolm.*

CHAPTER 16

Listening to her husband and mother-in-law argue over Glory's eighteenth-birthday parties might have been funny to Glory, except they were very serious.

"Mother, my wife is not a fashion doll that you can stick on a pedestal for everybody to gawk at!"

"Well, if you hadn't tricked her into marrying you, she would be! She'd be the talk of the town!"

Malcolm rolled his eyes and massaged his temples. "Chicago isn't a town. It's a huge city, and she doesn't need to be the talk of anywhere."

"But, son, can't you see the scandal brewing? The popular new girl is the talk of the season, and suddenly she turns eighteen and nothing? Folks are gonna wonder why. Everybody'll think she up and got pregnant or something."

"The only one who cares about this stuff is you, Mother."

Sitting in the Porters' conservatory on a sunny Sunday afternoon, Glory wanted to yell at them both. Not for the first time, she wished her birthday were anytime other than summer. That way, her friends could have decorated her locker at school and sung "Happy Birthday" in the bookstore. No dressing up and no fancy hall. Malcolm wanted a nice dinner at their favorite restaurant, but in the end, Anita counted herself the winner. Glory's first eighteenth-birthday party would be at Orly's in the private dining room, for her family and fifty of her closest friends. Malcolm would only put in a brief appearance lest the management remember Glory's and his impromptu wedding reception. The second party would be the lavish affair Anita wanted down in New Orleans.

"Miss Anita, I don't have fifty close friends. I don't think I even know fifty people." Glory sipped her vanilla iced tea and slouched in her seat. "And I don't know anybody in New Orleans."

"Don't worry, Precious. Everybody's gonna know you, and those that don't will want to. All you hafta do is be your charming, intelligent self. Now, sit up straight."

Malcolm stood up and started pacing around the table while Mrs. Beyers cleared their lunch plates. "And you're gonna have her out there... well, I hafta approve her dress, and that's final." Claiming his minor victory, he sat down hard in one of the white wicker chairs.

His mother raised an eyebrow. "Now, we've got three weeks," Anita said. "We don't have time for engraved invitations, but I'll pick something simple, maybe with an embossed border or something. You have a dress fitting tomorrow at nine, and we'll lunch at your little restaurant. I do hope they're not booked that weekend. If they are, we'll just hafta get a room somewhere downtown."

Malcolm sighed loudly and shook his head. Glory knew how he was feeling. His parents were taking over his life and now interfering in his marriage. He'd spent the past month trying to go to school, work full-time, and keep his night schedule at the mission. He was barely succeeding, and exhaustion was taking its toll.

"Mother, we hafta get going." Malcolm stood up from the table. "We've got things to do today."

"Oh, you're not preaching this afternoon?" Glory asked.

"Nah." Malcolm kissed his mother's cheek. "Dad can handle it. I deserve a day off sometimes."

Glory hugged her mother-in-law then allowed Malcolm to guide her from the conservatory to the front door. In the elevator, Malcolm pulled Glory into his arms. "Baby, I am so tired of them."

"Who?" Glory knew who he meant.

"Mother. Dad. Everybody."

She looked up at her husband. "Are you sure you can keep this up for seven years?"

"I have to." Malcolm squeezed his wife tighter. "And when babies start coming, it's gon' be even harder."

Glory stiffened. Babies again. Malcolm knew she didn't want children yet, but he kept bringing it up. He frequently forgot condoms and always prayed for *God's will* to be done. She had just started a new pack of pills and would continue to secretly protect herself and let God take the blame for their continued childless state. *God's will, indeed.* They separated as the elevator reached the first floor, and Malcolm ushered Glory through the lobby and out to the car.

ON THE MORNING OF HER eighteenth birthday, Glory awoke to smells of bacon and cinnamon. She slipped on a robe and followed her nose to the kitchen, where Malcolm was hard at work making breakfast. "Good morning, wife," he said.

Giggling, Glory took a seat at the kitchen table and watched Malcolm drop a pot of boiled eggs into one half of the sink, shake his hand, and then plunge it into the stream of cold running water.

"Dammit!" Malcolm cussed, sucking on the side of his index finger.

"Need any help?" Glory asked, unable to keep the laughter out of her voice.

"Woman, you just sit there and wait." Malcolm pulled a pan of extra-dark bacon from the oven, sighed, and dumped the greasy mess into the other half of the kitchen sink.

Glory watched with amusement and a bit of trepidation as Malcolm lay a few fresh slices of bacon on the stovetop griddle and turned it on. "Um, husband. Maybe you should..."

"Ouch! Dammit!"

"... put on a shirt. I think there's a law or something about frying bacon naked." Glory couldn't stifle her giggles, and Malcolm laid a dish towel over his bare chest and held it in place with his chin.

"Okay, that's it." Glory stood up. "You're gonna set yourself on fire."

"Leave me be, woman. I know what I'm doin'!"

Glory took her seat again, holding her breath to keep from laughing, and watched Malcolm slowly get a handle on things. Fifteen minutes later, she dug into toaster French toast, bacon, eggs, and fruit cocktail. Malcolm sat across from her, looking pleased with himself.

"So, how is everything?" he asked.

"Man, this is the best fruit cocktail you've ever opened. And the eggs... you peeled the heck out of 'em."

"Very funny, woman. Happy birthday."

After breakfast, Malcolm dropped Glory at the salon. She could tell Herschel was in the back room because the smells of hair frying and cooking were mingled with the floral scent of roses. She walked through the salon, greeting the usual Saturday-morning crowd and noticing that her mother hadn't arrived for her regular appointment.

Glory found Herschel in his usual place at the stove, distilling rose oil and rose water. "Good morning, birthday girl!" he called over the drone of four electric fans. "Happy rose day! How does it feel to be officially legal?"

"Honestly, it feels exactly the same as it did yesterday." Glory found her garden gloves and started pulling the heads off the flowers piled beside the sink. "Doesn't look like you got much this time. How many pounds?"

"Only ninety pounds. Rose-scented products are gonna be a tad expensive this season."

The two friends worked mostly in silence, occasionally laughing at the screaming and cackling coming from out in the shop. "So, what time is your hair appointment, Glory-Glory?"

"Not till two. The party's not till seven and—"

"And you decided to spend part of your birthday working? I mean, I love this place, too, but, girl, you wouldn't catch me here on my birthday."

"Well, I also came early 'cause I needed to talk to you."

"Okay, what's up?" Herschel placed a metal bowl of ice on top of a large pot of simmering rose petals. "Everything's okay, right? You didn't lose your pills or nothing, did you?"

"No... I need a new pack."

"Oh, really? You taking them now? Is this something you wanna talk about?"

"Well..." Glory gripped the edge of the sink. "Yeah." She took a deep breath. "Me and Malcolm did... it... a lot." She didn't turn around. She couldn't bear to see what she knew would be disapproval in her friend's eyes.

"I see." Herschel cleared his throat. "Are you okay? Is this something that you want?"

"Yeah, it is. I love him."

"Oh, really?" Herschel's voice was normal and matter-of-fact. To Glory, he didn't sound the least bit upset. "A few months ago, you were tryin' to break up with him. Now ya sleepin' with him. What happened to waiting for marriage?"

Glory turned around to face her friend and found she couldn't keep her eyes up. "Um, Herschel... we did wait for marriage." She spoke low and slowly, watching the truth dawn on the face of the man who'd been her best friend since she was a child.

Herschel turned away. He picked up a dish towel and began scrubbing the table, making tiny circles and large arcs.

"Herschel, it's really what I want. I'm happy with Malcolm."

"Really, Glory-Glory? You're happy to be stuck to a man who *won't let you cross the street by yourself*? That's really gonna make you happy?"

"Yeah, it does." Glory tried to keep her tone even, but she was starting to feel defensive. "And my mother is okay with it—"

"Well, first of all..." Herschel stood up straight, shaking a finger at Glory. "Yo' mama is crazy as hell, and we both know it." He held up a hand, cutting off Glory's interruption. "And secondly, as bossy as you say Malcolm is, Imma probably hafta kick his ass when he starts slapping you around. You just watch." He turned back to the stove. "Gon' make me hafta take my wig off and fight..." he mumbled.

Glory envisioned Herschel throwing his Jheri curl wig at Malcolm. She squeezed her eyes shut to clear the hilarious image. "Herschel, Malcolm loves me. He wouldn't hurt me." Glory kept her eyes down when she spoke, hoping that Herschel wouldn't see the truth.

Herschel blew out an exasperated sigh. "Darling, maybe not now because you take orders from him. But you're so young—"

"I'm not *that* young."

"Yes, you are, and that's the problem. You know what you want today, but as you get older, that's gonna change and grow. I mean, your whole world outlook changed in this one year. What's gonna happen in two years? Five or ten years?"

"But—"

"You're gonna change into a butterfly, and he's gonna lose control of you and not like it one bit. You just watch."

"So you're not happy for me?"

Herschel walked over and hugged Glory. "Darling, I'm always happy when you're happy, but I don't see you being happy in this forever. Sweetie, I love you, and I'll always be here for you."

Glory returned the hug. "I know you will... and everything is gonna be okay. Just watch."

Glory spent the rest of the morning sharing with Herschel the details of her wedding day, including Anita's dramatic hissy fit. Herschel roared with laughter at Anita's revenge of piling Glory's boxes at their front door.

"Girl, I told you she was a piece of work. Trying to be Alexis Carrington. Did she have on shoulder pads? I bet she was dressed like a pink-and-purple linebacker! Ah ha ha ha!"

GLORY ARRIVED AT THE restaurant promptly at seven thirty, but Anita kept her in the car until seven forty-five. "This way, your friends who come fashionably late will get to see your grand entrance."

"Why do I hafta make a grand entrance?" Glory looked down at her dress for the fifth or sixth time. The trendy shapeless dress—ivory with vertical beige stripes—covered her in the front from her knees to her collar bone. The V in the back at the collar and the six-inch split were the only concessions Malcolm made. He had vetoed anything showing more skin and had even demanded that she wear ivory hose to cover her legs. Of course, Anita obliged him... in her fashion. Glory's lace-top stockings were held in place by a black garter belt, and she felt positively sinful. To complete her outfit, Anita had insisted she try high heels again, so Glory teetered into the banquet room on red three-inch heels.

She couldn't help smiling as she made her grand entrance to the sounds of The Band of Brothers playing Stevie Wonder's "Happy Birthday." The gathered crowd joined in on the chorus, and Quentin stepped up to waltz her around the dance floor.

"No goddess uniform this time? You're making that gunny sack look pretty nice."

"Thanks. Oops, sorry!"

Quentin grimaced but didn't say anything as Glory stepped on his toe for the third time.

"How's Paula?" Glory asked, looking around. "Did you bring her?"

"Nah. She's too busy getting ready to go to school. I'm pretty sure we're breaking up this month. I see Malcolm is here, and he brought a date?"

"Where?" Glory tried to look around. Quentin helped by spinning slightly so Glory could see the door. Sure enough, there was Malcolm in a gray suit and white shirt. Glory would have bet that his blue tie was one of those she had given him this past Christmas. On his arm was Cheryl from church, looking like she owned the world. Glory stifled a laugh. She stepped away from Quentin and walked over to the couple.

"Hi, Malcolm. Hi, Cheryl." Glory's heels weren't nearly as tall as Cheryl's, but the two women stood almost shoulder to shoulder. "Thanks for coming."

"Hi, birthday girl!" Malcolm said over the music.

"So how does it feel to wear big-girl shoes?" Cheryl moved closer to Malcolm. "Is that your little boyfriend you were dancing with?"

Placing a hand on Malcolm's shoulder, Glory smiled. "No, Quentin's a friend from school. He's like a brother to me. Kinda like you and Malcolm." She wanted to laugh as she watched Cheryl's smile fade.

Cheryl turned to Malcolm. "Let's grab some refreshments." She pulled him toward the buffet.

Malcolm looked back at Glory, shaking his head. Glory covered her mouth to hide her giggles and then went back to join her other guests.

Forty-five minutes into the party, Glory gave up on high heels. Seated at a high-top table, she kicked her shoes off and massaged her bare feet. The waiter who was passing out hors d'oeuvres delivered her requested small plate of mini crab cakes and cold shrimp.

"Girl, you know, I had to chase that man down to get you that plate." Christy climbed into the seat opposite Glory. "And what's with all the snobs standing around with their arms folded?"

"Oh. Ignore them. They're jerks." Glory pulled the tail off a small shrimp. "Those are people Miss Anita invited. See those two in the red-and-green ties? Dexter told them they were risking their lives by touching my hand." She jingled the bracelets on her right hand. "He told them that my owner killed people for touching me. I punched him in the stomach for that. 'Just tryin' to help,'" she mimicked. "Yeah, right."

Tressa arrived and took the third seat at the table. "Um, Glory," Tressa whispered. "Why did your husband bring a date to your birthday party?"

Glory waved off the question. "She don't count. She only *thinks* she's his date." Her hand went to the silver beaded necklace that bore her engagement and wedding rings. "She's been after him for years, but he gave her no play at all. I'm not worried about her."

"I don't know, G," Christy said. "Her gold dress is dangerous—"

"And it can't compete with gold rings, so ha!"

"There you are, Glory-Glory!" Herschel's voice boomed as he waded through the crowd. Glory stood up to hug her friend. "Well, don't you look trendy. Lemme see your shoes!"

Glory pointed at her red pumps on the floor by her chair. "I'm not putting those things back on until it's time to go home."

The tall man laughed. "So you're gonna get your toes crushed while you're dancing the night away, huh?"

"Crushed toes, broken ankles." Glory shrugged. "It's all the same to me."

Herschel leaned in close to Glory. "That woman with Malcolm—is she the Fallon Carrington wannabe?"

Glory laughed. "Yeah, that's her. Want me to introduce you?"

"No, darling. C'mon, let's dance."

Glory let herself be pulled to the dance floor and fumbled her way through the "Bus Stop," much to the delight of her friends. Even the snobs joined in on the dance.

As the crowd thinned, Glory went to the pay phone and paged Malcolm. Part of their routine of sneaking into their home involved Glory paging Malcolm before she headed home. He would then go wait in his car for her to arrive at the church. If the coast was clear, they'd sneak into the side door and up the elevator to their fourth-floor apartment. If not, they'd go out or take a drive along the lake.

When Glory slid into the passenger seat of Malcolm's big brown Cadillac, he waited for her to get settled then pulled her into his arms. His kiss was soft and slow. "Happy birthday, Mrs. Porter."

Glory kissed her husband back. "Thank you, Superman. You're wearing a Superman tie, aren't you?"

"Yup. And the tie clip and bracelet. How did you guess?"

Glory smiled. "I just knew." She kissed her husband again. "Wanna stay here and make out in the car?"

"Woman." Malcolm laughed. "I'm not about to get caught by the cops acting like a teenager, especially with my wife. Besides..." Malcolm reached for the door handle. "I wanna get you inside. You still owe me a birthday dance."

The couple quickly slipped through the side door and into the elevator in the haunted hallway. On the ride up, Malcolm squeezed Glory's hand. "I'm sorry I didn't get to tell you how beautiful you look."

"Did you tell Cheryl how beautiful *she* looked?" Glory asked and then immediately regretted it. "I'm sorry. I guess seeing you with her bothered me a little."

In the quiet of their darkened living room, with the city lights reflecting off the polished hardwood floors, Malcolm pulled Glory into his arms. "Listen, woman, you know she's got nothin' comin'." He kissed her gently. "Now, tell me why."

Glory moaned a little as he slid his hands around her back and slowly unzipped her dress. "I am my beloved's, and his desire is toward *me*," she whispered, moving against him.

"Yes." He kissed her neck as he pushed her dress off her shoulders. "So?"

In response, Glory wrapped her arms around her husband's neck, and they swayed to silent music as he slowly undressed her. And when she kissed him, she wasn't a shy, scarred, and damaged girl—she was a beautiful eighteen-year-old woman.

INTERLUDE
JUNE 1980

In the Robinson Room, three eighth-grade girls leaned against a second-floor windowsill, watching the boys playing basketball down in the parking lot. There was one adult out there, the new youth minister. He wasn't that good, but what he lacked in skill, he made up for in height. He towered over the thirteen- and fourteen-year-old boys who ran circles around him.

"I don't see what the big deal is. We all know the Bible." Trina applied a thick coat of roll-on lip gloss, filling the air with the scent of bubblegum.

Andrea took her lip gloss from Trina. "No, he like really knows the Bible. Like every word of it. By heart." She rolled on lip gloss, smacked her lips, and offered the bottle to Glory.

"That's impossible." Glory rolled the sweet greasy ball over her top lip and then rubbed her lips together. She made a mental note to wipe it off before her mother finished choir rehearsal. "Nobody can know the Bible by heart. And which one? There's a lot of different ones."

"Yeah, and my daddy said he, like, knows them all." Andrea accepted the bottle back from Glory and put it down in her bra.

"Well, I don't care how much Bible he knows." Trina blew a small bubble with pink bubblegum. "He is fine! I bet I get him before y'all."

"You can have 'im." Andrea blew a bigger bubble than Trina's.

"Trina, why would a twenty-something-year-old man want a fourteen-year-old?" Glory asked, trying and failing to blow a bubble of any size. "That's just gross."

"Because I know how to rock his world," Trina boasted. "And I'm fifteen, so I know some things y'all too young to learn." Trina stood up straight with her chest out and her hands on her hips. "Y'all just little girls, but I'm woman enough for *Mr. Malcolm, the miracle man.*"

Glory and Andrea looked at Trina then looked at each other and burst out laughing.

"Laugh all you want. Y'all just watch me." Trina flounced out of the room.

Glory shook her head. "Why does she walk like that? She's gonna hurt her back."

"Her back'll be fine." Andrea snickered. "She, like, lays on it enough!"

Both girls laughed hysterically but quickly quieted down when they heard heels clicking in a nearby hallway. A few seconds later, they watched Trina switching across the parking lot to the basketball court, a bottle of pop in her hand. She walked straight up to Malcolm, held out the bottle, and shrugged. Malcolm smiled a little, took the bottle from Trina, and opened it and then held it out to her. Trina didn't take the bottle back. She placed her hands over his, threw her head back, and slowly turned the bottle up.

"Oh my God, would you, like, look at her?" Andrea moved to open the window. "She's, like, such a tramp!"

Glory pushed down on the window handle. "No! Let her make a fool of herself. She deserves it."

The two girls watched Trina slowly turn to walk away as a grubby orange basketball came flying and landed against her backside, causing her to stumble and dirtying her tight yellow dress. Trina screamed something rude, and JT yelled that girls weren't allowed on the court. Glory and Andrea slid to the floor, doubled over with laughter.

"Y'all sound like a couple of hyenas! What's so funny?"

The two girls stood up, and Andrea turned around. "Hi, Mrs. Bishop!" Andrea struggled to catch her breath. "We were, like, just watching the boys playing basketball with Malcolm."

"Yeah," Glory said, furiously licking her lips, praying that she could get all the shiny lip gloss off before her mother demanded that she turn around.

"Glory, you know you ain't supposed to be in here watchin' no boys. Turn around! Look at me! Where's yo' Bible at?"

Glory looked left and right then remembered that her Bible was across the room and she'd have to pass her mother to get it. She licked her lips some more and then moved to rush past her mother and get to her blue-denim-covered Bible. Mary grabbed her daughter's arm before she could get by.

"I said look at me! Wha's on your mouth?"

"Nothing," Glory lied. "Just ChapStick, that's all." Glory looked away from her mother, praying Mary accepted her explanation.

She didn't. "That ain't no doggone ChapStick! That look like that shiny lip-gloss stuff." Mary's grip on Glory's arm tightened. "You been playin' in makeup, girl? Answer me!"

Glory looked up at her mother. "It's not really makeup, Ma. It's just—"

The backhand knocked her to the floor. "Paintin' yo' face, and now you lying to me too!" Mary bent down, grabbed a handful of Glory's hair, and pulled her to her feet, shaking her head with every word. "You will not be a Jezebel in this life! Ya hear me! Answer me!"

"Yes, ma'am." Glory whimpered.

"Now, go clean that mess off yo' face!" Mary turned around, looking left and right. "Almost made me forget what I come in here for!" She grabbed her choir robe from a chair and stormed out of the room.

Glory stood still, staring straight ahead, willing herself not to cry. It was bad enough that Andrea had seen the slap. Glory was not about to add crying to the inevitable gossip.

"Glory," Andrea said softly, coming around to stand in front of her friend. She gently grabbed Glory's hand, but Glory snatched it away. "Glory, your lip is bleeding."

"Leave me alone," Glory whispered.

"Let me get you a napkin—"

"I said, leave me alone." Glory felt her lip swelling and sucked the blood from the small cut. She didn't look at Andrea. She just turned and left the room, going in the opposite direction of her mother.

"HEY."

"What do you want?"

"Nothing," Josiah said. "I knew you'd be up here."

Glory sat, arms folded, leaning against the wall on the third-floor landing of the haunted-hallway staircase. She didn't care that she had tears on her face, because it was too dark for anybody to see them.

"I know why you're hiding up here." Josiah sat down beside Glory.

"Andrea told everybody?" Glory asked.

"No, not everybody."

"Why'd she tell you?" Glory tried to keep the anger out of her voice. She honestly did appreciate Josiah's company.

"She knows we're friends—that's why."

"Oh." Glory had a funny fluttering in her stomach, sitting in the dark with this boy who was her friend.

"You should run away. I'm sure my mom would let you stay with us." Josiah slid closer until their legs were touching. "Or you could live with my dad on the West Side. She'd never find you there."

"Josiah, I'm not running away from home—"

"I hate your mother. Why would she hit you just for having lip gloss?"

Glory laughed a little. "Are you gonna use your robot karate moves on her?"

"I should." Josiah pouted.

Glory was surprised. He actually sounded angry. "Don't worry about it. I'm okay."

They sat in silence for a few minutes. Glory took slow, deep breaths and listened to Josiah breathing. She didn't jump when she felt his hand moving down her left arm.

"Josiah, what are you doing?"

"Trying to hold your hand. Is that okay?"

Glory didn't hesitate. "Yeah. If you want to." She held still while Josiah found her hand. She wondered if he could hear her heart pounding. Sitting in the dark on the dusty old staircase, Glory tried to breathe quietly. She didn't know why. It just seemed like a reasonable thing to do when sitting in the dark with a boy.

"Um, Miss Glory? Can I ask you something?"

"Yeah." Glory knew what the question was, and she knew what her answer would be. Back when they shared custody of her Barbie dolls, he'd started carrying around a Barbie shoe in his pocket. He gave her one every once in a while, when she was having a bad day. She knew he liked her *like that*, and she liked him probably just as much.

"Would you go with me?"

Glory squeezed his hand. "Yeah, JT, I'll go with you." She laid her head on his shoulder. "Should we kiss?"

"Only if you want to," JT said. "You don't have to. No, I mean I want to if you want to." JT stumbled over his words. "Do you want to?"

"If you do." Glory turned to face him in the darkness, inching closer until their foreheads touched, their noses, their lips. She tried to match her breathing to his like she'd read in the magazines at the salon. When he put his arms around her back, she moved her arms up around his neck. She had no idea how long the kiss lasted. She just knew that kissing Josiah T. Jackson was the best thing she'd ever done.

"SO THE BOY WHO WAS your husband is now your boyfriend?" Herschel stirred honey into his tea.

Glory blushed. "Yeah." She reached for a strawberry butter cookie. "And we kissed right there in church."

"Oh my, aren't you just a little vixen."

Glory's eyes went wide. "You really think so? It was only one little kiss. It's not like we were laying down or anything. Is kissing in church really bad?" Glory thought about the demons of lies and lust that must have gotten into her and silently vowed she would fight the demons of fornication.

"Glory-Glory, people kiss in church all the time. You've been to weddings."

"Yeah, but that's different. I opened my mouth, and our tongues touched!" Glory hid her face in her hands. "I'm goin' to hell, right?"

"Girl, quit it!" Herschel chided. "French kissing is the best kind. It's so romantic. You enjoyed it, right?"

"Yeah," Glory mumbled from behind her hands. "It made me feel funny, but yeah, I liked kissing JT."

"Well, darling." Herschel sipped his tea. "Kissing is real nice, but that funny feelin'—you gotta be careful with that."

"Oh God," Glory groaned. "I knew it was bad—"

"Calm down, girl. I didn't say bad. I said be careful!"

"But—"

Herschel held up a hand. "Just listen, okay?"

Glory nodded.

"That funny feeling feels real nice, right?"

"Yeah."

"Well, the thing is, the longer you feel that, the better it feels... and it gets to feelin' so good you wanna see how much better—"

"Herschel, what are you talking about?"

"You know what I'm talking about. Do I really hafta spell it out?"

"Oh." Glory hung her head. "That feeling." Sitting on the steps, kissing JT, Glory had felt her heart pounding and a strange pressure *down there*, kind of like she had to pee. It had felt weird but good at the same time—so good it had to be a sin. She'd gone home wondering if JT had felt the same thing.

"Yes, that feeling. You hafta be careful with that feeling. It makes you wanna have sex."

Glory gasped. "No, it doesn't!" She covered her ears and shook her head.

"Look at me, Glory-Glory." Herschel deepened his voice to the tone he used when he was deadly serious. "Yes. It. Does. And you do good to recognize it 'fore you wind up going too far."

"Oh, no. I'm not gonna do that until we're married," Glory insisted.

Herschel laughed. "Ain't you already married to him?"

"No!" Laughing, Glory threw a wadded-up napkin at her friend.

CHAPTER 17
October 1984

Glory and Malcolm left home every morning by six thirty, before the custodian opened the church at seven thirty, lest they be seen together leaving the parsonage. Immediately after they'd married, they had resumed their morning breakfasts at the Red Apple restaurant on the other side of town in the Englewood neighborhood.

"Malcolm, we really don't hafta do this if you don't want to." Glory stirred the decaf coffee that Malcolm always ordered for her but she never drank. "I mean, I never cared about a wedding at all, and if it's stressing you this much, why can't we just send out the announcements and skip the whole show? It's not like it's a real wedding anyway."

"Woman, Mother would freak out if we tried to cancel her big show."

The waitress brought their usual order of a little of everything on the menu, and Glory picked out her usual French toast, bacon, and fruit. She pushed her coffee away without drinking it. "Well, it's not supposed to be a big show anyway. Just immediate family and close friends." Glory lowered her voice to a whisper. "Did you know she ordered fifty invitations and *three hundred* announcements? It might be a small wedding, but she's not acting like it. I mean, really, who even knows three hundred people?"

Malcolm dug into his omelet, shaking his head. "I know I don't," he said when he finished chewing. "But after your birthday party down South, you remember how many calls she got asking for personal introductions and stuff. That's why I never wanted to be involved in that society stuff. I'da been trapped by some stuck-up debutante by my eighteenth birthday." He took another bite and laughed a little. "There's no way I was getting caught up in that mess. But this wedding is important to her, and it's one day. She's not getting all the engagement parties and stuff, so she's making the best of it. I guess I can give her that."

"Well, if you're sure," Glory said, "but I'm ready to bail anytime you are. Argh! I've got two dress fittings today, and I still can't convince my mother to go to her fitting. She refuses to consider anything Miss Anita wants to do. And the pink and purple, oh my God!" Glory paused for a deep sigh. "I don't know. I'm just tired of all this." She moved the food around on her plate. "I wish it was over already."

Malcolm looked into Glory's eyes. "Me too."

THE WEDDING AND RECEPTION outfits from Harlica's arrived two weeks before the wedding. Glory hated them both. Not that she cared about things like wedding dresses, but the dress was too tight and the sleeves too puffy. The reception suit—*Who gets separate clothes for the reception?*—was too tight and too low-cut.

Glory stood on a pedestal in her old bedroom at the Porters' while the seamstress tucked and pinned the hem of the wedding dress. Anita sat nearby, sipping tea, checking the guest list, and giving instructions that the seamstress ignored.

"Can you bring that waist in just a bit?" Anita asked. "She has such a perfect figure."

"Sure, I can." The seamstress stood up and grabbed a bit of fabric at Glory's waistline. "As long as you're okay with her passing out at the altar. Mrs. Porter, the dress is tight enough. She's gotta be able to move and breathe."

"Glory, stop slouching so she can fit the dress right. You *do not* want a saggy waistline when you're walking down the aisle." Anita sipped her tea and continued down the list. "I'm so glad Elder saw reason and let me plan a real reception. The Robinson Room, really? Out of the question. And your little restaurant's private dining room? Much too small. The 95th—at the top of the John Hancock Building—is the perfect spot, and a brunch reception with a view of the city in fall colors will be lovely..."

Glory tuned out her mother-in-law and turned her thoughts to her own family and friends. Jill as maid of honor and Tressa and Christy as bridesmaids. Everybody from Flora, Mississippi, would be there, even Mr. Espy—her mother's *friend*—and his son Darnell. Aunt Ruth said she'd be there, but Glory wasn't counting on it.

Uncle Bobby had so been angry when he got the invitation. He'd called and demanded that Anita's assistant have Glory and Mary call him. Glory sighed. It had taken almost an hour to convince her uncle that she wasn't pregnant. She'd stood with her mother at the pay phone, holding the receiver at a distance while he railed about "this foolishness." In the end, though, he did agree to give Glory away.

After the wedding dress was done, Glory and Anita lunched in the conservatory. "I do wish Mary wasn't so stubborn. There's no reason for her to wear her plain old church clothes to her only daughter's wedding." Anita swirled her iced-tea glass.

"My mother is really set in her ways, and she doesn't like attention," Glory said. "I'm honestly surprised she's coming to the wedding at all."

"And Malcolm still hasn't picked a second groomsman. The programs are being printed this week, and that line is still blank."

"Well, you know Malcolm isn't all in on this wedding either—"

"If he doesn't pick somebody by Wednesday, I'll just ask Deacon Strahan or somebody to stand in. But if he picks another homeless man, I'll just scream and maybe strangle him."

Glory laughed. She'd been surprised when Malcolm asked Dexter to be a groomsman, but the best reaction was Anita's when Malcolm introduced Tutu as his best man. After the shabby, toothless man had kissed Anita's hand, the poor woman took to her bed for two days.

THREE DAYS BEFORE THE wedding, the Mary and Martha Young Ladies' Circle Bible study ended at seven thirty in the evening, and Glory followed Andrea out to her car. The ancient green Nova had seen better days, and Andrea had no interest in keeping it habitable. Glory pushed the fast-food bags from the passenger seat and climbed in.

"Sorry about the mess," Andrea said as she climbed into the driver's seat. "I'm gonna clean this car out one day."

"Girl, you say that every week. If the cops ever decide to search your car—"

"Why you think I keep it this way? I got pulled over, and the cop looked in the back seat and said I was free to go. There's a method to my madness."

Glory just shook her head as the car stopped in front of Herschel's salon. Getting rides from Andrea on Thursday nights left Malcolm free to spend a little time at the mission. "Thanks, Andrea. If I ever get around to driving, I owe you a bunch of rides."

"No problem. It's on my way home. See ya!"

Glory watched her friend drive away then paused in front of the salon. It was dim, and all was quiet. Usually, there would be loud music and sparkling lights, but this time, there was only silence. Glory rang the bell and waited. No answer. She rang the bell again and also tapped on the glass with her key ring. She jumped when the buzzer sounded.

Glory turned the knob and pushed the door open on a dark salon. "Herschel? Is everything okay?" She took a half step into the room. "Herschel, answer me, or I'm calling the police!"

"Surprise!"

The lights came on, blinding Glory, and the sudden scream of Prince music possibly damaged her hearing.

"This is your bachelorette party, Glory-Glory!" Herschel's voice boomed over the music as his clients clapped and cheered, the men all in some version of bridesmaid dresses complete with hats, veils, and gloves and Herschel resplendent in purple silk pants with matching brocade jacket. "I get to be the MOB tonight—that's mother of the bride. Come in, darling! Let's get this party started!"

Glory threw her arms out and laughed, falling into her best friend's embrace. "Thank you, Herschel! You make a perfect MOB!"

Glory enjoyed pink champagne while her *bridesmaids* took turns draping her in white fabric of all sorts, creating their versions of the perfect wedding dress. She stood still while Herschel constructed an elegant multilayered veil dotted with crystal beads and silk flowers. She learned different dances from each of her guests. And she sat in the salon chair like a queen while two *strippers* gave her a manicure and pedicure and a third fed her chocolate-covered strawberries. Occasionally, Glory remembered to say quick prayers for forgiveness, because she was having the time of her life, and the party felt positively sinful.

"Okay, everybody, time for the serious part!" Herschel turned down the music and picked up a small wicker basket. "We're gonna play a little game." He handed the basket to one of the bridesmaids, who fished around and took a seashell from it then passed the basket along. When the basket finally got to Glory, it was empty.

"So, Glory-Glory," Herschel said, "before you got here, we all took a minute and wrote down a little pearl of wisdom on the shells. We're gonna share our pearls with you now. Who's first?"

Jaime, in a light-blue pastel gown, jumped up. "Me! I'm first!"

"Calm down. She ain't goin' nowhere yet!" Herschel waved Jaime off. "Hera, you go first."

The short man in bright pink stood up. "Okay, Glory. Here's my pearl. That man is gon' be whatever you tell him to be. If you call him good and smart and strong, that's what he'll be. But if you call him stupid and weak, he'll be that too. Always speak encouragement to your man." Hera walked across the room and dropped his shell into Glory's basket.

"Okay, how 'bout we just go around the room." Herschel turned his back on Jaime, who was still bouncing in his seat. "Your turn, Stevie."

"Okay." Stevie always tried to soften his deep voice. "Don't get ugly." He held up a hand to quiet the shocked murmurs. "Not in your body, not in your mind, and not in your spirit. That man loves everything about you. Don't let life turn you into somebody he don't recognize anymore."

Glory nodded at Stevie and held out her basket, accepting his pearl of wisdom. Each of the men, in turn, offered her a bit of advice and a blessing for her future.

"Okay, now it's my turn." Jaime was on his feet again. "Listen good, girl. This is real important. Coochie don't keep a man. Don't ask me how I know."

The room broke out in laughter and applause.

"Whatever yours does," Jaime continued, "I promise you it's a hundred others that do it better. What keeps a man is respect—respect for him and respect for yourself. If that mean you hafta tell him off sometimes, do it. Sometimes you hafta let him do stupid stuff too. But respect is the key. R-E-S-P-E-C-T..." Jaime danced across the room and dropped his shell into Glory's basket.

"And now it's my turn." Herschel dabbed at his eyes. "You know I love you like my own, right?"

Glory nodded, feeling herself tearing up watching Herschel get emotional.

"And I'll do anything for you, and all I want is for you to be happy."

Glory nodded again.

"As you continue to change and grow into the brilliant, beautiful, independent woman I know you're gonna be... don't let me hafta take my wig off over no mess, okay? Aha ha ha ha!"

Glory smiled and laughed through tears, but she knew her friend was serious.

The party continued until nearly eleven o'clock, when Herschel drove Glory to the Porters', where, much to Malcolm's dismay, she would be staying until the wedding.

"JILL, YOU CAN STOP crying now."

"I'm not crying." Jill sobbed, wiping her eyes with the back of her hand.

Glory looked at her favorite cousin and rolled her eyes. "Well, you're doing a great impression of crying. Geez! It's no big deal."

"No big deal—are you kidding me?" Jill sniffed loudly and wiped her nose. "My cousin baby is getting married tomorrow!"

"Is she gonna do this all night?" Christy asked. "This is gonna be a pretty sad pajama party. Tee, don't you dare start singing about parties and crying!"

Right on cue, Tressa started humming, and Christy just shook her head.

"So anyway, let's play." Glory placed a deck of cards on the coffee table. She spread the deck out and pushed the pile around.

"Um, Glory?" Tressa asked. "What are you doing?"

"This is the only way I can shuffle." Glory laughed. "I never learned how to do it the other way."

Christy looked at Jillian. "You never taught this girl how to shuffle cards?"

"It never came up." Jillian shrugged. "She didn't do much card playin' at Bigma's house."

Christy collected the cards and expertly shuffled them then set the deck in front of Glory. "That's how you do it. Now cut. That means take the top half and put it on the bottom."

Glory rolled her eyes at her friend and cut the deck. "So, I learned this game from the boy I met on the train." She pushed the deck to the center of the table. "Everybody draws a card and puts it faceup on the table. High card is the winner and gets to ask the loser any question they want. Loser picks another card, cuts the number in half, and has to answer for that many minutes."

"You mean like truth or dare but with no dares?" Jillian drew a card, and the other girls followed.

As the girls laid their cards on the table, Christy slammed down her jack. "Ha! I win, so what do I get to do?"

"You get to ask Jillian a hard question." Tressa opened another wine cooler. "Something good."

"Oh my God," Jillian groaned. "Not a—"

"Sex question!" Christy shouted. "So, Jillian, my new *play cousin*, tell us about your first time."

Jillian looked around at the expectant girls and drew a card. "Okay, five. That means I hafta—"

"Give us all the juicy details in two and a half minutes." Glory giggled. "Tell everybody the whole sordid tale."

Jillian sighed and rolled her eyes at Glory. "Fine. Okay... well... I was seventeen, and it was with a boy named Chuckie, and we did it in the back of his father's van. That's really all there is to tell."

"Nope," said Christy. "That wasn't even twenty seconds. You hafta go the full two and a half minutes."

"Yeah," Glory said. "Like, where was the van parked?"

"I don't like you right now, Cousin Baby. Not one bit." Jillian opened another wine cooler and took a long swallow.

"Yeah, right." Glory laughed. "You love me... and you're stalling!"

Jillian sighed again. "Okay, it was in a restaurant parking lot... and the restaurant was open... and the parking lot was full... and people said the van was rocking, but that's not true 'cause we didn't even do it right... if you know what I mean."

Glory, Tressa, and Christy all fell back howling with laughter.

Tressa was the first to catch her breath. "What do you mean you 'didn't do it right'?"

"Well." Jillian cleared her throat. "There was a lotta humpin' and bumpin' but no actual... you know..." She made a gesture with her fingers, sending the girls into another fit of laughter.

"Does that count?" Christy asked. "Humpin' and bumpin'? What, he was lost?"

Jillian laughed. "Yeah, he was lost and generally inept. But a few days later, we got it right. And trust me, it was no *big* deal."

With more screams of laughter, the girls continued their party of snacks and wine coolers, sharing stories of Glory's two times with JT in the back room of the salon and Christy's adventure in a closet at school. Even sweet, innocent Tressa told about the guy she met at the grocery store. Glory and her "sisters" talked and laughed until the sun started peeking over the horizon of Lake Michigan.

At dawn, Glory knelt at a bedroom window looking out over the lakefront and said a prayer. She prayed for forgiveness for lying to everybody about the timing of the wedding. She prayed for forgiveness for taking birth control pills and deceiving Malcolm. She prayed that she could be *the good wife* and that her thoughts of JT would somehow go away.

AT EIGHT THIRTY IN the morning on the second Saturday in October, Glory stood still while her mother-in-law fussed over her perfectly adjusted wedding dress. The layers of satin and chiffon combined with the tight bodice and puffy sleeves, Glory knew she looked like a fairy princess, but she'd rather have gone for something simple.

"Well, Precious," Anita said. "I'm gonna go wait in the narthex and give you and Mary time to chat." She air-kissed both of Glory's cheeks and tiptoed out of the Robinson Room.

Mary shook her head. "That woman is just too much." That was the closest thing to a real insult Mary Bishop would utter. As she adjusted the flowers in Glory's hair, she started humming a tune Glory remembered from Sunday school when she was a little girl.

"Wow, Mama," Glory said, "I haven't heard you hum that in a long time."

"Well, baby, I guess I'm just extra happy and extra thankful today. The Lord blessed you with a good godly husband, and now the whole church is gon' know. Are you happy, baby?"

Glory stepped back from her mother and twirled around. She couldn't say she was happy, because the wedding was just for show, but her mother's expectant look stopped Glory from telling the whole truth. "Of course, Ma. I've been married to Malcolm for five months, and everything is awesome."

"I knew you would be happy, baby." Mary clapped her hands. "After you walk down that aisle, the whole world is gonna know."

Glory hugged herself and moved slowly around the room. "I just never thought I'd be walking down the aisle to Malcolm."

"You not still thinkin' about that boy you was waiting for, are you? Ain't you glad you didn't waste yo' life waiting on him? Wouldn'ta been nothin' but heartache and misery."

"Mama." Glory sighed. "JT is out of my life. He's nobody to me. I'm married to Malcolm, and I have a good life." Glory took a deep breath and smiled at her mother. She really did have a good life with Malcolm, and they rarely argued, and she'd gotten used to the intimacy part, even if it wasn't all that much fun.

"Well." Mary smoothed her daughter's veil. "I'm just glad you didn't see no letters from that boy. Who knows what he wrote? Mighta turned yo' head or anything."

"Well, there's nothing to care about now—"

"Now, ain't you glad I threw 'em all away?"

"Wait. Threw what away?" Glory looked at her mother's self-satisfied face.

"Them letters. That's what we talkin' 'bout, right? He musta sent one every day for six months. Some days I was scared I mighta missed one..." Mary's voice trailed off as she moved around Glory, adjusting her veil.

Glory spun around and stared at her mother. "You did what? You threw away my letters from JT?" She looked around for the nearest chair to steady herself.

"Now, don't go gettin' all loud, baby. You said you happy with Malcolm, right?"

Glory turned away from Mary and held her head back, looking up at the ornate ceiling. She could feel tears burning behind her eyes and nose. "Mama, why did you do that?" she asked, her voice a raspy croak.

"You know I did it to protect you." Mary blew off her daughter's anger. "That boy woulda caused you nothin' but heartache. Nothin' but sin and pain, and you know it."

Glory closed her eyes, and try as she might, she couldn't keep tears from escaping. She felt a scream welling up from her gut, and she pressed a hand over her mouth, letting the scream out as a moan.

"Now, don't you go gettin' all funny actin', now," Mary said. "You know he wasn't really comin' back f' you no way. Boys just leave—"

"JT is different!" Glory snapped through clenched teeth. "If he wrote to me every day, you know that!" She snatched away from her mother. "Why do you need to control my life?" she wailed. "Why?" Glory didn't really want to hear her mother's answers. She didn't care that her makeup was ruined. "You made me marry Malcolm, knowing JT was waiting for me."

"But you love Malcolm. He's your husband, and he saved you, and he—"

"I wanted JT!"

"Baby, calm down. It's almost time for the wedding, and you messed your face all up—"

"You messed my life all up!" Glory hissed.

Mary stepped back and drew herself up to her full height. "Malcolm saved yo' life, and I saved yo' soul. And you not gon' stand here and talk to me like one of yo' little friends, you ungrateful, uppity... I wish I had the cord right now 'cause you got demons all up in you!"

"Wha's all 'a commotion in here?" Uncle Bobby, looking quite dapper in his gray tuxedo, came into the room. "They 'bout to seat the fancy lady, then it's your turn, Mary." He offered Glory his elbow. "Ready to take this walk, missy?"

Mary spoke up. "She certainly is. She's just a little emotional." She placed a hand on Glory's shoulder, and Glory shrugged her off. "I'm goin' to get in place." She squeezed Glory's shoulder again. "I know you gon' have a blessed life, baby."

Watching her mother leave the room, Glory choked back a sob. Her wedding day was supposed to be the happiest day of her life, but there she stood, feeling like her whole world had just exploded.

"Ya know, missy," Uncle Bobby whispered, "if you wanna split, the car is right out that door. Ain't nobody got to see. We could be halfway to Flora fo' anybody knows we gone."

If she weren't already married to Malcolm, she wondered if she would have called off the wedding. *Would I hop in Uncle Bobby's car and take off? Would I leave Malcolm? If I'd gotten those letters, would there even be a Malcolm?*

"You just say the word, and we gone." He poked her cheek, and she smiled a little for him, but Glory's insides roiled and churned so badly that she imagined swallowing knives might be less uncomfortable.

But she couldn't leave. She looked down at her bracelets and slipped a finger into the little space between the polished gold and her wrist. The outside was cold, but the side touching her skin felt warm. She'd had them on for almost a year, and there was no real way to get them off without Malcolm's consent. If she'd found out about the letters before May, she wondered if Malcolm would have let her go. *Would I have dared to ask? Would I have been prepared to leave home and go to JT?* Because that was what she would have had to do to get free from her mother. But now she was already married. She was Malcolm's beloved. He would fight for her and die for her and kill for her. And she was already married to him. This wedding was just a show.

Glory took her uncle's arm. "Let's get this show on the road." She sighed. *I'm sorry, JT.*

Glory and Uncle Bobby arrived in the narthex just after Lynette and Jermichael finished singing "Ebb Tide." New music began, and ushers came out to get Anita and then Mary. Glory exchanged glances with her best friends and her favorite cousin and didn't say a word when Christy rushed to her, pulled a compact out of nowhere, and touched up Glory's makeup. The door opened again, and Tressa, Christy, and Jillian filed into the sanctuary.

"Still got time to split," Uncle Bobby joked.

If only you knew. Glory shook her head and took a deep breath. Then the "Wedding March" started, and the doors opened, and Glory prayed that her tears looked like tears of joy. She laughed a little, remembering how she thought wedding ladies were crybabies. *That's good. Keep smiling.*

"Seriously," Uncle Bobby mumbled. "Squeeze my arm three times if you wanna split. I can fake a heart attack right here."

Glory looked to the front of the church. Malcolm stood there in his gray tuxedo, smiling his church smile. The uptight preacher's smile. The cold, serious smile. She smiled at him and shrugged. He appeared to warm up a little and mouthed, "Hi, Glory."

Glory mouthed the greeting back and forced down another sob. This man loved her, and she loved him, but marrying him was all wrong. She should be walking up the aisle to stand with JT, not Malcolm. Passing the front pew, she couldn't look at her mother, sitting there all proud like she had done a great thing.

"Last chance," Uncle Bobby whispered, kissing her cheek.

Glory stepped up to the altar and took Malcolm's hand. She closed her eyes. If this were a movie, she'd open them and see JT. She opened her eyes and looked into Malcolm's. She could see in the intensity of his gaze how much he loved her. And she loved him, but she wished he was JT.

The vows went quickly, and Glory barely kept from crying through the ceremony. Afterward, in the Robinson Room for coffee and pastries, Glory and Malcolm stood greeting the fifty or so guests who had been invited to the ceremony. Glory's grandmother, Bigma, hugged Glory and patted Malcolm's hand. "You look so pretty, Baby Girl."

Glory's aunt Martha, in flowing red and gold silk, chided herself for almost outshining the bride. Nobody agreed with her.

"Well, we did it," Malcolm whispered to Glory as the receiving line died down. "One more party, and then we're done. This wasn't so bad, was it?"

"Nah, it was okay." Glory wouldn't say she felt good, but her misery had lifted a bit. This was her life, and finding out about the letters changed nothing. "I'm just tired, probably from last night."

"Hmph... all that sniffling, I almost thought you changed your mind." He squeezed her hand and chuckled. "Not that it would matter if you did."

"Congratulations, Malcolm."

Glory looked up.

"I wish you all the best." Cheryl spoke to Malcolm like Glory wasn't even there.

Glory looked at the older woman. Her eye makeup was smeared, and she looked haggard, like she hadn't slept in days. Cheryl gave Malcolm a polite hug and walked away again, not acknowledging Glory at all.

"It's all right," Malcolm said. "She's still upset."

"I noticed." Glory kept her other comments to herself. She didn't want to sound like she was gloating.

It was nearing nine thirty in the morning when the "newlyweds" greeted their last guest and ran out in a hail of wildflower seeds. They drove off in Malcolm's brown Cadillac and headed toward Lake Shore Drive.

Malcolm reached across the seat and laid his hand on Glory's. "What was with all the tears? We've been married for five months... it's not like this was a *real* wedding."

Glory pulled down the visor and looked at the mirror. Her eye makeup was blackish circles around her eyes and left streaks down her cheeks. She pulled out her powder compact and touched up as best she could.

"I don't know why I'm so weepy." She tried to sound nonchalant. "I guess this is a more emotional day than I thought it would be. You looked pretty intense up there too."

Malcolm laughed a little. "I was shocked at your dress. Don't get me wrong, you look glorious... I just don't like people seeing you in all your *glory*."

"Well, you're gonna hate the reception suit. My glory is gonna be out there for all the world to see."

Malcolm sighed and shook his head.

"Well... okay," Glory continued, glad for something else to think about, "I guess it's not really that bad, but I just don't like it. I can't wait till this reception brunch is over."

"I'll reserve judgment until I see it."

Glory closed her eyes and laid her head back on the seat. That day was supposed to be fun, but it was turning out to be the worst day of her life. She twisted a bracelet on her left wrist—the bracelet that wasn't supposed to be there. *Why didn't I wait for JT? Why didn't I keep the faith?*

She thought about the pearl earrings and the hallway outside her apartment littered with Barbie shoes this past Christmas. He had left a message that he was coming back. *Why couldn't I have waited?* As the car turned onto Michigan Avenue, Glory turned her thoughts to other things lest she start crying again.

CHAPTER 18
November 1984

Glory sat in the front row, her usual seat for Thursday-night church services at the South Gardens Mission. Malcolm's message that night was about Pentecost and Jesus leaving and reassuring the disciples and sending the Holy Ghost. Glory waited for him to announce that this cold November night would be his last night working at the mission, but he never did. After service, he did as he always did—hugged a few people, shook a few hands, and turned out the chapel lights after the last congregants left.

He'd already packed up his office, so they went there to pick up the two boxes of his personal stuff. Glory followed him silently through the halls of the mission to the door that said Bro. Malcolm Porter. He slid the nameplate out of the holder, entered the office, and dropped it into one of the boxes on his desk... what used to be his desk.

Glory took a seat on the couch and watched him walk around behind the desk and sit down. "You know," Malcolm said, "Dad says the church saved my life, and I owe them, and he's right—they did, and I do. But this mission saved my soul. I woulda been dead a long time ago if this place didn't take me in... if Tutu didn't stop me from jumpin' that day... if people didn't need to hear what I had to say. You understand? I'd be dead. Long gone. Nothing."

Glory blinked slowly and nodded but didn't say anything. What could she say? He was right.

"Why is he making me do this? Why does he need to control my life?" Malcolm asked, but Glory knew he wasn't asking for an answer. "Why can't I work at the church and still have the mission? What's wrong with what I do here? There's more needy souls here than at that church!" He slammed his fist on the desk. Glory jumped.

Malcolm stared into space, a tear slipping down his cheek. He angrily wiped it away. She wanted to comfort him, say something soothing, but no words came to mind. She got up from the couch, walked around the desk, and held her hands out to her husband.

Malcolm stood and took her in his arms. His kiss was hard and angry. Glory kissed him back slowly, trying to absorb his anger and perhaps quell his ire, but Malcolm was not so easily calmed, and the kiss grew harder and deeper. "I want you right now," he said, his voice low and husky.

Glory kissed him again. "As soon as we get home, we can undress in the elevator," she whispered.

"No. Right now." He spun her around and bent her over the desk.

Glory tried to stand upright, but Malcolm kept one hand on her back, holding her in place. "Malcolm, no!" she protested. "Not here. Not like this. You're just mad right now, and this won't make you feel better!" Glory heard the jingle of his belt buckle and knew her protest would go unheeded, and when he lifted the back of her skirt, she groaned at his rough entry.

Her husband was angry. He was angry, and Glory knew this—sex—wasn't about love or even lust. This was the comfort Malcolm needed, his version of crying on her shoulder. She remained still while he worked out his anger, and she prayed that he would finish soon and that no one would knock on the door.

Malcolm was silent on the ride back home, and Glory only briefly wondered how many other women at the mission had bent over that desk in the past. She didn't know how she felt about what had just happened. She sat twisting the bracelets on her left wrist, reminding herself that she was Malcolm's beloved, and that even in anger, his desire was toward her.

IT WAS NEARLY TEN O'CLOCK the following Wednesday morning, and Glory had already spoken to Quentin in his dorm at MIT and Jillian down in Jackson, Mississippi. She slowly turned in circles, staring at her spotless kitchen. The dishwasher hummed softly, loaded with the morning's breakfast dishes, the self-cleaning oven was locked in a cleaning cycle, and the kitchen linoleum gleamed with a fresh layer of wax. In the dining room, she flicked invisible dust from the back of a perfectly dust-free chair. She'd completed every possible chore, and looking around the immaculate apartment, Glory was just plain bored.

She'd promised Malcolm that she wouldn't spend all day, every day at the salon, but for the third day in a row, Glory bundled herself up and walked the three blocks to Herschel's. The late-November winds whipped her hair around her face, and Glory kept her head down, pushing back against the wind. Inside the salon, she was greeted by the scents of the S. H. Hershey holiday products.

She made her way through the purple beaded curtain to the door marked Employees Only. Inside the back rooms that served as the lounge, Herschel's lab, and kitchen, Glory found her friend in his usual spot, standing at the stove, stirring a giant pot of something that smelled delicious but would most certainly be inedible. She greeted him while she hung up her coat.

"Glory-Glory." Herschel laughed. "This is not how you avoid spending every day here. Some days, you hafta go somewhere else or even just stay home."

Glory hugged her friend. "I'm just gonna be here a little while, then I'm going to hang out with Miss Anita. She's been bugging me about her offer to go to DePaul. Malcolm is against it, but I'm so bored I'm losin' my mind. Do you know I went to the liquor store and bought wine cooler when I left here yesterday?"

"Oh, you shameless hussy, you!" Herschel laughed again. "Next, you'll be hangin' off a bar stool, drinkin' brown liquor. Aha ha ha ha!"

Glory took a seat at the table in front of stacks of boxes, piles of tubes, and a collection of shiny silky drawstring bags. "Have you decided on the new scent yet?" She picked up a bar of soap and sniffed it. "You know, Herschel, I still can't get over these. Who woulda thought Southern greens would work as a soap for men?"

"Darling, all I did was think of how frisky holiday cooking made people. My daddy use'ta slap my mama's butt every time she bent over to check the turkey. He did it so much I thought she was doin' it wrong 'cause she kept gettin' spanked! Aha ha ha ha!"

Glory smelled the soap again. "How would macaroni and cheese smell?"

"Oh no! Cheese smells like sour milk. I'm not putting my name on that. But turkey and dressin' might work. A bit of sage and other herbs and a touch of wood and leather. Glory-Glory, I think that's the new scent! As soon as I finish filling these lotion bottles, Imma get started."

Glory started filling the bags with lotion tubes and soap bars, occasionally sniffing a bar and laughing to herself. The pound cake scent was her favorite, but her mother liked the peach cobbler scent, and Glory was still embarrassed by her aunt and uncle's giggly behavior with the Sweet Potato Pie and Southern Greens lotions. She shook her head and laughed a little.

"So," Herschel said, "I meant to ask you this yesterday, but did you figure out how to contact JT? Well, I'm guessin' you didn't, since you didn't mention it."

"No, I can't find anybody who has an address, and I really can't ask anybody at church now. And his mother stopped coming to church after Trina told that lie last year." Glory sighed. "And what would I say to him anyway? 'Sorry you didn't hear from me, but I'm married now, even though I promised to wait and marry you'?"

"Sweetie, you don't hafta stay married to Malcolm if you really still love JT—"

"No!" Glory snapped then lowered her voice. "I can't just divorce somebody 'cause I changed my mind—"

"Oh, honey, yes you can! It'll take some time, but you can do it."

Glory looked down at her wrists. Malcolm would never consider a divorce, and as much as she'd loved JT, Glory wasn't sure she wanted one. "I'm not gettin' a divorce. I'm sure JT moved on, and I'm gonna do the same thing."

"Well, darling," Herschel said, "you know I just want you to be happy, and you deserve a husband that *you* love as much as he loves you."

"I know, Herschel. I do love Malcolm. And I was a child with JT. We had all these dreams... but nothing was real... we were kids. Malcolm is a real grown man, and he's gonna make a good life for us."

"You keep telling yourself that if that's what it takes. We'll see when JT comes back. You know, he's gonna be a real grown man too."

"Isn't it time to pour that lotion?" Glory asked. She loved her husband, and the subject was closed.

"Yeah, it is." Herschel shook his head. "Start handin' me those bottles."

"WHERE YOU BEEN, WOMAN?"

Glory paused in the foyer and held up a shopping bag in each hand. "Hanging out with your mother. These are school clothes for January."

Malcolm raised an eyebrow. "School clothes?"

Glory walked into the living room and dropped the bags on the couch. "Yeah, I decided to take your mother's offer and go to De-Paul. It's the best chance at a university, and I—"

"I thought we discussed this." His voice sounded tight as he opened and closed his fists. "She's trying to control you, and you're just gonna let her?"

"Malcolm." Glory shook her head and went to hang up her coat. "She's not gonna control me. I'm a grown woman, and I make my own decisions. I'm just accepting her offer for school." At the sound of a slamming door, Glory turned around. Malcolm had walked away while she was talking.

Glory whipped up a simple chicken-and-noodle dish for dinner and sat beside Malcolm in the den. His favorite movie, *Buckaroo Banzai,* was playing in the VCR, and a tall glass of his favorite mix of strawberry and lemon Kool-Aid sat on the TV tray in front of him. He hadn't spoken to Glory in the past hour.

"So, how's dinner?" Glory asked.

"Fine."

"You want some more?"

"No."

Glory looked over at her husband. Though he faced the TV, he wasn't watching the movie. "Malcolm, I'm sorry." Glory sighed. "I'll tell your mother I changed my mind."

"Don't." He kept facing the TV.

"But if it upsets you this much, it's not worth it—"

"I'll get over it. She pulled strings to keep you outta Chicago schools. Now she's pulling strings to get you in. I just don't want her controlling you—"

"Malcolm, she won't. She wants me to major in all of these foreign languages, but I'm gonna make my own choice." Glory stood up from the couch to clear their dinner dishes. "She can't make me do anything I don't wanna do. I know her tricks now."

"Not all of 'em." Malcolm sipped his drink. "She's gonna start threatening to cancel your tuition checks if you don't do things her way."

Glory smiled. "That's why I'm applying for every scholarship I can. I might not get a full ride, but I'll get lots of little scholarships to keep me in school with or without her." She headed out of the den. "You want dessert?"

"Peach cobbler?"

"Yup."

Malcolm smiled a little. "Yeah, with ice cream."

Glory headed to the kitchen, shaking her head, but Malcolm was right to be concerned. Glory had given in about her beloved gold coat. One of those shopping bags contained a purple swing coat and pink accessories. She'd wear the purple coat to school and church, but she'd wear her favorite gift from Herschel everywhere else. She would take all her classes on two days a week. That way, Malcolm could drop her off, since he still wouldn't let her take the bus anywhere. Glory shook her head again. *Talk about controlling.*

Back in the den, Glory handed Malcolm his dessert. He had restarted the movie. "Glory, I'm not mad at you. It's not cool that you went against something I thought we settled, but I'm not mad. Just don't be goin' behind my back like that. That's the kinda stuff Mother does to Dad. She probably told you she would handle me, didn't she?"

Glory nodded.

"Well, she can't. We're not gonna play her game. If she causes trouble, we'll find another school and get financial aid—"

"Malcolm." Glory sat down beside him, her hand on his thigh. "She's not trying to separate us anymore, and this is DePaul. It's not like I'm going away or anything."

Malcolm stared into his peach cobbler. "You don't know what it's like to have people trying to control your life like this."

Glory looked down at her wrists. She didn't really love the gold bracelets anymore. Even though she'd only had them since last Christmas, they'd gone from feeling like a security-blanket symbol of Malcolm's love and protection to feeling like a symbol of his control.

"Malcolm, we're gonna be fine." Glory sighed. "And nobody is gonna control anybody, okay?"

Malcolm dug into his peach cobbler. "This is really good. I love your peach cobbler."

That meant the subject was closed. Glory shook her head and went to her library to curl up with a good book for a while.

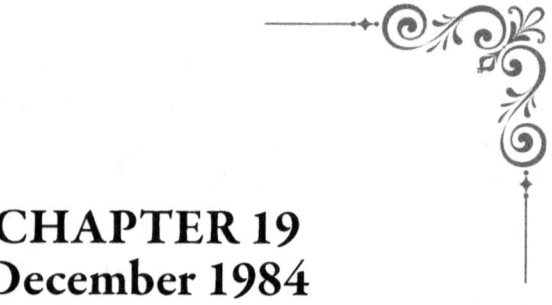

CHAPTER 19
December 1984

Glory tried to get comfortable in the tight, narrow seat. She pressed herself as close to the window as she could. Her mother sat squeezed in beside her, and Malcolm took the aisle seat. The previous Christmas, she and her mother had taken a luxurious overnight train trip from Chicago to Canton, Mississippi, and then a limo ride on to Flora. This year, because Malcolm had to preach on Christmas Eve, they took an airplane, leaving before dawn on Christmas day, and had to fly coach. Glory had taken many flights with Anita, always first-class, but this coach flight... though it was only ninety minutes, Glory would honestly rather have taken the overnight train trip than be this uncomfortable. She laughed a little at herself. She had definitely become spoiled in her travels with Anita.

Shortly after the captain turned off the seatbelt and no-smoking signs, the stewardesses came up the aisle with breakfast. The mushroom-and-cheese omelet and dinner roll wasn't what Glory was used to, but it tasted better than it looked. She tried to ignore her mother carefully picking the mushrooms out of the omelet.

"Why they cain't just serve plain ol' eggs? All this mess in 'em... things taste just like dirt," Mary complained.

"'Cause most people like omelets," Glory said. "You really should try it, Ma."

"Hmph." Mary snorted. "All this fancy mess..." Her complaining trailed off as she dug into her breakfast. Later, when the stewardess came down the aisle with coffee and hot towels, Glory tried to hide her face when her mother asked for a cup of hot water and then pulled a can of sage from her purse.

In the Jackson, Mississippi, airport, Glory and Mary hung back while Malcolm found a redcap to help with luggage. Stepping out into the cool December weather, which was still much warmer than Chicago, Glory spotted a familiar limo and elbowed her mother as a nicely dressed gentleman with a carefully trimmed silver beard and mustache approached them. Mary giggled and elbowed her daughter back.

"Merry Christmas, ladies," the man said.

"Merry Christmas, Mr. Espy." Glory shook his hand.

"Merry Christmas, Lee." Mary offered her hand, but Lee Espy pulled her into a hug and gave her a big kiss on the cheek.

Laughing, Mary squealed and waved him off. "Now, you know that ain't how Christian folk do!"

"Merry Christmas, Lee," Malcolm said. Glory often forgot that Malcolm was ten years older than she, and hearing him refer to Mr. Espy as Lee sounded strange to her. He shook Mr. Espy's hand and patted him on the shoulder. "Early-morning flights are the worst. Crowded, noisy, and don't get me started on the food."

"I'll be sure not to take an early flight when I come visit Ms. Mary this summer," Mr. Espy joked.

Mary giggled and swatted his arm. "I didn't say yes yet."

The drive from Jackson to Flora was uneventful, with Malcolm sharing the front seat with Mr. Espy's son Darnell, who drove the long black limo.

The streets of Flora, Mississippi, were just as gray as always. The town hadn't changed in years, and as they drove down the dusty road to Bigma's house, Glory found herself getting nervous about

Malcolm meeting her extended family. When they pulled into the front yard of the giant ramshackle house, Glory could see her Aunt Ruth on the front porch in Bigma's rocker, smoking what was probably not a cigarette.

"Look at that ol' heathen," Mary grumbled. "Smokin' that stuff on Christmas day."

"Aw, Mary, let her celebrate how she sees fit." Lee patted Mary's hand. "Tha's her business... 'tween her and the Lord."

Inside the house, Glory shook her head at the giant box just like the one Malcolm had sent the previous Christmas. They stowed their luggage in the extra bedroom.

"Well?" Glory said. "This is Bigma's house. What do you think?"

Malcolm pulled her into his arms for a long kiss. "I think this is exactly how I pictured your grandmother's house would be, right down to those homemade quilts."

"Well, they're not homemade." Glory laughed. "Aunt Ellie finds them at the thrift stores. Just like the pictures in here. She calls it 'instant ancestry.' Pretending like we have a long family history."

"What?" Malcolm looked around the bedroom with its flowered curtains and lampshades and throw pillows. "So this is all fake?"

Glory laughed. "Not fake... just not *my* family history. The Johnson-family history is in the living room and dining room on the walls. This is just Aunt Ellie's collection of thrift-store stuff."

Malcolm shook his head and pulled Glory in for another kiss.

"Not right now." Glory giggled. "They're waiting on us to open presents. What are they gonna think if we take too long?"

"They'll think we're newlyweds. They know we're in here making out." Malcolm entwined his fingers in the back of Glory's hair. "You're my beloved, and I want a real good kiss before we go out there." His eyes crinkled in a smile. "Better hurry, Mrs. Porter."

"Hey, you two!"

Glory jumped at the sound of Jillian yelling and pounding on the door.

"Bigma is gon' cut a switch if y'all don't get out here," Jillian yelled and pounded again. "Hurry up!"

Glory kissed Malcolm good and hard then pulled away and opened the door before he could stop her.

"'Bout time," Jillian said, heading into the living room.

"I think Supergirl is just jealous," Glory whispered as loudly as she could.

In the wood-paneled living room, Malcolm took a seat on the couch with Mary and Aunt Ruth. Uncle Bobby sat in the big chair with Aunt Ellie curled on his lap. Bigma sat in her rocker, and Glory took her traditional spot on the floor with Jillian.

"Let's get on with it." Uncle Bobby yawned. "I got meat on the grills. Folks be here in a little while."

"Dad, we've got four hours." Jillian stood up to pull the tape on the giant box. "This is for you, Bigma. Guess who it's from!"

"Is it from a nice young preacher who just married our Baby Girl?" Bigma asked.

"You got me." Malcolm laughed. "But I'm not gonna clutter your whole house up this year. This is the only box this time."

Bigma nodded thanks while Glory and Jillian lifted a giant Swiss Imports gift basket from the box. Uncle Bobby shook his head but said nothing. The Johnson living room was filled with love and laughter as gifts were passed around—except, of course, when Mary opened a box with a red negligee from Ruth, and Ruth opened a box with yet another Bible from Mary. Glory passed out the gifts from Herschel's, and Ellie smeared some of the new Turkey and Dressing scent on Uncle Bobby's neck and started giggling. "Oh my, my, my—"

"Y'all, please don't start," Jillian begged her parents. "My stomach can't take it."

AFTER THE GIFTS WERE all opened and the living room cleaned, everybody got busy preparing for the big family feast in a few hours, and Glory gave Malcolm a tour of Bigma's picture wall.

"Your daddy was a big man, huh?" Malcolm said when Glory pointed out his picture. "Maybe it's good I didn't get to meet him. He mighta crushed me."

"My daddy was a gentle giant." Glory sighed. "He wouldn'ta crushed you... maybe." Glory stood looking at the pictures. Her eyes stopped on the image of her daddy shaking hands with an eight-year-old JT.

"Do I know that little kid?" Malcolm asked.

"Yup. It's JT when he was about eight. My daddy said he was either brave or stupid." Glory touched the yellowing photo, careful not to let her finger linger too long on JT. "He told my daddy he was married to me."

"Oh, really?" Malcolm laughed. "If I remember right, I think that kid was brave *and* stupid."

Glory heard the smile in Malcolm's voice and looked up at him. She didn't like hearing Malcolm call JT stupid, not even as a joke.

As the house started filling with family and holiday guests, Glory watched her husband slip into church mode and work the rooms. He smiled and shook hands, quoted scripture, and turned down drinks. As the day wore on, Glory eventually made her way out to the back porch. She took a seat on the top step beside Darnell, Mr. Epsy's son. Malcolm stood out in the yard near the grills with Uncle Bobby and some other men. His plaid dress shirt and starched creased jeans only looked slightly out of place. Uncle Bobby had his Bible out, and the other men challenged Malcolm to recite verses. They were duly impressed.

"So that's the preacher who killed for you, huh?" Darnell nudged Glory with his elbow. "You know, I could take 'im, right? He ain't all that tough."

"I told you, he didn't actually kill... he just tried until I stopped him." Glory nudged Darnell back. She still didn't like to talk or even think about the *attack*. "So where's *your* girlfriend at?"

"She at home. I'm goin' to her place after a while. Yup, yo' Cousin Wild Thang missed her chance." Darnell flexed his muscles. "She coulda had all this."

Glory laughed. "Yeah, right. You'll never have a chance with Jillian, *ever*!"

"So, you know my pops wanna keep yo' moms here. Actually, he wants to *keep* her, if you know what I mean."

"Yeah, I know." Glory sighed. "You know she made that 'special' peach cobbler for him this morning soon as we got here. She's not tryin' to get married again, but she really likes your dad. They're so cute together. I wish she would consider it." Glory looked up to see Malcolm walking across the yard toward the house. She waved as he approached.

"What's up, you two?" Malcolm asked.

Glory was surprised to see Malcolm's church smile, the one that didn't reach his eyes. "We're talking about our parents getting together. Didn't you notice my mother smells like peach cobbler today? She's lovin' all the attention from Mr. Espy."

"Yeah, I guess I did." Malcolm laughed. "It's good seeing her happy."

Darnell stood up from the porch. "I'm goin' to get in on that Spades game. I'll talk to you later, *sis*."

Glory looked at Malcolm. His smile was gone. "What's wrong?" she asked.

"Is he still messin' with you? Do I need to talk to Lee again?"

"Malcolm, nooo," Glory said. "We're tryin' to be brother and sister. Besides, he's kinda scared of you."

Malcolm reached out and took Glory's hand. "Good." He sat down on the step beside her. "Your family is really cool, but the Bible grilling is gettin' tired. I wish nobody knew I know the Bible like this."

"Malcolm, it's kinda like a superpower." Glory squeezed her husband's hand. "It's really impressive."

"Yeah, whatever."

IT WAS NEARLY NINE o'clock when the guests were all gone, the leftovers were packed, and the women had finally finished cleaning the kitchen. Mary stood at the sink, drying dishes and smoking a brown-paper cigarette. Ellie put coffee and chicory in the percolator. Jillian nursed a drink. Martha sat sipping herbal tea, and Ruth quietly poured wine into Glory's teacup.

Bigma sat at the head of the kitchen table with a beatific smile. "Y'all don't know how good it is to see all my girls all grown up. Even you, Baby Girl, all married and making a home."

"Yeah, Glory, how's married life?" Jillian asked. "Not that I'm interested or anything... just curious."

"It's okay, I guess." Glory discreetly sipped her wine. "Probably like every other married couple."

"So how's newlywed life?" Ellie giggled. "If you know what I mean..."

"Ma, stop it!" Jill chided her mother. "Some things just ain't your business."

"I'm just askin' in case she needs some tips." Ellie winked at Glory and giggled again.

Glory kept her eyes down and sipped her wine again. "Lovely weather we're having, huh?"

"Oh, I'm sure they're happy," Martha gushed. "Look at her... she's actually *glowing*."

"Dammit, Martha, quit it," Ruth snapped as she added more wine to Glory's teacup. "She's goin' to school next month. She ain't tryin' to be pregnant. Bad enough she got married. She ain't stupid enough to be havin' no babies right now."

"My daughter is the good wife," Mary said. "God is gonna bless them any day now—I'm sure of it."

Glory coughed into her teacup, and Jillian patted her back.

"Well, I have the perfect teas for getting pregnant and a little something to keep your monthly regular. Maybe I'll pass some to Malcolm—"

"Aunt Martha, don't you dare!" Jillian stood up and wobbled a bit. "You want him to trick her into having a baby? Are you crazy?"

"Jillian Simone Ellis, you watch your tone!" Ellie snapped at her daughter. "That's your last drink."

Jillian sat back down, tossed back her drink, and defiantly poured more wine into her cup.

"So, Ma..." Glory took a shot at changing the subject. "What exactly are your intentions with Mr. Espy?"

Mary giggled and blushed. "You stop worryin' 'bout grown folks' business."

"Mama, I am grown folks now, remember?" Glory laughed. Her tactic worked, and her aunts and grandmother began grilling Mary about Lee Espy.

THE DAY AFTER CHRISTMAS, Malcolm hung out in the backyard, helping Uncle Bobby clean up, and Glory and Jillian said tearful goodbyes to Aunt Ruth, a trucker, who had accepted a load headed north. As Ruth's big brown truck pulled out of the yard, the girls hopped into Jillian's little red Chevette and headed to Canton Mall to catch the after-Christmas sales.

"So, Cousin Baby—can I still call you that—how's life? Excited about school?"

"Jill, Malcolm's tryin' to get me pregnant," Glory blurted. "And I didn't get to take my pill yesterday—"

"Holy crap, girl, you can't be doin' that. Missing just one pill could mess you up."

"I know." Glory hid her face in her hands. "And last night, I didn't want to do it—"

"Wait... wait," Jillian interrupted. "Y'all did it in Bigma's house? Really?"

Glory felt a knot tighten in her stomach. "More like, *he* did it. I just laid there, trying to keep quiet."

"Wow," Jillian said. "I don't know what to say. I mean, I'm kinda weirded out, but hey..."

Glory leaned her head back against the seat. The year before, when she'd spent Christmas in Flora, she'd ridden all over with Jillian and hadn't had a care in the world. This year, everything was so different. "Do you know where to get the tea Aunt Martha was talking about... the kind to get my period?

"It's probably stuff that she grows. You know how her garden is. We can stop by her house on the way back."

After the shopping spree and a stop at Aunt Martha's, Glory and Jillian got back to Bigma's with new clothes, and Glory had several brown packets of seeds and herbs. She went straight to the kitchen and made herself a cup of strong ginger tea, imagining she looked like her mother spooning the powder from the tiny can into a cup of hot water. Malcolm asked about the concoction and accepted Glory's explanation that it was her new favorite flavor. He even asked Bigma for a gingerbread recipe Glory could make.

They spent a total of six days in Flora, and on New Year's Eve, they said their goodbyes and headed back to Chicago.

INTERLUDE
JULY 1980

Glory watched the clock and paced from the kitchen to the living room and back again, counting each step. The red apple-shaped clock on the kitchen wall showed 11:40, and JT would arrive in twenty minutes. It had been two weeks since that first real kiss, two weeks of secretly being JT's girlfriend, two weeks of sneaking kisses at church and secret visits while Glory's mother was at work. When JT came to visit, they kept the back door open. Though there was little chance of Mary Bishop coming home early, JT could be gone by the time Mary unlocked the three deadbolts and called for Glory to unlatch the chains.

The doorbell rang, and Glory spoke into the hole in the wall near the door buzzer. "Who is it?"

When JT answered, Glory smiled, her heart skipping a beat. He was early. She couldn't press the buzzer fast enough.

Listening at the heavy wood front door, Glory waited for their secret knock. If there was anybody else in the hallway, JT would walk all the way up to the third-floor apartments, but if the hallway was clear, he'd knock, and Glory would quickly let him in. That day, he had two brown paper bags with him. The smell of her favorite lunch made Glory's mouth water. He handed her the bags and pulled cans of orange and grape pop from his jacket pockets.

"Happy birthday, Miss Glory." He pulled her into his arms, kissing her playfully on the nose. "I brought records. Birthday lunch is in the other bag."

Glory took the lunch bag to the center of the living room and sat down on the woven rug she'd laid out for their picnic. JT went to the stereo and placed a stack of 45s on the spindle. He kept the volume low lest the neighbors hear the worldly music and mention it to her mother.

"So, how does it feel to be fourteen?" JT asked, opening the orange pop and passing it to Glory. "What are you gettin' for your birthday?"

"Well, so far..." Glory took a sip. "I've got a pizza puff, fries, and orange pop."

"Wow," JT joked. "Somebody must love you a lot to get you all that."

"Actually, it's the best birthday I've had in a long time."

When lunch was finished, Glory packed up the garbage and placed it outside the back door, then she and JT played cards, the loser owing the winner a kiss. Soon, they gave up all pretense of card playing and just enjoyed each other. Their kisses started soft and sweet, in time to the beat as Prince sang a slow sexy song, and as the music changed and Glory got that feeling again, she kissed him harder, imagining they were the forbidden lovers in a romance novel, daring to steal a moment together.

JT's hands moved around her waist and under the back of her shirt, his rough hands warm and strong against her bare skin. He stopped and peeled off his jacket and tank top, his dark brown skin moist with sweat. Glory unbuttoned her pink blouse and let it fall from her shoulders like the women in the movies did. As warm as the apartment was, she shivered with goose bumps, blushing under her boyfriend's gaze.

When she went to remove her thin cotton undershirt, JT grabbed her hand. "Wait, um... wait a minute. You don't hafta take that off."

"But you took off yours, and I—"

"I don't want you to take it off." JT reached out with one finger and touched her left breast. "Keep it on."

"Oh." A wave of embarrassment washed over Glory, and she moved to stand up. "I'm sorry, I just thought—"

"No." JT grabbed her hand and pulled her back down to the floor. "I mean, it's okay if you take it off... I just think you look nice with it on." He reached out again and rubbed his palm lightly over the top and side of her right breast. "I like it."

Glory blushed again and shivered at his touch. She wrapped her arms around his neck and drew him down until they lay on the rug, facing each other, pressed together, devouring each other, hungry with the passion of young love. Glory rolled onto her back, and when JT moved on top of her, still kissing in time to the music, she realized that Herschel was right. That feeling, the pressure... it was so intense that all she wanted was for JT to touch her *there*.

Demons of lust and fornication. And JT held her so tight and pressed so hard that Glory understood he was feeling the same thing. "JT?" Glory whispered. "Do you feel funny too?"

JT answered with a deep, hard kiss, moving his body against hers, and Glory knew that with what she was feeling, she was definitely going to hell. *Filthy Jezebel.*

Groaning, his breath coming in short gasps, JT stopped moving, stopped pressing, stopped kissing her. "I gotta go," he said slowly. He stood up and turned his back to Glory then pulled on his tank top and tied his jacket sideways around his waist.

"JT, what's wrong?"

"It's getting late. I don't wanna get you in trouble." He went to the stereo and packed the stack of 45s back in the brown bag, moving quickly, his breathing still kind of funny.

"But—"

JT held a hand out to help Glory to her feet. He bent down and picked up her blouse. "You should put this on." Leaning in, he kissed her on the cheek. "I'll see you later. Bye."

Before Glory could stop him, JT was out the back door. From the porch, Glory watched him jog to the back gate. She felt the same funny feeling in her chest that she always felt watching him leave, the one that made her want to cry. *Is this what love feels like? Could I actually love JT?* That day, they'd gone further than they ever had before. She knew what Herschel meant about that funny feeling now. She'd been prepared to take off her undershirt. *What if JT had let me? How far would we have gone?*

Thinking about going all the way with JT, Glory felt that pressure down there again. She waved at JT's back as he went through the gate, and she whispered a promise to God that they wouldn't go all the way until they were married for real. By the time her mother arrived home from work, Glory had their apartment spotless, cleared of all evidence of JT's visit. She hung her rug over the back porch railing, sadly airing it out to remove the scent of JT's cologne. He wore too much, like all fifteen-year-old boys at church did. She wondered what the boys in high school would smell like.

"Ma, how old were you when you first had a boyfriend?" Glory set paper plates on the kitchen table while her mother unwrapped her special birthday dinner of Harold's chicken with french fries, fried okra, and white bread.

"Hmph!" Mary scoffed. "I was too young—that's how old I was. Fifteen years old, and thought I knew everything. Thought I had outsmarted everybody." She dished out wings and sides to both plates and set the container of mild sauce in front of Glory's plate.

"I ran off and married that boy too. But God showed me the error of my ways." Mary took a seat at her end of the table. "Worst mistake I ever made. Disobedient, lustful, shamed my family. I paid the price of Job for my rebelliousness. I know you ain't thinkin' 'bout no boyfriends, are you?"

"No, ma'am." Glory placed two glasses of her favorite fruit punch on the table and took her seat. "Some girls just talk about it a lot."

"Good. You don't need no boyfriend but Jesus, right!"

"Yes, ma'am. Nobody but Jesus." Glory poured the concoction of ketchup, barbecue, and a bit of hot sauce over her chicken and french fries and dug into her birthday dinner. She ripped apart a few wings, rolled the meat in the slice of white bread, and then dipped the sandwich in the puddle of sauce on her plate. After spending the afternoon with JT and then having her favorite dinner, Glory was sure this was the best birthday she'd had in a long time.

"So, baby, how ya feel now that you're fourteen, finna start high school and all?" Mary kept her wings dry, pulling them apart and twisting the bones loose from the meat until she had a pile of boneless wings on her plate.

"I guess I feel okay." Glory sipped her fruit punch.

"You know you can join the Young Ladies' Circle Bible study at church now. Surround yourself with good, godly young girls. None of that boyfriend mess."

"I guess I can," Glory mused out loud. "And hang out with Mother Porter. She's so elegant. I'm gonna be just like her."

"Child, I know she's first lady and all, but she's vain and prideful, and you should hear how she talks to the pastor. And when her own son was sick, folks say she only went to the hospital a couple of times. No, you *will not* be like her!" Mary picked up her glass and took a long drink.

"But, Ma, she's so smart—"

Mary put her glass down on the table hard enough to get Glory's full attention. "What I say? She worldly. All them fancy clothes and makeup and stuff. She vain and prideful... makin' me mad just talkin' 'bout that woman."

"I don't think she's that bad—"

"You got demons of disrespect and rebellion in you, girl?"

"No, ma'am." Glory answered quickly, opening her eyes wide. "No demons." She pressed her feet to the floor to keep her legs from shaking and wiped her hands on a napkin to hide their trembling. It had been at more than a month since her mother had used the extension cord to purge demons, and Glory would do or say anything to avoid another purging. "I'm not gonna be worldly or prideful."

"Tha's right, baby," Mary said between bites. "You gon' be a godly woman."

"Yes, ma'am... a godly woman."

CHAPTER 20
Spring 1985

Glory Hallelujah Bishop-Porter had changed. Now that her marriage was public, she didn't have to walk past Malcolm in church without speaking, and she could even touch him. She felt older and more accomplished than before. She was more than a high school graduate—she was a wife and second in church only to the first lady. She didn't want to feel proud, but she did.

Not only had she changed on the inside, but people treated her differently too. The Mary and Martha Young Ladies' Circle started avoiding her, but the Eves Women's Auxiliary welcomed her with open arms, and she called them all by their first names, like Sister Joy and Sister Kay. The men in the church called her Mrs. Porter or Sister Porter, and she was tapped to spend every Sunday that Malcolm didn't preach in the church nursery surrounded by babies.

Babies. Malcolm had given up all pretext of using protection. Glory kept a supply of rubbers in their nightstand drawers, but he always *lost* them. They talked about it often enough, and he assured her that he wanted to wait until after she finished college to start their family, but he nevertheless often reminded her that she could be a mother and still go to school.

Though Glory was still forbidden to visit her mother's apartment, Mary Bishop stopped by often, reminding Glory that her job was to be the good wife, and once a month, she'd blame Glory for not being pregnant. "You not takin' them pills, are you?" Mary asked. "I threw away them ones you had, but I know it ain't hard to get some more. Look at me, girl! You bein' a good wife, right?"

With the skill of a practiced liar, Glory would look into her mother's eyes and assure her that she was not *killing her husband's seed,* and Mary would squeeze her daughter's shoulder and assure her that she'd have a baby in God's time.

GLORY'S FIRST FEW WEEKS of classes went fairly easily. She'd decided on a business major so she could learn to do marketing for Herschel's salon products. Life was a bit hectic, though, with Malcolm driving her to school on Mondays and Wednesdays, her working at the salon on the other days, and being Church Lady on Sundays. Glory would never tell anybody, but she didn't enjoy being Church Lady, and sometimes she played sick to avoid church altogether.

At the sound of the front door opening, Glory pulled the covers up to her neck, scooched down in the bed, and glanced at the clock. She'd played hooky from church, and Malcolm was just coming home from first service. From the sound of his footsteps coming down the hall, she could tell he was not in a good mood.

He pushed their bedroom door open a little too hard. "Hey" was all he said. He took off his gray suit jacket and tossed it over a chair then lay on top of the bed covers beside Glory.

Glory looked at her husband staring at the ceiling. She freed one of her arms from the bedclothes and took his hand. "Tell me what happened."

Malcolm sighed and squeezed Glory's hand. "Dad and the deacons are coming to dinner. I told them you were sick, but Dad insisted we hafta meet now."

"Why can't you meet in the church?" Glory thought about Malcolm's favorite pot roast in the Crock-Pot. It was usually enough to have lunch and leftovers for a couple of days, but she wasn't sure it was enough to feed six people.

"'Cause there's an event after service today, and this is kinda off the record. Damage control. The good Reverend Blevins is probably the father of Trina's latest baby. She stood up and announced it during service."

"Wow." Glory looked over at Malcolm. "Do you believe her?"

"Yeah, I do. Everybody does, and Blevins didn't deny it—said, 'No matter who the father is, all babies are a gift from God.' You know how Dad is about scandals, and now he's looking at me funny." He rolled onto his side and placed a hand on Glory's belly. "He actually told me we can't conceive a baby till you're twenty-one. Talkin' 'bout how *unseemly* it looks having ministers impregnating teenage girls."

Glory sat up in bed. "I guess I should put more vegetables in with the pot roast and whip up a dessert—"

"Why does he need to control my life?" Malcolm asked.

Glory looked at her husband.

"Blevins's mess ain't got nothin' to do with me, but my dad still found a way to drag me in it."

"Malcolm, he's not trying to control you. He's trying to protect the church. If I got pregnant, then there would be two ministers with two pregnant teenagers, and people already think we *had* to get married anyway. And I don't think Denise is gonna—"

"Do you know that fool said Trina could live in his house, and Denise Blevins didn't say a word." Malcolm shook his head. "Talk about controlled. She'll do whatever that fool says."

Glory pushed the covers off and got up from the bed. Lying too long beside her husband, especially when he was in a bad mood, usually meant sex, and she didn't have time for that if company was coming.

"Woman, get back in this bed."

"Nope," Glory said. "I've gotta go work on dinner and get dessert on. Then I hafta freshen up. What time are they coming?" Glory slipped on a T-shirt and pulled on a pair of jeans.

"After second service, about four o'clock." Malcolm looked at his wife for a moment. "Don't be wearing that when they get here. Wear something nice." He placed his hands behind his head and closed his eyes. "You know I don't like you in pants."

In the kitchen, Glory whipped up the batter for a peach cobbler then found no canned peaches in the cabinet. With a quick change of plans, she peeled some apples, cooked them down a bit, and a few minutes later, slid an apple cobbler into the oven. Though Malcolm wasn't a fan of cornbread, Glory made some in an iron skillet using a little of the grease from the pot roast. Then she cut up a few more vegetables, simmered them in pot roast gravy, and added them to the Crock-Pot. She looked at the clock. Elder Porter was never late, so if he said four, they'd be there at four. It was three thirty. Just enough time to slip into something less comfortable.

In their bedroom, Malcolm still lay on the bed with his hands behind his head. His eyes were closed, but Glory could tell he wasn't sleep. "Your pants are gonna be really wrinkled," she said. "You should get up. Your dad'll be here in a half hour."

"Woman, don't tell me what I should do. I'll get up when I feel like it."

Glory sighed and changed into a blue denim skirt and left the room.

"DAUGHTER, THAT WAS the best pot roast I've ever had." Elder Riley Porter sat back in his seat and rested his hands on his ample belly. "Malcolm, boy, you better be careful. This lady'll have you as big as me." The men around the dining table all laughed and complimented Glory on her cooking, and when she offered apple cobbler and ice cream, she got an enthusiastic round of yeses.

Glory quickly served dessert then excused herself and retired to the library to study. She wasn't the least bit interested in the church scandal, but from what the pastor and deacons had been saying, Blevins was going to be stripped of all ministerial responsibility and privileges at Lake Shore Christian Fellowship Church. This was the part of church business that Malcolm always said he hated. Being a minister was one thing, but being a manager and dealing with politics always left him in a bad mood at the end of the day.

Glory opened her eyes in the darkened library. She'd fallen asleep on the couch, studying, an open highlighter pen in her hand, and the ink had soaked into the page she was reading. As her eyes adjusted to the near darkness, she could see Malcolm sitting across from her in the wingback chair. She couldn't tell if his eyes were open, but she knew he wasn't sleep. The way the hallway light fell on half his face, he looked sinister.

"Malcolm?" Glory sat up on the couch. "What's going on? What happened?" Glory remained in her seat. She didn't like to approach him when he was in a dark mood, and at that moment, she could just feel how dark his mood was.

"You went to sleep. We had company, and you just went to sleep. I had to stop the meeting to make coffee and serve more dessert."

"Oh, I'm sorry." Glory placed the cap back on the pen and closed her book. "I guess I was more tired than I thought—"

"If school and work," Malcolm said quietly, "are making you so tired that you can't be a decent wife, then they hafta go. Do you understand me?"

Glory stared through the darkness at her husband. *Is he serious?* "Malcolm, you're being unreasonable. It's not like you couldn't—"

"Do you understand me!"

"I'm sorry. Yes, I understand you." Glory stood up from the couch and went to kneel in front of Malcolm's chair. She took his hand in hers. "Now, tell me about the meeting. What happened?"

Malcolm sighed. "Since we don't excommunicate people—I wish we did—all we can do is forgive him if he asks. But who's he gotta ask?" Malcolm growled in frustration. "He sinned against his family and God and I guess his position as outreach minister... so does he hafta apologize to the church? And if we forgive him, does that mean we act like this mess never happened? 'Charity doth not behave itself unseemly, seeketh not her own, is not easily provoked, thinketh no evil. Rejoiceth not in iniquity, but rejoiceth in the truth.' Can we really just forgive and forget?"

Glory closed her eyes and briefly flashed to prom night. She had forgiven Malcolm, but she hadn't forgotten. Over the year and a half of their relationship, Glory had learned how to hold her peace and not provoke him to anger... because she forgave, but she couldn't easily forget. "I don't know. Maybe it'll just blow over. What's gonna happen to the outreach ministry?"

Malcolm ran his fingers through Glory's hair and sighed. "It's *my* job now. Dad thinks I'd be good at it 'cause of my work at the mission." He snorted a mirthless laugh. "So he's got me doin' service on weekends, Bible study on Fridays, shut-in visits in the mornings, and outreach every other minute. He thinks talkin' to a bunch of wayward teenagers at church is the same as working with the real needy people at the mission."

Glory looked up at her husband. "When is your day off? Where's your time for fun? What about life in general?"

Malcolm groaned. "*This* is supposed to be fun. He's trying to remake me in his own image. Dad lives and breathes this church, and that's what he wants me to do too. His *life in general* has always been church, and now he wants my life to be that way. You know, that's why Mother gets away with everything she does. He's always

been too busy to control her, so she just does whatever she wants."
Malcolm rubbed Glory's hair again. "I don't want us to be like
them."

LIFE AT CHURCH WENT on. As winter turned to spring,
Cheryl Cannon stopped coming to church, but she did keep up
her work at the mission. Reverend Blevins still came to church, but
he tried to butt in on the outreach ministry and always brought
new followers with him. And Andre Bradley's vulgar flirtation had
evolved into outright meanness whenever nobody was looking, but
Glory didn't want to tell Malcolm lest he blame her again for at-
tracting the young man's attention.

"You think you hot shit now, huh? Think you gon' be like
Mother Porter, huh?"

"Leave me alone, Andre." Glory tried to walk around her neme-
sis when he approached her outside the Robinson Room before
second service. "It's time for service." She looked around in vain,
hoping somebody was nearby or approaching.

"Act like you was all goody-goody, Miss Innocent and all that.
You ain't nothin' but a stuck-up secret hoe... and now you caught a
old preacher. Next, you gon' be poppin' out babies that prob'ly ain't
gon' be his—"

Glory never imagined herself capable of real violence, but she
lashed out without thinking, and before she knew it, her fingernails
had raised welts on Andre's cheek.

Andre's hand went to his face, and he took a step closer. "Miss
High-and-Mighty. I know all about bitches like you—"

"Andre, if you ever talk to me again, I will scream bloody murder, and Malcolm will kill you. He did it before, and he got away
with it. Don't try me." Glory turned and left for the sanctuary before Andre could respond. She was shaking—whether with rage

or fear, she didn't know. She'd just exaggerated a terrible secret to someone who was turning out to be her archenemy, and she'd lashed out and tried to hurt him out of anger. But Andre Bradley deserved it. He'd been tormenting her since the cotillion. Whatever liking he'd had for her in the past was long gone. Now he was just hateful. *Bless you, Andre.*

Service was the same as usual, but Malcolm's performance—and it was merely a performance—was off. He didn't have his usual energy. The congregation, of course, responded just as they always did, clapping and shouting and getting the Holy Ghost, but Glory could tell he was not feeling it. When they finally left the church, Malcolm was quiet on the elevator ride to the fourth floor.

Inside their apartment, Glory barely had time to turn off the Crock-Pot before Malcolm called her back to their bedroom. Glory sighed. Whenever Malcolm called her back to the bedroom, it usually meant one thing. It was not that Glory didn't enjoy making love with her husband, but lately it had become almost like a chore, his way of blowing off steam, and her job was to just... be there.

IN THEIR SLIGHTLY CHILLY room, Glory lay beneath her husband, sharing his kisses and enjoying his warmth. This was always her favorite part of sex—the afterglow. The issue, whatever it was, had been worked out, and he was happy, loving, and even a bit talkative. Glory was pleased that their lovemaking soothed and energized him.

"Malcolm, I need to go finish dinner." Glory moaned when she felt him stirring again.

"Aww... pleeease," Malcolm begged between kisses. "Just one more ride?" More kisses. "I promise I'll be quick."

"How 'bout instead of quick"—Glory tried to press her legs together—"we have dinner and then we have a really long slow, romantic ride..." Glory groaned. "Malcolm, that's not fair! You're always ignoring me! It's my body, and you always—"

Malcolm grabbed her hair and kissed her so hard she tasted blood. "Listen, woman," he grunted through clenched teeth. "You're my wife, so this is *my* body." He pressed into her and pinched her bottom hard enough for her to cry out. "Just like I'm yours, you... are... mine. Understand?"

"Malcolm, you're being a jerk." Glory pouted.

"But I love you, so it's okay. Now, quiet down, and let me love you."

Glory lay still and received her husband's love, and then, while he slept, she quietly showered and finished preparing their usual Sunday pot roast, cornbread, and an easy boxed cake for dessert. Glory was frosting the cake when Malcolm came up behind her and slipped an arm around her waist. He pushed her hair aside and kissed her neck.

"Woman, I love you so much," he whispered. "So much sometimes it scares me. Don't you ever even *think* about leaving me. I'll go crazy without you."

Though she was still annoyed with him, this was the Malcolm she loved—the passionate, unselfish, open, and honest Malcolm. "I love you, too, Malcolm. I'm not going anywhere..." Glory heard herself and paused. She'd said those same exact words to JT. "Dinner's ready. C'mon, fix your plate."

They sat at the kitchen counter for dinner, and try as she might, Glory couldn't push away thoughts of JT. Growing up together, playing together, his kisses, his touch... she could even imagine his scent. He'd used the same Polo cologne as every boy in the school, but on him, it had smelled manly.

"Hey... what's on your mind?"

Glory had been so lost in thought that she jumped at Malcolm's question. "Nothing, really."

"Uh-uh. There's something going on in that glorious head of yours. Tell me."

She sighed. "Just thinking about old things... childhood and stuff."

"Oh... like what?

Glory thought fast. "Like playing in the haunted hallway. And you living up here, and we never knew."

"Well, to be honest, I had probably moved when you were little. I used to play back there, too, though."

Glory laughed a little. "It was a great place for hide-and-go-seek, and... well, other games."

"Catch a Girl, Kiss a Girl?" Malcolm smiled and winked at Glory.

Glory feigned innocence. "Well, I never!" she huffed.

Malcolm laughed. "Well, I did, every chance I got."

"Okay... maybe a couple of times. Once I gave Andre a fat lip, and he wanted to fight, but JT stepped in. Wow, that was so long ago. I feel so old now."

"Yeah... you're an eighteen-year-old-old lady, huh, Grandma?" Malcolm got up to refill his plate. "Speaking of Andre, did you see him after service? Looks like he lost a fight. His face was scratched up."

"Oh, really?" Glory continued eating.

"Yeah. He said 'a secret hoe' did it. I wanted to punch him in the mouth, but I told him, 'Treat the elder women as mothers, the younger as sisters with all purity.'" Malcolm returned to his seat at the counter. "Is he bothering you at all?"

"I can handle Andre." Glory dug into her dessert.

"That's not what I asked you. Is he bothering you?"

"Malcolm, Andre is nothing and nobody. He's just a stupid boy who—"

Malcolm put down his fork. "Glory. Don't make me ask again." He leaned forward with his elbows on the counter, his fingers steepled.

Glory sighed. "Yes, Malcolm. He's bothering me. But he's not really a problem—"

Malcolm's eyes darkened. "Are you the 'secret hoe' who scratched him today?"

"Malcolm, this is silly—"

"Woman, answer me!"

Glory took a deep breath and got up from the counter. "Yeah, I slapped him... with my fingernails."

Malcolm leaned back in his chair and folded his arms. "Why?"

"He said really nasty things to me. I just snapped." Glory hung her head. "He made me so mad."

"He won't bother you again," Malcolm said.

"Honestly, I don't think he will. I told him if he came near me, I'd scream, and you would kill 'im." Glory laughed a little and looked at Malcolm.

Malcolm wasn't smiling. "He won't bother you again."

"Malcolm, I know you love me," Glory tried to keep the panic out of her voice. She walked around the counter and laid her head on his shoulder "But please don't do anything. He's just a stupid boy, and I can avoid him. He's a jerk—"

"I told you, I will come after anybody who's a jerk to you." Malcolm's voice was cold. "I will always fight for you... even in church. There's nowhere you can go that I won't fight for you."

That night, as Glory said her prayers, she added one for Andre and one for forgiveness for still thinking about JT.

CHAPTER 21
February 1986

M alcolm was changing. It was easy for Glory to brush off at first, but soon his testiness and temper flares were too frequent to ignore. He blamed it on the stress of having to spend more and more time at church and less and less time with Glory or his *hobby* of stopping by the mission every couple of nights. Glory had been able to predict his moods, and as long as she watched her tone and didn't disrupt his routines, he was always gentle and loving. But lately, the slightest things set him off.

"What's this?" Malcolm asked, lifting the Crock-Pot lid and sniffing.

"Leave it closed!" Glory snapped. "You're letting the heat out. It's gumbo."

Malcolm slowly replaced the lid on the pot. "Don't raise your voice at me, woman." He lightly patted her cheek. "You know I don't like that."

Glory took a step back from him, out of his reach. "And you know I hate when you do that." She touched her fingers to her cheek.

"Then watch your mouth, and don't make me hafta do it." Malcolm lifted the lid again and stirred the pot with a wooden spoon before returning utensil to the spoon rest and closing the lid. "You never cooked this before—"

"I was sick of pot roast. We've had it almost every Sunday for over a year. I wanted something different. I made bread and apple pie too."

"I like pot roast," Malcolm said. "And peach cobbler. Why are you tryin' to change things?"

"I'm not trying to change things. I just wanted something different for once."

"We have something different every other night of the week." Malcolm glared at her. "Oh, wait... we have leftovers every other night because school and work take up all your time!"

Glory opened a cabinet and began setting dinner dishes on the counter. She didn't look directly at her husband and didn't interrupt his brewing tirade. The previous Friday's tantrum had left her with a bruise that she'd had to cover with makeup on Sunday morning. Of course, he'd apologized. He even went out and came back with flowers and ice cream. And of course, Glory had forgiven him.

"I'm sorry I made gumbo. I didn't know pot roast was so important to you." Glory laid out silverware. "Your wish is my command," she mumbled. The silverware in her hands went crashing to the floor when she felt her head jerked back by her hair.

"Malcolm! Stop!" Glory's hands went to her hair as her husband pulled harder.

"Woman, don't be mumblin' under your breath at me!"

"Malcolm! Please, this hurts!"

"Don't you..." Malcolm's voice went quiet, and his grip on Glory's hair loosened, then he let go entirely.

Glory turned to face him.

"I'm sorry," Malcolm whispered. He pulled his wife into his arms. "I don't know what's going on with me. Every little thing makes me mad now. You don't deserve this." He pressed his lips to her forehead. "I don't deserve you."

As they sat down to dinner, Malcolm shared the latest behind-the-scenes shenanigans at church. "After Blevins finally left Lake Shore, he had the nerve to ask for a recommendation and severance. Of course, the board laughed in his face. Literally. He came into the meeting with a letter from his 'attorney'"—Malcolm made air quotes—"tryin' to make demands. Dad was real cool about it. He just said, 'It is your misfortune that we must deny your request.' Then he went on with the meeting. Blevins was mad, but he left quietly."

Glory shook her head. "Why would he think he deserved anything after what he did?"

"Well, because he really believes himself. This gumbo is pretty good. Almost as good as Mrs. Beyers's. But yeah, he's sincere in his belief that he's doin' the Lord's work and that by 'anointing' Trina—that's actually what he called it—a great prophet might be born. That guy is a real piece of—"

"Work!" Glory quickly interrupted him—not that she'd ever heard her husband cuss, but he was pretty unpredictable lately. "But what if he really tries to sue or something?"

"He doesn't have a leg to stand on." Malcolm used a piece of bread to sop up the last of the spicy gumbo in his bowl then got up and went for seconds. "Even if we were a regular employer, he got fired for a legitimate reason."

"So... um, Superman," Glory ventured carefully, "I haven't seen Andre in church for a while. Um... what did you do?"

Malcolm leaned back in his chair. "You'll know when they find his body." He winked at Glory.

"Malcolm, that is so not funny. Not even a little bit. Seriously, what did you say or do to him?"

Malcolm laughed a little. "I told him he didn't want me as an enemy... and I told his mother on 'im."

"You told his mother? Really?"

"Yup. And she went all the way upside his head. Thought I was gonna hafta pull her off him. You shoulda seen it."

"Nah," Glory said. "I woulda laughed too loud."

Their earlier tiff forgotten, the couple finished their dinner and retired to the den to watch TV.

AFTER THE GUMBO INCIDENT, Glory never again changed his Sunday dinner, and she made sure to have something on hand that she could make quickly for days she had classes. But that didn't seem to be enough for Malcolm. He was becoming the man he'd been right after he rescued her from the rapist, before he worked full-time at the mission. He was going back to being *old* Malcolm.

Glory would never use the word *abusive*. Malcolm was tired and tense and upset and overworked. Sometimes he got testy, and even when he got angry, it was only a rough squeeze here and a hair tug there. The slaps came only when she stepped way out of line, and they were never very painful.

Malcolm's temper flares were usually on Sundays after the dramas at church. Glory had begun maneuvering herself to be at his side whenever they were there, effectively keeping much of the petty drama away from him. Occasionally, though, like King Solomon, Malcolm was called upon to mediate disputes or minister to a crisis, and Glory might later find herself bearing the brunt of his frustration.

They'd been married almost two years when the first big fight happened. She'd challenged him, and he'd slapped her. Before they got married, Glory had accepted his "love taps," but as his wife, in her own home, their ten-year age difference didn't matter, and she would not be treated like a child. When she tried to move past him, more furious than hurt, Malcolm snatched her back by her arm. Instead of her usual passive silence, Glory pushed him away, which only earned her more blows until she stopped fighting. He left the apartment, and she stood under a cool shower to soothe her bruises.

When Malcolm returned, Glory lay on her side, pretending to sleep, while her husband undressed in the dark and slid into bed behind her, pressing his body against hers, kissing her neck and shoulders like the fight had never happened. When she felt him stirring against her, she sighed. He would not be put off that night. Even after the fight, he still expected his marital due.

"Malcolm," Glory said.

"Yes?" He softly caressed her shoulder and arm.

Glory winced as his hand brushed the bruised spots where he'd gripped her arms. "If you hurt me like this again, I will leave you."

Malcolm chuckled. "And go where? Back to your mother?" He kissed the thick deep scars on her back. "She'll beat you to death for real this time if you leave me. You know that, right?" He pressed a hand against her belly and moved closer.

Glory shuddered as his hand slid lower.

"Or maybe you'll go to Herschel's?" Malcolm whispered. "If I don't know where you are, I'll get worried and send the police looking for you. If they looked at Herschel's, what would they find? A lot of prescription meds and needles from those clinics on the North Side? They won't care that he's helping people... and what happens to fags in jail, Glory?"

Glory pressed her knees together, stiffening against her husband's probing hand.

Malcolm chuckled again and moved his hand up to her breast and squeezed. "I know. Try going to my mother's. She still thinks you're an idiot for marrying me before you finished high school, giving up all those college scholarships she arranged. Spitting on everything she did for you."

Glory tried to push his hand away, but he easily held her wrist and pulled her onto her back, pinning her under his weight. She turned her head, and his kiss pressed the swelling flesh under her eye.

"Hey, maybe you can go down South to your family. Your grandmother's rickety old wooden house, surrounded by fields of dry straw or... drunk Cousin Ricky's? Does his parole officer know he drives liquor around illegally?"

Glory cried silently as her own body betrayed her, responding to her husband's touch.

"Woman, understand. I *will* come after you," Malcolm whispered. "I'm Superman, remember? You are my lady, and I love you, and it's my job to protect you. No matter where you are, even in the middle of nowhere in Flora, Mississippi, I will always come to you. There's nowhere you can go that I can't get to you, nowhere that I won't come for you, okay?"

And as her husband moved inside her, marking his ownership of her bruised body, Glory submitted to his kisses and quietly sobbed at the exact words he'd once used to voice his love and calm her fears.

"You belong to me. Nobody—not your family, not your friends, not even that sailor boy that I know you still think about—can keep you from me. You're never leaving me. No matter how we fight, we will always make up, understand?" He pressed into her hard and deep, gripping her wrists, squeezing the bracelets against bone until she cried out. "Now, tell me why." He whispered. "Tell me what the bracelets mean."

"Malcolm, please." Glory begged. "This hurts."

"In his letter to the Ephesians," Malcolm said as he kissed her, "Paul tells us that the wife must 'see that she reverence her husband,' so tell me, Mrs. Porter. Now."

"I am my beloved's, and his desire is toward me," Glory whispered, almost choking on the words that had once thrilled her.

GLORY SLID A FRESH pack of birth control pills into the lining of her new designer purse. Her mother-in-law would be horrified if she had seen Glory cut the five-inch hole into the lining of her Christmas gift, but Anita was safely in the deep South, away from the vicious Chicago winter.

"So Malcolm isn't getting suspicious about why you're not pregnant yet?" Herschel sat across from Glory in the salon kitchen, sharing tea and pecan pie.

"Nope, and he can't even ask either." Glory squeezed honey and lemon into her tea and stirred. "He tries to act like he's just forgetful, so he won't admit he's trying to get me pregnant. I'll probably tell him I'm late sometime this year... keep him happy."

"So you're gonna deceive your husband and pretend to be almost pregnant. Glory-Glory, I'm surprised at you!" Herschel got up and added hot water to his mug. "Why not just tell him the truth?"

"Honestly, Herschel, I tried. He hit the ceiling. When we first got married, I suggested the pill when he *forgot* to use rubbers, and he went off about pills causing abortions and God's will and a whole bunch of other stuff. I decided to just drop the subject. But I'm not gonna be pregnant until I'm good and ready." Glory sipped her tea and cut herself another slice of pie.

Herschel shook his head. "What's gonna happen when he finds out? It's like you're cheating on him—"

"No, it's not! I'm protecting both of us from his stupid decision. I'm not trying to be anybody's mother anytime soon, and he's so busy with church he'd never see his baby. And I'm still practically a kid myself."

"I'm not saying you're wrong for taking the pills," Herschel explained. "I just think you're wrong for sneaking. What if you get sick, and he has to tell the doctor what meds you take?"

"Well, that's not gonna happen. And I've been taking them for almost two years with no problem. Besides, Malcolm is sneaking around too. He thinks I don't know it, but he's at the mission almost every weekday. He's supposed to do outreach ministry, but he visits the mission instead."

"Ooo... well, that's exactly the same, now, isn't it? You lying about taking pills and him sneaking and being a minister. Yup, exactly the same." Herschel sipped his tea. "Oh, your eye-rolling is perfect, and now I see you've added head rocking."

Glory got up from the table and took her dish and flatware to the sink. "I don't care what you say. I'm not having no babies no time soon."

"Oh, I almost forgot," Herschel said. "There's a package on my desk for you."

Glory wiped her hands on a dishtowel and walked over to Herschel's desk. On the desk stood a cube wrapped in brown paper. Glory guessed it was about eight inches high. It wasn't likely to be a comic book. It was from a PO box and addressed to Glory Porter. She stared at the neatly printed label and carefully peeled a corner of the tape.

"Aw, girl, just open it already!"

Glory jumped, nearly fumbling the heavy package. She hadn't heard Herschel walk up behind her. "I'm scared to. I think it's JT's handwriting."

"Well, I hope so, 'cause that's about the size of a bomb!" Herschel laughed at his own joke and took the package from Glory. "I'll open it for you, just to be safe." He quickly tore the paper off and handed her a small envelope and a taped Styrofoam cube.

"It *is* from JT." Glory gently picked at the corner of the wide strip of tape that held the two halves of the cube together.

"Well, go ahead." Herschel laid a hand on Glory's shoulder. "It's been almost two years. It's okay. You've moved on, remember?"

Glory sighed and peeled the tape away and set the cube flat on the desk with the imprinted side up. *F.A.O. Schwarz,* it said. She lifted the top half of the cube then carefully pulled out a heavy snow globe. Inside it, Barbie shoes rained down while a music box in the base played, "Isn't She Lovely." Glory laid her head against Herschel's shoulder and wept.

Dear Glory

When I saw this snow globe, I knew you had to have it. Something told me it would make you smile. Is it working? How are you? I hope you are safe and happy. After not hearing from you for two years, when I got the wedding announcement, and I don't know who sent it, I couldn't understand what I did to make you cut off communication and then marry Malcolm Porter. When you didn't answer any of my letters, I thought the rumors got to you, and you believed Trina's lies. I admit, I was pissed. But then I started thinking that it probably wasn't about me. I bet I can guess how bad your home life was. It had to be a whole lotta pressure for you to marry Malcolm. I hope he's a good husband. I came home last Christmas, but you were gone down South. I left you a message and a little something to make you smile. I hope it worked. When we were growing up, I never thought we wouldn't get married. I guess I took you for granted. I swear, I'm not mad. And maybe one day when we see each other, we can at least be friends. I will always love you, Glory.

Petty Officer Third Class Josiah T. Jackson

Glory read the letter five times before her tears stopped. Her head ached, and her eyes burned. "Isn't She Lovely" was one of the songs he'd tried to sing the night they made up... the night they made love. The night she promised to be his wife for real. *Is this why he's so heavy on my mind lately? Have I somehow known he's trying to reach me? Then why didn't I get that feeling a year ago when I thought he abandoned me?*

"Herschel," she said, finally. "Can I keep this here? I can't take it home."

"Of course you can, sweetie. But, darling, seems to me you still have some pretty strong feelings for that young man. How are you gonna—"

"I'm not gonna do or say anything. I'm not gonna contact him. If he thought to send this here to the shop, why didn't he send letters here?" Glory placed the snow globe back in the Styrofoam cube. "I have a good life now. I don't need to mess it up with childhood memories." She quickly went to fold towels lest she break down crying again.

It was two weeks before Glory decided to take the snow globe home and place it high up on a shelf in her library, next to her brand-new copy of the monster book and her ballerina jewelry box.

CHAPTER 22
May 1988

Glory watched helplessly as Malcolm lost control of his life. He spent nearly every waking moment on church business and at the beck and call of his father. He had finally had to cut ties with South Garden Mission, spending all of his time in ministerial duties for Lake Shore Christian Fellowship Church, and Glory watched her husband's frustration grow each time his beeper went off.

"Dammit," Malcolm said early one morning during breakfast as his vibrating pager danced across the kitchen table. He didn't cuss loudly or sound angry. He sounded tired.

"Let it wait." Glory poured him another cup of coffee. "Finish your breakfast. Whatever it is can wait."

Malcolm sat back in his chair. "No, it can't wait. I already ignored it once this morning."

"Well, at least eat a little something." Glory placed a plate in front of him. "You don't need to starve yourself—"

"Woman, don't tell me what to do." Malcolm pushed the plate away and stood up. "I don't need you trying to control me too."

Glory took a step back from the table.

He stepped closer, pulling her into his arms, and kissing her forehead. "I'm sorry I snapped at you. I know you don't mean it that way. I'm just tired. How 'bout we go someplace nice when I get home tonight?"

Glory relaxed in her husband's arms and kissed him lightly. "Sounds fun. I'll be home after six, though. Christy is in town. She's flying back to Alabama, and I'm riding with her to Midway. Her flight leaves around five thirty. We're gonna hang out for a while."

"Good." Malcolm squeezed her tighter. "Have fun. Tell her I said hi. Be home by six thirty, okay?"

Glory said goodbye to Malcolm and began cleaning the kitchen from his uneaten breakfast. By nine thirty, she'd thrown in a load of laundry and scrubbed their bathroom. By ten o'clock, she'd dropped a whole chicken into the Crock-Pot and changed into her favorite denim skirt. Satisfied that the apartment was spotless and perfectly organized, Glory called a cab and headed out.

Walking through the DePaul University library, Glory didn't feel the least bit guilty. If Malcolm asked, she wouldn't be lying. She *was* at a library, just not the neighborhood library. Last semester, when she'd had to drop out of school because *her wifely and church duties were being neglected*, Malcolm suggested she go to the library and had even bought her sets of *World Book* and *Encyclopedia Britannica* to help her feel educated. This was the same Malcolm who had bullied her mother into letting her go to college in the first place. Glory, of course, hadn't dropped out. She met up with classmates to get notes and visited her professors' offices to ask questions. She didn't attend classes regularly, but she took all three of her final exams and passed with an A and two Bs.

This semester was a little harder with all business-related classes. She'd already had to drop one class, but Glory was determined to finish school. She hadn't worked out what she'd tell Malcolm when graduation time came, but she wasn't really worried. After class and studying, she took the L downtown for a late lunch. She hadn't taken a bus in four years, but Malcolm never said she couldn't take the L.

Later, at the salon, Glory entered the backroom and was hit by the scent of fresh lavender. All the electric fans in all the windows couldn't clear the cloying purple smell of springtime. Herschel stood at the stove, distilling lavender oil and water.

"Well, hello, Glory-Glory!" Herschel shouted over the drone of the fans. "So nice of you to come to work today! Grab that mortar on the table and start crushing some of the flowers... just a little bit, now."

Glory hugged Herschel from behind, grabbed an apron, and got to work. "So what have I missed?" she asked as she plucked tiny flowers from long stems. "Anything interesting going on? Any new gossip?"

"This is a beauty salon. You know there's always gossip." Herschel laughed. "But the biggest question is where have *you* been? After a week, I had to actually clean up back here myself." He clutched the string of fake pearls at his neckline. "It was just awful."

Glory laughed at her friend. "Looks like you survived okay." She picked up a marble pestle and began bruising the flowers.

Herschel stepped away from the stove long enough to check and comment on her progress. "Not so hard, now. Don't want pulp yet... just a little oil out, then add a few drops of olive oil, and crush 'em some more."

Glory followed directions and created the lavender paste that Herschel would use in soaps and foot scrubs. They talked of the salon gossip, and Glory tried to explain away her absence. "Church-lady stuff takes up a lotta time. With school and everything, I'm not sure how long I can keep working here. Malcolm wanted me to quit when we first got married, but obviously, that didn't happen. Now I'm just so busy..." Glory let her voice trail off. She had told Malcolm months before that she'd quit the salon. So lately she just visited sometimes... and cleaned up... and got paid.

"Hmph." Hershel didn't hide his disdain. "So he wants you to quit your job? At least he's not interfering with school. Girl... well, you know how I feel. As long as you happy, I'm happy for you."

"Yes, Wonder Woman. I'm happy." Glory smiled up at her friend's serious face.

She really was happy most of the time. Marriage had taken some adjustments, and Glory knew beyond anything that Malcolm loved her. His bad days, even though they were more frequent lately, were always overshadowed by the good times. Each tiff was always followed by Malcolm begging forgiveness and being a perfect husband for weeks. And of course, Glory always forgave him.

SHE WALKED INTO THEIR apartment at five thirty, with plenty of time to wash off the lavender scent from the salon and finish dinner in case Malcolm had changed his mind about going out. She'd just locked the door when she felt her husband's hand on her shoulder. He spun her around.

"I've been looking for you all day. Where've you been?" he asked.

Glory looked in his eyes, trying to read his mood. "I told you where I was going today." Glory kept the annoyance out of her voice while she tried to remember exactly what she'd told him that morning.

The slap was so fast, she didn't see him move. "I asked you a question." Malcolm's voice was calm and cold.

Glory steeled herself and looked him in the eye. "I was at the airport with Christy—"

This time the slap turned her head. She staggered and fought back tears. Whatever had happened with him that day had turned him into this dark, angry...

"I had you paged. Lie to me again," Malcolm said.

Glory's hand went to her cheek as she tried to move around him. "Malcolm, I was at the library first, then I..." She saw his jaw clench and lowered her eyes.

"And Adam was not deceived, but the woman was in the transgression!"

She expected his anger to explode. What surprised her was that the backhand sent her flying into the door. She was still shaking when he grabbed the front of her blouse and pulled her to her feet. She tried to turn her face from the slap she knew was coming, but when he grabbed her hair, it was his fist that landed against her cheek.

"Please, God, Malcolm, *stop*!"

"I waited at the library for you." Malcolm grunted through clenched teeth. "I even called the salon. Now, where were you!"

"Malcolm, I'm sorry!" Glory begged as he dragged her by her hair with one hand and loosened his belt with the other. "I was at school!"

"Ye wives, be in subjection to your husbands!" In the kitchen, he tore the blouse from her body, breaking the strap on her purse and sending all its contents to the floor.

Pulling away, Glory tried to kick the compact of pills under the refrigerator before Malcolm saw.

"You're taking birth control pills!" Malcolm screeched. "This is why you can't get pregnant?" And then his rage boiled over. "Surely as a wife treacherously departeth from her husband, so have ye dealt treacherously with me!"

It was no longer the rough leather of the belt but the cold steel of the buckle digging into her, knocking against bone where she tried to shield herself with her hands. The prongs on the studded belt tore into her and stung where they drew blood, and Glory begged for mercy until Malcolm dropped the belt.

"Oh God, Malcolm! Please!" Glory sobbed through swollen, bloodied lips. "I'm sorry!"

"Wherefore will ye plead with me? Thou hast transgressed against me!"

With her hair clenched in his fist, her face pressed against the kitchen table, slick with tears and blood, Glory felt him push into her. "Nooo!" she cried. Her own husband was now the monster he'd rescued her from.

"And God said unto them, 'Be fruitful, and multiply!'" His was not the passion of a husband working out his anger but the righteous fury of God punishing a sinner, driving out the demons of rebellion from the inside, pounding her womb into submission... forcing his children into her despite her protests... demanding her body deliver sons in his image.

"Thy way and thy doings have procured these things unto thee. This is thy wickedness, because it is bitter, because it reacheth unto thine heart!"

"Please, Malcolm, no!" Glory sobbed. "Stop! This hurts!" Reaching across the table, she tried to pull away from the pain and depth of his assault.

Gripping her hair tighter, he slammed her face against the table, pulling her closer, sinking himself deeper. "I will greatly multiply thy sorrow and thy conception. In sorrow thou shalt bring forth children, and thy desire shall be to thy husband, and he shall rule over thee!"

Glory screamed, and he pressed on, relentlessly, shredding her resistance, breaking her will, binding her demons...

Demon of lies.

Demon of selfishness.

Demon of rebellion.

And when she could no longer scream, she cried, and her insides ached, and her husband destroyed the last of her innocence. This was worse than the beatings she'd gotten as a child.

This was the beating that had made her mother.

This was the beating that made godly women... the beating that only the strongest, godliest of women endured and lived with and by the grace of God forgave.

GLORY AWOKE TO THE smell of sage and burning paper. She was lying on the kitchen floor with a cover laid over her. Her head ached and her neck and her shoulders. Her whole face hurt, and her lips felt numb. She tried to open her eyes and found she could only open one. She moved to sit up, but intense pain in her belly and her head made her lie down again. She took slow, deep breaths, feeling a sharp pain in her right side where she remembered falling against the doorknob. Whatever body part she moved ached and burned.

"Mama?" Glory's throat was sore and her voice all but gone. She rolled over onto her stomach and then pushed herself to her knees and finally reached up onto the kitchen table to pull herself to her feet. "Mama?" Glory called again, this time a little louder.

"Yes, baby?" Mary entered the kitchen carrying one of their fancy teacups and a rolled paper cigarette. "You up, I see. I woulda put you to bed, but I cain't lift you like I used to."

"Where's Malcolm?" Glory took a step and felt the floor stick to her feet. Leaning on the kitchen table, she lifted her right foot from the spots of semidried blood on the floor. There was dried blood on the back of her hands. Had she tried to defend herself? Had she actually fought back?

"Malcolm's not here, baby. He had to go out. I came straight from work." Mary laid a hand on Glory's shoulder. "You go clean yourself and get in bed. I'll put some soup on."

Glory knew she must look like hell, but of course, her mother would never say. Godly women accepted beatings and prayed to be even godlier. She made her way down the hall to her bedroom. *Did that really happen?* In the bathroom, she looked in the mirror and gasped. Her left eye was swollen shut, and a patch of dried blood streaked through her right eyebrow. Her swollen lips were crusted with blood. She peeled off her torn underclothes and wasn't surprised to feel fluids running down her legs. It burned.

Assault. That was what it was.

Like a young girl walking down the street, minding her own business and dragged into a gangway...

Malcolm was out of control. Glory was the last thing in his life that he thought he could control, and she'd shown him that was not true. Forcing himself on her... in her...

Glory stood under a warm shower, her black-and-blue body stinging with cuts and welts, her tears mixing with the falling water, just like when her mother used to purge her demons with the extension cord. Malcolm had used his whole body to beat her, to punish her... to subdue her. *Inside and out... inside and out... inside and out...*

This was not a man demanding submission of an ungodly wife. This was a vile and evil... Glory couldn't finish the thought.

"Baby, your soup is ready," Mary called through the bathroom door.

Glory moved slowly, not looking in the mirror again, drying herself carefully, applying ointment to her cuts and welts. She wasn't interested in soup. She went into her library and lay on the couch.

"I see you still got demons of disobedience," Mary said when she came into the library with a tray.

"I don't want it. My throat hurts." Glory didn't know why she was even telling her mother about her pain.

"Well, it's your own fault. I tried to get all that rebellion outta you, but you just too stubborn. Take a whole lotta devilment make a man beat you like that. I saw them pills you had... course he gon' lay the hand 'a God to you..."

"Shut up, Mama," she whispered as her mother continued her lecture on how ungodly Glory was. While Mary talked, Glory drifted in and out of nightmares, plagued by visions of her husband as the monster who had pulled her into the gangway so many years ago.

GLORY OPENED HER EYES. She was still on the couch in the library. The plastic ice bag over her eyes was now a bag of cold water, and the hot water bottle on her stomach was lukewarm. She tried to sit up, but her whole body ached, and she could still feel cramps deep in her belly. Malcolm sat across the small room in a chair, arms folded, legs outstretched and crossed, his chin on his chest... sleeping. The first time she'd seen him sleeping like that, watching over her, had been in the hospital after he'd saved her from... *a monster*. When she moved, Malcolm opened his eyes. He looked into hers a long time before speaking.

"I'm sorry."

Glory's usual response was "I know," but this time she just stared at him, trying to see her husband as something other than the *thing* who had just brutalized her. Glory believed Malcolm was sorry, but she didn't have absolution to offer the monster he'd become.

"You hurt me." Glory sat up, turning her face to the light falling in from the hallway. The swelling around her eye had gone down enough for her to be able to see, but her face still ached. As badly as she wanted to hide, she wanted Malcolm to see what he'd done.

"I know." Malcolm lowered his head, keeping his eyes down. He always did that when he bruised her face—kept his eyes down, not looking at her.

"Real bad, Malcolm." Glory slowly moved to the end of the couch. With great pain, she knelt in front of him, lifting his chin, forcing him to look at her. She took some satisfaction in seeing tears in his eyes.

"God, I'm so sorry." Malcolm moved to pull her into his arms, but Glory leaned away. She knew he was truly sorry, and she wasn't afraid of him, but she had no comfort for him this time. She could not meekly accept this... assault and go on as usual.

"I know you are." She laid her hands on his knees and pushed herself up to her feet. "I just don't know that I can forgive you."

Malcolm grabbed her wrist. "If you hadn't lied to me... those pills—"

Glory snatched her arm away. "Malcolm, this wasn't just a fight," she whispered. "This wasn't a little tiff." She looked him in the eye again. "You marked my face like a stranger on the street... like an enemy. You... you... violated me. I shouldn't even still be here."

Malcolm grabbed her wrist, his hand closing over her bracelets. He looked into her eyes. "You're my beloved. My desire is toward you. You don't get to leave me."

Glory snatched her hand away and walked out of the library and into the guest bedroom, slamming the door behind her. She climbed into bed, pulled the covers up over her head, and drifted off to sleep, only to be awakened a while later by Malcolm climbing into bed behind her, pulling her aching body close to his.

GLORY AWAKENED TO THE smell of fresh coffee and frying bacon. She also detected a whiff of cinnamon, but when she moved to stretch, her husband in bed beside her pulled her close and wouldn't release her.

"Malcolm, why do I smell breakfast cooking?" Glory tried to sit up, but he held her down and kissed her swollen and bruised cheek. "Malcolm Porter, don't you dare try to touch me. I'm still sore and bleeding from what you did to me." Her words came out slightly slurred because of the swelling around her mouth. She rolled over on her side, turning her back to him.

He pressed closer to her and moved his hand over the curve of her hip. "Woman, do you know how fine you are to me... even now?"

Glory didn't answer. She got out of bed and pulled on her bathrobe. She wasn't sure whether she should go into the kitchen and let Mrs. Beyers see the mess that had been made of her face or if she should lock herself in their bedroom until the housekeeper left. She was still considering when Malcolm came up beside her. He took her hand and pulled her to the kitchen.

"Good morning, Brother Malcolm, daughter," Tutu said. *Okay, not Mrs. Beyers.* He had his head down and appeared to be chopping vegetables. "Your omelets will be ready in a minute or two. I added a touch of cinnamon and vanilla to the coffee. Both flavors are very calming." The old man with skin like tree bark and the musical Caribbean accent seemed to glide around the kitchen in his spotless white apron, never taking his eyes off his task. "Sit down. I'll pour your coffee."

Malcolm led Glory to the kitchen table and held her chair for her. Glory took her seat, her eyes silently questioning her husband.

"Tutu's gonna be working for us now. He'll take over cleaning and cooking and stuff, so you have more time for important things." Malcolm looked up and nodded when Tutu appeared beside him with the coffeepot. "I know how much you like the library and stuff. He'll drive you around so you don't hafta take cabs."

When Tutu leaned down to pour Glory's coffee—which she wouldn't be touching—he paused and looked at her, blinking a couple of times, but otherwise said nothing. Glory stared at Malcolm. Household help was definitely not necessary, and though Tutu had been like a father to Malcolm, he hadn't always been sweet to Glory and had even gone so far as to threaten her when he thought she might betray Malcolm.

"Malcolm, we need to talk about this." Glory felt the forming scab at the corner of her mouth crack when she spoke.

"There's nothing to talk about." Malcolm rubbed his palms together as Tutu set a plate in front of him. "He's moved into the maid's rooms, and he'll have a car by the end of the week. Or you can just spend all day every day with me."

The old man seemed to ignore their conversation as he set a plate in front of Glory. He placed a bottle of hot sauce she didn't recognize on the table in front of her. "This is the best Jamaican hot sauce you'll ever find." He smiled, showing all the brown stumps where his teeth used to be.

Glory looked down at the plate in front of her then at the bottle of hot sauce. Her hand went to her swollen lips and sore cheek. She got up from the table and went back to bed in the guest bedroom.

TWO WEEKS LATER, GLORY stood at the bathroom mirror applying a thick coat of foundation to her face. Malcolm stood behind her, watching. "It looks like you have a stocking over your face." He laughed a little.

Glory glared at him but didn't speak. She hadn't been to church in a few weeks. This would be her first Sunday back since... *the assault*. She looked in the mirror at herself. She did look like a stocking face, just like Denise Blevins had... and Katie Merrill... and even Trina Toliver-Bates. Glory gasped. All "godly" women with thick makeup. She remembered laughing at the stocking-faced women, wondering why they did their makeup like that. Now she knew. They were *godly* women. She lowered her head so Malcolm wouldn't see her cry.

Malcolm slipped an arm around her waist and rubbed against her, kissing her neck and shoulder. "I miss you. It's been weeks. You should be okay now." He lifted the back of her dressing gown and moved his hand up her thigh. When his fingers slid between her legs, Glory pushed away from him and threw up in the sink.

CHAPTER 23
Winter and Spring,
1989

Church Malcolm and the good wife... that was who they were: the perfect godly couple. Malcolm read the scriptures on Sundays during first service and preached the sermon at second service, and Glory minded the babies in the church nursery during first service and sat front and center at second service. While Malcolm made his ministerial rounds through the week, Glory prepared meals for shut-ins, changed diapers in the daycare center, and took piano lessons so she could play an instrument like a proper first lady in training.

What Glory also did was clip leaves from the herb garden growing in planters in her library. Her husband's touch turned her stomach. She thought it would go away, but Malcolm had succeeded where her first attacker had failed, so she would just bear his affection and then go and vomit. The herbs did their job, and even if her period was a day or two late, a week of strong ginger tea seemed to *clear out anything.*

It was near Christmas when Glory found herself throwing up at odd times. She took the herbs and ginger tea as usual, but her late period didn't come. Malcolm noticed in January and made an announcement in church even before she took a home pregnancy test. After service, she stood in the Robinson Room, receiving well wishes as long as she could stomach it. Some women confessed that they'd been wondering what was taking so long. Glory just shrugged and hoped she looked appropriately content. When the home pregnancy test result was finally positive, Malcolm immediately made a series of doctor's appointments for Glory and, when he couldn't be by her side, charged Tutu with her care.

"HI, HERSCHEL... IT'S Glory."

"Hellooo, Glory-Glory! So now, why haven't I seen you in months? What's goin' on?"

"Herschel, I'm pregnant."

"Oh." Herschel went quiet.

"Hello? Herschel, are you there?" Glory thought they had been disconnected.

"Yeah, I'm here. How are you feeling?" He cleared his throat. "How do you feel?"

"I'm fine. I'm nauseous, and Malcolm doesn't want me going out because of germs and stuff. He's kinda paranoid." Glory laughed. "I'm bored, and I'm gonna try to sneak by to visit later."

"And... how's your brain? You're twenty-two. This is almost ten years earlier than you planned. Did you miss a pill?"

Glory sighed. "I don't know what happened. I really don't want a baby, but Malcolm is ecstatic."

"So, how far gone are you?" Herschel asked. Glory could hear him moving around. She imagined he was working on beauty supplies like usual.

"I'm thirteen weeks. At least that's what the doctor said." Glory shifted herself on the couch as Tutu entered the library with her third cup of ginger tea. She'd told him she needed five cups a day, hoping against hope that it could still work. "I really hate this." Glory didn't want to cry again. She'd been crying for months. "I don't know what to do, Herschel."

"Well, darling, what *can* you do? Seems to me like you already did it."

"I thought about not having it," Glory confessed. "I'm probably goin' to hell."

"No, sweetie. You're not going to hell for anything. Listen." Herschel lowered his voice. "All you hafta do is say the word, and I'll make any arrangements you want. What you choose to do with your body is your business."

"I don't think I can do *that*, Herschel." Glory sighed. She swallowed hard as tears pushed at the corners of her eyes. "God, why me?"

GLORY RECOGNIZED THE constant bad feeling. The pressure in her stomach and chest and throat. The feeling she'd gotten when her daddy had died. She sat in the armchair beside the window in her library, watching the early-spring rains turn everything a grayish green. She'd been crying a lot as she felt the waistline in her clothes tighten despite her frequent vomiting. She dreamed of falling on knives or falling down stairs or falling to the sidewalk from their fourth-floor apartment.

She missed school. She hadn't been back since... *the assault*. She snorted at the irony. Malcolm had made her quit school so she'd have more time to be a proper wife, but Tutu did all of her wifely duties except sit in the front pew on Sundays and lie beside Malcolm at night. She missed Herschel. They'd spoken twice since she told him about her pregnancy, and every day, she thought about his offer to "make arrangements," and every day she prayed for forgiveness for actually considering it. She hated Tutu. Even though the old man waited on her hand and foot, he moved silently around the apartment and reported to Malcolm her every move, and Glory was positive he listened in on her phone calls. And her mother's frequent visits grated on her last nerve. Every day, she asked herself why she didn't just leave, but Malcolm's promises to harm her family and friends terrified her, and when she saw him torture Tutu because she'd gone to the salon for a few hours, she didn't dare try him again.

But it was Malcolm's loving and solicitous behavior that truly sickened her. When he was home, he seemed to always be behind her, his arms wrapped around her, humming to their unborn child. In bed, he'd lie beside her with a hand gently stroking her belly, and when he made love to her, it was soft and slow, and Glory wanted to die because her desire *was* to her husband, and he did indeed rule over her.

THAT FEELING OF ANGST and dread was back, and when the phone rang, Glory sat down and took a deep breath before answering. A second after she picked up, she heard the telltale click of Tutu picking up an extension. She shook her head.

"Hello?"

"Hi, Cousin Baby." Jillian's voice sounded exhausted.

"Hey, Jill. What's the matter?" Glory looked at her watch. It was just after nine o'clock in the morning, and Malcolm had left for the day. She looked out the window, down onto Seventy-Fifth Street, listening to the staticky sound of cars moving on wet pavement coming in through the slightly open window.

"Glory, Bigma's gone." Jill sighed.

Glory hung her head, surprised she didn't burst into tears. "I knew it," she whispered. "I've been feeling it all morning."

"You sure it's not something else? I mean—"

"Yeah, Jill, I'm sure. I felt the same thing when my daddy died. I gotta go."

Glory hung up the phone before Jill could speak again. She thought about calling her mother at work, but she was sure Aunt Martha would be spreading the news. Aunt Ellie would likely be a basket case. *Dammit!* Glory realized she should have asked about Aunt Ellie. She wondered how Bigma had died. In her heart, she felt it was peaceful. Looking out the window, Glory sat back in her chair, sipped her tea, and ignored the tears on her face and the flutter in her belly.

HER AUNTS, RUTH, MARTHA, and Ellie—it seemed like it had been ages since she'd seen or spoken to them. Actually, it had only been about three months, and it wasn't like they spoke often anyway, but Bigma's death had brought them all together. Aunts, uncles, cousins, and well over a hundred friends converged on Flora, Mississippi, to pay their respects. The big new church was packed, and the social hall overflowed with food and sweet tea and people passing out hugs and swapping stories of the legendary Augusta Johnson.

After the repast, family crowded into the Johnson family home, filling every room except Bigma's. People stood in the doorway and stared, but nobody would cross the threshold. Nobody, that was, except Glory. At Aunt Martha's suggestion, Glory walked into the small room and let up the shades just the way Bigma liked it. The electric fan in the window filled the room with the moist spring air and the scent of early magnolia blossoms. According to her eccentric aunt, Glory would feel the love of her grandmother by being in her room. Glory didn't believe it, but she'd longed for the privacy and the time away from Malcolm. She shed her simple black dress and pulled back the layers of quilts. Snuggled in bed, Glory wrapped her arms around Bigma's pillow and inhaled her grandmother's combination of blue hair grease and menthol pain salve.

Glory tried to cry, lying there in the softest, warmest bed ever, but no tears would come. The loss of her grandmother, as painful as it was, was not the worst she'd ever felt. She stared at the pill bottles on the bedside table. Pills for pain and sleep and stomach trouble. She felt a flutter in her stomach. Not nausea or hunger pangs but a flutter of hope. As she drifted off to sleep, Glory dreamed of walking in a cotton field and holding Bigma's hand.

"WHERE ARE YOU GOING?" Malcolm sat up in bed, and the covers fell to his waist.

"I'm just going for a walk." Glory pulled her grandmother's hand-knit wool sweater over her head. She'd be taking that back to Chicago with her no matter what Aunt Ellie said. "Go back to sleep."

"Wait up." Malcolm swung his feet to the floor. "Lemme get dressed." He stood up, shivering, and pulled the shade down, blocking out the breeze and the early-morning sunshine.

"Malcolm, please. I really wanna go by myself. I promise I won't go far." This was the protective Malcolm that she used to love. "I'm just taking a walk around the garden. You can see me from the back porch."

"You know I don't like you out alone. You hafta be careful. What if you fall or something?"

"Then I'll get muddy." She walked over and laid a hand against her husband's cheek. "The ground is soft—it won't hurt. Malcolm, please? I dreamed I was in the cotton field with Bigma. I feel like I need to go say goodbye there." She stared into Malcolm's eyes, willing only sadness to show in hers. "Please?"

Malcolm sat on the side of the bed, pulling on his pants from the night before. "Okay. I'll go in the kitchen and figure out that percolator, maybe sit on the back porch, have coffee with Bobby."

Heading out through the back garden, Glory tried to move slowly and watch her step. She took deep breaths and let the early-morning air fill her lungs. For the first time in a long time, she felt peace. She felt hope, and when she got to the edge of the cotton field, Glory pressed her hands into the cool soil and began to dig up a cotton root. As she dug, she thanked Bigma for leading her there and said her last prayer to God.

Part 3

INTERLUDE
April 1983

That day's work had been the usual: do a couple of loads of towels in the washer, clean up and mop the kitchen area, and straighten and vacuum the lounge. The sound of the closing door made Glory jump. She wasn't actually concerned, just surprised. Herschel usually left her alone after all of her work was done, and Thursday nights, he was always extra busy with his special clients, getting ready for the weekend.

Glory sat up straight on the couch and blushed a little. The book she'd been reading had quite a few steamy passages, and she had been in the middle of one of them. She looked up and saw not Herschel but JT.

He crossed the room in four steps, grabbed Glory's hand, and pulled her to her feet and into his arms, crushing her mouth with a kiss so long and deep Glory could hardly breathe. He paused only long enough to take a breath and resume the kiss.

Glory tried to pull away. Not that she didn't love kissing JT, but he was different that evening. When she broke the kiss, he pulled her closer, held her tighter, and buried his face in her hair. His breathing sounded almost like he was crying.

"God, Miss Glory, I love you so much... I loved you since we were babies. I loved you my whole life." He pressed his lips to hers again.

Glory pulled away and got a glimpse of his bloodshot eyes before he squeezed them shut, forcing tears at the corners. "JT, what's wrong?"

He tried to kiss her again, but Glory pulled away from him. "JT, what's the matter? You're scaring me."

He pulled her back into another embrace, pressing her head to his chest. Glory could hear his heart pounding.

"Nothing's wrong. I just had a rough coupla days, and I realized how stupid life can get. The thought of losing you scares the hell outta me." He kissed her again, pressing her body to his. "Oh God, if I ever lost you, I would die."

Glory wrapped her arms around her boyfriend. "I love you, too, JT. I don't know what's wrong, but I'm not going anywhere."

"I dream about us together forever—being married, husband and wife. Our kids and a house and a dog—"

This time, Glory kissed him softly, gently, praying he knew how much she loved him, praying he was reassured. Then she sat down on the couch and reached for him, beckoning him to join her.

JT knelt in front of her, not even pretending to hide the tears that slipped down his face. "God, I love you so much. You're all I ever wanted my whole life. Before I knew what makin' love was, I knew I only wanted you." He reached out and unbuttoned her blouse, pausing to kiss the valley between her breasts through her undershirt. "Girl, I want you so bad." He pushed her blouse down and off her shoulders, tossing it aside. Taking a leg in each hand, he pulled her to the edge of the couch.

Glory pressed her lips to his, caught up in his passion, shuddering as his hands moved up her thighs. She held her breath as his hands traveled farther. He'd touched her like that before, but this time... Glory tried to pull herself away.

"Girl, I love you so much. Please let me show you." He kissed her again, begging, pleading, sucking like he was starving. "Please, Miss Glory. I need you."

Glory was consumed by conflicting emotions. She loved him and wanted more than anything to be with him. But giving in, giving her whole self, accepting his whole self, falling into the trap of demons of lust was a sure way to eternal damnation. *How can love be wrong?* Glory knew he would be her husband one day, and she loved him... *But is now the right time?*

Glory broke the kiss. "JT," she panted. "We can't. Not here. Not like this."

"Please, Miss Glory. You want me too. I can feel—"

"No," Glory said a little more firmly. "We are not doing it on this old couch in the back room of a salon." She pressed her hands against his shoulders. He was shaking.

JT wrapped an arm around her waist and pulled her closer, pressing her to his chest, seeking her mouth with his, his strength overpowering her resistance.

"JT, I said no!" Glory said, raising her voice and pushing away from him. She sat back on the couch and clamped her knees together. "I'm not doing it with you in here."

JT sat back on his heels, staring at her. Glory would have sworn she saw the fire in his eyes slowly fade. He shook his head as if shaking off a spell. "I'm sorry, Miss Glory. I don't know what I was doing. Oh God, did I hurt you?" He got up from the floor.

Glory stood up from the couch and took a couple of wobbly steps. "No, I'm fine." She leaned against him. He'd stopped shaking, and his heartbeat was coming back to normal.

He wrapped his arms around her, this time gently. "I love you, Miss Glory." He kissed the top of her head. "I always have, and I always will."

"I know you do, JT." Glory took a deep breath. "You weren't wrong. I want you, too, sometimes so bad it hurts, but we can't do that back here." She paused, but JT only held her tighter. "You'll come visit me Monday, right?" Standing there in JT's arms, Glory said a quick prayer, asking for forgiveness. She knew with every fiber of her being that JT would one day be her husband, but come Monday, he would be her lover.

CHAPTER 24
SPRING 1989

When she got dressed, pulled the hospital gown on over her clothes, and then padded down the hall in blue footies, carrying her shoes and purse in a plastic hospital bag, Glory still wasn't sure she'd go through with it. When she stepped onto the empty elevator and shed her disguise, she didn't know what she would do. Blending in with the crowd of people leaving South Shore Hospital after the morning shift change and then walking toward Seventy-Ninth Street, Glory could have easily just gone home, but it felt like the world was moving at high speed and slow motion at the same time. She didn't need to watch where she was walking because it seemed like even the trees were stepping out of her way. She didn't run... she didn't even walk very fast. She felt herself just moving. And still, she could have turned back.

Glory climbed onto the bus, put two dollars into the fare box, accepted the super-transfer slip, and moved all the way to the back. There was no real crowd, but it was darker back there, and nobody was likely to notice her. It was her first bus ride in five years, and she'd forgotten how loud it was. The diesel smell made her at once nauseated and nostalgic.

Even back when she'd been allowed to ride the bus, Seventy-Ninth Street was a route she never took. Looking down on the unfamiliar shops, Glory imagined herself a tourist, watching the few commuters on this chilly Easter Sunday morning. None of the stores were open, and the bus made very few stops on its way to wherever it would eventually end up. As the bus headed west, leaving the South Shore area, Glory was sure her decision had been made.

When they passed over the Dan Ryan Expressway, Glory's watch showed eight o'clock in the morning. At church, Easter Sunrise service was probably long over, and breakfast was being served. Malcolm would dispatch Tutu to pick her up from the hospital while he stayed at church. She hoped Tutu would only be fired for returning without her. Glory prayed he would just quit and leave. The last time she'd managed to get away for a few hours, Malcolm made her watch while he crushed Tutu's fingers and nearly broke the old man's arm, sending Glory to her knees, begging him to stop, promising not to sneak out again. But Tutu's loyalty was only to Malcolm, and while Glory protected him by being "the good wife," the old man always turned a blind eye and deaf ear when Malcolm was upset with Glory.

She got off the bus at Seventy-Ninth and Halsted then took the Halsted bus to Sixty-Third Street, an area she hadn't seen in more than four years. It felt almost like coming home. Glory stood in the line at the doughnut shop under the L station for a glazed Long John and a cup of tea. She took a corner seat facing a wall and enjoyed her breakfast alone... in public... without Malcolm.

At nine o'clock, she went into Kresgee's and bought a white blouse, fresh stockings, a hairbrush, wristbands, makeup, and a backpack. She ducked into the ladies' room, changed clothes, applied dark lipstick and eye makeup, and did her best to cover fading marks on her face with powder. She slid the wristbands over the bracelets that she couldn't take off without a special screwdriver, the constant reminder that she was Malcolm's beloved. She tied her hair back and looked at herself in the mirror. Malcolm always insisted she keep her hair loose and unbraided—his interpretation of biblical law. But whenever she was away for more than a minute, Glory tamed the thick unruly mess. She hated the way she looked now. A thin, hairless scar cut through her right eyebrow. Her light-brown complexion, normally clear, showed the mark of Malcolm's recent displeasure. Her usually thin waist had thickened during the short four-month pregnancy, and since the miscarriage two days before, Glory noticed that her breasts had started filling out and aching.

Maybe Tutu would wait until after Malcolm finished teaching the men's Sunday-school class before telling him she was missing. Her plain white blouse wasn't Easter Sunday finery, but if she chose to turn back, she could just show up at church and act like it was the plan all along. Malcolm might be upset that she wasn't dressed as elegantly as the assistant pastor's wife should be on Easter Sunday, but maybe he'd excuse it because she'd just left the hospital, and then her mother and mother-in-law would whisk her home and straight to bed.

Glory got on the Sixty-Third Street bus and continued west, the route that just five years before, when she was seventeen, had taken her to high school every day. As the bus headed farther west, Glory knew she was getting closer to the point of no return. It would soon be too late for her to turn back. Maybe she could blame her wandering off on stress from the miscarriage. Publicly, her husband would mourn the loss of their first baby and praise God for her safe return. Privately, he would punish her rebellion and disrespect and continue his relentless drive to build their family with or without her consent, and it was her duty as a godly wife to consent.

At the Cicero Avenue terminal, Glory got off the bus and looked around. The northbound Cicero bus sat idling behind the eastbound Sixty-Third Street bus that would take her back home. There was still time to turn back, minimize the damage, protect her friends and family, protect herself...

WHEN THE BLEEDING HAD started, Glory had gotten into bed, expecting to quietly ride out the event, but by the time Malcolm came home, her body was wracked with cramps, and she was nearly delirious with fever. Despite Glory's protests, Malcolm called an ambulance and then carried her down in the elevator to wait for the paramedics. At the hospital, Malcolm was livid when the emergency room doctor told them the miscarriage couldn't be stopped. He demanded to speak to whomever was in charge and railed against the incompetence of their treatment. Even when the doctor admitted Glory for observation, Malcolm was still not satisfied.

"I told them not to bring us to this raggedy hospital!" Malcolm growled.

She heard her husband pacing beside her hospital bed.

"Everybody here is stupid! Cain't do one simple job..."

Glory didn't really listen to Malcolm's tirade. She lay back in the bed with her eyes closed, pretending to sleep as he raged... until the woman in the next bed started singing "Precious Lord." Glory opened her eyes and watched Malcolm's pacing and raging slow and then stop. He reached out and took his wife's hand and squeezed. Their eyes met, and then Glory looked away. Malcolm's pain was more than she wanted to bear. She just wept quietly. She'd cried because of her pain, she'd cried for her lost son, and mostly, she'd cried because it was all her fault, and she was surely damned to hell.

FROM THE BACK OF THE northbound Cicero bus, Glory watched the eastbound Sixty-Third Street bus depart back toward her home and prayed that she was doing the right thing by not contacting her family. She'd write them when she figured out what to do and somehow try to warn Herschel and Ricky that day.

Glory glanced at her watch. It was ten o'clock in the morning, and Tutu was no doubt telling Malcolm she'd left the hospital. There was really no reasonable way for Malcolm to blame the old man, but Malcolm was rarely reasonable. Ideally, Tutu would be okay. Glory could imagine Malcolm walking into the hospital, his long stride crossing the lobby in maybe ten steps, his black leather coat fanned out behind him. He'd have a couple of men from church with him, and he'd smile at the nurses, but it would be a cold dark smile. In the room, he'd pull up a chair next to her hospital roommate's bed and pretend to ask the old prostitute friendly questions. Gladys would pretend to check her purse and say her money and bus ticket to California were missing. Glory prayed that Gladys wouldn't try quoting the Bible at Malcolm. He knew the Bible by heart, and Gladys knew just enough to probably make him mad.

As the bus rolled north, Glory was surprised to find the neighborhood becoming familiar. She recognized the gray buildings that sort of looked like her own neighborhood but not quite and the boarded-up storefronts, some still scorched from riots of twenty years before. This was the westside neighborhood where she and Herschel used to go on their Saturday trips to distribute condoms and needles. When the bus slowed down at Madison Street, in front of O'Reilly's Restaurant, Glory pulled the buzzer and stepped off the bus into the chilly late-morning sunlight and looked around. Across the street, the Hotel Toledo had the Vacancy light on. Herschel had once told her it was cheap and nasty, but for Glory, it would be home for at least that night.

WHEN GLORY WALKED IN, O'Reilly's Restaurant was busy but not overly so. It looked exactly the same as it had the last time she'd been there, at least three years before, with the same dark wood and green vinyl everywhere. Waitresses in beige dresses with brown aprons rushed around with their arms loaded with dishes. The crazy old lady behind the cash register was still chewing an un-lit cigar and cussing loud enough for everyone to hear. Glory took the help wanted sign from the window by the door and approached the old lady at the cash register.

"What the hell you think this is—TV? Gal, you betta go put that sign back! What if we need more than one person?"

"Oh, I'm sorry," Glory said. "I thought—"

"Folks always thinkin'! G'on! Put it back! Ain't nobody playin'!"

"Mama!" a woman's voice called out from somewhere. "What're you fussin' about now?"

"Come over here and see!" the old woman answered. "Why e'rybody wants a job keep movin' that damn sign? Tol' y'all to tape it down!"

Glory replaced the sign in the window and came back to the register.

"Hi. Call me June," the waitress approaching the cash register said. The short woman with an afro puff and heavy brass earrings carried herself and spoke like she was tall. "Got any experience?"

"I've been taking orders and serving people all my life." Glory laughed a little then quickly regretted it. It sounded so much better when she'd rehearsed it in her head.

"So, no real waitress experience at all?" Even though she could see over June's head, Glory felt like the lady was looking down at her.

"No, ma'am," Glory said. "But I'm smart and a fast learner. I'm really good at cleaning too."

"Mm-hm."

Glory stood still, respectfully averting her gaze, feeling June stare at her. She tried not to fidget and too late realized that while she'd covered Malcolm's bracelets with wristbands, the hospital band was still visible on her wrist.

"Follow me," June said. "What's your name?"

"Gloria, ma'am." Her heart pounding, Glory followed June through the restaurant and then through a side door into a back room. June went to a rack and flipped through a few uniforms, looking back at Glory a few times, before finally pulling out one and grabbing an apron from a hook.

"So." June handed the uniform to Glory. "We'll see how you do just for today. It's Easter, so we gon' be swamped. You keep coffee in everybody's cup. Keep all the waters full. You don't take orders. Just help the waitresses. They'll tip you if you do good, got it?"

"Yes, ma'am." Glory accepted the uniform with trembling hands and followed June through another door into a different part of the back rooms.

June pointed at a bathroom door. "Go in there and change, then come to the break room over here." She pointed at another doorway. "Deedee will get you a locker and get you punched in."

"Yes, ma'am. Thank you." Glory willed herself to show no emotion other than polite professional interest.

Inside the bathroom, Glory steadied herself against the sink. Her heart pounding, her whole body shaking, she struggled to steady her breathing, realizing just then that she'd had no idea what she was doing and no way to last more than a few days before her money ran out. But even if she wanted to go back, she couldn't. By that point, Malcolm would be worried, but since he had to preach that day, he would hold his peace until the afternoon and then explode, and if he found her...

Glory couldn't complete the thought. She would concentrate on one day at a time. For the moment, she had a job and a place to stay—somewhere Malcolm would never think to look for her.

Glory changed into the uniform. It smelled of fabric softener with a hint of bleach. She tied on the brown apron and checked her reflection, barely recognizing herself. With her hair held back in a thick ponytail, she looked normal, just like a waitress.

Glory tried to freshen her makeup, realizing June probably saw the bruise showing through her smudged powder. There would be no going back. No more Mrs. Malcolm Porter, no more good wife, no more pretending to be a godly woman. It was done. It was really done. Her vision clouded by her tears, Glory marveled at the bitter irony of sacrificing her baby on Good Friday and resurrecting herself on Easter Sunday.

CHAPTER 25

Glory glared at the shoes from which she'd just pried her swollen feet. One-inch heels were not supposed to cause this much pain, but then again, the gray designer pumps weren't exactly meant to touch the floor for three straight hours either. When she'd walked into the restaurant and asked for a job, she was shocked, but grateful, to be hired immediately, but after being so long on her feet, Glory wondered if she should have asked to start the next day.

The small break room in the back of O'Reilly's Restaurant was fairly clean, but it looked like it hadn't been painted since opening day. On the butter-mint-green walls, streaked from recent wiping, hung signs explaining minimum wage and employee rights. A bulletin board on a wall over a low counter was covered with postcards, photos, and a handwritten sign reminding Glory that her mother didn't work there and that she should clean up after herself. From the condition of the counter and the small table in a corner, Glory guessed that nobody else had read the sign.

Seated in the hard folding chair, Glory rubbed her aching feet on the cold floor, not caring how dirty it might be. When she stretched, she felt something creep down the inside of her thigh and jumped out of the chair. The more she moved, the faster *it* ran down to her ankle, and before she could get a look at it, she felt another one. But this time, she recognized the sensation as she felt still another thread give way and create a run down the inside of her cheap pantyhose.

Cheap pantyhose. She'd forgotten what such things were like. Her mother called them proper stockings, but Mother Porter called them, "tacky nylons, not fit to touch the legs of a Porter woman." Glory had grown up in nylons and knew well the feeling of threads snapping and runs heading up or down her leg. Only the magic of clear nail polish could stop them. But at seventeen years old, when she'd gone to live with the Porters, the first thing Mother Porter had taught her was, "satin for nighties, silk for undies," and Glory hadn't worn a pair of nylons in five years... until that day. She thought about the silk stockings tucked away in her bag that was stuffed into a tiny beige locker. She could put them on, ease the friction, stop the burning where her thighs rubbed together. *No.* She was a normal woman now, just plain Glory Bishop. No more silks and satins and designer pumps. The next day, she would go to Woolworth's and buy more pantyhose and a pair of cheap gym shoes, maybe even some plain earrings, and start her life without Malcolm... *if* she did a good enough job and *if* she was hired.

With fifteen minutes left on her lunch break, Glory stood in a phone booth outside the restaurant, dropped the quarter in the pay phone, and dialed the number she'd wanted to dial for the past month. An answering machine picked up on the seventh ring.

"Herschel! It's Glory!" she yelled over the background music and the friendly voice asking her to leave a message. "If you're there, please pick up!" At the beep, Glory tried to keep her voice calm. *But what if Malcolm already sent the police to Herschel's? What if he isn't answering because he can't?* "Herschel, please! If you're there, pick up—"

"Well, hellooo, Glory-Glory!" a delighted voice finally answered. "Hold on, let me shut off this stupid machine."

Glory listened while Herschel fussed about, trying to find the off switch. She wanted to laugh, but mostly, she wanted to collapse into her friend's arms and cry her eyes out. She wanted to tell the man who'd been like a sister to her the whole truth. But for the moment, Glory would have to be satisfied with protecting him from Malcolm.

"Glory-Glory, why haven't I heard from you in months? Being a church lady made you too good—"

"Herschel, I'm sorry I haven't called, and I promise I'll tell you everything one day." Glory looked up and down the block then glanced at her watch—ten minutes left. "But I don't have a lot of time to talk. I left Malcolm today, and he's gonna send the police to your place, looking for me. You hafta do something with the needles and birth control pills and stuff."

Glory listened to a few seconds of silence before Herschel cleared his throat and finally spoke. "I see," Herschel said in the deep male voice he only used when he was deadly serious. "Where are you right now? I can come—"

"No, Herschel. Malcolm is serious. He'll have the police rip the salon and your place apart just 'cause he can—"

"Glory-Glory, you just let me worry about that." He was back to his normal voice. "I've paid enough cops to keep the FBI and the CIA outta my wig. My only concern is you. Where are you?"

"I'm at a rest stop on my way to California." Glory hated herself for lying, but the less Herschel knew, the better. "I'm taking the bus." A police car cruised up the street. Glory turned her back and ducked her head. "I hafta go in a minute. I do need a favor, though."

"Anything, darling."

"There's a box in the last cabinet under the counter by the back door. It has some special stuff in it. Will you please keep it safe for me? Hide it in case the police do come? I don't want Malcolm to get it."

"So you've been planning this for a while, huh? Okay, darling. You call me from the next rest stop. I'll take care of things here. You be safe now!"

Glory could hear the wheels turning in Herschel's mind. She was right to call and honestly surprised that Malcolm hadn't gone after her friend yet. Hanging up the phone, she looked at her watch. No time to call anybody else.

Back inside the restaurant, Glory scurried behind the counter, grabbed a pitcher, and filled it with ice water. She topped off the water glasses of the customers seated at the counter, grabbed a fresh pot of coffee, and moved out to the dining room floor. In the crowded restaurant, the waitresses moved like a troupe doing a well-choreographed dance, ducking and dipping around each other with the occasional shout of "Behind you!" or "Coming through!" Glory waited for an opening and took her place in the dance, moving among the tables offering coffee and ice water at each table and sidestepping rushing waitresses and busboys.

Even though her feet hurt, Glory found herself smiling more often than she'd smiled in the last year. Every customer's mumbled "Thanks" lifted her spirit and gave her hope. When she occasionally caught Miss June's eye, the older woman would just nod at her. The crazy old lady at the cash register—Gram—laughed and joked with the customers, sometimes causing Glory to blush and prompting Miss June to yell, "Mama, would you stop it?" Gram would just rock back and forth and laugh.

"Why she alla time get so riled up?" Gram would ask whoever was in earshot. "I just be havin' a li'l fun."

"Hey, Gram." A customer stopped at the register to pay. "Why you be chewin' on that cigar alla time?"

"Aww, baaaby." Gram affected a feeble voice. "You know Gram like to keep her lips wrapped around a thick one."

"Dammit, Mama! It's Easter Sunday!"

The customers just laughed, and Glory hurried past to fill more water glasses.

By the sixth hour carrying water and coffee, the crowd had thinned out, and the three waitresses who'd left for the day had each tipped Glory ten dollars. Even though she was exhausted and her feet hurt, she sat in the breakroom and carefully counted the single dollar bills—the first money she'd actually worked hard for. She didn't count her years at Herschel's salon as work. She'd mostly just done a couple of loads of laundry and swept up a bit there. The rest of her work time had been spent reading the books her mother would never have allowed. But that day, being on her feet for six hours, dealing with rude customers, ducking and dodging speedy waitresses, Glory had worked up a real sweat.

"Girl, you did pretty good today!"

Glory jumped. She hadn't heard Roz approach. The tall, heavy-set woman had looked imposing as she moved gracefully among the tables, but she was the nicest and most patient of all the waitresses.

"So, how much ya get?" Roz asked. "You were working pretty hard out there."

"Thirty dollars." Glory tried to act nonchalant, folding the money and hiding it in her bra. "It wasn't hard at all. Can I ask you a question?"

"Yeah, what's up?"

"Do you think I did good enough to get hired? Will Ms. June let me work here?"

Roz leaned down to Glory's level. "June wouldn't a gave you that uniform if she wasn't gon' hire you... but you didn't hear that from me."

Glory bit her bottom lip but couldn't keep the smile from breaking through. "For real?"

Roz moved to the wall of small square lockers. "Yup. That's how I started here ten years ago." She opened a locker and pulled out a white cigarette case. "She gave me a uniform to 'try out.' I been here ever since. Even met my old man here." Roz grinned. "When he found out I made all the bread and desserts, he asked me to marry him. I said 'Sir, what is your name, and ain't you already married?' Aha ha!"

Glory laughed at Roz's tale of her courtship and marriage and having the reception in the restaurant. "So, you make all the desserts and bread? Really?"

"Yup. I'm about to go set up some dough for in the morning. Gotta bake a few cakes and some pies too." Roz lit a cigarette and sat down in a chair across from Glory. "Remember the blizzard in '79? We were open 'cause folks was stranded and needed to eat, but the bread and dessert trucks couldn't get through. I went back in the kitchen and whipped up some cornbread and a coupla carrot cakes. Now I do all the baking. I just wait tables sometimes for pocket money."

"Hey!"

Both women looked up as another waitress entered the breakroom. Tall and curvy, Stacey didn't walk—she sashayed. "Why you gotta pollute the air today?" she asked Roz. "It's Easter Sunday. Cain't you take that outside?"

"I can," Roz said, not moving from her seat. She took a long drag and blew the smoke in Stacey's direction. "But I'm not."

Stacey fanned the smoke away. "Imma have you arrested for assault and attempted murder!" She coughed dramatically. "What's her name, here, is a witness." She turned to Glory. "I'm sorry, what *is* your name?"

"Um, Glory—uh. Gloria," Glory stuttered.

"Okay, fine, Glory—uh," Stacey mimicked. "You're my witness."

Roz took one more puff on her cigarette, crushed it out in an overflowing ashtray, and blew her last bit of smoke at Stacey. "Too late. No evidence."

The women's laughter and playful argument was interrupted when June appeared in the doorway and cleared her throat. Glory had no idea how long she'd been standing there, but from the slight smirk on her face, Glory guessed she'd heard quite a bit.

"You were a big help today, Gloria," June said. "Keep the uniform, and come back tomorrow, say, ten o'clock. We'll see how you handle waiting tables. Okay?"

"Yes, ma'am." Glory dug her fingernails into her palms to keep from bouncing in her seat and bit her bottom lip to keep from smiling too big. Actually, she was so happy she wanted to hug the woman.

When June walked away, Glory fought down the urge to pray and praise God. She hadn't prayed since Bigma's funeral... since she'd knelt at the edge of the field beyond the garden and dug up a cotton root. Not since she made the tea and drank it for a week... and killed the little piece of Malcolm growing inside her.

THE HOTEL LOBBY SMELLED of cleaning chemicals. The peeling wallpaper, stained with years of smoke and neglect, barely hinted at the hotel's former classic elegance. Unembellished wood that once might have been highly polished was now covered with years of grime. Worn carpet in the middle of the lobby was held together by duct tape. Ancient furniture was stained with God only knew what.

Glory approached the plexiglass-enclosed front desk, tapped on the glass, and waited. After what felt like a reasonable amount of time, she knocked loudly.

"Hey! He can't hear too well," a man's voice said. "You gotta ring the bell up there!"

"Thanks." Glory looked around. The lobby was empty except for a person hidden behind a newspaper. High up on the plexiglass was a sign Glory couldn't believe she'd missed. She pushed the button below it and was answered by a sound somewhere between a gong and a clashing cymbal.

The man who made his way to the window was a lot younger than Glory expected. Tall and thin, the gaunt man smiled, showing jagged teeth. "Well, hello there! How can I help yo' fine self this evening?"

"Um, I'd like a room, please." Glory's heart was pounding. Her hotel experiences had only been four star and above. This place and this desk clerk were unlike anything she'd ever seen.

No. Wait. Glory pushed the uppity thoughts away. This man looked like anybody she'd see on the South Side—the men in front of the liquor store who called her church girl, the taxi driver she sometimes called when she could sneak out, and Tutu, her chauffeur, butler, and *keeper*. She was a normal woman now, no better than this man in front of her.

"Heh, heh, heh... you workin'?" the man asked.

"Yes, sir." Glory looked at the man's shirt, hoping to find a name tag. She didn't see one. "Across the street at the restaurant—"

"Ha ha ha ha!" The man laughed loudly, slapping the counter. "Woo, girl, you funny. I guess you ain't from around here, huh?"

"No..." Glory looked around for a name tag again, "Sir. Um... I just got into town."

"Um-hm." The man smirked. "New in town, and you land at the fabulous Hotel Toledo." He spread his arms and bowed, nearly hitting his head on the counter. "That's the story you're going with, huh?"

"I'm sorry?" Glory asked.

"Are... you... working?" He made a gesture with his fingers "You know, sellin' tail, peddlin' poontang, dancin' on dick!"

Glory's eyes went wide. Laughter came from the corner. "Boy, don't you know a lady when you see one?" the voice behind the newspaper asked. "Do she look like any hoe you ever seen?"

The desk clerk burst out laughing. "Ha ha ha! I'm just playin! I know she ain't no hoe, but you should see the look on her face! Ah ha ha ha!"

Glory smiled a little, letting the two men enjoy their joke at her expense. Between guffaws, the clerk checked Glory in and charged her a dollar for a plastic baggie of toiletries. "You need a key to get up here," he explained as they rode a rickety elevator to the fourth floor. "Elevator don't come up here without a key. You wanna come downstairs, you gotta walk down or call the desk." He opened the door to room 406. "People up here been here a long time—some for years. It's safe up here. Don't go on two or three. Tha's where people get rooms by the hour. Understand, Miss Gloria?"

"Yes, sir," Glory said. "Thank you."

She looked around the small wood-paneled room. The double bed sunken in the middle and the faded bedspread had obviously seen better days. Glory made a mental note to place a towel on the single flattened pillow. An old electric alarm clock rested on the scratched nightstand below a bedside lamp with a stained shade, next to the coin box to make the bed vibrate. The beige threadbare carpet, patched in places with duct tape, surprisingly matched the drapes and bedspread. At least, Glory hoped the bedspread was meant to be beige.

"Bathroom's in there." The man gestured toward a doorway on the other side of the bed near a window with metal bars. "The window bars got a latch. It's easy to open. Fire escape right out there." He pointed at the window and the open metalwork of the fire escape. Glory wondered if she could see the stars from there. "Phone's down the hall. If you want one in the room, it's a twenty-five-dollar deposit—"

"I don't need a phone," Glory said.

"Um-huh. Don't plan on callin' nobody, huh?" He looked Glory in the eye until she looked away. "No cookin'," he continued. "No pets and no overnight guests. I'a come knock on your door if yo' company stay too long. Tha's how we keep the riffraff away from up here."

"I won't be having any company."

"You get hungry, there's a shortcut to the bar next door right in the lobby. Through the door and down the hall to the Knotty Pine. They got good burgers sometimes, when the cook ain't drunk."

Glory guessed the clerk didn't get to talk to guests very often. He went on and on about the hotel's features and then began telling her about her neighbors in the other rooms on the fourth floor. As tired as she was, Glory politely listened to the man talk until her loud yawn interrupted his monologue.

"Oh... I guess you tired, huh? I'll leave you alone now."

"I'm sorry." Glory yawned again. "I am really tired. It's been a long day." She placed a hand on the loose doorknob. "Thank you for your help."

"You welcome, Miss Gloria. Don't forget to leave your key at the desk when you go to work tomorrow."

"I won't. Good night."

Glory shut the door behind the desk clerk, turned the deadbolt, put the chain on, and closed the second door latch. She leaned against the door and breathed a sigh of relief. She'd signed the register Gloria Jackson. The clerk hadn't asked for any ID, and Glory didn't know what she would have done if he had. She'd put Herschel as her emergency contact and hoped he'd never have to be called.

Taking in her surroundings, Glory detected the smell of pine cleaner and something else she didn't quite recognize. The bathroom was the smallest hotel bathroom she'd ever seen. Actually, the room was the smallest hotel room she'd ever seen. There was no actual closet, only a wall-mounted rack with wire hangers—some still with the paper from a local dry cleaner.

She pulled the drapes closed and slowly peeled off her uniform. Using half of the tiny bottle of shampoo, Glory washed her uniform and underwear in the sink and hung them on hangers on the rack. Careful to keep her hair dry, she showered quickly and wrapped herself in a towel. It was only six o'clock, still too early for bed, and Glory was sure she wouldn't be able to sleep anyway.

By that point, Malcolm would be worried. He'd have yelled at everybody in the hospital and probably called every bus station between Chicago and California. Glory shook her head. Malcolm had always underestimated her. Quiet, mousy little Glory. The good wife. Humble and obedient. He probably thought she'd just wandered off. Even if he believed she had purposely run away, he'd never think to look for her on the West Side. She wondered what her hospital roommate had told him. She'd be forever grateful to the older woman for her advice and for the two hundred dollars that had made her escape possible.

Opening the drawer on the nightstand, Glory found a phone book and a Bible. She ran her hand over the fake-leather cover and traced the gold lettering with her index finger. Part of her wanted to open it and read her favorite psalm, but she didn't dare. By causing the miscarriage—by aborting her pregnancy—Glory was no longer a child of God. Reading the Bible, praying, worshiping—they were all blasphemy. She'd committed an unforgivable sin.

Placing a hand against her belly, Glory felt only emptiness. Not just the emptiness of her womb but an emptiness in herself.

SHE WASN'T SURE WHAT pulled her from sleep. It could have been the window-shaking thunder or the knocking on her door. Glory stretched and looked around. The green glowing clock showed 8:13 p.m., and the sun had long ago set, leaving the room in total darkness except for the seconds when flashes of lightning cast the room in eerie blue. Another violent thunderclap was followed by more knocking on her door.

Turning on the bedside lamp, Glory fought down panic. It didn't make sense that Malcolm could have found her so quickly. All she had to do was not answer. She quietly slipped out of bed and found her clothes. With every thunderclap and lightning flash, the knocking grew louder and harder until the visitor was actually banging. After quickly pulling on her skirt and blouse, Glory opened the window latch.

"Yoo-hoo! New girl? You in there?"

Glory stared at the door. Okay, so it wasn't Malcolm.

"Yoo-hoo hoo! I'm Willow Aspen, your neighbor down the hall!" More banging. "I'm not a pervert or anything!"

Glory tiptoed to the door. Through the peephole, at the exact moment of an especially bright lightning and loud thunderclap, she looked into a gray-green eye. She thought she should probably scream and maybe be afraid. Instead, with the chain and latch still in place, Glory opened the door.

"Can I help you?" Glory asked the tiny woman in the bright-green footie pajamas—the same green as her hair.

"Hi, I'm Willow." The strange-looking woman stuck her hand through the narrow space. "Nice to meet you." She moved her hand up and down. "You know, knights always shook right hands 'cause that was their sword hand. It proved they didn't have a weapon and meant no harm."

Glory smiled in spite of herself and shook Willow's hand. "Hi. Nice to meet you too."

"I brought cookies and hot chocolate and marshmallows. I'm the welcome wagon! I even brought my coffeepot... but you hafta supply the water."

"Okay." Glory pushed the door closed, unhooked the chain, and opened the latch.

So far, her day had gone better than she'd dared to hope. Sharing hot chocolate with the little green woman seemed like a good finale. She opened the door.

"Hi, I'm Glory... ah." She stepped back and ushered Willow in. "Welcome to my very humble home."

"That's not your name," Willow said. "I know exactly who you are! I knew it the minute I saw you moving in. You don't belong here."

Glory took a step back. The woman was probably half her size. Glory was sure she could take her—she'd fought Malcolm before. *But then what?* Glory thought about the $160 in her purse. Maybe she could buy the woman's silence.

"Yup," Willow continued, "You're Balsam Pine."

Huh?

"The most beautiful of the evergreen family."

"Okaaay?" Glory didn't pretend to understand.

"Balsam Pine is used to make Xmas trees. No, it's not bad to say Xmas 'cause in Greek, the first letter of Christ is *chi*—the Greek letter *X*—so Xmas is okay. And you're beautiful like a balsam pine tree. Totally not a hooker or dope fiend. Am I right?"

Glory almost laughed. "You're absolutely right, Miss Willow—"

"Oh, I'm not Miss anything. Just plain Willow."

Glory smiled at the elfin woman who was barely as tall as her shoulder. Willow looked to be in her mid to late twenties, and Glory guessed that she was a performer of some sort, which turned out to be correct. Willow told stories of playing her instruments in the subways, and Glory talked about her first day at work and what she could of her own story.

"So you just up and left home and came to Chicago?" Willow sipped her third cup of hot chocolate. "What about your boyfriend? What if he comes back looking for you?"

Glory absently twisted a bracelet on her left wrist. "He won't come looking for me. Especially not here."

"You know, you talk kinda funny. You're from Mississippi, but you don't have an accent. You have this Southern dialect—like you said 'real good' instead of 'very well'—but you talk like you're from Chicago."

Glory stood up from the corner of the bed and stretched. She glanced at the clock. The two women had been talking for over an hour, and the storm showed no signs of letting up.

A loud thunderclap caused Willow to jump, nearly spilling her drink. "I hate storms. It's like God is yelling at us."

Glory pulled back the curtain and looked out into the night. "You scared of storms?" It wasn't so much a question as an observation. "I've learned to love storms. The rain washing all the bad stuff away. It's like a loud party in the sky, with bumping music and flashing lights." Glory sipped her cocoa. "I sleep real good in storms."

CHAPTER 26

Waiting tables came naturally to Glory. After only three days, she was balancing seven dishes on her arms or carrying five water glasses without spilling a drop. After being reminded about pop refills—not free—and coffee refills, which were free, Glory sailed through each day, and her tips grew larger. On her fifth day, she accepted a second uniform and a full-time position at O'Reilly's Restaurant.

"Hey, Gram!" Glory greeted the elderly cashier as she entered the crowded restaurant to start her shift, the lunch rush in full swing.

Though most of the other waitresses complained, Glory enjoyed the hustle and bustle of the afternoon crowd. The radio, tuned to WGCI, blared out the noontime news update then switched to a bit of smooth jazz. She wove her way through the commotion to the back room, pausing to watch Mr. Perry and Zac at the grill. Though Zac was twice his father's size, the two men moved in perfect sync. When Zac went left, Mr. Perry went right. Sometimes, Miss June had to come back to the kitchen and tell her husband and son to slow down—the waitresses couldn't get the food out to the tables fast enough. Since he'd been there since morning, Zac's apron was stained with the colors of the day, while Mr. Perry, having just arrived, was neat and pressed and clean as a whistle. Glory loved watching the father-son duo in action.

She quickly stuffed her backpack into her locker, checked her face in the mirror, and rushed out to the dining room. Over the past couple of days, Glory had been letting Willow do her makeup, and she barely recognized herself. The heavy bright colors created a pink, purple, green, and black mask around her eyes. Sharp rouge defined her cheekbones, and her neutral-colored lips dazzled with frosted lip gloss. Her hair, bound in a fluffy side ponytail with feathers attached to the end, completed the look.

"Girl, you lookin' like Rainbow Brite up in here," Gram had said. "Why you tryin' to hide your pretty face? Lookin' like all the rest of these painted-up—"

"Mama, hush!" June called from somewhere in the dining room.

Gram laughed. "Hee-hee-hee. Miss High-and-Mighty don't know I steal a quarter every time she get to hollerin'. I'm finna be a millionaire! Ha ha ha ha!"

Glory laughed with Gram and then carried a water pitcher to refill the glasses at her tables. Her section included six booths of different sizes, including one right behind the cashier station with four cops talking and laughing rather loudly. Occasionally, one of the other waitresses would stop by to chat with them, but Glory tried her best to serve them quickly and then move on.

When she delivered their desserts, one of the cops, Max, grabbed her hand. "Gloria, what's the hurry? You never stop to chat with us. You should get to know us, maybe have a little fun some-times."

Glory pulled her hand away. "Excuse me, I have other customers to check on." She wiped her hand on her apron as she moved to the next table.

"Man, that's one uptight broad," Max said.

Glory busied herself drying a table that the busboy had left too wet.

"She just needs a little lube," another cop said. "Slap her on the ass a couple of time—that'll do the trick!"

"Nah," said a third. "Just grab her by the hair and slob her down. She'll be all yours!"

The fourth cop chimed in. "Ha! She'll be runnin' outta here, crying like a baby!" All four cops laughed loud and long.

"Heh heh heh." Gram joined in their laughter. "Tha's real funny. Know what else is funny?"

"Ha. Naw, Gram. What else is funny?" The group of men snickered as Glory moved another table away.

"Heh heh, y'all lay a finger on that girl, I 'a whoop yo' ass till God don't know you! Ha ha mutha—"

"Mama," June growled through clenched teeth. The owner and head waitress stopped at the cash register. "If you don't stop cussin' so much..." June left her threat hanging in the air and moved on to greet a customer.

"Heh heh heh. She said not to cuss so much. That mean I can still cuss some. Hee-hee-hee!"

"Aw, Gram, how you gon' beat up a cop?" A regular customer stopped at the register and handed Gram a guest check. "You cain't walk, and that man got a gun."

"Ha! So what?" Gram shot back. "I got two guns. One under this counter and one right in here." She reached down into the front of her striped duster.

June's hand slammed on the glass-topped counter, causing everyone nearby to jump. "Mama, don't you dare!"

"All right, all right," Gram mumbled. "That girl ain't no fun at all. Just for that, I'm taking two quarters."

When seven o'clock rolled around, Glory began her side work: replacing ketchup and mustard bottles and filling salt and pepper shakers. Wiping the tables, she was reminded of her time cleaning the back rooms of Herschel's salon—the exotic scents of Herschel's beauty treatments, the noise of the customers and stylists, and the parties on Thursday nights. She'd been away from home for less than a week, but it had been months since she'd last seen the salon, and she so missed it. After that one phone call to Herschel on Easter Sunday, Glory hadn't contacted anybody else. Sometimes, she thought about who besides Malcolm might be worried about her. She wondered about Tutu but forbade herself to care about his fate as he had never cared about hers. Glory tipped the busboys and thanked them for their help and then started cleaning up behind the counter. Humming to herself while wiping the shelves under the counters with bleach water, Glory bumped her head when somebody touched her shoulder.

"Sorry, didn't mean to scare you," June said. "Come find me when you finish up."

"Yes, ma'am." Glory glanced at her watch. "I'm almost done." She picked up her pace, and minutes later, she pulled her tightly packed backpack from her locker. She looked around the back rooms for June, unable to imagine what could be the matter.

She found June in the back office. "Grab one of those boxes. Help me get these upstairs."

Glory followed June through the kitchen and out to a door marked Not an Exit that was, in fact, a well-lit exit to a wooden back porch. Climbing the stairs, Glory was surprised at how sturdy they were. She'd expected the creak and bounce of an old building structure, but this porch and staircase felt solid.

"This is all new," June said.

Glory nearly stumbled as June answered her unspoken question.

"Yeah," June said. "We got this building in '74, few years after the riots. Most everything was still burnt out and boarded up. Restaurant was one of the only things still open on this block."

They reached the landing on the second floor and paused. "Why didn't the restaurant get messed up?" Glory asked.

June laughed a little. "Oh, it got messed up, just not burnt up. Windows smashed, cigarette machine and pay phone stolen. Broke a lotta glass... a whole lotta glass."

"That was in '68, right? When Dr. King passed?"

"When he was *murdered*." June spat over the rail and continued their upward journey. "Yeah. Whole West Side was burning except the black-owned businesses. That's how we saved the restaurant. Old Mizz O'Reilly let me tell folks I was the owner and she was just a front. She sold me the restaurant in '72, and then when she went to Florida in '78, she sold me and Perry the building."

"Oh." Glory didn't know what else to say.

Reaching the final landing on the third floor, June pulled out keys and unlocked a black metal gate on a gray-painted door. Down a long dim hallway, the two women walked, June humming to herself and Glory taking notice of the chipped stucco walls and bits of cigarette ash and butts on the floor.

"Damn riffraff!" June said. "Messin' up other people's property!" She stomped her feet a few times for emphasis.

They passed two sets of doors marked *G, H, I,* and *J,* then through a heavy wood door with a small cracked window, then past doors marked *D, E,* and *F.* finally stopping at door *C.* June used her keys on a metal gate and two deadbolt locks. "Come on in. Set that box down anywhere." June pointed at a small kitchen area. "Maybe right there on that counter."

Glory dropped the box on the counter with a loud *thunk.* She cringed when she heard the rattle of glass and metal, hoping she hadn't broken anything.

June placed her box on the window seat of a tall narrow bay window then joined Glory in the kitchen at the counter. "Put down your bag. Have a seat. This gon' take a minute."

"Um... okay." Glory put down her bag and took a seat on a wobbly orange vinyl-covered stool at the orange Formica counter. The panels in the cabinet doors had been painted bright orange, as had the window and doorframes. Though orange was not her favorite color, Glory could see how someone could find the space cozy.

June turned on the water in the sink. The faucet sputtered a bit before spitting out a stream of grayish water. She then pulled a small pot from the box, filled it with the eventually clear running water, and set it on the stove. "How you like your tea? Strong? Sugar?"

"Uh, yeah," Glory answered. "That's fine." The dark wood-paneled walls matched the kitchen cabinets and the floor. The gold stove and refrigerator gave Glory the impression that someone had carefully decorated the studio apartment.

"So, what's your real name?" June asked.

"Pardon me?" Glory had no idea what she'd been expecting, but it definitely was not that question.

"You heard me." June placed two mugs on the counter and bowed her head in quick prayer. "You been on my clock for almost a week. If Imma give you a paycheck, it has to have your real name on it."

"Oh." Glory hung her head and took a deep breath. She'd made over a hundred dollars in tips that week. If she needed to find somewhere else to go, she would. But as quickly as the thought of leaving entered her mind, she pushed it away. In the short time she'd been there, Glory felt like she was making friends at the diner and at the Hotel Toledo. She really didn't want to leave.

"My name is Glory Bishop," she said.

"Nice to meet you, Glory." June sipped her tea. "Where you from?"

"Nowhere near here." Glory hoped she could evade any other questions.

"I know that, but you ain't from too far outta town. Suburbs? Evanston? Up north somewhere?"

"No, ma'am. I lived on the South Side, South Shore."

June leaned forward and placed her elbows on the counter. "What you hiding from, Glory?"

For some reason, Glory was near tears. *How can I tell this good, Christian woman I killed my baby and left my husband? How can I tell June I'm hiding from God?* Glory twisted a bracelet on her left wrist. "I left my husband."

"You the one on the news this week. Distraught woman that wandered away from the hospital?"

"I don't know," Glory answered honestly. She hadn't watched TV all week. "Maybe."

"Well, you don't look too much like the picture. All that make-up, and your hair is different. Are you in trouble? Cops after you? Gangs?"

"Oh, no, ma'am." Glory blushed. "Nothing like that. I just couldn't live with him anymore."

"Didn't tell *him* that, huh? What if he finds you?" June sipped her tea again.

Glory lifted her cup with shaking hands and tasted the tea. Smooth and sweet. No bitterness. "He won't come to the West Side. I had a friend tell him I was goin' to California."

"You think he believes that?" June smiled a little. Glory breathed a sigh of relief.

"I hope so, ma'am." Glory locked eyes with June for a moment and then looked away.

"Mm-hm." June stood up straight and drained her cup. "Deedee told me you stayin' across the street at the Toledo. You need a real address on your paycheck. You can use this one. Rent is a hundred fifty dollars a month. Includes utilities. Deedee is across the hall, and Zac and Renee are next door. They pay a hundred fifty too. I charge you same as I charge my kids."

Glory stood up and walked around. On the right side of the room were two doors, one to the bathroom and the other to a large closet. The daybed near the window against the wall had a somewhat discolored mattress and two drawers at the bottom.

"Had a girl in here for three years," June said. "She went to DePaul. Just graduated in January. She kept the place pretty clean." June ran her hand over the counter. "She picked the color for the appliances."

Glory walked over to the tall bay window and looked down on the intersection of Madison and Cicero Avenues. When she squinted, the colored lights looked just like Seventy-Fifth Street, and the sounds coming up from the street sounded like the neighborhood where she'd grown up. She opened the window and leaned out. Looking up, she could only make out the brightest stars, but the smells of the diner and the thumping music from across the street... when she closed her eyes, she was back home.

She closed the window and turned back to June. "I don't know what to say." Glory's voice was just louder than a whisper. She cleared her throat and tried again. "I mean, yes, I want this apartment. I just don't know... why? Why are you being so nice to me?"

June laughed a little. "Girl, I knew you were in trouble when you first came in here. You still had on that hospital band, and it looked like everything you owned was in that backpack. All that makeup didn't cover the spot under your eye. I just had a feeling about you, and when the Lord gives me a feeling about somebody, I listen."

"Oh." Glory's mind raced. She would need some more chairs and a table and pots and pans and dishes and linens. She looked at June again, and this time she smiled. "I don't know how to thank you. When can I move in?"

"You can move in now if you want. The box on the counter has a few things to get you started. The other box has towels and stuff for the bed. You can give it back when you get your own stuff."

"Um... can I hug you, Miss June?" Glory didn't actually wait for an answer. She walked up to the older woman and gently wrapped her arms around June's neck.

She felt a familiar pressure building up inside her chest, the same pressure she felt when the music or the message at church was especially stirring. Pressure like something pushing and pulling on her heart at the same time. Pressure that used to force its way up and out of her throat as thanks and praise to God. This time, though, now that she was no longer a child of God, Glory swallowed her thanks and praise, squeezed her eyes shut to stave off tears, and tried to compose herself.

"Thank you so much, Miss June." Her words came out garbled as she choked on a sob.

"You're welcome." June rubbed Glory's back. "I got a good feeling about you, girl. The Lord is gon' take you through whatever trials you got."

After June left, Glory more closely inspected her new home. The wood paneling and floor were rough in places where the varnish had rubbed off, but mostly, the place was in good condition. She found wire hangers and a folding table with three chairs deep in the long narrow closet. The stained-glass window in the back of the closet cast blue light from a nearby streetlamp. Glory imagined a musician standing in that blue light and smiled a little. She unpacked the box on the kitchen counter and wasn't surprised to find two sets of dishes from the restaurant, but she was quite pleased to find a few utensils and a three-piece set of red aluminum cookware with wooden handles.

In the box on the window seat, Glory found a set of mismatched sheets, a bedspread, towels, and a can of spray disinfectant. She twirled and danced around the apartment, using the can as a microphone, singing the words to the happiest song she knew. Spinning and spraying, Glory disinfected the closet and hung up her clean new uniform. She sprayed the mattress and then made her bed and emptied her backpack into the two freshly disinfected drawers. She always carried her belongings with her, leaving nothing in her hotel room, not even the soap, reasoning that she'd have everything she needed if she had to run away again.

"Well, Daddy, that was easy," Glory said into the empty space. "I'm glad I have tomorrow off. I need to do a little shopping." She laughed at herself, wondering why it was okay to sing to herself but silly to talk out loud to herself. Glory shook her head and went to stand under a warm shower.

WHEN SHE REALIZED SHE was waking up, Glory pulled the blanket up over her face. *There's no way it's morning already!* With her eyes closed, she pulled the cover down slowly, until morning sunshine forced its way through her eyelids. She groaned, sat up in bed, looked around, and smiled. She leaned over the side of the bed, opened a drawer, and dug out the stolen hospital gown that served as her robe. Pulling the gown over her shoulders and tying it in the front, she swung her feet to the cool floor and stood up. She made a mental note to buy a rug. Looking around the one-room apartment, Glory decided that she'd keep up with the orange motif and get orange curtains and towels and whatever else she could find. She'd eventually get a TV, but she decided against getting a phone right away.

At twenty-two years old and after five years of marriage, Glory felt like an adult for the first time in her life. She got dressed in the only outfit she had, including a new pair of nylons. She opened the window to check the weather and decided against wearing her coat.

Going out, she tried the locks three times, smiling uncontrollably each time a lock clicked open and closed.

Her first stop was the Hotel Toledo to officially check out.

"You know you paid for the whole week, right? No refunds, workin' girl!"

"I know, George." Glory laughed. "I don't want a refund. I just wanna check out. I got an apartment!" Glory smiled at the front desk clerk behind the acrylic glass.

"Nobody checks outta here, girly." The voice behind the newspaper laughed. "They just leave or get carried out! Ah ha ha ha! Tell her, George! Remember the trick on the second floor? Died in the saddle! Woo! Now, that was funny!"

George laughed a little and shook his head. "Yeah... some freak in a real saddle playin' cowboy. We found him after a few days—"

Glory held up a hand to interrupt the story. "That's okay. I don't need that picture in my head."

"Yup! Ass up, saddle on his back! Ah ha ha!" The voice behind the newspaper went from laughing to coughing.

"That's what you get!" George yelled. "Girl said she didn't wanna hear it! 'M sorry, Miss Gloria. You the first real lady we had in a long time. Hate to see you go."

Glory was grateful for the plexiglass barrier. Otherwise, she might feel obliged to hug the scruffy man, who seemed to have cleaned himself up a bit in the week she'd been there. "Thanks, George. But you'll see me around. I'm still workin' across the street. See ya!"

Glory's next stop was Woolworth's. She decided to walk the two blocks and explore her new neighborhood. The shops on Cicero Avenue looked just like the ones on Seventy-Fifth Street. Even the people looked the same. There were a few more boarded-up storefronts than on the South Side, but otherwise, Glory felt right at home.

"Hey, Miss, can I talk to you?"

"Sorry, I'm in a hurry." Glory picked up her pace, not looking at the young man keeping up with her.

"Oh, that's okay, then. I see you workin' in that restaurant. I'll come talk to you there, okay?" the young man called to Glory.

Glory shook her head and kept walking. She smiled a little. She'd forgotten how it felt to be flirted with—boys vying for her attention, telling her she was special. She fanned a fly away, and the clink of her bracelets interrupted her pleasant thoughts. *I am my beloved's, and his desire is toward me.* Just thinking about the bracelets' inscriptions made her heart ache. That verse from Song of Solomon—she'd read it out loud four times the night Malcolm locked the bracelets on her wrists. Glory had felt so loved that night, and Malcolm had loved to hear her recite the verse.

"Whose beloved are you?"

"Yours."

"And who is my desire toward?"

"Me."

After a few years, though, Glory grew to hate that verse. All the times they fought, he reminded her that she belonged to him. Glory shook her head again, shaking off the melancholy that threatened to darken her day. Malcolm was not there and was not coming to the West Side to find her.

Inside Woolworth's, Glory bought a rolling shopping cart and a few other things, then she made her way a little farther up the street to the grocery store. She laughed at herself a bit, imagining she looked like an old lady dragging that shopping cart behind her.

CHAPTER 27
Summer 1989

"Your hair looks great like that, Gloria." Willow sipped her iced tea. "Like an African princess or something."

"You really think so?" Glory almost ran her hand over her netted hair but caught herself. "Thanks."

Her cornrows had been Deedee's idea. Since Glory had confided in the Parnells' daughter, Deedee had been helping Glory to change her look. Her cornrows were wound and braided with white and gold beads, making Glory feel like she wore a crown.

"I'll be right back." Glory yawned, reminding herself, not for the first time, why she'd accepted this five o'clock Thursday-morning shift. She liked the early mornings, and her regular customers seemed to like her too. Glory left her friend sitting at the counter and ran back to the kitchen to check the bacon.

"Anybody out there?" Zac stood at the slicer, cutting a turkey breast into thin slices. Next, he'd do the roast beef and corned beef brisket. With Zac in the kitchen, preparing for the lunch rush, Glory came in and cooked the breakfast meats, since he wouldn't touch pork.

She went to the fancy oven with double doors and checked on the three pans of bacon. "Just Willow and the one other person," Glory said.

The bacon was almost ready. She closed the oven doors, set the timer for four minutes, and decided to wait. After these three, she only had six more pans of bacon and five pans of sausage to cook. That would be enough to get through the breakfast rush until the other cooks and Roz arrived at eight.

Just as the timer dinged, the bell over the front door out in the dining room jingled. Glory carefully pulled the pans from the oven and quickly replaced them with three more. She used a spatula marked *pork* to transfer the meat to a tray lined with grease-absorbing brown paper. As she headed back out to the dining room, she ignored Zac mumbling about her leaving "swine juice" lying around his kitchen.

Willow looked up from her comic book. "As I was saying, that's a really nice look for you. Now you look like a real Chicago girl."

Glory shook her head at her friend. "Yeah, I look different all right, but I'm not sure. The braids are so tight it's itchy, and sleeping on these beads is miserable."

"Well, you said you wanted to look different. You look nothing like you did a few months ago. Your skin is even different."

The new customer approached the counter. "Y'all still got that two-dollar breakfast?"

"Yes, ma'am," Glory said. The woman wore an army-green backpack over a tattered flannel shirt, which was over at least two T-shirts. Her cornrowed hair had grown out to a fuzzy afro with lint and other bits of debris visible. "Have a seat anywhere." Glory motioned around the dining room. "How you want your eggs? You want coffee?" Glory picked up a coffeepot.

"Why cain't I sit here at the counter with y'all? Yo' customers too good to sit next to me?"

"No, ma'am," Glory said smoothly. "I just figured you'd wanna have room to set your bags next to you." Glory leaned over the counter and looked toward the floor. "Looks to me like you're carrying a pretty heavy load."

The woman looked down and then looked back up. "Yeah, I guess. Imma go set in that big one in the corner. That okay with you?"

"Anywhere you want. Need some help with your bags?"

"Nah, I got—"

"Lemme help you with those, ma'am." Another customer had gotten up from the counter. The short heavyset man grabbed two of the woman's bags and headed for one of the large circular booths before she could finish her protest.

The bag lady mumbled something about pushy men as she followed him to the corner booth.

"So, how you want your eggs?" Glory called.

"Scramble hard! Decaf coffee!"

After about six minutes, Glory placed a breakfast plate on the table in front of her third customer of the day.

The lady slid two dollars in change across the table. "Take that. Ain't gon' need nothin' else."

"Yes, ma'am." Glory scooped up the money and dropped it into her apron pocket. "I'll leave you alone. Just holler if you need something."

The bag lady grunted a response as she dug into her breakfast. Back at the counter, Glory prepared herself a cup of tea and leaned against the counter. She probably drank too much tea, but after years of Malcolm always ordering coffee for her, she relished the freedom to drink tea whenever she wanted.

"Well, I gotta get going." Willow got up from the counter stool and smoothed her skirt. She wore a simple white skirt and yellow tank top, but her hair was flaming red.

"Where are you playing today?" Glory asked Willow. She glanced down the counter at another customer, who was reading the newspaper.

"I'm going to the Clark and Lake L station for a while." Willow stood up and grabbed her trumpet and violin cases. "Then to the subway or the Metra if it starts raining again."

"Have a good one!" Glory called as her friend left the restaurant. She then headed into the kitchen to attend to the bacon.

By ten o'clock, the breakfast crowd had come and gone, and O'Reilly's Restaurant was gearing up for the lunch rush. All of the condiments on the tables were refilled, and a few of the waitresses stood at the counter, rolling flatware in paper napkins. Gram had taken up her usual spot at the cash register, and in the kitchen, Roz was busy baking, and Zac was arguing loudly with Joe, the prep cook, about baseball.

"Hey, hey, Gloria! You know what Big T wants!" The big round man's voice boomed through the dining room, drowning out the jingle of the bell over the door. "Put some more sugar in that sweet tea this time. You was kinda off yesterday!"

"Heeey, Big Daddy," Gram said as Tom pushed a table aside and rolled his bulk into the booth across from her. "When you gon' come and get some 'a this-here brown sugar?"

"Aww, Gram." Tom huffed, settling into the seat. "You know you too much woman for a young buck like me."

Glory shook her head as Gram and Tom laughed. She placed a tall glass of sweet tea and a cup of ice on his table. "Here ya go, Tom." Glory refused to call him *Big* anything. "I'll tell Zac to get your steak on—"

"Make sure he burn it and gimme some mashed potatoes with it. None of that powder stuff either. Just mash me up some hash browns with a little butter and black pepper, maybe some onions."

"Sunny-side up?" Glory knew the answer, but she asked anyway.

"Yup but only three today. This booth gettin' a little tight."

"You got it, Tom." Glory patted his shoulder and headed off to put the order in. Back in the kitchen, Roz stood watching Zac slam down his spatula.

"I'm not doing it! That's the third time this week, and I refuse to burn another steak for that... that... heathen!"

"Zac, man, you say that every time." Joe picked up Zac's spatula and held it out to him. "C'mon man. Just give the customer what he wants."

"By the time y'all finish arguing," Roz said, "that steak'll be nice and burnt. Just don't set the alarm off again!"

"Don't forget the black pepper in the mashed hash browns—" Glory began.

"You better not dump no pepper on my grill!" Zac said.

His tirade was cut short when his father walked in. "Boy, what you fussin' 'bout now? You worse than yo' mama." Perry Parnell bumped fists with Zac and Joe and tipped an invisible hat to Roz and Glory. "Man want a burnt steak at least four days out the week. He payin' yo' salary. You better burn the hell outta that steak." Mr. Perry laughed, but everybody knew he was serious, and Zac pressed the juicy T-bone on the broiler rack.

Back out in the dining room, Glory carried the coffeepot around and greeted her regular customers. The ten o'clock crowd was mostly seniors and a few families out for a late breakfast. Big Tom sent his compliments to the chef for another perfectly burnt steak and mashed hash browns. Marcus came in with his grandson, Li'l Man. The Alexander sisters relaxed in their usual booth. The three women met twice a week, read the obituaries out loud from three different newspapers, and planned the funerals they'd attend. Gram called them the old biddies.

"Good morning, ladies." Glory poured coffee for two of the sisters and placed a small pot of hot water in front of the third. "Anything different today?"

"Yes," the middle sister said. "Could you sprinkle a little cinnamon sugar on my English muffin, sweetie?"

"Yes, ma'am." Glory didn't need to write down their order. In a couple of weeks, she'd learned it by heart: bacon and eggs times two—scrambled soft—and hard buttered white toast. The middle sister always ordered hard-boiled eggs, an English muffin, and hot water with lemon. Listening to the three sisters bicker, Glory imagined that would be her, Tressa, and Christy in a few years.

Glory pushed away pangs of guilt when she thought about her best friends. No doubt Malcolm had contacted them, and they would be worried. She thought about telling her friends that not only had she left, but she was also in hiding... and she wondered what they would think about the miscarriage.

ON A WARM FRIDAY AFTERNOON, Stacey set a cup of tea on the counter in front of Glory. "'Bout time you got here. Don't look around, but two dudes been in and outta here all day looking for you. One kinda young, he's a regular—pretty buff, dark skin. The other one older, earring, purple shirt with ruffles... said he was your sister."

Glory spun around and jumped down from the stool. "Herschel!"

Across the dining room, a tall man unfolded himself from his seat. "Glory-Glory?"

Glory and the man rushed toward each other, scooting around patrons and dodging waitresses. Glory flung herself at her best friend in the world, not caring about the spectacle they made. Herschel caught her up in a bear hug and lifted her off her feet.

"Glory-Glory! Oh, hallelujah, Glory-Glory!" Herschel sobbed. He hugged her and kissed the top of her head before setting her back on her feet.

"Herschel, how did you find me?" Glory asked, wiping her own tears. "How?" She looked up at the man who'd been like a sister to her and hugged him again.

"You remember my cousin Allen? You met him the first time I brought you to the West Side."

"Yeah..." Glory took a good look at the handsome young man she recognized as a frequent customer. "Is that him?" She waved to him.

"Yup, that's him." Herschel took Glory's hand and pulled her toward the booth. "He told me you were here, but I didn't believe him, and he said you didn't recognize him."

Allen stood up. "Yeah, I tried to talk to you a couple months ago, but you were moving too fast." He offered his hand and that devastating smile.

Sliding into the booth, Glory hung her head. "I'm sorry. I didn't remember you. I was goin' through some stuff a couple months ago. How have you been?"

Allen smiled again. "No biggie. I probably sounded like a flirt or something." He sipped his pop. "Herk didn't believe me when I told him you were here. Said you were in California or somethin'."

"Well, that's what she told me," Herschel said accusingly. "You've got some explainin' to do, girl." He slipped an arm around Glory's shoulders and squeezed. "I missed you so much." Herschel squeezed Glory again. "Did you ever go to California, or have you been here all along?"

"I started seeing her here a couple of months ago," Allen said. "I thought she looked familiar and was gonna reintroduce myself, but she was always too busy."

"Now I'm embarrassed." Glory blushed. "I should've recognized you—"

"Why? You only saw me that one time... and it was what, five years ago?"

"I guess, and we only talked for, like, five minutes. But you recognized *me*. How's your grandmother doing—"

"And a good thing he recognized you too," Herschel said. "I thought you were long gone, and I told Malcolm and the police you called me from somewhere between Chicago and California. Malcolm was crazy worried, Glory-Glory. What's going on?"

Glory looked from Herschel to Allen. "Nothin' important enough to talk about now. Stacey said you were here all day?"

"Yup," Allen said. "I wouldn't let Herk leave. He told the waitress he was your sister." Allen laughed. "I don't think she believed him. Anyway, I'm gonna get going and leave y'all to catch up. My work here is done."

Herschel slid out of the booth, and Glory stood to hug Allen. "Thank you so much. It's really good seeing you again."

Allen laughed. "You see me at least once a week."

Glory punched him in the shoulder. "Well, it's really good knowing you again."

After Allen left, Herschel took the seat across from Glory. "So, now, tell me the truth about how you got that scar through your eyebrow."

Glory's hand went to her face. She sighed. "Me and Malcolm had a fight."

"Oh, really?" Herschel's voice deepened. "When?"

"Know what?" Glory said. "Let's get out of here." She got up from her seat. "Let me show you my apartment."

"Oh no, you're not getting out of this. I've been too worried about you for too long—"

"Okay." Glory took his hand. "I'll tell you when we get upstairs."

She paid their bill and led Herschel through the back rooms to the stairway and up to her apartment. Glory opened the door with a flourish. She'd recently finished decorating with orange and goldenrod accessories that matched the kitchen cabinets and appliances.

"Girl, this is adorable." Herschel gushed. "Looks like the Great Pumpkin blew up in here. Why is it so hot?" He went to the window and opened it. "See, tha's a nice breeze comin' in. Nice view too!"

Glory watched her friend flit around her one-room apartment, touching and rearranging things, chattering all the time. She poured two glasses of iced tea and grabbed a box of strawberry butter cookies from the cabinet.

"So, no roaches or nothin'?" Herschel asked, taking a seat at the counter.

"Nope. Nothin'." Glory raised her glass. "Free at last!" She touched her glass to Herschel's and took a sip.

"So, you and Malcolm had a fight, or did Malcolm just fight you?"

"Well," Glory began, "you were right..."

An hour later, Herschel sat dabbing his eyes. "I knew it, I knew it, I knew it. Last year when you stopped comin' around—always busy with church or somethin'—I knew somethin' was wrong. Dammit, Glory-Glory, why didn't you say anything?"

Glory hung her head. "The first time he hit me, I was shocked, but I married him anyway. Then I was just embarrassed, and... I didn't know better. I thought that was just being married. I thought if I just acted better and listened better... if I was more godly..." Glory looked up at Herschel. "At first, he just hurt me when I was rude or when I messed up, so I tried to be good. And I loved my husband, I promise I did. But he... he... Herschel, he raped me... over and over again. I didn't know that's what it was. I thought he was entitled to my body whenever he wanted. I was being the good wife." Glory wiped a tear. "*His desire was toward me.* God, I hate him so much."

Herschel blew his nose loudly. "Do people here know you're in hiding?"

"I told just the Parnells and Roz. I don't know—maybe everybody knows by now."

"What are you gon' do when he finds you? If Allen recognized you, somebody else might."

"He won't find me." Glory said confidently. "He hates the West Side so much I think he's actually scared of it. He always talks about how it's nothing but evil over here. There's no way he'll come this way looking for me. He thinks I'm in California, right?"

"Glory-Glory, you didn't see him. He was actually screaming that I was hiding you. The cops had to hold him back. Almost took off my wig then. That man will go anywhere to find you. He's obsessed."

Glory held up her wrists. The bracelets clinked. "He thinks he owns me. I'm his most prized possession. You can't love somebody and do what he did to me." Glory let out a deep breath. "Waking up with my mother telling me it was my fault..."

Herschel placed a hand on Glory's and squeezed.

Glory waved him off. "I'm okay. When I wasn't okay, I prayed to die, but I'm okay now. I'm just mad. I'm mad at myself for being stupid enough to get manipulated."

Herschel slammed his hand on the counter. "No, girl. You cain't blame yourself. That was a grown man movin' in on a seventeen-year-old child. He was wrong—"

"Oh, I know. Him and my mother. It's their fault. I was a child," Glory spat. "All I knew was that I wanted to have my own place and be a normal girl. Malcolm promised me that... and his mother actually gave me all that. But I threw it all away and married that... that..." She growled under her breath. "Oh my God, I was sooo stupid."

"No," Herschel snapped. "Don't you dare beat yourself up. Already beat up enough as it is. The important thing is you got away."

"Not really." Glory shook the bracelets on her wrists. "He still has the key. You know, I didn't love him when he gave them to me. I let him put these shackles on me—my uncle went ballistic—but I thought it was so loving and romantic. And he was so powerful it was almost scary. I was such a child."

"Yeah, you were," Herschel said. "You know you can come back home. I'll always have a place for you. I ain't scared of Malcolm."

"But I am. The last fight... when he really hurt me... I didn't know who he was." Glory sighed. "But I'm okay now. I've got a good place to live and a new family that loves me. I'm gonna get back to school one day soon, and even if I never take these bracelets off, Malcolm is outta my life."

"Well, I can get some bolt cutters, and we can have those things off in a jiffy."

Glory looked down at her wrists. "I keep 'em covered with wristbands usually. Sometimes I almost forget they're there. Other times, even though I hate what they mean, I feel safe with them. Like as long as I have them, somebody is lookin' out for me. I don't know what's wrong with me. Maybe I'm crazy. Cutting would destroy 'em. I don't think I want to do that."

"Or we can go to the pawnshop. I know you'll get a pretty penny for 'em, and they'll gladly figure out how to get 'em off."

Glory twisted the bracelets on her left wrist. She'd worn them for six years. She couldn't imagine being without them. "I don't know..."

Herschel just shook his head and squeezed Glory's hand again. "I know you'll take 'em off one day."

Glory blinked back tears. "I missed you so much. I was scared to call 'cause I didn't know what Malcolm was doing. What if he had your phone bugged or something? I wanted to see you, but I'm scared to drive on the South Side 'cause somebody might see me. Yeah, I know how big the South Side is, but still..."

"So, you're finally driving now? Really?"

"Yup! A real nice customer named Greg taught me." Glory beamed. "He kinda likes me, but we're just friends. I just got my license today."

"Oh, really." Herschel got up and poured himself more iced tea. He held the pitcher out to Glory. She declined.

The two friends sat and talked until long after sunset. Glory told of the people she knew now, and Herschel told of the goings-on at the salon. They went back down to the diner to have a late dinner and talked some more.

"You hafta come back next Saturday, okay? I want you to meet Miss June. She's really nice." Glory looked somber. "She knew I was in trouble when she first saw me, and she still gave me a chance. And Gram? You told me she was crazy the first time you brought me here. She's not crazy, just funny." Glory laughed a little. "Did you know she has two guns?"

"I wouldn't be surprised if that old lady had a sword and a switchblade too." Outside the restaurant, Glory hugged Herschel again. "I guess now that I know where you are, we can hang out again," Herschel said.

"But what if Malcolm has you followed or something?"

"Darling, if he was gonna do that, he'd have done it a long time ago and found out everywhere I go." Herschel squeezed Glory's hands. "And I'm sure my phone isn't bugged, so you can call sometimes."

"I promise I will." Glory hugged him one last time and wished him good night.

Back in her apartment, she washed the iced tea glasses and wiped the counter and made plans to see about getting her own telephone... and if she would be having company, maybe a small TV too.

CHAPTER 28

From the time she started at O'Reilly's, Glory had been fascinated by Zac and Renee. Renee didn't really work at the diner, but she would take orders and fill coffee and water when she was there. Zac, the meanest man in the kitchen, was all sunshine and rainbows when Renee was around. And Renee, usually all spit and sass, would wipe the sweat from his brow and tighten his apron when he got busy. Anyone could see that they adored and brought out the best in each other. That was why the night of the fight, Glory and everybody at the diner listened in stunned disbelief as Zac and Renee raged at each other.

"Well," Renee said, "If you don't like it, you know what you can do! Don't nobody do you like I do, and yo' life would still be a damn mess if it wasn't for me!"

Glory banged on the kitchen door while Stacey turned the music up and chattered loudly with the few customers seated in the dining room.

"Oh yeah?" Zac yelled back. "My life would be a helluva lot quieter, tha's fo' damn sure."

"Oh hell. You couldn't find yo' own ass without me!"

"Why are they doing this now?" Glory asked Stacey. "They have a perfectly decent apartment where they could scream all they want."

"Woman, you know what?" Zac yelled. "I'll be just fine without yo' naggin' all the damn time—"

"Oh really?" Renee shot back. "Keep it up, and Imma marry yo' ass and then nag you till you die!"

"See," Stacey said to Glory, "every few months, they blow up at each other. After this, they'll stop speaking for about a week then get all lovey-dovey again."

"Oh yeah?" Zac yelled. "I dare you!"

Suddenly, there was no sound coming from the kitchen.

"Did I hear that right?" Glory asked.

Stacey went to the kitchen door and looked through the glass. "Yeah, I think you heard it right, and I think she's callin' his bluff. They're back there kissin.'"

Glory laughed, but she suddenly felt weepy.

IT WAS DEEDEE WHO INSISTED on red as the theme for the night. Renee's bachelorette party was across the street at the Knotty Pine, and all the ladies would wear red. The dress was simple really—plain cotton, sleeveless, drop waist, snaps down the front—but it was bright red, and everything in Glory screamed *No!* Her mother had always told her red was for whores who let the sunrise catch them.

Glory looked at herself in the full-length mirror on the inside of her closet door. The dress wasn't tight or anything, but the softly falling fabric accentuated her curves. Her cornrowed hair twisted up into a bun and gold hoop earrings completed the look.

"Come on out in yo' red dress! Sho' lookin' good tonight! I said come on' out in yo' red dress! Sho' lookin' good tonight. Don't nobody do it like you. Girl, you sho' *is outta sight*!"

At ten o'clock, the evening sounds floated through the open window, the late-summer breeze making the curtains dance to the music. Glory took a long swallow of her rum cooler and swayed a little from side to side.

"Way you move in yo' red dress, girl, you sho' do walk that walk! Way you move in yo' red dress, girl, you show do walk that walk. Way yo' hips be swayin' make a grown man talk baby talk... ha ha ha ha!"

Glory spun and danced around the room in her stocking feet, watching herself in the mirror. She had to admit, as she opened another bottle, that she did look and feel pretty in the red dress. The cool peach flavor with just a hint of rum made her feel light on her feet and a little giggly.

"Look at you drinkin' that evil liquor, face all painted up like a whore in that nasty red dress!" Her mother's voice broke through Glory's reverie, and she looked around.

Of course, Mary wasn't there. Glory was safe in her own apartment, being an adult getting ready for a party. She took another swallow and set the bottle down a little too hard.

"You done turnt into a vain and prideful filthy Jezebel! I didn't raise you like that! You gon' pay the price of Job for all this sin and rebellion!"

Glory pressed her hands over her ears. "God doesn't punish you for having a red dress!" Glory yelled into the air. "I'm not doing anything bad!" She looked in the mirror again. The dress went nearly to her ankles. At the scoop-neck collar, when she leaned forward, she could just see the thin lace trim on her white cotton slip. She even had on plain brown pantyhose. With the long-sleeved sweater on, it looked like something she might wear to church. But her mother's voice haranguing her, berating her, cursing and condemning her... try as she might, she couldn't block it out.

At ten thirty, Glory grabbed her coat. She picked up her red high heels and thought better than to try walking all the way across the street in them. She laughed a little. No good could come of that. Down in the foyer, she paused and looked through the heavy wood-and-glass door. There were people outside of the liquor store and a few people waiting at the bus stops. All she had to do was to go out of the door, walk to the corner, and cross the street. It was really a short, simple trip, but suddenly, Glory felt overwhelmingly self-conscious. The dress hung a little longer than the coat. *What if somebody looks? What if there are men in the tavern on ladies' night? Do they even let in men on ladies' night?*

She pulled the door open and stepped out into the hot September night. She clutched the shoes close to her chest and headed for the corner.

"Damn girl, ain't you hot in that coat?"

"I'm fine," Glory mumbled.

"I can see that!" The catcalling man laughed.

"Look at you, all that stuff on yo' face... got men hollerin' at you on the street! Nasty Jezebel!" Her mother's voice was back.

Leave me alone, Mama. I'm covered all up.

"They can still see that red dress, and you got them red whore shoes in yo' hands!"

Shut up, and leave me alone, Mama.

"You got demons all up in you! Pride and vanity, sin, rebellion. I oughta take the cord to you!"

Mama, you can't hurt me anymore.

At the door to the tavern, Glory paused and looked around. Nobody seemed to notice that she was preparing to enter a tavern for only the second time in her life. The door opened, nearly hitting her, and a laughing couple came out. Glory grabbed the handle and waited for them to pass before ducking in. What she noticed first was the smell—a deep, rich tobacco mixed with the smell of the brown liquor her parents used to drink.

"Gloriaaa!"

Glory looked deeper into the room and then headed over to where Renee and her friends sat, having started the party a bit earlier.

"Congratulations, Renee." Glory took a seat at the cluster of round tables. Most of the waitresses from the diner were there and some of Renee's other friends too. "Looks like you started the party without me."

"Girl, why are you carrying yo' shoes?" Stacey asked while Renee waved the barmaid over.

Glory laughed. "'Cause I cain't walk in heels. I woulda broke my neck tryin' to cross the street." She dropped her high heels on the floor and kicked off her gym shoes then slipped on the bright-red pumps with sparkly toes. She held her legs out and admired her feet, grateful that her mother's voice was silent.

"Whatcha drinkin'?" the barmaid asked, setting cocktail napkins in front of Glory.

Glory looked around the table at the various glasses. "I don't know. A Coke, I guess?"

"Nope! Bring her a sloe gin fizz." Renee nodded at Glory. "You'll love it. It's just like fruit punch."

"Okay." Glory shrugged. "Bring me what she said. But just a little." The barmaid patted Glory's shoulder and headed for the bar.

Glory looked around the big dark room. The windows looking out onto Madison Avenue were trimmed with white holiday lights and neon beer signs. As her eyes adjusted to the darkness, she saw a cigarette machine and a jukebox near the front door beside the mirrored bar. In a corner across the room from the bar, a few couples stood, swaying, on the raised dance floor. The tavern wasn't crowded, but most of the tables were occupied by groups of fancy-dressed women while the bar was lined with well-dressed men facing into the room, checking out the ladies.

Glory blushed and turned her head when she accidentally made eye contact. *Please don't come over here.*

When her drink arrived, she took a tentative sip. It *was* exactly like fruit punch—cold and fruity with just a touch of fizz. By the time Glory finished her drink, the barmaid was setting another one in front of her. "This is from Clem over by the bar."

Glory looked toward the bar. A man in a black-and-white suit with a white coat and scarf worn over his shoulders like a cape lifted his glass in a toast in her direction. He motioned toward the dance floor. Glory smiled and shook her head. Dancing was not on the agenda.

"Look at you flirtin' with somebody's husband, you Jezebel!" Even inside the tavern, her mother's voice haunted her

Please, Mama. Just stop. Glory took a deep breath and a long swallow of her second drink. As the night wore on, she joined the ladies on the dance floor to dance the Bus Stop, stepping and turning, jumping and clapping, laughing and having the time of her life. As she finished her fourth sloe gin fizz, the buzz finally kicked in, and Glory let the man in the white coat lead her barefoot to the dance floor.

She didn't know what the dance was—she just shifted her weight back and forth between her left and right foot, doing a dip or a spin when her partner placed a hand on her hip or held her hand. By the end of the song, Glory's buzz was gone, and she was ready for another drink.

"Slow down, girl," Deedee said as Glory returned to her seat. Glory had danced up a sweat and was waving the barmaid over.

"You want another fruit punch?" the barmaid asked.

Glory giggled. "I'm tired of fruit punch. What's a good grown-up drink?"

The barmaid laughed. "I'll surprise you."

"Gon' be out all night, drinkin' and shakin' yo' tail like a whore!"

Glory stood up and went to the ladies' room. It smelled of pine cleaner and a hint of bleach, with a strong overlay of lemon air freshener. Obviously, the Knotty Pine tried to keep it clean, but the floor in both stalls was damp.

"Look at how low you done sunk! In this stinkin' hole, walking yo'self straight to hell..."

Glory pressed her hands over her ears and hummed, but her mother's voice still tormented her. "Arrgghh!" Glory screamed. She shook her head until her mother's voice went silent.

Two women came in, looking around. "Hey, you okay in here?"

"One of these fools messin' with you?"

Glory shook her head and opened her eyes. "I'm okay. I just saw a big spider, that's all. It scared me."

"Oh, okay," one of the women said. "Then hurry up. I gotta pee!"

Glory finished up and washed her hands. Her mother's voice stayed silent. Looking in the permanently marked mirror, Glory checked her makeup as best she could and left the ladies' room, determined to continue having a good time. Returning to her table, she sat down in front of a tall brown drink.

"It's a Long Island Iced Tea," Deedee said. "It's a little stronger than a sloe gin fizz."

Glory took a sip. "It tastes just like iced tea with a little alcohol in it. I like it." She took a long swallow and coughed. "It's a little strong, but it's good."

Glory enjoyed her drink and laughed at the ladies' dirty jokes. She didn't really understand all of them, but the liquor made everything funny. When "The Bus Stop" came on again, Glory was ready, and she danced and clapped with the crowd, and when the dance ended, she went to the bar and ordered another drink.

"You sure you want another one?" the bartender asked. "Don't seem like you do this too often."

Glory swayed a little to the music. "Yeah, but this is the last one." Glory took her drink and danced her way back to the table.

"Girl, why you still ain't got no shoes on?" The man in the white coat, Clem, appeared at her side as she sat down. "You ain't danced that much yet."

Glory giggled a little. "I guess it's time to dance some more!" She took a long swallow of her drink, stood up, and steadied herself against the table.

Deedee laughed and shook her head. "I'm glad you ain't driving tonight!"

Out on the dance floor, the music changed to something slow, and Glory let the man in the white coat hold her close. "Mmm, you smell good enough to eat," he said.

Glory giggled a little. "It's Pound Cake body spray."

"So that's why them fat boys lookin' at you like dessert, huh?"

"I don't know about all that." Glory laughed. "A boy I once knew called it a love potion." Glory found it easy talking to Clem, but when he asked for her number, turning him down was easy too.

"So you just swoop in here, get all up in my head, and then break my heart?" Clem slowly twirled Glory on the dance floor. "What if we were put here tonight to change each other's lives? Maybe you supposed to belong to me."

Glory stiffened a little. She glanced at the bracelets sitting low on her wrist. "I doubt that. I only belong to me. I'm just here to hang out with my friends." She took a step back. "I think I need to go sit down now."

"I could show you a real good time... if you give me a chance."

Glory sighed. Clem was likely a really nice guy, but the thought of a man in her world still made her a little queasy. "Maybe some other time," she said, extricating herself from his arms. "I need to go sit down for a while."

"I understand," Clem said, stepping back and raising his hands slightly. "Maybe some other time."

Back at her table, the party had grown louder. The ladies still standing were all on their third or fourth shots, and the barmaid appeared at Glory's side with another round of drinks. Her buzz was subsiding, and she could feel her mother's presence trying to intrude. *Up in this hellhole with a bunch of dirty Jezebels!* The tall thin glasses with whipped cream on top looked like dessert. Glory took one and dabbed her finger in the topping. She tried to take a sip, but the fluffy white cream got on her nose.

"That's not how you do it." Renee laughed. She leaned forward and put her mouth over the entire rim of the glass, picked up the glass with her mouth, then threw her head back and swallowed.

Glory stared in shock. "I don't think I'm gonna do it like that." Using two fingers, she scooped up the whipped topping and giggled, slowly licking her fingers, earning cheers and applause from a man at a nearby table. She then sat back in her chair and sipped her drink like a lady. The creamy liqueur was almost too sweet, but she quickly finished the shot, and when the barmaid came to clear their glasses, she ordered her last Long Island Iced Tea... again.

Sometime during the night, the top few snaps of her dress had come undone, and as the temperature in the crowded bar rose, the beat of the music moved her. Wailing blues—if she didn't listen to the lyrics, she would have sworn it was gospel. The bass, the sax, and the moaning and groaning of the organ and the steel guitar all called to her, stirring her soul like the church music did. It was all Glory could do not to rip off her dress and dance on the bar.

It was nearly four in the morning when Glory stood up from the table. The room listed slightly to the left, and when she tried to order just one more drink, she was reminded that it was actually Sunday morning. The party had evolved into a few rousing games of Spades, and most of the other tables had people talking loudly and drinking from bottles hidden in brown paper bags. A few couples moved slowly on the dance floor, and the barmaid went around collecting glasses and wiping tables. The DJ had long since left, and somebody kept playing blues on the jukebox. Glory tried to listen to the conversations, and Renee suggested for the umpteenth time that maybe it was past her bedtime, but the music and the crowd and the smells and the whole atmosphere held her, and all Glory knew was that she wanted to be there forever. And when the party eventually ended, that was where the sunrise found her... her mother's voice finally silent.

INTERLUDE
April 1983

"I think tha's her grandbaby."

"I wouldn't be surprised. You know that boy of hers is the devil."

"Mm-hm. Always been, always will be."

"The devil, jes' like his daddy."

Glory waited silently in the bathroom stall for the church ladies to finish their business and leave. She didn't mean to eavesdrop, but they had started talking before she could get out of the stall. When they left, Glory washed her hands and took her time, taking the long way to the sanctuary. The young men's Sunday school was letting out, and she lingered at the water fountain, waiting for a glimpse of JT.

It had been three years since their first real kiss—three years of brushing fingertips and stolen glances. She and JT had kept their relationship secret. There had been a few close calls, like the time her mother came home early and JT hid under Glory's bed until Mary left for choir rehearsal. Glory had been on her best behavior that afternoon lest her mother find it necessary to purge demons while JT was there. There was another time when JT left his hat and Mary found it. Glory said it belonged to Kevin Flowers from church, and the purging of her demons of lust and deceit and dishonor felt like it took an hour, leaving marks that took days to heal.

Glory pushed her hair back and leaned over the water fountain for the third time. JT still hadn't appeared. Maybe she'd missed him. In the sanctuary, Glory climbed the stairs to the balcony and looked down at the gathering congregation. Her mother was already in her seat. The church mothers took up the front row, with Mother Porter sitting a little apart from the older women. The teenagers sat beside their parents, scattered throughout the sanctuary. Glory even saw Evelyn Jackson, JT's mother, but apparently, JT hadn't come to church that day.

"You know JT got arrested again?"

"Huh?" Glory spun around. "When?"

"Last week," Andrea said. "Wednesday, I think."

"Oh well." Glory casually smoothed her hair. "What happened?" She didn't want to appear too interested or encourage gossip, but if anybody knew the truth, Andrea would. Her mother and Mrs. Jackson were best friends.

"He, like, got caught smoking reefa and was, like, drunk too."

"Oh really?" Glory scoffed. "That don't even sound like JT."

"I know, right?" Andrea blew a medium-sized pink bubble and cracked her gum.

Glory looked around, hoping nobody saw.

"So, like, yeah. His old boy left him in jail overnight. His mother was like totally pissed."

Glory winced at the P-word, praying that nothing bad would happen because Andrea had cussed in church. *So, was that why he was so upset Thursday night? Was he that scared of going to jail and losing me?* Lost in thought, Glory barely heard anything else Andrea said.

Once she was seated beside her mother, Glory paid little attention to the service. Her thoughts were on JT and their time together at the salon. He had been so intense. Now Glory knew why he'd kissed her so hard her lip had swelled—why he was so hungry for her. She smiled a little. Well, he wouldn't be hungry much longer. Just the thought of being with JT caused a shiver. Glory knew she would be breaking her promise to God, but what if JT had gone to jail? Or what if he got killed? His last memory of her would be being pushed away. He might be gone before she had a chance to prove her love to him.

Glory sat up straight and squeezed her legs together. Over the years, she'd already read all the books in the salon's back room, but Friday and Saturday, she again flipped through the pages of *The Joy of Sex*, studying the pictures and planning her Monday morning with JT. First Glory would take a bubble bath. The book said no perfume or deodorant, so she would add vanilla to the water. She hoped he wouldn't mind the soft hairs in her armpits. Her mother had purged her demons of vanity and pride when she'd tried to shave. With the windows covered, her bedroom would be dark as night. Glory knew she wanted him to touch her but wasn't sure she wanted him to see her naked. *Will we taste each other?* The book said it was a good idea. She made a mental note to buy fruit on the way home from church. The book said fruit was good because it wasn't filling, and doing it on a full stomach was uncomfortable. Glory shivered in her seat. Tomorrow, she and JT would take the next step.

After service, in the Robinson Room for coffee hour, Glory looked around again for JT. Sometimes, on days he didn't appear at church, he would come to pick up his mother after service, drawing lots of glares for wearing gym shoes in church, but that day wasn't one of those times. She made her way over to her friends. Of course, they were talking about JT's adventure. She moved away from them and wandered over to the serving table to make a cup of tea.

"Of course, I was mad. I was mad as heck, but when I saw his little face, I just fell in love."

"When is his dedication?"

"We're not having one."

Glory didn't know all the women talking nearby in a tight circle, but she recognized Mrs. Jackson's deep alto tones. JT's mother always seemed a little extra nice to Glory, and some days, Glory was positive the kind woman knew about her and JT. That day, she sounded exasperated.

"His daddy's not gonna ask the church's forgiveness, so no dedication. But tha's okay, ain't it?" She cooed at the bundle in her arms. "Grandma can dedicate you all by herself." The other women in the circle reached in to touch the son of...

No.

Glory stepped around the circle to get a better look.

Please no.

Over the shoulders of the clucking church ladies, Mrs. Jackson met Glory's eyes. Glory took a step back, shaking her head. *Is that pity?* A sudden pain punched her in the stomach like a fist and knocked the wind out of her. *Oh my God, nooo.* She was choking, suffocating, dying. With shaking hands, she set the cup of tea down on the serving table, slowly turned, and looked for an exit. The nearest one led to the haunted hallway.

One foot in front of the other.

You let me kiss you. That means we're married.

Just a few steps.

Please, Miss Glory. Trust me.

Almost there.

Miss Glory, would you go with me?

As she climbed the stairway, Glory retreated into the darkness of her favorite childhood hiding place. At the third-floor landing, she lay down on her side, wrapping her arms around herself.

Before I knew what makin' love was, I knew I only wanted you.

She knew she was going to hell because she prayed for God to make the baby not exist so she could keep loving JT.

Glory didn't remember coming home from church or going to bed. The only reason she woke up and got out of bed Monday afternoon was the incessant ringing of the doorbell. Her bedside clock showed 12:09. She considered not responding—she didn't want answers.

She eventually made her way to the door buzzer. "Who is it?"

"It's me. Can I talk to you?"

Hearing his voice wasn't like another gut punch. It was a gentle caress against her cheek. But she couldn't let him in. She wouldn't be able to stop herself from loving him and needing him... and making love with him... and not being able to breathe without him.

"No, leave me alone."

"Glory, don't do this. I love you. You know that." His words rushed out like his life depended on it. "You the only girl I want. Glory, please. JJ can be *our* son, yours and mine. We can still have the family we want. We can get through this. I love you, Miss Glory. Please. I need you."

"Josiah, please just go."

"Nooo!"

Josiah's pleas tortured her. His cries touched her soul. But his betrayal destroyed her whole spirit. Willing herself not to give him entry, Glory lay down on the floor beneath the door buzzer while down in the lobby, Josiah leaned on the bell. She hugged herself, digging her fingernails into her arms. The physical pain was less than the ache of her breaking heart.

For the next three days, minutes after her mother left for work, the doorbell would start ringing, and Glory would lie beneath the buzzer and not answer, hurting more and more each day. The following Thursday night at the salon, the music was loud, and the customers and stylists danced around and bounced in their chairs. By the time Glory had arrived for her shift, Herschel had already heard the gossip and was waiting for her in the back room.

She took one look at him and finally broke down crying. "You know what? We almost did it last week, right here in this room. He said he loved me sooo much, and I could feel it." Glory sat on the saggy old couch, her head against Herschel's shoulder.

"Well," said Herschel, "you wouldn'ta been the first—I know that."

Glory didn't want to think about how many virginities had been thrown away on that couch. "How could he do that to me, Herschel?" she cried.

"Darling, if you want the answer to that, you gonna hafta listen to him." Herschel held up his right hand. "Now, I'm not saying you *should* listen to him, but you might wanna consider it."

Glory shook her head and wiped her eyes. "No. There's nothing he can say. He's been cheating on me for who knows how long. I mean, he only said he loved me 'cause he knew I was gonna find out he was a liar and a cheat."

"Well, we know he was at least once a year ago—"

"And he's been lying to me for at least a year." Glory sobbed again. "Herschel, I hate him!"

Herschel rubbed Glory's hair. "No, you don't. You don't hate him. You're hurt—for good reason—but that's all. And every day, it's gonna hurt a little less—"

"I never wanna see him again!"

"You don't really mean that either. You love a man that cheated on you, and it hurts so much 'cause you wanna keep loving him, but you wanna punish him too."

"I was actually gonna do it with him Monday, in my house, in my bed. I even read *the book* again to make sure I did everything right. I loved him so much." Glory broke down again, and Herschel handed her tissue after tissue until she stopped crying.

"Well, sweetie, I gotta tell you, he's been calling here every night this week, and he said he was gonna come by tonight—"

"Tell 'im I'm not here. Tell 'im I quit. Tell 'im I died!"

"Well, I guess that answers my next question. I'll do whatever you want, but I'm not gonna lie. I'll tell him you don't wanna see him, okay?"

"Yeah, but he's not gonna go away. What was he trying to do last week, get a baby outta me too?"

"I don't think that was it. I think he wanted to prove how much he loved you before you got the news. That's a man's power. A good time might make you forgive anything—"

"I don't need to hear that right now." Sniffling, Glory stood up from the couch and looked around. She hadn't been at work all week, and the mess had piled up. "I'm gonna get to work. Please don't let him back here. I can't take it."

By the time Glory finished her shift, JT had not come, and she wasn't sure how she felt about it. She definitely didn't want to see him or hear anything he had to say, and apparently, he'd given up, but the thought of never seeing him again only widened the hole in her heart.

As spring turned into summer, Glory found herself hurting less and less. She definitely thought about JT and dreamed about him, and her heart skipped a beat every time she got a glimpse of him playing basketball in his backyard. Sometimes, they'd make eye contact, but he would hang his head and turn away. Though Mrs. Jackson brought the baby to church with her every Sunday, JT never came. He had obviously given up and probably moved on. After two months, Glory let go too.

CHAPTER 29
December 1989

The Saturday morning before Christmas Eve, O'Reilly's Restaurant was filled with last-minute shoppers and husbands with kids who'd been kicked out of the house so Mom could cook. Gram was at the register, trading barbs and dirty jokes with anybody who stopped for a chat. Roz's Christmas cupcakes were a huge hit, and Glory packed box after box. In the kitchen, Perry and Zac battled it out over who was the fastest, and the poor waitresses struggled to keep up. Miss June walked around, handing everybody their Christmas bonuses, and in the break room, the table was piled high with grab-bag gifts and homemade treats from the staff. And WGCI had started its all-Christmas-all-the-time block, filling the air with soulful holiday tunes.

"Hey, Marcus. Hi, Li'l Man." Glory poured coffee for Marcus and set a Styrofoam cup of apple juice on the counter in front of Li'l Man.

"Morning, Gloria," the older man said. "Got big plans with the family this weekend?"

"Nah." Glory pulled out her notepad. "I'm gonna be working. Usual?"

"Yup, but the Li'l Man here got something for you." Marcus elbowed his grandson.

Li'l Man smiled, showing a huge gap where his front teeth used to be. "Yup, I got a present for you. It's a surprise."

"Boy, you look like a jack-o'-lantern." Glory laughed. "What's the surprise?"

"Close your eyes, and hold out your hand."

"Hmmm..." Glory eyed the little boy. "Okaaay, but I don't usually trust little boys who tell me to close my eyes."

"It's okay. Trust me." Li'l Man smiled even bigger.

Glory closed her eyes. She didn't have words for what she felt when small fingers pushed a pinchy plastic ring onto her index finger. She took a deep breath before opening her eyes to see a huge diamond perched on her finger. She didn't know whether to laugh or cry. She placed the coffeepot on the hot plate, walked around the counter, and lifted the boy in a big hug, kissing him on the forehead.

"This is the prettiest ring I've ever seen," she said. "I'm gonna keep it with me forever."

"See, Grandpa, I told you she would." Beaming, Li'l Man hugged Glory back. "Now we can get married!" Glory put the boy down, and he scrambled back onto the counter stool. "All we hafta do is—"

"Hold up, Li'l Man. I think you tricked me. The last little boy who tricked me into marrying him, I beat him all the way up." She gave him a playful noogie.

"Oh, you did, did you?" A slow smile spread across Marcus's face. "Is that a fact? Why'd you do that?"

"'Cause he tricked me into letting him kiss me. I think I was five or six. I got him real good, though. Somebody had to pull me off of him. That boy had me fighting in church." Glory laughed at the memory.

"Well, I'll be damned," Marcus mumbled. He cleared his throat. "You just don't seem like the fighting type. Well, Li'l Man, maybe you should rethink this. Ain't right to trick a lady into marrying you. 'Specially one that can kick yo' ass." He went back to sipping his coffee.

Glory tilted her head, staring at the old man.

Li'l Man hung his head. "I wasn't trying to trick you." Big tears spilled from his eyes. "I just..." He sniffed loudly, wiped his nose with the back of his hand, and laid his head against his grandpa.

"Oh, sweetie, don't cry." Forgetting her consternation, Glory hugged the little boy. "I love the ring, and I am gonna keep it with me forever, but one day, you're gonna want to give a ring to a girl your age. I'll be an old lady when you're a young man. You don't want your wife to be old, do you?"

"You're not gonna get old." The boy pouted.

Glory hugged him again. "I love you for wanting to marry me, Li'l Man. This is the best Christmas present I've had in a long time."

The boy smiled. "See, Grandpa, I told you she loved me."

Smiling, Glory shook her head and headed off to put their order in.

Moving through the restaurant, Glory got hugs, big tips, and even a gift or two from her regulars. Big Tom pulled her into a bear hug. "Tell that man back there that was the best steak he ever cooked. Don't know how he be gettin' it tender and burnt at the same time." He dug out his wallet and handed Glory two fifty-dollar bills. "Merry Christmas. I hate shoppin'. Give one to that man in the back."

"Oh? Thank you!" Glory tried not to bounce on her toes. "Merry Christmas, Tom."

"Nah tha's a man and a half right there!" Gram blew a kiss to Tom as he put on his Santa hat and headed for the door. "You know I'm waitin' on ya, Big Daddy!"

"Ol' lady, you need to quit!" Herschel's voice carried through the restaurant as he entered. "Merry Christmas, everybody!"

"Ha." Gram laughed. "How you just gon' gank Santa Claus's pimp coat?"

Herschel did a twirl in his plush red-velvet maxi coat with white fur trim. Glory suspected the trim was real fur, but she didn't want to think about it.

"I bet you know a lot about pimps, don't you, ol' lady?" He leaned over the counter and planted a big kiss on Gram's forehead.

"A li'l lower, I might change yo' life!"

"Okay, Mama, that's enough!" June shouted. "One more dirty joke..."

"He he he," Gram giggled just loud enough for Glory to hear. "Imma take a whole dollar this time."

Glory hugged her best friend, and Herschel lifted her off her feet. "Merry Christmas, darling! Are you almost done here? I've got a big surprise for you. I think you're gonna love it!"

"Well, I've got something for you too." Glory reached into her pocket and pulled out her sparkly unicorn, rainbow, and shooting star keychain collection. She handed Herschel her door keys. "You can have a bite down here or go upstairs, and I'll be there in about an hour."

"I'll go upstairs, darling. I cooked a little something for us, and I need to heat it up. I think you're gonna looove your gift."

Glory shook her head, watching her friend sashay out of the restaurant. She quickly finished her side work and soon said good-bye to her last two customers. In the breakroom, she counted her tips—over a hundred fifty dollars—and shared some with the bus-boys. This was her first Christmas season as a waitress, and the tips were phenomenal, better than any Saturday she'd ever worked. She had been slightly worried that she'd overspent on Christmas gifts, but her tips over the last few days had put her mind at ease. She'd considered going to the Century Mall on the North Side, dressed in a hat and dark glasses, but Miss June had convinced her that she should lie low and told her she'd find everything she wanted in the Sears and Spiegel catalogs.

Climbing the stairs to her third-floor apartment, Glory thought about her family... her *real* family. It had been eight months since she ran away from home, and she had contacted only Jill. This would be her first Christmas without them. She would have none of her aunt's sweet potato pie. *How can I go the rest of my life without Bigma's pecan pie?* She laughed a little at the thought of Uncle Bobby dozing off at the grills and wondered if her mother and Mr. Espy were still a holiday couple. *Will there even be a Christmas in Flora this year? Without Bigma, what would be the use?*

Glory opened her apartment door, and the smells of Christmas down South hit her like a big fluffy pillow. Herschel stood at the sink, washing dishes. "Everything is heating, darling. Chicken and dressing, and macaroni and cornbread is in the oven. Aunt Rosie and Allen are bringing the pies and onion rolls. I told them about four o'clock would be good. Since you have plans for Christmas day, we're having our Christmas dinner right now. Surprise!"

Glory walked over to the stove.

"Greens and sweet potatoes," Herschel said, rinsing the last dish. "I thought about bringin' chitlins, but honestly, I'd rather watch you cry than gag."

Glory put her arms around Herschel and laid her head against his back. "Herschel, this is the best present I ever got." She cleared her throat. "I don't even know what to say."

"Girl, you never know what to say. The words are 'Thank you,' and then I say, 'You're welcome.' See how simple that is? Now you try it. Thaaank yooou. That's right, darling. You can do it."

Glory laughed and thanked her friend. Her little Christmas tree stood on the window seat with a few new presents around it. Her card-dining table was draped with a Christmas tablecloth and an old lawn chair at the fourth-place setting. The scent of holiday cooking and the sounds of holiday music filled the air.

After a quick shower, Glory pulled on her favorite pair of Gloria Vanderbilt jeans and a red-and-gold-beaded sweater. Her mother and then Malcolm had never allowed her to wear pants, and for Glory, buying the tight jeans was a great rebellion. She considered wearing shoes, or at least socks, but at the last minute decided to go barefoot.

A little after four, Glory pressed the buzzer and then opened the door as Miz Rosie and Allen arrived. "Woo, child," Miz Rosie said. "Why you all the way up here? I'm too old for this mess. Merry Christmas, baby."

Glory hugged the old lady and helped her off with her coat. "Al, ask Herschel where to put the stuff. So. Miz Rosie, welcome to my castle." Glory laughed.

"One-room castles is kinda nice. Only need one heater, and you can see the TV from anywhere." Rosie hobbled over and sat on Glory's daybed. "Get the game on, would you?"

"Yes, ma'am." Glory arranged throw pillows behind her guest. "Who's playing?"

"Oh, I don't care who playin'. Just a bunch of boys throwing a ball and hittin' each other. I cain't hardly see no way, hee hee."

"Hey, girl, how you doing?"

Glory turned around and hugged Allen and accepted his kiss on her cheek. He was still as good-looking as the day she first met him, and he still reminded her of JT. She squeezed her friend tight and shook off the memory. "All is well. I'm just a little tired from working today. What you been up to?"

"Me? Nothing much." Allen took a seat on one of the counter stools. "Just workin' and coaching. Can I ask you a question?"

"Sure." Glory took a seat beside him.

"Why y'all women go crazy with wedding plans? Weddin' ain't for three years, and she already making guest lists and stuff. What's that about?"

Glory laughed. "Allen, she's been planning this wedding probably since she was four years old. I bet she already has names picked out for your kids."

"Yeah," Herschel said. "You best just go along with it, and she'll be happy. But don't you dare let her put you in a light-blue suit. Ooo wee, Aunt Rosie, these pies look good!" Herschel unpacked the box on the counter. "What's this?" He pulled out a square plastic storage container.

"I just thought we needed a li'l banana puddin' too," Rosie called across the room. "Cain't never have too many desserts!"

Herschel laid their Christmas dinner out on the counter, and Miz Rosie came and stood with them to say grace. Glory kept her head up and her eyes open.

Herschel received high praise over dinner, except Miz Rosie said he should have left the ham-hock fat in the greens. Glory and Allen disagreed, and Glory set one of the onion rolls aside for Roz to try. It might be a great addition to the restaurant menu. And the pies... oh, the pies. The sweet potato and pecan pies were so close to her family's recipes that Glory almost cried. After dinner, much to her chagrin, she admitted that she couldn't play spades or bid whist, and after everybody gave up on teaching her, they had a rousing game of Go Fish then returned to the kitchen for round two of dinner.

Standing beside Allen, drying the dishes while he washed, Glory tried to push away images of washing dishes with Malcolm. He'd always insisted on drying. Glory hadn't really cared, but now, given the opportunity, she chose to dry.

"So, Allen, what exactly does a chess coach do?"

"Umm... I mainly coach chess." Allen laughed a little. "The kids are great, and our best player is this twelve-year-old girl. She's phenomenal." He passed Glory a wet pan. "So, what's up with you? Ready to tell why you're hiding on the West Side?"

"Man, I'm not hiding. I'm right here, and you found me easy enough." She sighed, turning around and placing the pan onto the counter. "So how about your other players? Are they any good?"

"Aaand she changes the subject." Allen shook his head and smiled as he handed her the last pan. "Okay, fine. They're all pretty good on some level. I even got a seven-year-old whose game is really tight."

"Time to open presents," Herschel called. "Y'all quit slowin' around. Aunt Rosie is falling asleep."

Glory and Allen joined Herschel and a loudly snoring Miz Rosie, who woke up to thank Glory for a rose-embroidered scarf and Herschel for a rose-imprinted housecoat. Though she was very grateful, Glory couldn't help but laugh at the box of twelve pairs of nylon pantyhose from Herschel, and she loved *The Ebony Cookbook*, which she got from Allen and Miz Rosie.

After Allen and his grandmother left, Glory dug out two more gifts. "Herschel, I have a couple more gifts for you." She took a seat at the counter and laid a brightly wrapped package on it. "I wasn't sure which you'd like better, but I thought you might like both, so I got you two more things."

"Oh really, Glory-Glory." Still sweeping up, Herschel made his way over to the counter. "Well, I have one more gift for you too."

Glory watched her friend's face as he opened the purple silk tie embroidered with purple raindrops.

"Girl, you know me so well!" He picked up the other box and shook it a little. "I think I know what this is," he sang as he ripped the paper open. "Aha ha ha!" He threw his head back laughing at the action figure—a Barbie doll dressed as Wonder Woman. "Oh my goodness! This is classic! Where did you find it?"

"I found it in a toy catalog months ago. I've been holding it for Christmas for you."

"Well, I love it. Now for yours." Herschel placed a small red velvet pouch on the counter. "Take it out carefully. You don't wanna drop it."

Glory poured the contents onto the counter and gasped. "H-H-Herschel, is this what I-I-I think it is?" With trembling hand, Glory picked up the gold bead chain with the gold screwdriver attached.

"Yes, darling, it is," he said softly. "It's time."

"Oh my God, Herschel," Glory whispered. She squeezed her eyes shut. "What did you do? How did you get it?" She cleared her throat, but it was too late. Tears were forming, and she could hardly breathe.

"Nothing really dramatic, sweetie." Herschel handed her a paper towel. "I saw those bracelets of yours in a store window and went in and bought just the screwdriver." He reached out and took Glory's hand in his. "It's time for you to take these things off. Whatever happens, you're not going back to Malcolm, are you?"

"No, I'm not," Glory said in a raspy whisper.

She always figured she'd get the bracelets taken off one day, but it had never occurred to her that it was actually in her power to do it herself. *How many other things did I believe just because Malcolm said so?*

She took a deep breath and held out an arm to Herschel. "Go ahead. I'm ready."

Herschel shook his head. "No, darling. You hafta free yourself. It won't count if I do it."

Glory rotated the bracelets on her left arm and pressed her arm against the counter to hold them in place. Then she took the screwdriver in her right hand, carefully inserted the golden tool, and turned the screws. Hands shaking, she and Herschel sat in silence as it took her nearly fifteen minutes to remove three of the bracelets, and as she loosened the last screw on the fourth one, Glory let her tears fall and prayed she wouldn't accidentally slip and stab herself with the screwdriver because she could hardly see.

"I am my beloved's, and his desire is toward me," Herschel said, reading the inscription from one of the pieces of gold on the counter. "Interesting choice of verse."

Glory stared at the pale-brown rings where her wrists hadn't been exposed to the sun for six years. It was almost exactly six years to the day since Malcolm had locked the bracelets on her. He'd made her feel beautiful and desirable, and then he'd told her she had to go home because he wasn't strong enough to resist her. He'd told her he loved her.

While Herschel put the bracelets and screwdriver in the red velvet pouch, Glory sat rubbing and staring at her wrists. They looked so naked. They *felt* naked. She covered her face with her hands and didn't hear the melodic jingle of the bracelets. The silence startled her at first. She flapped her hands then her arms. Then she stood up and spun around, all without the constant jingle of the bracelets.

Glory looked at her friend, who sat watching her with tears rolling down his face. "Thank you, Wonder Woman," she whispered.

Glory walked down to the first floor with Herschel and stepped out into the cold December night. As he drove off, she waved goodbye, again surprised by the silence.

After an exhausting day and a wonderful evening, Glory finally got ready for bed, marveling at how quiet her world seemed without the constant jingle of the bracelets. She lay in bed, looking at the back of her hands without the dazzle of gold. After an hour of trying to drift off to sleep, Glory climbed out of bed and went to the kitchen counter. She picked up the red velvet pouch, pressed it to her cheek, and listened to the muffled jingle of the bracelets. Shackles, her friends and her uncle had called them. But Glory had once loved those bracelets. She took the pouch back to her bed and easily fell asleep to the sounds of Malcolm's love and protection.

CHRISTMAS EVE BROUGHT the beautiful soft snowflakes that children caught on their tongues, and all the customers entered the restaurant stomping and slapping off the thick heavy snow that seemed to stick to everything. The breakfast crowd had been light, but the lunch and dinner crowds were heavier than the day before. Even Gram was too busy to cuss and tell dirty jokes. Back in the kitchen, Zac and Perry continued their battle for grill supremacy, and Roz packed takeout trays for delivery to the tent cities along North Lake Shore Drive.

By the time the restaurant closed at six o'clock in the evening, the whole staff was busy cleaning and organizing. While the waitresses took care of the dining room, the busboys took care of the kitchen. Gram helped as much as she could, wiping the glass surfaces as far as she could reach.

Glory took her time clearing the tables in her section. She still wore her wristbands, but now they felt strange against her bare skin. She had even dropped a couple of cups, amazed at how light they seemed. This would be her first Christmas Eve without family and her first in five years without Malcolm. Glory couldn't decide how she felt. The Christmas after JT left, she'd imagined she'd be miserable, but Malcolm's attention had taken up all her thoughts. The Christmas Eve after she and Malcolm married had been spent at church, and Glory hadn't been happy until they were aboard a plane heading south. But this Christmas Eve she would be with the Parnells.

She tried not to sigh. The Parnells knew her story and had basically adopted her, and she felt grateful, but she wondered about Malcolm. Glory had no doubt that he was still looking for her, and she asked the universe every day to not let him find her—but he'd told her enough times that there was nowhere he wouldn't go to get to her. She shook her head. She would not allow thoughts of Malcolm to disrupt what promised to be a joyous holiday.

GLORY FELT LIKE SANTA, lugging her packages down to the Parnells' first-floor apartment. Besides the gifts for everybody, there were also leftovers from the previous night's Christmas dinner. Standing at their door, Glory couldn't help moving to the Christmas blues coming from the apartment, and when Deedee opened the door, the sounds and smells took Glory back to Bigma's kitchen in Flora, and she wanted to laugh and cry at the same time.

"Merry Christmas! Put your stuff under the tree," Deedee said, dancing her way out of the room. Glory did as she was told and then followed the music and laughter back to the kitchen. She nearly tripped over a Styrofoam cooler with a huge turkey marinating.

"Girl, betta' watch yo' step," Gram called from her spot at the kitchen table, picking bunches of greens. "Come get some 'a this here wine fo' June drink the whole jug."

"Leave me alone, ole lady." June exaggerated emptying her glass and loudly smacked her lips. "Ahhh! Gimme a little more, Glory." She placed her glass on the counter. "I don't wanna touch the bottle with chitlin' juice on my hands."

Glory laughed and poured June's glass and then filled a coffee mug with the sweet red wine for herself. She took a sip. The taste took her back to Christmas Eve a few years back—her grandmother's kitchen with her mother and her aunts. Delicious, almost like plain grape juice. She took a seat at the table with Gram and grabbed a bunch of collards.

"This is a whole lotta of food. Is it gonna be a lotta people tomorrow?" Glory easily pulled the stems from two leaves at the same time.

Gram smiled and nodded. "Not too many. Just us and maybe my sister Patty and her kids—"

"Her badass kids." Renee lifted the lid on a large pot on the stove. "Deedee, the water is ready for the corn."

"I cain't stand them kids." Deedee poured a handful of salt into the boiling water, then carefully dropped broken ears of sweet corn into the pot. "I'm glad I don't hafta babysit them monsters no more. They mama crazy too."

"Girl, you know that was too much salt," June chided. "Pull some of that water out and add some fresh water. Tryin' to kill the whole family with high blood pressure."

"Yeah, Ma." Deedee used a small saucepan to dip saltwater from the big pot. "And them chitlins is real healthy, right?"

"Don't worry, li'l girl. These ain't for the kids' table."

As the women in the Parnell kitchen laughed and talked, Glory fought a pressing melancholy. The last time she'd cooked in a kitchen full of women at Christmas was the year she learned the extent of what her mother had suffered. Aunt Ruth, the cool one, had tried to force Glory's mother to admit her second marriage was a mistake, but Mary Bishop did no such thing. She insisted the abuse she suffered was well deserved and that Glory wouldn't suffer the same fate because she was better behaved.

"Glory, you mighty quiet over there. What's wrong?" Gram cut through the rubber band on another bunch of greens.

"Nothing really," Glory answered. "I guess I'm just tired. Today was pretty busy." She pulled the stems on the last two leaves in front of her and started gathering the discarded stems while Gram worked on the last bunch. "I guess I'm kinda missin' home too. I usually spend Christmas Eve at church then go back home to Flora for Christmas Day."

"Yeah, being away from home, especially at holiday, is tough," Deedee said. "Remember when I spent Christmas in the hospital, Ma?"

"Girl, you were a mess." June started moving chitlins from the sink to a big stainless-steel pot. "That's when you lost faith in Santa 'cause you was the only kid in the hospital he visited. Made us both kinda sad."

"That is sad. How old were you?" Glory asked.

Deedee checked on the corn, stabbing into the pot with a carving fork. "I was ten. That was the worst Christmas ever."

"I think my worst Christmas was moving up here from Tennessee," Gram said. "As bad as it was down South, I thought the cold up here was gon' kill us. Tha's why I got so many kids. Me and Jasper stayed in bed, tryin' to keep warm. Let all the kids sleep with us too. The more heat, the better."

"You know, Mama, I coulda lived the rest of my life not knowing that." June cut two large onions and three large green peppers in half and dropped them in the pot with the chitlins. She added some salt and a handful of black pepper and closed the lid. "Now, these'll be ready 'bout two, three hours. Renee, what else you need for the dressing?"

"I need you to not put your chitlin hands in it." Renee took the wooden spoon from her mother-in-law and stirred minced celery, onions, and green peppers into the seasoned cornbread batter.

"You know," June said slightly louder than necessary, "I got some real good dressin' from Soul Queen on the South Side. They make theirs with sausage—"

"Mama June, I told you, I'm not about to put pork in the poultry dressin'," Renee snapped as respectfully as possible. "And just because you say it again and again in front of people ain't gon' change my mind."

"Well, okay." June headed back to the sink. "I guess some people like dry dressin'."

"Zac ain't gon' eat dressin' with pork in it, and you liked it just fine last Christmas and Thanksgiving, and seem like every other Sunday you asking me to make dressin'. Now, 'cause you been to some fancy restaurant..." Renee's voice trailed off as she quietly continued her rant, stabbing into the mixing bowl with the spoon.

"June, you know that girl's dressin' is damn near perfect." Gram held her cup out to Glory and pointed at the wine jug. "You just tryin' to mess it up 'cause it's better than yours."

"Hmph." June went back to stirring the pot of chitlins, fanning some of the putrid aroma in her mother's direction. "My worst Christmas was the one after the riots. Most everything around here was still boarded up, and business was real slow. On top of that, I hadn't heard from Perry in a month. I didn't know how we was gon' make it."

"What did you do, Miss June?" Glory tore open a bag of sweet potatoes, found a couple of paring knives, and went back to the table with Gram.

"I did what I always do," June said. "I prayed and kept on pushing. Just seems like God gives me whatever I need whenever I need it. But Lord, I was scared. Mrs. O'Reilly was trying to sell the restaurant, and I couldn't see a way to buy it without using up all our savings, and I couldn't reach Perry to talk about it. I just stepped out on faith."

"Um, Mom," Deedee interrupted. "Where's the bad part? Sounds like you really won that Christmas."

"Ha. We didn't win at Christmas. I was scared half to death at Christmas. Yeah, it got better and turned out all right, but that wasn't a good holiday at all."

"Well, it still doesn't sound all that bad. I mean, you did have me. What more could you want?"

"Girl, you stupid." Renee laughed at her sister-in-law. "My worst Christmas was the year Zac got out. I was at home with my family, and the bell rings, and it's Zac. Problem was, my boyfriend was there, and we were celebrating our engagement."

"Oo daaamn!" Gram laughed. "Did Zac whoop his ass?"

"Mama, hush!"

"No, Gram. He didn't fight at all. He just looked at me and then saw the ring and left. I couldn't enjoy anything for the rest of the holiday."

"So what did you do?" Deedee asked.

"Obviously, I called off the engagement. Well, my *fiancé* called it off. Come to think of it, he probably was a little scared of Zac." Renee laughed a little. "I guess it turned out okay for me too. Your turn, Glory."

"I've never had a bad Christmas," Glory said. "Well, taking those long bus rides down South was pretty bad. Nasty bathrooms, funky people, nothing to read—yeah, my mother only let me read the Bible. I hated those trips, but really nothing bad ever happened." She thought for a minute. "But the best one I ever had, me and my mother took the train down South, and I made out with a boy I met on the train." She giggled. "He was so cute. He drew a picture of me as a supervillain—"

"Oh, you slut!" Deedee laughed. "Making out with strangers on the train."

"Not a slut, Deedee. I'm a supervillain. I'm the Weak Femme Fatale. My superpower is that men just give me goodies... but then I feel guilty and give them back."

"Yeah, that's pretty weak, all right." Renee poured the dressing batter into two pans and covered it with plastic wrap and foil then set it out on the enclosed back porch, where the temperature was thirty-two degrees.

Deedee lifted the pot of boiling corn from the stove and started pouring off the hot water.

"Girl, why you pourin' out the corn water?" Gram yelled across the kitchen, startling everybody. "You should save it for the corn-bread."

"Gram! When have we *ever* saved corn water for cornbread?"

"Mama, would you quit it?" June stepped back from the sink so Deedee could finish pouring. "Girl, dump that water out and ignore that crazy old lady."

The women all laughed, drank wine, and shared their best-Christmas stories. Glory told of her childhood holidays with her daddy, but she could not speak of many holidays after he died. When they started talking about romantic holidays, Glory talked about getting pearl earrings from JT when she was seven.

What she couldn't talk about was the Christmas Malcolm had really hit her for the first time and forced her to get her ears pierced. She couldn't talk about the night he locked the bracelets on her wrists and almost made love to her. She couldn't talk about that past Christmas when she missed her period.

Even though there was plenty of food cooking for Christmas Day dinner, Renee ordered Chinese, and Glory served Herschel's leftovers. As Perry blessed the food, Glory kept her eyes open. She hadn't prayed in eight months, and hearing the prayers of others stirred feelings in her that she quickly squashed. She whispered a quick thanks to the universe for allowing her to remove the bracelets, but she didn't pray.

After dinner, seated around the living room with the Parnell family, Glory watched in amusement as June passed out Christmas Eve gifts. Each of the boxes was the same size but wrapped in different paper. Glory was pleasantly surprised when a red box was placed in her lap.

"Oh, thank you!" Glory waited until everybody had torn into their wrappers to begin carefully opening hers. If somebody had gone through the trouble of wrapping it, she figured the least she could do was respect it.

"It's pajamas," Deedee explained. "We get 'em every year. I told Ma what color to get you."

Glory opened the box and pulled out a set of big fluffy green footie pajamas, while Deedee pulled out pink ones.

"Wait a minute." Renee held up her red set, slightly different from Glory and Deedee's. "Why mine got a flap that open in the back?"

"'Cause y'all newlyweds!" Gram said. "Why you think? I want me some great-grandbabies! Aha ha ha ha!"

"Dammit, Mama! It's Christmas Eve!"

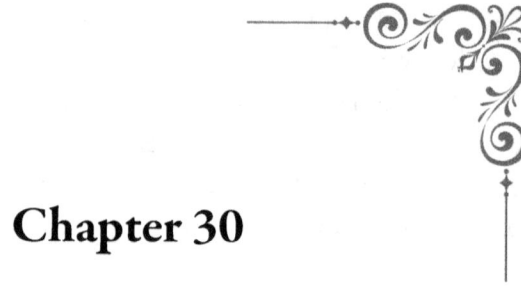

Chapter 30

Waking up, Glory needed a minute to remember that she was on the couch in the Parnells' living room. Deedee was curled up on the love seat and Zac and Renee laid out on the floor a little too close to the Christmas tree. Christmas Day. Glory sat up and looked around. The wall clock showed four in the morning. She stood up and tiptoed over to a window. The lone car traveling up Madison Avenue left tracks in the fresh snow, its sound all but completely muffled. There was too much light to look up and see stars, but the streetlights reflecting off the white world gave what her daddy used to call a heavenly glow.

"Hey."

Glory turned around.

Deedee stood up from the love seat and stretched. "Why you up so early? We don't hafta get to the restaurant till five thirty."

"I just couldn't sleep. I don't know. I just feel weird." Glory went back to sit on the couch. She wished she could fold her legs like Deedee, but she'd never been allowed to sit that way. "Maybe I'm just thinking about stuff too much. Is it possible to be too happy?"

"Ha, nope."

Both girls looked over at the Christmas tree, where Renee was propped up on an elbow.

"It's not possible to be too happy... but you can mess it up by overthinking it." Renee placed a hand gently on Zac's chest. "I've never been this happy in my life, and it gets better every day."

"Well, yeah... but what happens when the honeymoon is over?" Deedee looked from Glory to Renee.

"I guess you keep living," Glory said. "You take it like a woman and keep living."

The ladies talked until nearly five o'clock, when Zac admitted he'd been listening for at least half an hour. Glory and Deedee laughed when he grabbed Renee and rolled her over with a loud kiss.

"Dammit, man!" Renee fussed. "Not in front of the kids!"

The laughter and holiday merriment continued as everybody got up to open the restaurant and begin the day. On Christmas Day, things were different at O'Reillys'. Mr. Perry and Miss June stayed in bed while the kids and Roz ran the show. They were only open from seven until noon, and the only food cooked was the two-dollar breakfast. People who wanted it could buy a two-dollar bag lunch for the road. Deedee said usually they got about twenty customers for the whole morning, but it was a time for the kids to crank the music all the way up and laugh with their customers.

"So, how you likin' Christmas at O'Reilly's?" Roz asked Glory while they stood washing the large bacon pans. "Real quiet, huh?"

"I guess." Glory lost her grip on a pan, and it went crashing to the tiled floor, echoing throughout the kitchen and, no doubt, out into the dining room. "Dang it!" Glory picked up the pan and slid it back into the dishwater.

"What are y'all doing back here?" Renee came through the dining room door. "You scarin' the customers. All three of 'em. Glory, you got customers askin' for you."

Glory dried her hands and headed out to the dining room. She grabbed a coffeepot and headed for the table where Deedee stood talking to two men. She recognized the one waving her over from his frequent six a.m. visits.

"Hey, Gloria, my boy wants to meet you!" the customer yelled.

Though she was tired, Glory put on her best waitressy smile. "Well, good morning and merry Christmas—" Her words caught in her throat. With a shaking hand, she placed the coffeepot on the nearest table.

The new customer rose from his seat, took off his shades, and smiled. "Merry Christmas, Mrs. Porter. It's time to come home."

She trembled. Bile rose in her throat. The room swayed under her feet. "No," Glory whispered.

"Yes." Malcolm pulled her into his arms. "Everything's gonna be okay. 'Rejoice with me. I have found my lost sheep. I tell you that in the same way there will be more rejoicing in heaven.'"

"Oh shit!" Deedee ran to the kitchen door. "Zac! Get out here now!"

Glory pulled herself out of her estranged husband's embrace and took a step back. "No," she whispered again, more to herself than to him. "I can't go back." Sweat beaded at her brow.

Malcolm wrapped his arms around her again. "It's okay. I know you're scared and confused, but we're gonna get you whatever help you need. 'Do not be afraid—I will save you. I have called you by name—you are mine.'" He pressed her head to his chest. "When guys at the mission said they saw you, I couldn't believe it. I've had cops all over California looking for you."

Listening to Malcolm's pounding heartbeat, Glory forced down the panic rising in her gut. It had been months since she'd last seen her husband, but here, in his arms, it felt like only yesterday. "I can't go with you. I hafta work." Her own words sounded weak to her, but her mind was a jumble and her only clear thought was *No*.

He lifted her chin and looked into her eyes. "It's okay. I'm here now. You don't hafta stay here." He hugged her again. "God, I've missed you so much. Whatever they've done to you, we're gonna fix it. 'I will give up whole nations to save your life, because you are precious to me and because I love you and give you honor. Do not be afraid—I am with you!'"

"What's going on?" Zac came out into the dining room. Roz, Deedee, and Renee stood in the kitchen doorway.

Glory pulled away from Malcolm and took a step back out of his immediate reach. "I'm not going with you. This is my home." Glory heard herself and wished she'd sounded more forceful, but truthfully, she was terrified. *What if Malcolm insists? What if he threatens the Parnells like he threatened Herschel? What if I have no choice?*

"I don't know what all she told you, but she's been traumatized real bad," Malcolm said to Zac. "I'm not sure she realizes I'm her husband." He offered his hand to Zac, who shook it. "I'm Malcolm Porter. We've been married for five years." He reached inside his coat and pulled out his wallet. "I've got our wedding picture if you wanna see it."

Deedee and Renee moved to stand on either side of Glory, each holding a hand. Glory took a deep breath, drawing strength and courage from the two women. "I know who you are, Malcolm." Glory looked him in the eye. "I know we're married, but I'm not coming with you." She saw his flash of anger and flinched. She could see the seething darkness hidden behind his smile.

"Yes, you are," Malcolm said slowly. "Wives, submit yourself unto your husbands as unto the Lord." He reached for her hand.

Glory shrank away and saw his fist clench.

"Brotha," Zac spoke up. "We finna close, and my sista here don't wanna go with you." The big man moved to stand in front of Glory and his wife and sister. "Maybe you should come back another time."

Malcolm opened and closed his fists. Glory knew he wasn't used to hearing the word *no*, especially from her.

"Please, Malcolm," she begged. "Just go."

"Glory, I don't know what these people did to you, but you're not yourself. You're sick, and you need help." Malcolm tried to reach around Zac. "Please, woman, let me help you. 'Do not cling to events of the past or dwell on what happened long ago. Watch for the new thing I am going to do. It is happening already—you can see it now. I'm a different man.'"

Glory looked into her husband's eyes. Behind the pleading that almost broke her heart, she saw the darkness that would brutally punish her if she went with him, the darkness that had left her bruised and scarred, the darkness that had tried to force her to bear his children.

Glory shook her head. "No, Malcolm. I'm not coming with you."

Malcolm hung his head, rubbing his gloved hands together. "My brotha," he said to Zac. "Did I just see a roach? How often does the health department come through?"

Glory's eyes went wide. "Malcolm, please don't do this."

"Or the fire marshal, and how 'bout the IRS?"

Zac laughed a little. "You really that desperate for a woman that don't want you... *my brotha*?"

"Who can find a virtuous woman? For her price is far above rubies," Malcolm recited. "This woman belongs to me, and I have a right and responsibility to take care of my wife."

Zac stood toe to toe with Malcolm. "Now, tha's where you're wrong, my brotha'. This woman belongs to Allah. If she don't choose you, you need to step off and move on."

Renee laid a hand on her husband's shoulder.

Malcolm looked at Glory incredulously. "You're consorting with Ishmaelites and Canaanite women? 'Hast thou also committed fornication with the Egyptians thy neighbors, great of flesh, and hast increased thy whoredoms, to provoke me to anger?'" He reached around Zac and grabbed the front of Glory's uniform.

"Malcolm, no!" Glory pulled away.

Everything happened so fast. Glory snatched herself out of Malcolm's reach, and Zac shoved Malcolm hard enough to send him backward over a table.

Malcolm jumped to his feet. "Woman, I said it's time to go!"

"Get her outta here!" Zac yelled, moving to block Malcolm's path. "Renee, call 911!"

"Yeah, call the cops!" Malcolm tried to push past Zac. "You're holding a sick woman against her will!"

"Malcolm, just go!" Glory pleaded as Deedee dragged her toward the kitchen door. "Please, just leave me alone!"

Malcolm looked past Zac and met Glory's eyes. "You know, there's nowhere I won't come for you. No place you can go that I won't get to you."

Back in the kitchen, Glory cried on Deedee's shoulder, waiting for Zac to come back. The jingling of the bell over the front door signaled another customer's arrival or Malcolm's departure. Zac pushed through the kitchen door, and Renee went to him.

"He's gone?" Renee asked.

"For now," Zac said. "Glory, does he always talk like that, in Bible verses?"

"Yeah." Glory wiped her eyes. "He knows the Bible by heart and talks like that when he gets excited."

"Damn, girl, that fool is crazy. I see why you left." Roz handed Glory a cup of hot tea. "What're you gonna do?"

"Obviously, I hafta go." Glory accepted the tea. She sniffed and lifted her chin. "He's gonna come back, and it'll just get worse. He wasn't joking about the health department and stuff. He's not gonna give up. He hates hearing the word *no*."

"ABSOLUTELY NOT! YOU'LL do no such thing." June tucked a dish towel into her apron.

"But, Miss June, he's never gonna let me go."

"Girl, that's what restraining orders are for. If he comes near you, he goes to jail." June unfolded a shiny gold tablecloth and laid it over the dining table.

"But his father is so—"

"And nobody on the West Side gives the slightest damn who his daddy is. I never heard of your church till you mentioned it. You in a whole different world over here."

"But, Miss June, what if he calls the health department or somebody?"

The petite woman stopped laying out napkins and looked up at Glory. "Then let 'em come. All our stuff is tight, and we never have any problems."

"Yeah," Gram said from her favorite seat in the living room. "And he step up in there again, he gon' get popped."

"Mama, hush. But seriously, Glory, we can handle this. He's only a man, and we can ban him from the restaurant. He don't know where you live, and it's the holidays. He can't call the health department before next week. Maybe he'll calm down by then."

"Miss June, Malcolm is worse when he's calm."

Glory spent two nights with the Parnells before going home to her own apartment. Her first night back, she still slept with the red velvet pouch that held the bracelets. She'd tried sleeping with the radio on and the window open, but only the quiet jingle of the bracelets could lull her to sleep. In her dreams, Malcolm came to her, pulling her from the grip of a monster, wielding a sword, raging scriptures. In another dream, she ran from him, but he drew her in by a gold chain. And in yet another dream, he made gentle love to her, and his kisses were warm and sweet, and Glory woke with her cheeks wet from tears.

Chapter 31

"Malcolm told me yo' mind ain't right. That you think you cain't leave here."

Glory looked across the counter at her mother, who took a can of rubbed sage from her purse and stirred some into her cup of hot water. Glory tried not to breathe too deeply. The smell took her back to a time she tried every day to forget. "Mama, I'm fine. There's nothin' wrong with my mind."

"Then why you ain't come home with Malcolm?" Mary Bishop sipped her tea and drummed her fingers on the counter.

"Excuse me." Glory grabbed the nearby coffeepot and went to greet another early-morning customer. After the drama of Christmas Day, Glory hadn't been surprised to see her mother walk in two days later at six o'clock in the morning. What had surprised her, though, was how calm Mary had been. There was no hug or big emotional display. Mary had just nodded, taken a seat at the counter, and waited until Glory finished serving her first customer of the morning.

Back behind the counter, Glory topped off her mother's tea and placed her two-dollar breakfast in front of her

"You know," Mary began, "people sayin' you had a nervous breakdown from losing the baby. They say Malcolm sent you away to get help." She sipped her tea. "A couple folks say you ran away. That Cheryl came back to church, been real friendly to yo' husband."

Glory stood patiently, listening to her mother go on about the rumors and life in general at church. Malcolm had been lost without her. He prayed for Glory in church every Sunday and Friday. A parade of women had delivered food to him daily for the past eight months. Glory just nodded acknowledgement. She would not be drawn into a conversation or debate about the life she had escaped.

"So, Mama..." Glory wiped the counter and tried to keep the tremor out of her voice. "Did you come all this way to tell me church gossip?"

"No, baby." Mary's voice went soft, almost like she was talking to a child. "I came to get you. It's time you came home to your husband. I know losing the baby was bad, but you and Malcolm can get past that—"

"Mama, I am home." Glory kept her eyes down.

"I see you got demons of rebellion and disobedience in you."

Glory looked at her mother, her eyes wide. "No, ma'am. No demons." She heard herself and coughed. "Mama, I'm a grown woman, and I don't have demons. I never had demons—"

Mary reached across the counter, grabbed Glory's hand, and squeezed. "Demon of lies and deceit, I bind you in the name of Jesus!" she hissed. "Demon of rebellion, I bind—"

Glory snatched her hand back, upsetting Mary's teacup, spilling its contents across the counter and onto the floor. "Dang it!" she said, reaching for a rag.

Mary's eyes went wide. "Jesus! You cussin' now too?" She stood up and reached for Glory's hand again.

When Glory pulled away, she nearly knocked Mary's purse from the counter. That was when she saw the brown extension cord coiled in the purse like a snake.

Glory froze.

Mary's eyes went to the extension cord and back to Glory's. "See... I said it's time to come home. I'm not leaving here without you. You got a husband and a home and a whole life that you just tryin' to throw away. I can see the demons all up in you, makin' you rebel and cuss and disobey—"

"Get out," Glory whispered.

"I bind you in the name of Jesus." Mary reached into her purse.

"Get out!" Glory screamed. "Get out! Get out! Get out!" Glory grabbed a steak knife from under the counter. "I said get out!"

Zac appeared at the kitchen door. "Sista, you all right out here?"

"Mama, you get outta here right now, and don't you ever come back!" Glory waved the knife from side to side. "I bind *you* in the name of Jesus!"

Zac came up behind Glory and grabbed her wrist, causing her to drop the knife. The two early-morning customers dropped cash on their tables and quickly left.

Glory struggled against Zac's grip on her wrist. "I said get out! Zac, let me go! Get her outta here!"

Mary pointed at her daughter. "You got demons all up in you. Me and Malcolm be back to get you. Bind up all those demons. Bring you home where you belong. Didn't raise you to be no waitress!"

"Get ooouuutt!" Glory screamed until Mary left the restaurant. Then she ran to the window and watched her mother cross the street to the bus stop. She pressed her forehead to the glass and exhaled, surprised that she had no tears. All Glory felt was a dark, boiling anger. She took deep breaths and let her rage subside, walking around the restaurant, wiping tables and rearranging condiments, occasionally slamming down ashtrays.

During the breakfast rush, Glory watched Miss June and Deedee moving around the restaurant. She could never imagine working with her mother, being in sync, laughing and talking about life. Even in their lightest moments, Glory had needed to watch her words carefully lest her mother see demons in her.

After the lunch rush, Glory sat down in the break room and put her feet up. Her shift would be over as soon as her side work was done. *Fill the condiments, wipe the salad and dessert case, and scrape gum from under the tables.* Counting her tips, she set aside her usual ten dollars for each of the busboys and then headed out to the nearly empty dining room to get back to work. She'd grown used to the jingling of the bell over the door, so she didn't look up when she heard a customer enter.

"Sit anywhere you want," Gram said. "Sit over here, right by me."

"Thank you, ma'am, but no. I won't be staying long."

Glory dropped the saltshaker she was holding, loosening the lid and spilling salt all over the table she'd just cleaned. She didn't move. She kept her back to the room and begged the God she no longer worshipped that *he* hadn't come back.

"Glory, you need to stop this foolishness now." Malcolm stepped close to her, using his calm, loving voice.

She felt Malcolm's hand on the small of her back and stepped to the side away from him.

"I spoke to your mother a while ago," he said, following her. "She said you were screaming and hysterical. Clearly, you're not well."

Glory tried to maneuver herself closer to the kitchen door, but Malcolm blocked her path. The few customers in the dining room chatted among themselves, and the waitresses didn't seem to notice Malcolm and Glory's quiet confrontation.

"You know, as your husband, I'm responsible for you. I can call an ambulance, and they'll take you to a psych ward—"

"For what?" Glory snapped. Customers and waitresses looked in their direction, and Deedee ran into the kitchen. Glory turned to face Malcolm. "Because I wanna be on my own?" She lowered her voice. "Because I wanna be away from you, you think I'm crazy?"

"Woman, you obviously don't know what you're doing." He placed a hand on her shoulder, and she snatched away, taking a step back. He reached out and grabbed her wrist. "And as long as you wear these—"

Glory watched Malcolm's face change from a patient, concerned husband to the angry monster who had so viciously raped her. "You took them off," he whispered, squeezing her wrist until she wanted to cry out.

Glory looked around the restaurant. The customers had gone back to their meals, but Stacey stood nearby, holding a pot of hot coffee. Zac and Deedee stood at the kitchen door, while Gram watched silently for once.

"Yes, I took 'em off," Glory hissed through clenched teeth. "I hate them. I don't belong to you—"

The kiss stunned her. She'd always had a weakness for Malcolm's kisses, but this time his kiss was hard and angry. Glory tried to pull away, but he grabbed her hair and wrapped it around his fist. She felt his teeth press against her lip. When she pushed him away, he caught her wrist before her fingernails could rake across his cheek.

"See," Malcolm said calmly. "You've got violent tendencies now. You might be a danger to yourself." He squeezed her wrist again as Zac moved to stand behind him. "I'm going to have you treated, and there's nothing you can do about it. You *will* be back home, and we *will* have our family." There was no light in his eyes when he spoke. Only the cold smugness of a man who knew he would win.

Glory wanted to destroy that smugness. She wanted to spit in his face. "What're you gonna do, Malcolm?" Glory said a little louder than she intended, but she didn't really care. "Are you gonna beat me up and rape me every day?" She saw his facade crack just a little. "It won't matter, 'cause I'll kill any baby of yours, just like I killed the last one—"

Malcolm's calm shattered, but Zac grabbed him in a bear hug, pinning his arms to his sides. "Did you hear that?" Malcolm yelled. "She's talking about killing babies. She's already killed one, and she wants to kill more."

Zac turned Malcolm around and moved him toward the door.

"Can't you see she's sick? My wife needs help! You all heard her!"

"Shut up, and git yo' crazy ass outta here!" Gram yelled over Malcolm's ranting. "Fo' I hafta pop you. You don't wanna try me!"

Glory watched Zac *help* Malcolm to the door. She could tell he was hurting, but Malcolm had always channeled his hurt into rage, and Glory had spent five years bearing the brunt of that rage. She knew he believed she needed help... and that it was his responsibility... and that he owned her. And though she still slept with the bracelets on her pillow, Glory knew she would never be with Malcolm again.

She didn't go to the door, but she watched through the window as Malcolm got into his car and laid his forehead against the steering wheel for a minute before driving off. He was hurt and angry, and she'd humiliated him in front of people. He would definitely be back.

Every day after Malcolm's visit, she went to work, wondering where she could go and what she should do. Now that she'd dealt with her mother and Malcolm, Glory again considered going away... leaving her home and the people who loved her like family. Each day that passed without incident made Glory more and more nervous. In just a few days, she grew to hate the bell jingling over the restaurant door.

Chapter 32
January 1990

The weather was too bad for anybody to be out this first Saturday of 1990. At O'Reilly's for her usual Saturday-night shift, Glory sat at the counter, reading a novel in the spotless and empty restaurant. When she heard the bell jingle and saw the woman in a familiar mink coat, Glory knew, just like Ebenezer Scrooge, that this would be the last of her three holiday visitors.

"So, you're calling yourself Gloria now, hmmm?" The woman with the thick Southern accent walked over to a booth by a window and removed her coat. "Come join me, and bring us some tea."

Glory folded down a corner of the page she was reading. She poured two small pots of hot water and added a tea bag and lemon to each. She placed the tea on the table then took a seat across from her mother-in-law. Glory had to admit she was surprised. Anita was usually headed back home to New Orleans by January 2.

"How are you, Precious?" Anita asked. "I doubt you missed me, but I certainly missed you."

Glory took a sip of her tea. "I'm good, Miss Anita. I'm happy here."

"You look happy. And I see you took off those ridiculous bracelets. I bet my son was fit to be tied."

Glory remained guarded. "He wasn't too happy." She took another sip of tea. "I think I know why you're here, but you wasted a trip. I'm not going back. Please tell Malcolm to give up—"

Anita held up a hand. "Malcolm doesn't know I'm here. He thinks I'm back South by now."

Glory raised an eyebrow and stopped stirring her tea. "I don't understand."

"It's really very simple, Precious. I got on the train and got off after a couple of stops."

"But if Malcolm didn't send you, why are you here?"

"Why, to visit you, of course."

Anita reached into her purse and pulled out a snakeskin cigarette case. Glory watched in shock as her mother-in-law, first lady of her former church and consummate Southern belle, pulled out a long thin cigarette and lit it with a gold lighter. "I know, it's a nasty habit. That's why I indulge only when I go South for the winter." She inhaled deeply, burning a significant portion of the cigarette, then took her time exhaling.

Glory just stared.

"Close your mouth, Precious. Unless you wanna breathe in my smoke." Anita tapped the ashes into an ashtray.

"I'm sorry," Glory said. "It's just so..."

"You think that's shocking, watch this." Anita reached into her purse again, pulled out a fat envelope, and slid it across the table to Glory.

Glory looked into the envelope and gasped. The two stacks of twenty-dollar bills wrapped in two-thousand-dollar bands was more cash than Glory had ever seen at one time in her whole life, but it was not enough to get her to go back to Malcolm. She slid the envelope back across the table. "Miss Anita, there's not enough money in the world to get me to go back to Malcolm. I think I'm insulted that you thought you could pay me—"

"And I'm honestly insulted that you think I would stoop so low as to try to bribe you to stay with my son." She laid her hand over

Glory's. "The money is for you to get away." She took a long drag on her cigarette. "I don't want you back with Malcolm."

Glory was incredulous. "You're trying to pay to get rid of me?"

Anita rolled her eyes and squashed out her cigarette. "Before you married Malcolm, you were headed for college. You had a full ride and a happy, healthy life ahead of you, but you threw it all away. Now, I admit, I went about things badly, but, Precious, I was trying to protect you." She lit another cigarette. "You think I don't know my own son? You think you're the first girl he's ever hurt?"

Glory stared at the woman sitting across from her, her tea forgotten. "Protect me?"

"Yes, protect you. And I'm here to try to protect you again."

"By paying me to leave?"

"Malcolm told me what really happened to the baby."

Glory hung her head. She'd been angry when she'd said that, and now she regretted sharing that secret with him. She had never been okay with taking the cotton root, but she'd felt like her life depended on it.

"He's hurt and angry. He says you owe him children."

Glory closed her eyes and shook her head.

"He's not gonna give up. He's gonna have you committed. He's got doctors at church who'll agree with him that you're a danger to yourself."

"No," Glory said.

"And when he has you drugged and compliant, he'll punish you and torture you and breed you like a mare until you kill yourself or you kill him. But either way, he's gonna win, and your life will be over." Anita took another long drag on her cigarette and blew it out in a thin stream. "My son is sick. There's a reason why he's an only child. I didn't want another like him."

"Miss Anita, why can't he just let me go?"

"He loves you... in his way." She pushed the envelope back across the table. "That's enough to get all the way across the country, even to Hawaii. When you get settled, I'll send you more... a little every month till you get on your feet—"

"Miss Anita, I can't." Glory felt tears coming, but she would not allow herself to show weakness. "I have a life here—"

"And you'll make a life somewhere else."

"But I can't just run away. I have friends and family here—"

"Glory, do you understand that you can't win this? Do you understand that he'll destroy you if he can't have you?"

"If he's so dangerous, why don't *you* have *him* committed."

Anita took another drag on her cigarette. "Elder would never allow it. Malcolm is his miracle. He'd trade me for Malcolm in a heartbeat. I'm actually glad he loves my son like that." She squashed out the cigarette.

Glory stared at the envelope on the table. It was enough to get away and start a new life, but could she? She laid her hand on the envelope and jumped when the bell over the door sounded. She slid out of the booth to greet her new customer. "Sit anywhere." Glory stood up.

Anita slid out of the booth, too, and the man approached their table. Glory watched him brush a bit of hair out of Anita's face and place a hand low on her back.

Anita looked up at the man. "Earl, this is the young lady I was telling you about—my daughter-in-law, Glory Bishop Porter. Glory, this is my old friend Earl Malcolm."

Glory choked back a gasp. The tall dark-skinned man's features were so familiar. The short afro haircut, perfect teeth, sharp cheekbones... and his eyes, the light brown that she knew so well.

He offered his hand to Glory. "Pleased to finally meet you, Miss Glory."

Glory shook his hand but stared at Anita.

"C'mon, gal. We need to hit the road," Earl said to Anita. "Wanna get some miles on before the snow comes." He headed to the door while Anita grabbed her coat. Glory helped her put it on.

"Now, Precious, you think about what I said." Anita brushed a hair out of Glory's face. "I want you to be good to yourself. Think about what's best for you in the long run. Now, give us a hug, Precious."

Still in shock, Glory hugged her mother-in law.

"See," Anita whispered. "I told you my big black buck was fine." She giggled and patted Glory's cheek then headed out the door with her friend.

Glory watched through the window in awe as they climbed into a brown Cadillac parked at the curb. She took the envelope off the table and stuffed it into her apron pocket. Maybe she would leave—tell the Parnells and Herschel she was going to California for real this time. Malcolm would surely go after her family and friends. Hawaii or some other island might be the answer. *But can I run forever?*

Glory cleared the table and looked at the clock. It was nearly closing time. She headed back to the kitchen to wake the sleeping cook.

"HELLOOO!"

"Hi, Herschel."

"Well, hello, Glory-Glory. I was just thinking about you."

"I'm sorry to call so late, but Malcom's mother just left the restaurant."

"Well, you had your mother, Malcolm, and now his mother. I wonder who's next. The daddy maybe?"

"I doubt it. Malcolm and Anita aren't always honest with the pastor. But, Herschel, she gave me four thousand dollars to get away—"

"What? That hankty heffa is tryin' to buy you off?"

"Nooo," Glory said. "She knows Malcolm is dangerous. He's gonna try to have me committed." She heard Herschel gasp. "She gave me the money to get away from him."

"Glory-Glory, are you sure she can be trusted? I mean, she did try to get you outta town once before."

"I know, Herschel." Glory sighed. "But she said she was trying to protect me. She knew Malcolm was crazy and—"

"And she couldn'ta told you then?" Herschel's voice had dropped a couple of octaves. "She coulda saved you a lotta heartache."

"I don't think I would've believed her. I was too brainwashed by Malcolm."

"Well, what're you gonna do?"

Glory stood up and grabbed the phone base. She paced around the apartment, the cord trailing behind her. "I don't know, Herschel. If I leave, you think he'll give up?"

"Honestly, I don't know, Glory-Glory. He thinks he owns you. Maybe you need witness protection... or he needs to die."

"Herschel, don't say that. I don't wanna be with him, but I don't want him to die."

"Nah, I guess not, but he needs to be in jail at least."

Glory sighed again. "It's like I spent all year waiting for him to find me but dreading it... and now he's got doctors that'll say I'm crazy. Can he actually get me locked up?" Glory felt herself tearing up. "And if I try to leave, what's he gonna do to my family and friends?"

"Glory-Glory, you let us take care of ourselves. I know you *think* he's powerful, but he's only a man, and his only power is in the little circle of the South Side. There's a whole big world out there, and he don't run nothin'!"

"I really wanna believe that. I guess the brainwashing was too good." Glory switched the phone receiver to her other ear. "But let me tell you this other part..."

Glory shared with a shocked Herschel her suspicions about Anita's *friend*, and Herschel laughed long and hard. "I can't believe she called him a big black buck..." More laughter. "Maybe she gave you the money to keep you quiet."

"Nah... it's like she wanted me to know, but I don't know why. That's the second time she's told me a major secret."

"Girl, your life is gettin' like a soap opera." Herschel laughed again.

When Glory went to bed that night, she automatically reached for the pouch with her bracelets... Malcolm's bracelets. She held it for a minute then dropped the pouch to the floor beside her bed.

Chapter 33

Glory wove her way through the dining room, her arms loaded with dishes for the Alexander sisters. Big Tom bantered back and forth with Gram, and the cops laughed a little too loud, prompting Gram to threaten them and Miss June to yell at Gram. It was the regular late-morning crowd, and the unusually mild winter weather brought out the best in everybody.

Back in the kitchen, Glory laughed as Zac complained yet again about burning a steak for Tom. She'd just taken the plate from Zac when Deedee rushed in.

"Glory, you hafta get outta here! Malcolm is back and—"

"And I'm okay. He doesn't scare me anymore—"

"But he's brought people with him this time." Deedee grabbed Glory's arm.

Zac handed his spatula to Joe and walked with Glory and Deedee out to the dining room. Through the window, Glory could see an ambulance, its lights flashing, idling behind Malcolm's car at the curb. She guessed the two men standing by the door were the paramedics. She served Tom his steak with a smile and collected her tip from the cop's empty table.

Standing by Gram's checkout counter, near Tom's table, though she refused to show fear, Glory wanted to kick herself. She'd become complacent. It had been about a week since Anita's visit, and she hadn't seen or heard from Malcolm. But now he was back, and Glory accepted that she needed to take the money and make a new life for herself somewhere else. That day, she would pretend to agree to go with Malcolm and head into the back to get her coat, and while he waited, she would sneak up the back stairs to her apartment and wait for him to leave. Since he didn't know where she lived, she could hide in her own home for as long as it took to wait him out. Then she would get to O'Hare Airport and take the first flight to anywhere.

Malcolm approached her slowly, one hand out. "Come on, Glory. Let's go home."

Glory took a deep breath.

Malcolm moved closer. "Is there somewhere we can go to talk privately? Just me and you. I won't hurt you."

"Malcolm, stop talking to me like I'm crazy." Glory shook her head.

"I've got papers here that say you *do* need help." He reached into an inside pocket and pulled out a sheath of papers. He nodded toward the window. "There's my car and an ambulance. You're getting into one of them. Please don't make this hard." Malcolm seemed to beg, but the look on his face was triumphant. "The health department and the fire marshal are coming through here today, too, and things might get a little... uncomfortable."

"You need some help, Gloria?" Tom grunted, pushing his table away a few inches.

Glory patted the big man's shoulder. "No, Tom, I'm okay." She held up a hand, stopping Zac's and Deedee's approach. "I'm going with him to get this cleared up."

Malcolm smiled.

Glory had once loved that smile. "I hafta go get my coat and purse."

"I'll go with you," Malcolm said. He placed a hand on Glory's shoulder.

"I don't think so." At the unmistakable click of a gun being cocked, all eyes turned to Gram. The old woman stood, her right arm outstretched, holding an old revolver. "It's just like me... kinda old but definitely still works."

"Oh God, Mama, no!" June begged. "Please put that away. She's going with him—"

"You want her to go?" Gram snapped. "Naw, you don't. You know what'll happen if she go with him. He gon' lock her up and have her doped up and still beat the hell outta her. Tha's how muthafuckas like him get they jollies." She held the gun steady. "Not this time, though. Boy, you gon' get the hell outta here, and if you come back, I *will* put a bullet in yo' *ass*!"

"Gram, please, it's okay," Glory said gently. "I'll be okay."

"I said no! Don't you go nowhere wit' him." Gram waved the gun. "This crazy muthafucka is gon' wind up killin' you. Women al-la time thinkin' they can handle him, wind up with broken bones, burnt up, dead." She leveled the gun again at Malcolm.

"Mama, think what you doin'," June pleaded. "He's not worth it."

"This ain't just about him. I been knowin' muthafuckas like him all my life. Beatin' a woman make 'em feel strong, in control. Hell, shootin' him'll be like squashin' a roach... killing a rat... takin' out the trash."

"Gram." Glory moved out of Gram's line of fire. "He's not worth goin' to jail for the rest of your life..."

"I ain't goin' to jail 'cause this muthafucka is finna get outta here."

"I'm not leaving without my wife," Malcolm said calmly. "So you're just gonna hafta shoot me."

"You heard the man," Gram said. And she pulled the trigger.

Everybody in the restaurant flinched—everybody except Malcolm. And Glory.

The gun just clicked.

Malcolm looked into Glory's eyes, a sad smile on his face. "You really don't care if I die, do you?" The papers slipped from his hand and fluttered to the floor.

"Malcolm, please." Glory ignored the tear sliding down her own cheek. "It's over. Let me go."

"Okay." Malcolm reached out and wiped the tear. "If that's really how you want it." He gently stroked her face. "But you know you can't *live* without me, don't you?" he whispered softly.

The world slowed down. Glory didn't understand the sharp pain, but she saw the darkness in Malcolm's eyes.

He grabbed her hair and pulled her closer. "And he rose up from among the congregation and took a javelin in his hand... thrust... them through... the woman through her belly."

When he pulled the steak knife out of her side, blood spreading over her uniform, Glory was too short of breath to scream. She tried to push away, but his hand in her hair held her fast.

"She is hardened against her young ones as though they were not hers..." He plunged the knife into her breast.

"Malcom, *no*!" Glory finally screamed, her voice a raspy croak.

The knife struck her sternum. "And the Lord spake unto Moses, saying... smite them..."

Glory coughed, spraying blood onto his face and light-brown suit. Darkness clouded the edges of her vision. Open wounds burned where the serrated knife sliced into her arms as she tried to fight him off.

"The rest of the people will hear of this... never again will such an evil... among you."

Even in blinding pain, beneath the sound of her own heartbeat and Malcolm's calm recitations, she heard the screams and shouts of people around her. But nobody would be able to stop him before it was too late.

When Malcolm pulled her head back and raised the knife, Glory closed her eyes.

"And Moses said unto the judges of Israel, 'Slay ye every one...'"

INTERLUDE
JUNE 1983

As she stood folding towels and occasionally wiping sweat in the back room of Herschel's Salon, Glory didn't turn around when the music from the shop suddenly got louder. The Thursday-night party was going strong, and whoever it was that had opened the door probably wanted more wine coolers from the refrigerator.

"Hello, Miss Glory."

Glory froze. She hadn't heard him—wanted to hear him—say her name in two months. Maybe if she acted like she didn't hear him...

"I said 'Hello, Miss Glory.'"

How can he just show up after two months, like he isn't a two-timing devil? She heard the door close and hoped he'd gone... but wondered if that was really what she wanted. And then he was behind her with his arms around her waist, kissing her neck and shoulder, whispering of their childhood wedding and their first real kiss. He showed no remorse, only the cockiness and bravado that always got him exactly what he wanted. But not this time. Glory stiffened her resolve and her back and refused to face him. Of course, that did not deter him. When he let go of her waist and moved to the couch, Glory knew he would not be put off this time, and when he started singing, that was the last straw.

"Josiah Jackson, you leave me alone! Right now!"

"Oh... so you're talking to me now, huh? I win big. I get to hear your pretty voice and look at your fine a—"

"No!" Glory turned to face him, arms folded, seething, channeling every bit of hurt and anger into a glare that she wished would burn him to cinders. "No. I'm not talking to *you*! I'm asking the devil to leave me alone! I'm asking *Satan himself* to leave me alone and never speak to me again!"

"Well." He stood and moved toward her. "Your prayer is gonna be answered. I'm leaving for the navy tomorrow."

And Glory's resolve crumbled. She blinked a few times and then squeezed her eyes shut. She would not cry in front of him. "How could you do that to me?" she whispered. "How?"

"I'm sorry, Miss Glory." He tried to take her hand, but she pushed him away. "I'm leaving in the morning, and I need to make things right with you. Please, just listen to me. You don't hafta talk to me. You don't hafta forgive me. Just listen. Then, if you still hate me, I swear I'll never bother you again."

Taking a seat on the far end of the couch, Glory couldn't imagine what he'd possibly say to make this right. He'd cheated on her. He had another girlfriend somewhere. He had a baby that was not hers. "Do you love her?"

"Who?"

Glory folded her arms and just stared at him.

JT hung his head. "No. I don't even know her—"

"You're doing it with a stranger? And then you wanted to do it with me?"

"No, I'm not doing it with nobody. I mean, I did do it with somebody, but it was only once... and I don't even remember her—"

"Were you gonna forget about me too?" When he knelt in front of her, she pushed him away.

"Please, no. I told you, I've been lovin' you my whole life. Even if you hate me, I'm never gon' stop lovin' you." He reached for her hand. "Me and my cousins was next door to his house on this girl's porch, and we had some wine and some bud."

"You were high?" Glory pulled her hand back. She didn't hide the disgust in her voice. "Or drunk?"

JT hung his head again. "Probably both, and her sister came out asking for somebody to come in and help her move something, so I went in to help her."

Glory just shook her head. That was always how it started in the forum magazines—a woman needed help and the man got sex instead of money.

"Did you kiss her?"

"No. I didn't. I don't think I even touched her... with my hands, that is."

"Were you naked?"

"No, I didn't take anything off."

Glory didn't know why she was relieved, but she was.

"It was only one time, and it was so fast I wasn't even sure it had happened. I mean, like, I completely forgot about it until my mother heard about JJ." JT reached out and took Glory's hand.

She didn't pull away. "Why did you say you wanted me?"

"I do want you. I guess I wanted to prove myself before you... found out."

"Why didn't you tell me when it happened or when you found out about the baby?" Glory asked. "Why did I hafta hear it whispered in church from those stupid gossips who think you're the devil?"

"I was scared. I didn't want to hurt you." He dropped his head and laughed a little. "I was outta Barbie shoes." JT laid his head on her lap, and despite herself, Glory began stroking his hair.

"You stopped coming to church. Are you ashamed?"

"No." He sounded a little angry. "Nothin' to be ashamed of. I just don't believe in that kinda *God* no more. My God forgives me when I mess up. That church don't. You said it yourself—they think I'm the devil. They want me to apologize to them like my son is their business. I apologized to my mama and you."

Glory pushed him away and stood up. "JT, I hate it when you talk like that. How can you question God?"

He followed her to the dryer and helped move warm towels to the folding table. "I'm not questioning God. I just think it's real disrespectful to act like what God makes is bad."

"What's her name?" Glory would pray for him, but she wouldn't listen to him blaspheme. "JJ's mother. What's her name?"

"Um... it's Michelle." JT stumbled over his words. He had sounded all confident challenging God, but now he seemed embarrassed. *Good. He should be ashamed of himself.*

"You could marry her. Give your son a proper fam—"

"Girl, are you crazy? God, no! She don't want no part of this baby, and... well... just no." Before Glory could pick up another towel, JT pulled her into his arms, mischief shining in his eyes. "And besides... I'm already married, remember, *Mrs.* Glory?"

"Well, actually," Glory said to that smug, self-satisfied smile that she loved and hated, "my daddy said that since you didn't ask him first and you didn't have a job, we're not really married."

"But you let me kiss you, so we are." He kissed her lightly on the lips. She didn't pull away.

"But you tricked me, and we were five. So we're not."

This time, when he kissed her, Glory's heart was whole again. There was no doubt in her mind that he loved her, and in the back room of the salon on the saggy old couch, Glory and JT made love.

Chapter 34

Glory was dead. She had to be. And hell appeared to be a hospital. There was no other explanation. But that didn't make sense. She, of course, was in hell because she didn't worship anymore, but every time her eyes opened, she saw Herschel and her daddy, and there was no way they would be in hell. *But wait. Why would Herschel be dead? Did Malcolm kill him too?* She tried to call out to Herschel or her daddy, but they couldn't hear her.

As Glory drifted in and out of consciousness, she slowly became aware of the oxygen mask over her face, and the pain. She couldn't pinpoint where she was hurting, but she couldn't move, her arms hurt, and breathing felt funny. She tried to talk, and the two men rushed to her bedside.

"Don't try to talk," Herschel said. "You're in the hospital, but you're gonna be just fine."

Glory wanted to smile at Herschel, but she couldn't stop staring at her daddy. Obviously, she was alive, which meant the man wearing her daddy's face wasn't her daddy. She knew she should be relieved that she wasn't dead and in hell, but all she felt was sadness and confusion.

"Who are you?" Glory whispered, looking into eyes identical to her daddy's.

"She wants to know who you are," Herschel said to the man.

The big man smiled her daddy's smile. "I'm Paul Bishop IV. I'm your big brother."

446

Glory's eyes went wide, darting from Herschel to Paul and back.

"Yes, darling," Herschel said. "It's true. I checked his pedigree and everything. You have a long-lost brother."

Glory closed her eyes and drifted off to sleep again.

"I SPENT THE LAST TWO years trying to find you," Paul said. "I'm sorry. I don't mean to keep staring, but you look exactly like my aunt and my cousin. I just can't get over it."

Sitting up in the hospital bed, her lunch of meat loaf, congealed gravy, carrots, and peas all but ignored, Glory still couldn't stop staring at the man calling himself her big brother. He looked so much like her daddy, except his hair had less gray than her daddy's had. He and Herschel had been in her hospital room every day for the past few days, not intruding but making it obvious that they weren't going away anytime soon.

"That's okay," Glory said, sipping her lukewarm tea. "I keep staring at you 'cause you look just like my daddy. How did you find me?"

Paul chuckled a little. "You were all over the news. When a big fancy preacher gets shot trying to kill his wife, it's big news."

"He really did try to kill me, didn't he?" Glory hung her head. "Is Malcolm dead? How'd he get shot?"

"No, he's not dead." Paul sighed and shifted in his chair. "He's on another floor, but he's going to jail. An old lady shot him—"

"Gram really shot him? But her gun was empty."

"That crazy old lady had two guns," Herschel said. "Pretty good shot too."

Glory adjusted the cannula in her nose. "But Elder Porter is just gonna—"

"He's not gonna do a damn thing." Herschel interrupted her. "There was at least ten witnesses, including two paramedics."

"Wow," Glory said. "They were supposed to take me to Manteno or someplace. Wound up bringing us both here, huh."

Glory laughed a little, and her chest hurt. The doctor had said a punctured lung was the worst of her injuries. She'd have some scars, but she would recover. "First it was my daddy, and then Malcolm was my biggest protector. Malcolm always said he'd fight for me no matter what." Glory looked at Paul. "You know, he almost killed somebody for attacking me once. Almost beat him to death with a steering-wheel lock. I had to beg him not to kill. He always said he loved me and would always fight for me." Glory felt tears coming and leaned back in the bed. She would not cry over Malcolm again.

"You know," Paul began. "I'm a social worker, and I work a lot with abusers. A lot of 'em can't separate love and control. They need to own everything they say they love... even people."

"That sounds like Malcolm all right," Herschel said. "Your mama called while you was sleep. She didn't wanna wake you. Said she would come take you home when you get released—"

"I'm not going with her. She just—"

"Don't worry, Glory-Glory. You don't hafta do nothin' you don't wanna do. You can come stay with me for a while till you can get up and down your stairs."

"I know you don't know me, but you my baby sister," Paul said. "I'll make sure you have whatever you need."

Glory looked over at the man with her daddy's face. "I still don't understand how or why you've been looking for me for two years. Did we meet when I was a baby or something?"

"Naw, we didn't meet. I think we almost did once. When I was about sixteen, seventeen, I think Daddy tried to tell me about you. See, we wasn't real close back then on account of the divorce when I was little. Daddy stayed gone, and I stayed mad." Paul clasped his hands together and shook his head. "Anyway, when I was a teenager, he took me on a day run with him—I don't remember where. South, I think. He tried to talk to me, but I wasn't really listenin'. He said God was givin' him a second chance to be a good father. I *thought* he said God gave him glory." Paul laughed a little. "I mostly tuned him out. I had a pretty bad attitude for a lotta years, but him and Mama stayed close friends. I didn't see him much after that. I figured he gave up on me. You know, when Daddy was sick, he couldn't really talk, and he couldn't write what he wanted to say either. But he could point, and he always pointed at me and said, 'Glory.' I thought he was just happy to see me."

"Was this when I was a baby?" Glory asked. "I don't remember Daddy being sick."

"Naw, you had to be about nine or ten when he got sick. The stroke took a lot from him. He couldn't walk or talk for about a year. Then he—"

"Oh, I'm sorry. You look so much like my daddy, I really want you to be my brother, but my daddy died in 1976. I was nine. He wasn't sick. He was burned up in an accident... a truck accident."

Paul looked at Herschel and then back at Glory. "Why do you think that?" he asked, a look of consternation on his face. "Where'd you get that idea?"

"When I was nine, I stayed home at the babysitter's after lunch 'cause I was feeling sick." Glory looked at the ivory blanket covering her lap. "When I got home, Mama told me he was dead. She told me about the fire a couple days later." Glory dabbed her eyes with the corner of the blanket. Talking about her daddy's death always made her cry. "It wasn't even a funeral, just church service with a piece of paper with his picture."

Paul looked shocked then upset.

Herschel watched Paul's face change in demeanor. "Let's go get some coffee," Herschel said. "Maybe grab a bite. That ugly meat loaf is making me hungry." He laid his hand on the big man's shoulder. "C'mon, I'll buy." He turned to Glory. "We're goin' down to the cafeteria. They have decent burgers. I'll see if I can sneak one up to you, okay, Glory-Glory?"

"Okay." Glory watched the men leaving the room. Paul even moved like her daddy. Glory closed her eyes and rested her head back against the pillow. Maybe they were cousins. Maybe Paul had been named after his uncle Paul III, and Paul's daddy actually did have a stroke. That could be why they looked so much alike.

Glory dozed off and woke in time to see Herschel pulling a White Castle sack out of his handbag and placing it on her tray table. "The grill was closed, so we went out. Hope you're hungry."

Paul took his regular seat, holding a brown shoebox on his lap. "While you eat, Imma tell you a story. That okay?"

Glory looked over at her new friend—possibly cousin—and nodded. She'd expected him to be disappointed that they weren't siblings, but he looked more resigned than anything. Herschel pulled his chair close to Glory's bedside and started unpacking their meal. Glory almost gagged when the smell of onions hit her, but she didn't tell Herschel that.

"Well, after my daddy had the stroke," Paul began, "he couldn't do anything, really. He was always a big man—that's where I get it from—and strong as an ox. Heh, I remember him carrying in giant watermelons when he'd come back from a run down South."

"My daddy used to do that too," Glory said between bites.

"I say all that to say," Paul continued, "Daddy didn't have it in him to stay down, not even from the stroke. He would sometimes get so frustrated he'd cry. Then one day, he got his arm to move, then a few months later, his hand was kinda working. It wasn't perfect, but he could do letters. He wrote just one thing: Glory. I thought he was celebratin' being able to write, and I told everybody Daddy was getting better and praising the Lord."

Glory smiled. "That's why my mama named me Glory... to praise the Lord."

"Well, every time I went to see him—see, he was in a nursing home—he would hand me another note. Seem like all he did was write the praise notes, but he would cry when I tried to pray with him. Some days, he'd just be mad and shut down. Then the speech therapy lady tells me he's tryin' to talk, and the doctor had said he probably wouldn't be able to. Well, Daddy showed them. Got to where he could point, and he would make sounds. Took us a minute to figure out he was saying 'Glory.' Then he would point at me and say it." Paul laughed a little. "I thought he was thankin' the Lord for me. Then one day he wrote 'Get Glory.' And that was a hallelujah day 'cause I finally understood him. I promised him I would get glory.

"Now all this time, I'm still thinkin' he's praisin' the Lord and gettin' better, but he wasn't. But I was out gettin' glory like I promised. I got back in school, finished my degree. Patched things up with my wife, even joined a church. But all the time I'm showing and tellin' Daddy that I'm gettin' glory. I'm being a better man... the man he always wanted me to be." Paul grabbed a tissue from the box on the windowsill and dabbed at his eyes.

"If this is too hard..." Glory began.

"Naw. I'm okay." Paul looked up and nodded at Herschel and tapped the lid of the box. "You need to know this stuff. Anyway, Daddy died in '81, and my mother gave me this box of stuff that came out of his truck after the stroke. Meantime, I'm doin' everything I can to be the kinda man my daddy was. I'm out gettin' glory. I forgot about that box and found it again two years ago." He held the shoebox out. "Take a look."

Herschel cleared the tray table, and Paul handed Glory the box.

"Now listen, Glory-Glory..." Herschel gently patted the top of the box then turned away and sat down. "Just open it."

Glory heard the catch in his throat and was suddenly afraid of what she would find inside the box. Lifting the lid, she saw that it was a box of photos and other papers. Glory rifled through familiar images—copies of the photos her mother had cut up so many years ago.

"How did you get these?" she asked, staring at a photo of a wild-haired toddler hiding inside a giant work boot... a copy of an image that had been on her grandmother's picture wall. Glory looked at Paul and then at Herschel. "Did you give these to him?"

Herschel sighed and shook his head.

"I don't understand—" Glory tried to form the words. What she was seeing was not possible. There were her baby pictures and photos of her with her daddy and then ones of her daddy in a hospital bed and in a wheelchair. Digging deeper into the box, she found a checkbook for Paul and Mary Bishop, a copy of her own birth certificate, and a copy of the obituary and death certificate of Paul Bishop III.

"Daddy died calling your name, and I never knew it." Paul's voice cracked. "I'm out trying to be a better man—wasn't till I opened that box that I knew what he was gettin' at. I knew I had to find you. I promised my daddy I'd come get you—" Paul's shoulders shook as he sat sobbing.

Herschel handed him a tissue. "Glory-Glory, you okay?"

Glory couldn't talk. For just a moment, until she'd seen the obituary, Glory had had her daddy back. She looked over at Paul Bishop IV... her big brother who had spent years trying to find her. Glory lay back against the pillow. The evidence was right there on the table in front of her. *But why?*

"Paul," Glory found her voice. "Why did my mother tell me Daddy was dead?"

Paul sniffed and blew his nose. "I don't know. When he had the stroke, I tried to call her, your mama, almost every day... even called her job. Tried coming to the house. Wrote letters... I guess she didn't want him by then. Maybe they had split up."

"That doesn't make sense. Mama loved Daddy. She woulda took care of him. She woulda let me see him."

"Maybe she didn't think you could handle seeing him sick?" Herschel offered. "She mighta thought it was too traumatic for you."

"After he died—after she *told* me he died—she got rid of every sign of Daddy in the house. His clothes and pictures, even his books. Made it like he was never there. That's when she took the phone out and cut the TV cord." Glory pressed her hands over her eyes. "Why would she lie to me like that?" She looked over at the two people who seemed to love her most in the world... one of whom she'd only just met.

PAUL BISHOP IV DROVE like an old lady, and he wouldn't stop talking. Glory tried not to let it get on her nerves, but it did. Since meeting her big brother, she'd heard stories of aunts, uncles, cousins, and even nieces and nephews. The idea of having a big family on her father's side was a bit overwhelming. She searched her memories and only had vague recollections of her daddy maybe mentioning his relatives, but she'd grown up with her mother's family.

"You know, the doctor said for you to rest. How about we go on to Herschel's and get you settled in, and you make this visit maybe next week. You should be takin' it easy and not getting too excited—"

"Paul," Glory said, "I appreciate your concern, but I'm fine, and I hafta do this now. If I wait, it'll eat at me, and that'll be more stressful."

She leaned her head back against the seat. After two weeks in the hospital, mostly lying down, Glory had been elated to finally be released on Saturday morning. Riding from the West Side back to the South Side, Glory realized how much she'd missed her old neighborhoods. As they exited the Dan Ryan Expressway at Seventy-Ninth Street, Glory tried to relax. Breathing too deeply caused pain, and most of the stitches in her arms and chest had been removed, but she still felt a little delicate and weak.

"You really want me to come in with you? I don't think your mother is gon' be happy to see me."

"I'm trying not to be too harsh," Glory said, "but I'm not really caring how my mother feels right now."

When Paul stopped the car in front of Mary's apartment building on Seventy-Fifth Street, Glory realized she hadn't given him directions. "I guess you *have* been here before, huh? I'm honestly still hoping all of this is a huge misunderstanding." Glory covered her face with her gloved hands. "I just can't imagine why she would do this."

Paul reached across the seat and patted Glory's hand. "Well... let's go in and find out."

At the heavy wood-and-glass front door, Glory turned the knob, and Paul reached over her head and pushed the door—just like her daddy used to. It felt weird being back inside the hexagon-tiled foyer. She tried her old key on the deadbolted inner door. It still worked. The knot in her stomach that had started in the car grew tighter. Up the three stairs to the hallway outside the door of her mother's first-floor apartment, Glory couldn't help but notice specks of orange and pink wedged between the floorboards and baseboards—the last of the Barbie shoes JT had left sprinkled on the floor six years before.

The security gate across the door looked closed, but Glory saw that the padlock was only locked onto the gate. Mary Bishop was home. The knot in Glory's stomach tightened to a genuine cramp, and she tried to relax with Paul's steadying hand on her shoulder.

"You don't hafta do this," Paul said. "No real good can happen. In this case, the truth is just as bad as the lie."

"You're probably right." Glory sighed. "But I gotta know." She knocked lightly on the door. "Mama, it's me!"

"Oh, your arms still not working all the way? Let me." Paul knocked loudly.

"Mamaaa... it's me, Glory!" From her side of the door, she could hear the familiar sound of her mother fussing as she undid several locks and latches and opened the door.

"Don't you still got a key?" Mary said opening the door. "Out here yellin' like you crazy. How you get here from the hospital, anyway—" Mary's jaw dropped. The brown-paper cigarette in her mouth fell to the hardwood floor, where Glory quickly stamped it out. Her hand shaking, Mary pointed at Paul. "I rebuke you in the name of Jesus!"

"It's good to see you too, Ms. Mary," Paul said evenly.

"Glory, don't you bring that son of a no-good, lying, two-timing devil in my house! I bind him in the name of Jesus!"

Glory tried to take her mother's hand, but Mary snatched away. "Mama, I need to talk to you," Glory pleaded. "And Paul does too—"

"I ain't gon' hear nothin' he got to say!"

"Please, Mama?" Glory pushed the door open and stepped past her mother and into the apartment. "I have questions. I need to know what really happened to Daddy."

Mary turned her back on Paul at the door, walked across the living room to the kitchen, pulled a brown-paper cigarette from her bosom, and lit it on the stove. She took a long puff and then blew it out slowly. "I told you. Yo' daddy's dead. Been dead a long time." Another long puff.

Paul came into the apartment, closed the door behind himself, and secured one of the locks. Glory motioned for him to have a seat on the plastic-covered couch.

"But *when* did he die, Mama?"

Mary leaned against the kitchen doorframe, slowly puffing her cigarette. "He been dead since the day I tell you he died."

"Ms. Mary," Paul said. "Our father died in 1981, but you told Glory he died in '76—"

"That low-down devil been dead to me since the day I told you he died!" Mary snapped. "He been dead since May 26, 1976, and I hope he suffered and burnin' in hell!" She turned and tossed the still-burning cigarette into the sink and lit another one.

"Why, Mama? What are you talking about? Daddy was a good man. He loved you—"

"You know... I thought he did." Mary shook her head. "He told me and showed me he did. And I loved him so much you was conceived in sin. Tha's why you got all them demons."

"Mama, I don't have demons." Glory moved to sit in a plastic-covered armchair. She wasn't prepared to argue, but she would never again allow that statement to go unchallenged.

"But we got married, and you was the miracle. Thought I couldn't have no mo' babies—thought God was still punishin' me—but you was the miracle." Mary blew smoke in Glory's direction. "I didn't even get a call 'bout the accident. I saw it on the way to work. Jackknife truck on the Dan Ryan... Thirty-Fifth Street... I knew it was him. *Ambulance* and fire trucks out there." Mary shook her head again. "I thought he was burnt up or worse. I got to the hospital, St. Bernard's, right there by the expressway. That nurse told me he had a stroke and only family could see him. Then she told me his *wife* was wit' 'im!"

"Oh God, Mama, no!"

"Yes! *His wife!* That no-good, lyin', two-timin', son-of-a—"

"Mama, no! That's not possible. What did Daddy say? Did you talk to the other lady?"

"What for? What could he say? I just turned around and left."

Glory stared at her mother as she lit a third cigarette. This couldn't be happening. Her daddy, even if he wasn't perfect, couldn't be *this*. Glory cleared her throat. "Mama, you knew Daddy wasn't dead?"

"Yeah, I knew. I checked the paper every day, waitin' for him to die. Took him five long years... and now you come up in here with his son, lookin' just like that ol'—"

"Stop! Stop! Stop!" Glory heard herself screaming at her mother, then she heard herself crying. "Oh God, just stop! You took my daddy from me! How could you do that? What gave you the right—"

"God gave me the right!" Mary yelled at her daughter. "Yo' daddy wasn't a godly man when we met. He joined church and acted godly, gave me everything I wanted, said everything I wanted to hear... I bet that poor woman thought she was his only wife too. Love be makin' women foolish. Tha's why I kept that ungodly boy offa you! Tha's why I found you a godly husband, but you got all them demons up in you, messed him all up!"

"Mama," Glory said through clenched teeth, "the only demons anywhere is you and Malcolm. You took my daddy from me. You took JT from me—"

"I protected you! And you still got demons of disrespect!" Mary advanced on her daughter, holding out the lit cigarette. "I bind you in the name of Jesus!"

Glory stood up. "No! You don't get to torture me ever again." Glory slapped the burning cigarette from her stunned mother's hand. Paul quickly moved to stand between the women, crushing out the cigarette on the floor.

"Ms. Mary," Paul said gently. "That lady was my mother, his *ex*-wife. They divorced when I was ten... back in 1960. Long before he married you."

"You a lie, and the truth ain't in you!" Mary snapped. "Why that lady say she was his wife? Huh!"

"She made a mistake. She had old paperwork from his job. I don't know—"

"No! I'm not gon' stand here and listen to yo' lies! You jus' like him!"

Glory stared at her mother, concentrated on breathing, and tried to push away her own hateful thoughts. "Mama, you always told me pride was a sin... but you left Daddy 'cause you was too proud to ask a question?"

"I wasn't proud. I was shamed!" Mary hissed at her daughter. "I was so shamed I came home and cried my eyes out. I tore my clothes and put ashes on my head. I knew God was still punishing me for my sins, and I promised God I would keep you pure and clean and godly... keep you from the same sins as me... keep you from the same punishment."

"Mama, God isn't punishing you," Glory whispered.

"Lies! God took my babies. He took my husbands. I been payin' the price of Job for my sins my whole life! I shamed my family, and God is still punishin' me."

Glory looked into her mother's eyes, expecting to see tears, but she saw only anger and madness. "Mama, God isn't like that. God loves us and forgives our sins. And Job wasn't punished. He was tested and rewarded—"

"Blaspheme! You don't know nothin' 'bout God. You turnt on God when you left yo' family. Yo' sinfulness took away yo' baby!"

Glory stared at Mary, feeling her heart breaking. Her mother truly believed God was punishing her and that she deserved it. She watched her mother pray silently, her lips barely moving—the ritual that usually calmed her when she felt attacked by demons. Glory watched her mother embrace the madness that was her version of God and accept punishment for her own imaginary sins. No amount of truth would open Mary's eyes.

She reached out and touched her mother's shoulder. "We finna go, Mama." She felt her brother's hand squeeze her own shoulder. She knew she should feel reassured, but Glory only felt empty. Mary didn't respond. She continued her silent recitations. Glory and Paul walked to the door.

"Goodbye, Mama," Glory said. Mary still didn't move.

Glory and Paul stepped out into the hallway, and Glory used her old keys to lock the door.

Chapter 35
April 1990

After a month off work then a few weeks of light duty, Glory finally felt back to herself, moving around the diner on her usual Saturday-night shift. Two couples sat in the big booth, making plans for the night. A young man sat in another booth, studying and downing coffee like water. And to Glory's great surprise, the bell over the door rang, and in walked Marcus and Li'l Man.

"Well, what a surprise!" Glory glanced at her watch. It was after nine o'clock. "Isn't it past somebody's bedtime?" she chided.

"Yup," Marcus said. "It's way past my bedtime. I'm tired as hell... but *somebody* just had to see you." They took their regular seats at the counter, and Glory went to prepare Li'l Man's chocolate milk then moved to pour Marcus's coffee, but he held up a hand. "I'll take decaf this late."

"I'll make a fresh pot." Glory headed to the coffee station. "So, Li'l Man, what's so important that you hafta keep your grandpa up so late?"

The little boy sighed. "My dad said I hafta break up with you."

"What? Why?" Glory let disappointment show on her face and in her voice.

Li'l Man sighed again. "He said you already married." He pouted. "You can't be married to two people."

"Well, now, what does your daddy know about me?" Glory asked. "Has he ever been in here?"

"I don't know," Li'l Man said. "He just said you're already married to him." He groaned a loud sigh and put his forehead on the counter.

With a trembling hand, Glory set the decaf coffeepot back on the burner. She looked over at Marcus. The old man was beaming.

"JJ?"

Marcus nodded.

"What?" The child pouted. "I'm not happy right now."

Glory turned her back to the counter as the bell over the door rang again. She fished a napkin from her pocket and dabbed her eyes. Little JJ was a six-year-old now. *But...*

"Hello, Miss Glory."

No.

"I said, 'Hello, Miss Glory.'"

Glory turned around, and her feet started moving before she could form a coherent thought.

"Remember the first time you let me kiss you? You said you'd be my wife."

Glory moved around the counter, not trying to hold back tears, facing the boy who had owned her heart her whole life.

"Ugh!" Li'l Man groaned. "You kissed her?"

"Boy, quiet down." Marcus thumped his grandson.

"Remember the second time you let me kiss you?" JT reached out and took Glory's hand. "You said you'd be my girl."

"You kissed her two times? Double yuck!"

"I'm sorry I didn't wait," Glory tried to whisper, but her words came out as, "I never stopped loving you..." And then she was in his arms, and he was kissing her, and she was kissing him... her hands on his face, the back of his head, her arms wrapped around his neck. Glory tried to inhale him in that kiss. She could hardly breathe through her tears and runny nose, but she needed that kiss to never end.

"Oh God! Why are they kissing now?"

GLORY TURNED THE LOCK and leaned against her apartment door, listening to JT's footsteps as he headed down the stairs. In a movie, she would count to ten and then open the door, and he'd still be standing there in the hallway. They would kiss, and next thing, they would be in bed. But this was real life, and when Glory had said good night to JT after their third or fourth date, she meant it. In the dark apartment, she rushed over to the bay window and looked down onto the corner of Cicero and Madison Avenues. She watched JT pause and look up at her apartment window. He waved. She wondered if he could see her. She watched him turn and head to his car parked around the corner.

Glory laughed a little. Once an apartment overlooking a city street and being with JT had been the be-all and end-all of her dreams. But as she watched the cars go by and listened to music oozing out of the Knotty Pine across the street and breathed in the cool-spring-night air, she found herself saying a prayer of thanksgiving. In the summer, she would be a bright young student at Columbia College. She had a job, an apartment, and friends who were like family. She had JT... and she had choices.

Acknowledgements

A whole lotta people had a lot to do with helping me finish Glory's story.

Red Adept Publishing, especially Lynn, Jessica, and Sarah for their faith, time, and infinite patience.

Carol DaLuga and Geraldine Cunningham, my sixth- and seventh-grade teachers respectively— the only teachers who actually let me exercise my imagination and write whatever I wanted

My "sisters," cousins, and friends: Angela, Cheryl, Jennifer, Rae, Miranda, Jilon, Nicole, Della, and Simone, whose beta reading, critiques, editing, and genuine love and support helped me make sense of Glory's life and get the story told

The awesome, incredible women of The Woolfer, especially the ladies in the Writer's Room

The creative writing department at UW Madison for guidance and encouragement, especially Christine, Kristin, Laurie, Chris, Kathy, and Laura.

The great writers and instructors at The Novel-In-Progress Bookcamp & Writing Retreat

And finally, Jovanda, Joseph, Jeremy, Marcus, and James. The lights of my life and my reasons for living. Thank you for your patience with me. I love you.

Don't miss out!

Visit the website below and you can sign up to receive emails whenever Deborah L. King publishes a new book. There's no charge and no obligation.

https://books2read.com/r/B-A-OIII-YSTSB

BOOKS 2 READ

Connecting independent readers to independent writers.

Did you love *Glory Unbound*? Then you should read *When Robins Appear*[1] by Densie Webb!

With a lucrative freelance career and a loving family, Deborah Earle has a life many women would envy. But her daughter, Amanda, is heading to college soon, and Deborah worries about having an empty nest. She thinks another child might be the answer. Her husband, Richard, however, may not be willing to start over so late in life.

Amanda is excited about attending NYU next year, but she meets Graham, a handsome older boy, falls hard, and considers postponing her education to stay close to him. Her mother takes an instant dislike to Graham, but Amanda refuses to let her keep them apart.

As Deborah watches her daughter rush headlong toward heartache on an all-too-familiar path, the secrets lurking in Deborah's past continue to echo in her present. When tragedy strikes, Deborah faces a future she could never have imagined.

Read more at https://wordpress.com/view/densiewebb.com.

Also by Deborah L. King

.

Glory Bishop
Glory Unbound

Watch for more at deborahlking.com.

About the Author

Growing up, Deborah L. King always wanted to be an author. She published her first short story when she was seven years old. When she's not writing, she can be found enjoying cooking, photography, and watching cartoons and *Star Trek*.

Born and raised in Chicago, Deborah has managed to achieve all her childhood dreams and still lives in the area with her husband and two youngest children. According to her daughter, she has "literally aced her life"!

Read more at deborahlking.com.

About the Publisher

Dear Reader,

We hope you enjoyed this book. Please consider leaving a review on your favorite book site.

Visit https://RedAdeptPublishing.com to see our entire catalogue.

Don't forget to subscribe to our monthly newsletter to be notified of future releases and special sales.